The Dawlish Chronicles

Britannia's Innocent
February – May 1864

Britannia's Interests
July – November 1866

Britannia's Guile
January – August 1877

Britannia's Wolf
September 1877 - February 1878

Britannia's Reach
November 1879 - April 1880

Britannia's Shark
April – September 1881

Britannia's Spartan
June 1859 and April - August 1882

Britannia's Amazon
April – August 1882
(Includes bonus short story *Britannia's Eye*)

Britannia's Mission
August 1883 – February 1884

Britannia's Gamble
March 1884 – February 1885

Britannia's Morass
September – December 1884
(Includes bonus short story *Britannia's Collector*)

Britannia's Rule
September 1886 – April 1888

Being events in the lives of:

Nicholas Dawlish R.N.
Born: Shrewsbury 16.12.1845
Died: Zeebrugge 23.04.1918

Florence Dawlish, née Morton
Born: Northampton 17.06.1855
Died: Portsmouth 12.05.1946

Britannia's Interests

The Dawlish Chronicles
July – November 1866

By

Antoine Vanner

Library of Congress Cataloguing-in-Publication Data:

Antoine Vanner 1945 -

Britannia's Interests / Antoine Vanner.

Paperback: ISBN: 978-1-943404-47-6

Paperback Binding Type: Perfect Binding

Kindle: ISBN: 978-1-943404-48-3

Cover design by Sara Lee Paterson

Published by Old Salt Press

Old Salt Press, LLC is based in Jersey City, New Jersey with an affiliate in New Zealand

For more information about our titles go to: www.oldsaltpress.com

Britannia's Interests

Introduction

Mexico gained independence from Spain in 1821 and the following decades saw political turmoil, civil war and foreign intervention. Texas was lost in 1836 and the 1846-47 war with the United States was ended by ceding California, Arizona, and New Mexico

Conflict between Liberals and Conservatives dominated politics. Liberals were dedicated to modernisation, legal and economic reform, and lessening the power of the Catholic Church. Conservative opposition led to the "Reform War" of 1857-1861. It ended in a Liberal victory that brought Benito Juarez to the presidency.

In 1862, French forces invaded Mexico, ostensibly to collect debts on which the Juarez government had defaulted, but with the larger objective of establishing a client state as a. new "Mexican Empire". It imported Ferdinand Maximillian, younger brother of Emperor Franz-Josef of Austria, installing him as their puppet Emperor Maximillian I of Mexico. The measure gained Conservative support. The French, and Mexican forces supportive of the new empire, gained control of much of central Mexico. In the north and south however, "Juarista" armies, loyal to President Juarez, remained in the field. In the following years regular armies and guerilla groups waged merciless war.

Emperor Maximillian, a well-meaning but weak man, was prevailed on to sign a "Black Decree" that authorised court martial and execution of anybody found aiding or joining the Juarista guerrillas. Some 11,000 Juarez supporters may have been killed on the grounds of this decree. In a quixotic gesture, a small "Belgian Legion" volunteered to fight for Maximillian, whose wife Carlota was a princess of Belgium.

When the American Civil War ended in 1865, the United States Government, sympathetic to the Juaristas, supplied them with arms and put diplomatic pressure on France to withdraw. By 1866, the French were recognising the war as unwinnable and evacuation as inevitable.

But there would still be cruel and relentless fighting, and scores settled, before the whole sorry episode could be brought to an end . . .

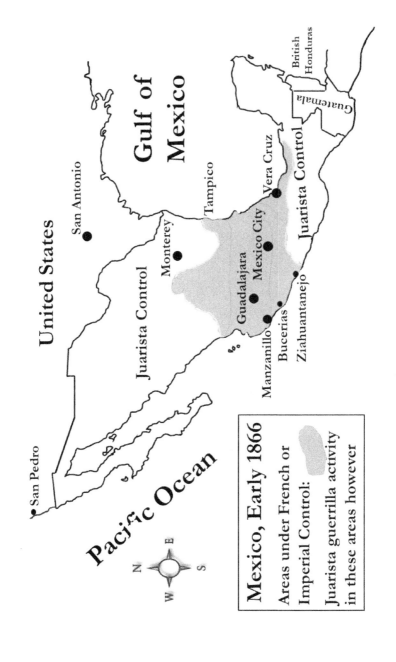

Pacific Ocean

United States

Gulf of Mexico

San Pedro

San Antonio

Monterey

Tampico

Vera Cruz

Mexico City

Guadalajara

Manzanillo

Bucerias

Ziahuantanejo

Juarista Control

Juarista Control

British Honduras

Guatemala

N
W E
S

Mexico, Early 1866

Areas under French or
Imperial Control:
Juarista guerrilla activity
in these areas however

Prologue

23rd July, 1866
The Village of San Ramón Nonato
27 miles south-west of Guadalajara, Jalisco State, Mexico

He had not foreseen this, had not come to kill and to burn in villages that had known only misery long before this war had begun. He'd been told, when he'd volunteered, that the country was unsettled. It was a passing phase, he was assured, and the installation of a new and enlightened ruler would bring tranquillity. He'd expected ceremonial guard duties at the palace of Chapultepec, horseback-escorts of the empress's carriage as she passed among a grateful people, levees and banquets staged with all the dignity of centuries of Hapsburg protocol.

But not this.

Half the houses in this village – adobe shacks – were already blackened shells and the thatched roofs of the remainder were blazing. Upwards of forty men stood penned by a hedge of bayonets against the church wall and the priest, though exempt from the roundup, insisted on staying with them. A sergeant – a Fleming who might have a memory of being pious back in Ghent or Brugge – had allowed the priest to bring a stool on which he now sat hunched, listening to the confessions of those who had already abandoned hope. A few others crouched, weeping. Some were calling empty reassurances to the women and children standing behind the half-circle of Belgians before the wall but the majority waited in stolid, mute, acceptance. They had never expected much of life.

Delay makes it even crueller, a small internal voice reminded Major – and Baron – André Damseaux de Vérac. *You can't escape it. You must choose nine of them.*

It could all have been avoided if a young husband had not split a private's skull with an axe during house searches the previous day. Already badly beaten, his mouth bleeding and teeth knocked out before he was dragged in front of Damseaux and he pleaded his wife had been

8

molested. She might well have been – it happened more frequently now as hope and discipline eroded – but the dead man's corporal and comrades denied it and remained adamant under questioning. There was no option but to enforce the Black Decree to the letter. The young husband and nine others must be shot.

It would have been easier if weapons were found but there had been nothing more lethal here than the man's axe. The report that brought this Belgian patrol here had proved to be correct. A Juarista band had spent two nights in the village a week before and been no more welcome than the Belgians. The community knew nothing of the emperor installed by the French two years before and cared just as little for the republican Juaristas who opposed them. It was too poor to want anything other than be left in peace.

The Kingdom of the Belgians was a new one – not yet thirty years old – and it lacked the prestige of older monarchies. The marriage of the king's daughter, Princess Charlotte, to the brother of the Austrian Emperor had been welcome evidence of its acceptance by Europe's older royal houses. Nobody expected she would soon be Empress Carlota, consort of the ruler of a new and exotic empire, with an emperor selected for it by the French. Nor that she would bring Belgian volunteers with her as her personal guard, her own legion. Major Baron André Damseaux was one of them.

"Have you signed it, sir?" Anselme, the lieutenant who entered now was hesitant. It would be his first time to command a firing squad.

"No," Damseaux said. "Come back in ten minutes."

He was sitting at a rough table in the priest's two-room house, the only one not yet burnt. He had read and reread the proclamation that one of his lieutenants had drafted for him. A literate sergeant had made ten copies. It did not matter that the Spanish was less than elegant – it was unlikely anybody here but the priest could read. Posting it on charred fence posts, and bringing back one copy to Ciudad Guzmán for the records, would grace the miserable business with legality. All that was needed now were his signatures.

Hell must have something of this, he thought. Smoke and fragments of burning thatch were drifting across the small and crowded

9

plaza outside. The men might be awaiting their fate in sullen resignation, but the women were not. Some wailed in despair and others screamed hatred and abuse at the troops holding them back. The decree authorising such savage retribution achieved nothing but win fresh adherents to the Juarista cause.

Another officer entered.

"We shouldn't wait much longer, sir." Captain van Maarkedal, Damseaux's deputy, said. There was a hint of contempt in his voice, as there had been for the last week. That he was Flemish, not Walloon made it worse. "The men want to finish and be gone. They're sick of it. We shouldn't count too much on their patience."

And not just on their patience. On their loyalty too, Damseaux thought. French forces had abandoned the city of Guadalajara two weeks before and retreated eastwards towards the Gulf coast. The city's occupation by Juarista forces had cut off this small Belgian unit and the nine depleted French battalions between here and the Pacific Ocean to the west. Only the few ports there offered the chance of evacuation. Even the humblest Belgian private knew the situation was desperate and, worse, that his officers lacked the battle-hardened resolve of their French counterparts. Only fear of what Mexican irregulars did to stragglers made desertion unattractive. But van Maarkedal was right. It was better not to test patience beyond a limit that had already been all but reached.

"Five minutes," Damseaux said. "There are a few items to address first."

Once van Maarkedal left. Damseaux took his revolver from its holster and laid it on the table. He had been thinking about this moment ever since the unit's commander, a Colonel de Broqueville, was killed in a skirmish a week before. The command then devolved on him. He'd not desired the responsibility, never wanted more than the ceremonial duties he enjoyed at Chapultepec. He waltzed well, rode elegantly, was admired for his skill as a fencer, and acquaintance with an Austrian countess held every promise of a satisfying liaison. In Belgium, the loss of his wife in childbirth – the baby, a daughter, died a week later – induced him to volunteer. Service at the emperor's court had indeed helped him forget.

If civil war had not ended in the great republic to the north, if arms had not flooded in from there after it to breathe new life into the Juarista cause, he would still be at the emperor's palace. French defeats, and French desperation, demanded use of Empress Carlota's Legion in the field.

It was then that he learned what he really was. Not a physical coward, as he'd feared, even expected – which was a relief – but something worse. A man whose vanity had led him to pledge his word with so little heed to a cause he should have recognised as hollow. A man who did evil because he could not face loss of what the world saw as his honour.

And a man who was drinking more heavily each day to forget what he had become. He'd finished the cognac he'd carried on this patrol and turned to local tequila. He'd heard himself sometimes slurring his words, had seen his hands shaking.

His gaze kept returning to the revolver. The longing to be free of this moment, to reach out to the weapon, put it in his mouth, was a torment. What must happen here this morning would be small by comparison with what had happened at three other villages before. But there had been genuine resistance in them and, even if some innocents had fallen before a blood-spattered wall, there were Juaristas with them who were yet more merciless when they took prisoners.

He tore his eyes away from the pistol and looked out through the glassless window. Through the grey haze of acrid smoke, he saw that the women were more frantic now, screaming, raising children above their heads to see their fathers, pushing towards the troops who held them back. A sergeant, face bloodied by a woman's fingernails, had lost patience and smashed her to the ground with his rifle butt. Beyond the thin rim of troops, the men penned against the church wall were less passive now, their voices rising in defiance. Older children were beginning to throw stones. If even one Belgian private yielded to exasperation and fired back, the consequence would not be just a riot, but a massacre.

Let van Maarkedal handle this, the internal voice urged. *He won't hesitate and the responsibility won't be yours, not anymore. You'll feel nothing, you'll be gone.*

And then, suddenly, something like love for his men – he had never felt it before – stirred in him. Their once glorious uniforms, his too, were by now ragged and patched, boots and gaiters of untanned leather, tall-plumed shakoes replaced with straw sombreros, but their discipline was holding, if only just. Fear dominated them – not of just death but of capture and mutilation, fear of the Juaristas and yet worse fear of the bandits in the hills. And fear most of all of abandonment by the French who had never disguised their contempt for Empress Carlota's Legion.

Without him, these men would be lost. And not just their lives, but something more, something deeper – something like human worth itself. They were men drawn from simple homes on the Flanders coast or in the Ardennes forests, men driven to enlist as an alternative to drudgery on farms or in the collieries of the Pays Noir. They had been scarred in mind by what they had been forced to do here and had been made all but monsters. They deserved better.

And these villagers deserved better too, even if it would be at the cost of his honour.

He stood up, pushed the revolver back in its holster, buttoned down the flap, reached for the proclamation and the copies and tore them into pieces. Then he went out.

"You've signed, Sir?" van Maarkedal met him. "We can go ahead now?"

"What's the name of that man who killed Lejeune?"

"I don't know. Does it matter?"

"Have Anselme fetched. He must know."

The young lieutenant did know. It was Jorge Morales.

"Rewrite the proclamation," Damseaux said. "The copies too. One name only – that one."

It had to be that one. Good reason or not, he had killed a Belgian soldier. It could not be let pass, not if discipline were to be stopped deteriorating further.

12

"Nobody else? You're releasing all the others?" van Maarkedal said. "You're sure of that, are you, major?" His tone was just short of insolence. "You know that Colonel Durand's orders were explicit."

"Let me worry about Durand," Damseaux said. "He's in Ciudad Guzmán and I'm here." *I've let that French butcher use me for too long.* "As I said. We'll just shoot this Jorge Morales."

It was over quickly. The doomed young man, limping, face even bloodier since last night, was separated from the others and pushed against the wall. The priest stayed with him, whispering in his ear, though he seemed not to hear. Lieutenant Anselme selected five men from what would have been a larger firing party. Those released from it looked relieved. Troops drove the remaining captives to one side – they were surprised, confused, uncertain whether they should hope or fear. Silence descended on the crowd, broken only by crying children.

Damseaux went forward, pressed through the throng, felt spittle fall on his face but no hand was laid on him. He stood beside Anselme, noticed that he was trembling.

"It's on my head, not yours, lieutenant" he said. "Take your time. Do it properly. It's kinder that way."

A jerk of his head told the padre it was time for him to go but, before he did, the old man made the sign of the over the condemned man. Jorge Morales seemed to understand what was coming. He drew himself as erect as he could as a corporal bound his wrists behind him, his eyes searching the crowd for a last sight of the wife for whom he was dying. Then he was pushed to his knees, face touching the wall. It was as on previous occasions, but this time only one man.

Anselme had spaced his five privates in a line, each two paces from the next, ten from the victim. He called the order to load, checked each rifle when they had, then walked to the end of the line and drew his sword. An eternity passed after he gave the order to aim. At last, the blade swung down, and he shouted the command to fire.

The young lieutenant was ashen faced when he moved toward the body, sheathing his sword as he did and fumbling with his holster flap.

"Stand back, Anselme." Damseaux had taken out his own revolver. "I'll do it."

He could see no sign of life but he fired into Jorge Morales' head anyway.

*

The column trudged through four more villages before it reached the first fortified French position, some fifteen kilometres north of Ciudad Guzmán, three days later. There was no resistance in any of them, no reason for house-to-house searches – there had been no Juarista presence this far south, not yet, though bandit activity could not be discounted. But fear and surly hatred were palpable in each place, women sweeping their children indoors, men slinking away down side-alleys, eyes cast down in impotent resignation, as the Belgians plodded past. It was better to take no chances, Damseaux thought, and he bivouacked his force far away from settlements each night, clothing and boots worn during sleep, rifles loaded, sentries posted.

They started again in the cool of each dawn, the pack-mules as weary as the men. Damseaux trudged on foot himself to spare his horse, the only officer's mount remaining, and he let his orderly lead it. They moved faster when they reached *El Camino Real*, the royal road that dated from Spanish days and ran, by endless meanderings, through the mountains towards the Pacific coast.

The sight of the two small French redoubts that flanked the road was heartening, even if the welcome there was a cold one. They were not intended to offer anything but token resistance, here only to provide warning of a Juarista thrust before falling back on Guzmán. The French major who commanded the Algerian zouaves holding the positions extended no invitation to Damseaux to dine with him and did no more than indicate that he could camp nearby.

Safe now inside French lines, they marched next day along the last few kilometres to the city. He had decided to face Colonel Adolphe Durand, commander of all French and Imperial forces between here and the Pacific, as soon as possible. He'd report what he had done – or rather, not done – at San Ramón Nonato. He was resolved to state what he would refuse to do again.

Come what may.

Though he'd drunk heavily, he'd been unable to sleep, had rehearsed his defences in his mind, had accepted at last that none had validity, were not even worth making. The decree he would refuse to implement again carried the full authority of Emperor Maximillian, even if that well-intentioned but weak man had been talked into it by the French commander-in-chief. Durand would be within his rights to have him shot, though he doubted he would. But disgrace would await him back in Belgium if he ever reached there alive. Lifelong disgrace, an officer who had betrayed his word.

The column pressed on through the heat of the day. Tired as they were, the men did not complain. They were looking forward to respite in Guzmán, however brief and meagre, cantinas, drink, girls to be had for almost nothing.

"Cavalry coming to meet us, sir," Lieutenant Anselme was pointing towards the city.

Damseaux shook himself from his reverie. The temptation his revolver urged was as strong, maybe stronger, than before. He saw immediately that the riders were immaculately uniformed, scarlet-topped kepis, blue tunics, red breeches, pennons fluttering from upraised lances, members of a troop selected by Durand as his personal guard. It was said that most had campaigned with him before in Algeria and Italy, that they'd vied for selection and that he had their absolute loyalty. He never left his quarters without an escort drawn from them. And one of the two riders trotting ahead in similar colours, could only be the colonel himself.

"Have my horse brought," Damseaux said to a sergeant. He was reluctant to meet Durand on foot, to be looked down on by a man whom he suspected already despised him. His orderly brought the miserable creature and he heaved himself into the saddle.

He was glad he had done so when he saw the rider accompanying the colonel was a woman. Mounted side-saddle, the red of her skirt matching that of her lover's breeches, and wearing a frogged blue tunic modelled on an officer's, Madame Sapin rode with an assurance a veteran cavalryman might envy. Her face was heavily veiled against the sun and Damseaux could not make out its features. He'd been told she was beautiful, and French, but had never seen her, much less spoken to her.

His mount managed a canter, a weak one, and he drew rein and saluted just ahead of the colonel and his mistress.

"A successful patrol, major?" Durand said.

"Successful, sir. Very successful." Impossible to say anything else in the presence of this woman.

She remained silent and was looking away. He imagined contempt in her eyes as she'd taken in his ragamuffin state.

"And not too happy to be back, I'll wager, Major Damseaux." Durand's tone was laced with sarcasm. "Longing already to be out on patrol again soon, are you not?"

The Belgian column was coming close, shambling like exhausted beggars, the caricature, Damseaux knew, of what a fighting unit should be, fit for nothing better than burning villages and shooting hostages.

Like me.

"These Belgians are fire-eaters, desperate fellows," Durand said to Madame Sapin. "Longing for combat. It's hard to rein them in. Isn't that so, major?" He laughed.

She said nothing and Damseaux hoped she didn't smile, though it was impossible to see through her veil. He'd heard she must be fifteen years, at the least, younger than the colonel and he wondered how he had found her, how she could bear him.

"We're proud to be Empress Carlota's men." Damseaux could not think of any other reply on the spur of the moment. He had never felt more wretched, more of a fraud. And the colonel was what he would never be. A soldier, a real soldier, even if a brute.

"And Her Imperial Majesty will be even prouder when you go south, major, you and your heroes. An assignment they'll welcome."

"May I enquire where to, sir?"

"Oh, just a little way. See me tomorrow. Nine o'clock. We'll discuss it then. You'll like it."

Damseaux saluted, bowed to Madame Sapin, and turned away. He was almost out of earshot then he headed the colonel speak to her in a stage whisper.

"Out of the firing line. The only place I can trust them."

And he laughed again.

HMS Sprightly

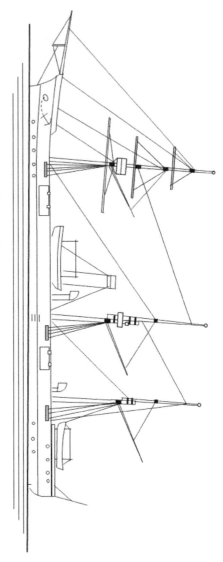

First Class Gunvessel , *Cormorant* Class
Builder: J Scott Russell, Millwall
Launched: February 1861
Completed: July 1862
Displacement: 877 tons
Length: 185 feet overall
Beam: 28 feet
Draught: 12 feet
Armour: None

Machinery: Single Expansion Engine,
700 Horsepower, Single Screw
Speed: 11 Knot (Max.)
7 Knots (Cruising)
Armament:
1 × 7-inch/110-pdr Armstrong breechloader*
2 × 20-pdr Armstrong breech-loaders*
*Behind hinged bulwarks
Complement: 90

Chapter 1

"This has been the best year of my life," Nicholas Dawlish had written on the last page of the journal he'd kept during every day of 1865.

He had not expected it to be so. Few welcomed a posting to the Pacific Station, a virtual backwater, nor had he done so himself when, as a newly promoted sub-lieutenant, he was appointed third officer of HMS *Sprightly*. There were reasons why some powerful people in Britain wanted to forget Princess Alexandra's Legion had ever existed, much less participated in the recent war in Denmark. Dawlish had been a very minor player and, while he'd been sworn to secrecy, it was expedient that he, and more senior volunteers, would remain far from Europe until the affair was forgotten.

From the station base at Esquimalt, on Vancouver Island, the gunvessel departed in early April to cruise down the western coasts of the Americas as far south as the Magellan Straits. Her duty had been to show the flag at ports where there were British commercial interests. Most visits had been little more than social occasions, with an opportunity at times to explore ashore for a few days, but several had more serious intent. Small as she was, *Sprightly's* presence was enough to serve notice to Peru, Chile and Spain that, regardless of the intermittent war they were fighting over guano reserves, British investments and British commercial interests were sacrosanct. Resent it as they might, none challenged that assumption. With an efficient but approachable captain, Commander Frederick Weatherby, and a contented crew, the long cruise that brought *Sprightly* back to Esquimalt in late September seemed more of a holiday than a duty. Dawlish spent much of his off-duty time studying Spanish and practising when he could go ashore.

The next year, 1866, had begun well with a visit in February to Nazareno, on Bolivia's short Pacific coast, but nobody had relished heading north in May to Novo-Arkhangelsk. Magnificent though its location might be, and grandiose the snow-capped mountains about it, the capital of Russia's American colony was mean and squalid.

Settlement of a dispute over sealing-rights boundaries had been protracted and increasingly ill-tempered. A seaman's death in a vodka-sodden affray in a foetid tavern had soured relations further. It had been a relief to crawl back south to Esquimalt with an increasingly sickly engine. The last three hundred miles were, of necessity, under sail alone and made worse by a violent storm.

The inner surfaces of *Sprightly's* cylinders were too scored and pitted for further piston-packing to make much difference. Reboring was beyond the capabilities of Esquimalt's limited machining facilities. There was no option but to bring the gunvessel to an American dockyard. Its location, San Francisco, was unfortunate, if unavoidable. Tempted by wages they could only dream of elsewhere, four seamen had disappeared and, worse, an artificer from the engine room with them. The Central Pacific railroad, now pressing eastwards through the Sierra Nevada, was insatiable in its demand for labour, skilled or unskilled. The shiploads of bewildered Chinese workers arriving almost daily attested to that. In this teeming city there was no hope of capturing the deserters, even if the American authorities been interested in cooperating. With its civil war behind it, the United States was growing and thriving again. The least of its concerns was a naval inconvenience for a European nation that had demonstrated sympathy for the losing side.

*

On Wednesday August 8th, the now-repaired *Sprightly* was coaling for her return to Esquimalt when a steam launch with 'Western Union' stencilled on its side delivered a telegram. Weatherby called Dawlish to his quarters soon after. He handed him a sheet with pasted-on strips of print. There were no breaks in the string of letters.

"From the Station C-in-C, I'll warrant," he said. "You'll sort it out for me, will you Dawlish? Thanks. Good fellow! You like codes and ciphering and all that sort of thing, don't you?"

It was true. He did, ever since his consumptive uncle, a retired naval officer, had taught him the Playfair system, for he was too debilitated to do much else. The clear Pyrenean air of the French spa-town of Pau had slowed, but not halted, the illness. The memories of those days when he was twelve years old was poignant, not only of the dying man who had made him his heir but of the kindness of his mistress – now dead herself – and of her daughter Clothilde, who became like a sister to him. That she had disappeared after her mother's death made recollection all the more painful.

Five minutes were enough to reveal a coherent message. Seventeen words only. The brevity, and the demand for immediate sailing, were indication enough that there was no room for questioning.

Sprightly to repair to Manzanillo with all despatch and take appropriate measures to protect British interests.

"Damned if I've heard of the place," Weatherby said. "Have you?"

Dawlish hadn't either. The captain's steward was sent to the chart house to fetch a gazetteer and summon Ashton and Sanderson, the first and second officers, along with Grove, the lieutenant of marines.

"Be careful when you hear that damn word 'appropriate', Dawlish," Weatherby said. "Nothing can destroy a man's prospects faster. The decisions will be yours and there'll be scant thanks if they're successful, and repudiation if they're not." There was a hint of bitterness in his voice. Officers who made mistakes – or enemies – often found themselves posted to the Pacific Station.

The steward returned with the gazetteer. Manzanillo proved to be a small port on Mexico's Pacific coast, almost two thousand miles from San Francisco. The book was eight years old and identified the place as used by local coastal traffic only. Anything could have happened in the meantime, especially in a country riven by civil war and foreign intrusion.

"What are the British interests there, sir?" Ashton had arrived, the other officers also.

"You know as much as I do," Weatherby said.

Telegrams were expensive but three days would have been enough for the regular coastal mail to carry a package from Vancouver, Dawlish thought. He suspected Weatherby was thinking the same. It should have been possible to send more specific instructions. That they hadn't been, implied somebody in London had no intention of being embarrassed should there be failure. Neither was the Station C-in-C in Esquimalt.

"Who's holding this Manzanillo place, sir?" Ashton asked the most important question. "The French, the Mexican Imperial army, or the Juaristas?"

That wasn't known either.

"We'll sail on the morrow, regardless," Weatherby said. "Mr Ashton, you'll see to that. And coal – not just the bunkers brimming but all the sacks you can stack on deck. I'll sign for them. God knows when or where we can coal again."

"Are the men to know where we're going?"

"Not until we're at sea. And, Lieutenant Grove, just in case the word gets out, have your men posted, and watching like hawks. I don't want anybody slipping over the side before we leave. Mr. Sanderson, and Mr. Dawlish, you're to get ashore immediately and find out all you can about Manzanillo. Our consul here must know something."

Dawlish felt a surge of elation. Opportunities for ambitious young officers to earn distinction often started like this.

*

Above the entrance to a building shared with several commercial enterprises, the enamelled plaque carrying the crown, lion and unicorn identified the British consulate.

"I think you can handle this business quite well on your own, Dawlish," Sanderson stopped as they were about to mount the steps. His tone was hesitant, almost apologetic. "The captain asked me to see to another matter." He wasn't looking Dawlish in the eye. "I'll meet you here again in a couple of hours. Five o'clock, say. That'll give you time enough."

Whatever it was, it would not be business of the captain's. It could be women, or it could be drink. Maybe both. Sanderson's weaknesses were known and, all the worse, apparent to the lower deck. He couldn't be more than thirty but his face was already flushed and bloated. It was no surprise that he was serving on the Pacific Station.

"Very well, sir," Dawlish said. "I'll do my best."

The consular appointment here was official, not honorary. William Arnott proved to be a stout, florid fifty-year old who was not only welcoming but more than willing to help.

"It's a change not to meet an Englishman whose goods are being held up in customs, and like to spoil there," he said, "or one who's had every possible misfortune and indignant that I won't advance him a hundred dollars to get him home to his starving wife, children and invalid mother."

His office was comfortable but untidy, with large maps pinned to the walls. Framed photographs – officers in mess uniforms in posed groups – indicated an army background.

"Manzanillo?" he said. "I know where it is. Not much more, though. I recall something happening there a few years ago. But I haven't heard anything about it recently – we haven't got a man there. It's hard to know what's going on in Mexico nowadays."

"But you must hear a lot about it here, sir."

"Less than you'd think and damn near nothing that can be trusted. But the general opinion is the French have seen the writing on the wall. I'd be surprised if there'll be a single one of 'em there in a year's time. If Emperor Max has any sense – and by the looks of it, he hasn't – he'll be gone with them. God knows that Juarez and his people have a lot of scores to settle."

"So what was happening in Manzanillo a few years ago, sir?" Dawlish wanted to draw the conversation back to the port. Arnott's predictions were no different to those he'd read in American newspapers, all of them in full sympathy with the Juarista cause.

"There was to be a railway running inland from Manzanillo. It was to link the Pacific coast with Mexico City and beyond. All the usual hyperbole about such ventures – vast opportunities for trade and industry, opening the country for exports to the Orient and so on. It was eight or ten years ago. I don't know how far it got before the

French arrived and the chaos began. That put paid to a lot of undertakings like it. The investors must have taken a bad beating."

"British investors, sir?" Dawlish said.

"The short answer's 'yes', but I can't recall the company's name. There must be something in one or other of the trade directories or yearbooks."

Arnott rang a bell on his desk and a clerk appeared. He was sent off and returned two minutes later with an armful of thick volumes. Several were Board of Trade publications, others commercial listings. Dawlish felt suddenly aware of a complex world of industry and commerce of which he knew nothing.

While the clerk waited, Arnott scribbled two notes. "Take this to Anderson at the *Chronicle* and this one to Webster at the *Clarion*. Wait for the replies – it won't take long – and get back as quickly as you can."

When the clerk was gone the consul said, "They're editors. Anderson's got good army contacts. The *Clarion's* only interested in business." He pushed half of the volumes across his desk to Dawlish. "Just scan the indices for mentions of railways, railroads, Mexico, Manzanillo. D'ye speak any Spanish? Good! Take this one too then." The *Annuario Universal* for 1862, published in Mexico City. "I'll skim through the others."

It was a half-hour before either found anything of value since most of the documentation referred to the United States. A British directory did however indicate the Occidental and Pacific Railway Investment Company Limited was registered in London in 1856. Shares and debentures had been issued to support construction of a link, *El Ferrocarril del Pacífico,* from Guadalajara in central Mexico to the western coast. Dawlish was too embarrassed to admit he did not know what debentures were.

"They must have had a damn good man in Mexico to smooth the way," Arnott said. "Look at the list of directors – by their names, half of 'em must have been Mexican politicians, though I doubt if one of 'em ever set foot in London. That's how it's done, young Dawlish! No wonder the government granted a hundred-year concession within six months."

Another, more exuberant, publication confirmed, as Arnott had foreseen, that the line would open limitless prospects for economic development and that its profitability would be stupendous. A survey completed in 1859 identified a practical route that reached the ocean at Manzanillo.

"Let's look at a map," Arnott said.

The small scale of the only map of Mexico to hand did not hide the mountain range that ran parallel to the coast. Guadalajara lay 5000 feet above sea level and a hundred and twenty miles inland. Many of the range's peaks were higher but the railway route surveyed dropped southwards through a wide valley towards the ocean. Though special provisions would be required at a few points, gradients were said to be moderate over most sections. Dawlish suspected that 'special' might be as treacherous a word as 'appropriate'. Averages over the total distance were meaningless. What mattered was whether there were obstacles at those few sections – steep climbs that might demand zig-zags or walls of rock necessitating tunnelling. He knew this because he had devoured the illustrated papers that were full of the problems facing the Central Pacific and the ingenuity of the engineering solutions that needed armies of labourers to implement.

The *Annuario Universal* revealed that work had been suspended – temporarily, it stressed. Starting from Manzanillo, the line had reached the town of Colima and extended for a few miles beyond. Dawlish found the place on the map, checked the scale.

"About forty miles, as the crow flies," he said. "But it looks like the actual route's twice that or more."

"I doubt if anything's been done since then," Arnott said. "Not with the upheaval in the last four years. The work will start again when things have been resolved. I can't see the investment's at any serious risk."

"Why's that, sir?"

"A republican government issued the licence six years before the French showed up. Once the French are gone, Juarez and his people will want to be seen honouring agreements made by their republican predecessors. If they don't, there won't be another penny of foreign investment in Mexico. A lot of Juarez's eloquent apostles of democracy will be looking forward to remunerative seats on boards."

"But we're to head to Manzanillo urgently," Dawlish said. "There must be something at risk."

Arnott shrugged. "Probably British residents knowing they'll see the Juaristas arrive sooner rather than later and a few of 'em panicking about the prospect. It's good your vessel's on the way. There's nothing more reassuring than the sight of a gunboat."

The clerk was back. "Mr. Anderson says this is the best he's got for now," he said.

Arnott ripped the envelope open, scanned the single sheet and passed it to Dawlish. "It's a damn good summary," he said. "No surprises though."

The *Chronicle's* editor had dashed off four handwritten paragraphs in haste. French forces abandoning whole states and major towns, Guadalajara among them, and retreating towards Mexico City. Garrisons along the road from there to Vera Cruz reinforced. The Juaristas' advance was south and eastwards, not yet toward the Pacific. Manzanillo had probably little to fear for now.

"There's something interesting here." Arnott held up the note brought from Webster of the *San Francisco Clarion*. "A silver mine. Plutus Mining Limited. British. Somewhere near Colima – wasn't that place on the railway? Expected to start production soon." He passed the paper across. "But you see the date of the licence, do you?"

"1864."

"Two years ago. And which government could have issued it?"

"The French?"

Arnott shook his head. "No, but it might just as well have been – it was Emperor Max's Imperial government. And in a few months' time it won't be worth the paper it's written on. Whoever's put their money in Plutus has damn good reason to be worried. Some American company will be more than glad to take the licence over and make a few of Juarez's cronies rich on the way."

"But it's a British company and –"

"And I'll wager investors in London are getting cold feet. Influential people, no doubt. Then a word or two in certain ears in Whitehall and a telegram to the Minister in Washington – with that new ocean-cable in place it could be done within a day. Maybe a telegram from the Admiralty too, through to its people at Esquimalt. And your captain's at the end of the line, poor devil."

"What can he do?"

"His judgement, his decision, and a bloody sensitive one at that. I wouldn't wish it on my worst enemy. Scylla and Charybdis, Dawlish, Charybdis and Scylla, French and Juarista. It's no wonder that he hasn't received any clearer orders."

Dawlish waited outside the consulate for Sanderson's return. Two labourers, Irish by their accents, catcalled from across the street when they saw his uniform. One crossed to spit at his feet. Passers-by laughed and he felt angry and humiliated while he waited longer than agreed by *Sprightly's* second lieutenant. It made it worse that, when Sanderson arrived a half-hour later, his voice was slurred and his face red.

"Found out anything useful, Dawlish?" Once more, Sanderson did not look him in the eye.

"Yes, sir. Very useful."

"Tell me the gist of it while we walk back to the jetty. I'll let you deal with the details if Weatherby's interested."

And the captain was interested – very interested – and as he listened to Sanderson's confused summary and Dawlish's clearer exposition, he looked worried.

With good reason.

Chapter 2

Manzanillo possessed a splendid anchorage, a semi-circular bay, beach-fringed, with a small rocky peninsula extending out from its centre into deeper water. Smaller craft could moor directly at the wharves there, close to the warehouses and workshops behind, but larger vessels must lie further out, dependent on lighters to carry freight to or from shore.

It surprised Dawlish that it was so empty – only a single brig lying along a wharf, empty lighters clustered close by, nothing at anchor, no movement on the calm blue water other than a small fishing boat pulling seawards, another dozen hauled up on the beach. At the peninsula tip, a green, white and red tricolour, with some symbol on the central stripe, flapped lazily over what was typical of the small stone forts with which Spain had protected its colonial ports. A black barrel jutted from only one of the embrasures, but it must be an antique, for there had been no response to the salute *Sprightly* fired on approach.

Dawlish was at the bow with the mooring party and his gaze kept returning to the bridge, waiting for the signal to let go. Weatherby and the other officers were still scrutinising the buildings ashore. There was activity there, but no bustle, just a few figures emerging from the shadows of the warehouses – rust-streaked corrugated-metal barns – to watch the gunvessel's arrival. A large steam-crane stood idle and an inactive string of wagons – no locomotive – showed that rails ran along the frontage. The heaps of coal further back must have been brought here at vast expense. A little further on, were what looked like wooden offices and the railway workshops – more rusting metal sheeting, open-fronted sheds. A wisp of smoke drifted from a single smokestack, a boiler kept at pressure, perhaps for powering machine tools. *El Ferrocarril del Pacífico* must still have some life in it, but no puffing clouds of steam indicated movement in what might be the shunting yard.

Beyond lay the town itself, another tricolour flying above a grandiose yellow building. The low white housing surrounding it seemed identical to those in every port between Valparaiso and

California, and more substantial than the huts behind the beaches that arced away from either side of the peninsula. Green-clad mountains lay behind, an unbroken wall extending north and south.

The gunvessel anchored. With all now secured, Dawlish was summoned to the bridge.

"Your Spanish is damn useful," Weatherby said. "I'm going ashore and I want you with me. Better get into full rig."

It was surprising how few officers bothered to learn even a smattering of languages, Dawlish thought. Private study, and practice when ashore, had given him more than basic capability but still not as fluent as he was in French. He sensed Ashton and Sanderson didn't like that he had made the effort. They lived in a state of general resentment, even at the best of times.

He was already sweating heavily in his formal uniform as he sat with his captain in the sternsheets and the gig approached the wharf.

"If this place is under threat, nobody here seems to being doing much about it," Weatherby said. "We saw more activity in Novo-Arkhangelsk."

A small group of uniformed men had emerged from the fortification and were hurrying at a fast shamble towards the wharf. The figure ahead of the twin files must be an officer and he was glancing over his shoulder at intervals as to assure himself that he was being followed. He reached the landing steps just before the gig and a sergeant was yelling for the men to halt and form ranks. By the time Weatherby and Dawlish had landed, the troops were presenting arms in something resembling a salute and the officer, in a faded uniform that must once have been gaudy, managed scarcely better.

Salutes returned, introductions made, Dawlish translating. Teniente Robles commanded the town's garrison of Mexican Imperial troops. The British ship's visit was unexpected but welcome, he said. He only regretted that His Imperial Majesty Maximilian's warship *Quetzal* had not been here to return the salute. And might he enquire about the reason for the visit?

While he translated, Dawlish noticed that several of the soldiers were barefoot. Wide-brimmed hats outnumbered battered shakoes. He saw a few modern rifles, but most were armed with flintlocks probably abandoned by the Spanish more than four decades before. Dark skin and high cheekbones indicated Indian ancestry and there was a deadness in the eyes that Dawlish found disturbing. These were men who expected nothing because they had never had anything, or ever would, and who wore these pitiful uniforms only because they had been conscripted into them. Men who would cast them off and fade away at the first opportunity. And Teniente Robles – Spanish-looking, not Indian – must know that too, must be wondering whether his Imperial commission might now be a death warrant.

"The fellow wants to know why we're here, does he, Mr. Dawlish?" Weatherby said. "Tell him we're want assurances about the safety of British life and property."

Robles might not speak English, but he seemed to detect the contempt in the captain's tone. Dawlish was diplomatic when he answered. With the town obviously well garrisoned, he said, and an Imperial warship patrolling the coast, there were no British concerns about the situation at Manzanillo itself. But little was known about matters further inland. Would the teniente be able to assist?

No, with infinite regret, the teniente could not help. His authority was in Manzanillo only. But the alcalde would know more about the matter, and he would be happy to escort *el capitán inglés* to meet him. He would have to leave him there since he had urgent business to attend to at the fort.

And as they passed through narrow cobbled laneways to the *alcaldía*, – the yellow building glimpsed earlier – Dawlish wondered how long it would be before Teniente Robles would himself be casting off his uniform and finding a new allegiance.

*

The same device as in the white central stripe of the tricolour appeared on a plaque behind the alcalde's desk, an Imperial crown above, dark eagles below flanking an image of another eagle devouring a serpent.

And the words *Equidad en la Justicia*. Maximilian's empire had promised much.

The alcalde – no obvious trace of Indian blood – seemed like a man who might also be calculating when to turn his coat. They learned almost nothing from him. The railway's presence was valued, he said, even if it reached scarcely past Colima. He believed the weekly train was valued by traders there no less than in Manzanillo. He knew of the Plutus mine – *El Glorioso* – and would be proud if its silver shipments were made through this port.

Dawlish asked if such shipments had been made already. And no, the alcalde said, they hadn't, but no doubt they'd come in due course. There was no Juarista threat here and he believed that His Imperial Majesty's forces, with welcome French support, were in full control of this state – as they would soon again be in all Mexico. But his own authority was confined to this town, and it would better for the honoured *capitán inglés* to raise the matters that had brought him with the state governor.

"Ask him where we'll find that fellow," Weatherby said.

"Where may we find His Excellency, señor?" Dawlish translated.

"In Ciudad Guzmán. I can provide you a letter of introduction."

A memory of the map on the consul's wall. Guzmán was halfway between Colima and Guadalajara. The railway had not extended that far.

"Can you advise us on how to reach there, señor?"

The alcalde shrugged. "It may be difficult. It's beyond my jurisdiction. But Señor Turnbull of the railway may be able to help you. The letter of introduction to His Excellency will be sent to your ship."

A few meaningless courtesies before they left. And the alcalde – for however longer he might hold the title – looked relieved to be rid of them.

*

A man in oil-stained cotton shirt and trousers had just left one of the wooden offices and was hurrying towards an open shed where a small steam engine powered overhead shafting. The slapping sound of belting told of some drill or lathe in use. The face beneath his frayed straw hat-brim was brown and leathery.

Dawlish hailed him. *"Quiero hablar con el jefe. Donde esta?"*

"No sabe las palabras 'por favor', señor?" The man had stopped, was offended. Nothing here of the passivity seen in the eyes of Robles' pathetic soldiers.

"What's the fellow saying, Mr. Dawlish?" Weatherby said.

Dawlish was interrupted as he was starting to reply.

"He's saying courtesy costs nothing," the man replied. And any 'fellow' deserves to be called 'Sir'. The words were English, the tone angry and the accent strong Yorkshire. "If you're looking for the *jefe*, that's me, Harry Turnbull, general manager of *El Pacífico*."

Weatherby introduced himself, apologised for Dawlish's unfamiliarity with the language and extended his hand. Turnbull wiped his own on his oily trouser leg and then shook it.

"I'm busy, captain," he said. "If you've anything to say to me, you can say it while we walk."

He didn't wait for a reply but strode on towards the shed. Weatherby paused, then joined him. Dawlish felt angry, humiliated, as he kept pace with his captain, and felt it all the worse since he had brought the rebuff – well-merited – on himself.

Rails entered the shed from the shunting yard and ended at an inspection pit. A small black saddle-tank, most likely for shunting-yard-use, lay over it, several men working beneath. Despite the multiplicity of tools and benches and chain hoists and racks of stacked components, there was no impression of clutter. The lathes of various sizes, a shaper and two large pillar drills stood in regular rows. The floors were clean. Turnbull ran a tight ship.

He had stopped to view the activity in the pit.

Weatherby stood by him, began to speak. "There's concern that –"

"We've seen nothing of the navy in eight years, captain, not since we started surveying the line and then building it." Turnbull cut him off. "We've managed well enough without your navy. So I suppose it's the mine that's brought you here now."

"Not just that, Mr. Turnbull. The safety of the railway too." Weatherby said, "And of British employees and dependents."

"Damn few employees anymore. A half-dozen English lads – like Bill Kemp down in the pit – just enough to keep everything from falling apart, two of 'em married to locals. Still lots of Mexicans, good workers. And I presume the Americans won't be any of your concern."

"Americans?"

"They probably don't like being called that anymore. Rebels, Confederates, damned if they'd live in the re-United States. Lots of 'em came south when the war ended. Emperor Max welcomed them with open arms – land grants and the like. A few that hadn't any taste for farming drifted here."

"What do they do?"

"For me? They're under contract to patrol the railway. Do it damn well too. No half-measures. Just what's needed here. And there are another couple of 'em on that Imperial ship we see here now and then."

He turned away, walked on, stopped by a large lathe, the only machine working. What Dawlish recognised must be a locomotive's steam cylinder was clamped to the faceplate and rotating slowly, thin slivers of metal falling from the cutting tool inserted to graze the inner surface. It was the same job, though on a smaller scale, as the reboring carried out in San Francisco on *Sprightly's* cylinder. The operator, eyes fixed on the tool, adding drops of oil to its tip from a can, did not look up.

"Any better, Jack?" Turnbull said.

The operator didn't turn his head. "Sharpening the bloody things every five minutes. Near wore out, they are, whole bloody lot of 'em." Another Yorkshireman.

"You mean the cutting tools, Mr. Turnbull?" Dawlish said. He saw Weatherby glaring at him for speaking out of turn.

"Aye. We don't owe them much though," Turnbull said. "Had good use of them, we did, but there's an end to everything. More've been ordered but nothing's arrived."

Dawlish turned to Weatherby. "If I may, sir, might I have a word with you?"

They stepped aside a few paces.

"What is it, Mr. Dawlish?" Anger and impatience in the captain's tone.

"Mr Sherwin could help. There's a good stock of cutting tools on board. He could share a few."

It was true. *Sprightly's* commissioned engineer kept his stocks and ruled her engine and boiler rooms with a rigour equal to that which Turnbull imposed here. Despite that, Weatherby, like so many officers, swore he'd be damned if he'd ever want to see a mechanic in a wardroom. But Dawlish, fascinated by machines, spent much of his off-duty time in the engine room. Gentleman or not, Sherwin was worth learning from.

"You're sure, Mr. Dawlish?"

"Certain, sir. I thought it might be appreciated." He nodded towards Turnbull, who was still talking to the craftsman.

Weatherby did not reply but he went back to Turnbull and made the offer. Dawlish would bring *Sprightly's* engineer across later to see what he could do.

Mood altered, the manager invited them to share coffee and cigars in his office, but first led them through another shed – a cupola for cast iron, now cold, and equipment for sand-moulding standing idle. Another shed, opening on the shunting yard, contained three tank-engines, much larger than Dawlish expected. They needed to be powerful, some of the gradients were steep, Turnbull said, and traction demanded brute force. There were also, on sidings, many open wagons and a half-dozen wooden passenger coaches.

Turnbull's office was in one of the huts. It seemed saturated with tobacco smoke but here too was an impression of efficiency. Ledgers stood stacked in neat rows on the shelves behind the desk. What looked like technical manuals filled a bookcase. A large drawing table stood in one corner. Dark cloth hung like curtains over what were probably blueprints on the walls to protect them from light.

"Have you been here long, Mr. Turnbull?" Weatherby had sat back and was savouring his cigar.

"From the beginning. I've liked it here – you can get things done. Difficult at times, but you can get 'em done. We made damn good progress until we suspended construction when the French arrived and Juarez and his people resisted and the whole damn country went to hell."

"Have you been home?"

"Home's here. Never wanted to go back to England. Too damn much forelock tugging there."

Dawlish sensed Turnbull relished talking with a lack of the deference he would have to adopt in Britain with as obvious a social superior as a Royal Navy captain.

"The alcalde told me that the state governor's in Ciudad Guzmán. I've business to discuss with him." Weatherby said. "How far can your railway bring us, Mr. Turnbull?"

"As far as it reached before construction was suspended. That's about twenty miles short of Guzmán," Turnbull said. "But you don't need to go there to get reassurances from the governor about protection for *El Pacífico*. Don't bother, captain. Emperor, or Juarez, or the French, it makes no odds. We're just keeping what we've got in order. Once the present bedlam ends, then whoever'll be lording it in Ciudad Mexico – and I don't give a tuppenny damn who that might be – will want the line, and the finance from London for its completion all the way to Guadalajara. There's no need for Her Majesty's Navy to worry itself about that."

"And the mine, Mr. Turnbull?"

"The Plutus mine? *El Glorioso*? I've never seen it but there's good business carrying equipment to it from the port here. And I'll be happy to take even more of its money whenever it starts shipping silver."

"But could you help us get to Ciudad Guzmán, Mr. Turnbull?"

"I'll get you past Colima to the railhead where the track ends. It's near *El Glorioso*. And a day's hard travel can get you to Guzmán from there too. Sorderer can give you advice about that."

35

"Sorderer?"

"Colonel Sorderer, he likes being called. He'll remind you if you don't. Colonel Isaac Sorderer, CSA. One of the Confederates who came south. But if you're heading there, you'll need an armed escort of your own. It can be bloody dangerous north of Colima."

"Dangerous?"

"Everywhere's someway dangerous now. Not just Juarista raids but bandits too, just as bad, usually worse. That's why I need Sorderer's boys. It's also why you'll need an escort."

"How large?"

"A half-dozen men if they're any good and three times as many if they're not. And before you ask, I can't spare anybody from the track patrols and the bold Teniente Robles won't be volunteering anything either. You'd better bring your own people. And don't ask the alcalde or anybody else here for approval. With things as they are, nobody approves anything. Just do it."

Weatherby looked uncomfortable. The time for the first dreaded decision about 'appropriate measures' was upon him. He turned to Dawlish.

"I've details to discuss with Mr. Turnbull," he said. "Return to *Sprightly*. Bring Sherwin back immediately. He can go straight to the workshop and see what's wanted there. Then you can report what he says."

"Are you an engineer, Mr. Dawl, or whatever your name is?" Turnbull ignored the captain. "No? Then let the Sherwin man come an' speak for himself. He's got a tongue in his mouth, hasn't he?"

At any other time or place, Weatherby would have taken offence. But instead, he said to Dawlish, "That seems reasonable, very reasonable. Bring Sherwin here after he's seen the workshop."

The engineer might never be welcome in a wardroom but at this moment his services would be the price of transport as far as the railway reached. And then, a visit to the Plutus mine before pressing on to Ciudad Guzmán.

Far inland, through the mountains of a land in turmoil.

Where *Sprightly's* guns could offer no protection.

36

And where whatever decisions Weatherby could not avoid must later be deemed appropriate in Whitehall offices.

As there'll be in my future too, Dawlish thought. *But not yet.*

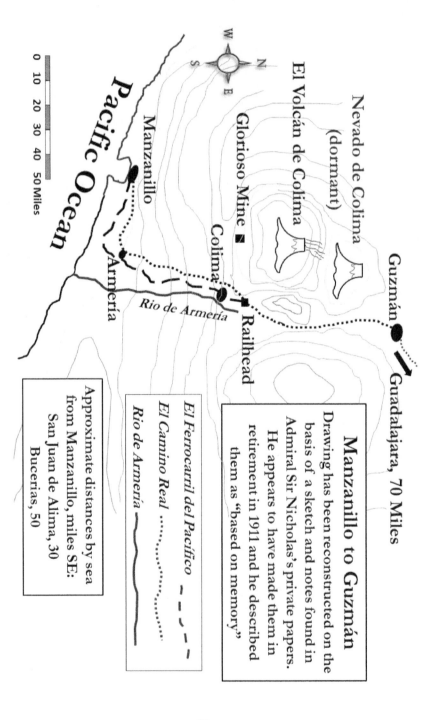

Nevado de Colima (dormant)

El Volcán de Colima

Glorioso Mine ■

Manzanillo

Colima

Railhead

Armería

Rio de Armería

Pacific Ocean

Guzmán ●

Guadalajara, 70 Miles

0 10 20 30 40 50 Miles

N
W   E
S

Manzanillo to Guzmán

Drawing has been reconstructed on the basis of a sketch and notes found in Admiral Sir Nicholas's private papers. He appears to have made them in retirement in 1911 and he described them as "based on memory"

Rio de Armería ——

El Camino Real ·········

El Ferrocarril del Pacífico – – –

Approximate distances by sea from Manzanillo, miles SE:
San Juan de Alima, 30
Bucerias, 50

Chapter 3

"What's in the kegs?" Dawlish asked.

Ox carts had brought them from the brig moored at the wharf – the *Sarah Norton*, registered at San Francisco. The effort they demanded of the labourers loading them into a boxcar looked disproportionate to their size.

"Mercury," Tom Bryce said. "Heavy stuff."

He was Dawlish's age and his accent reminded him of another American Southerner he had known. Mutual trust and regard had been forged on the cold waters of the North Sea two years before.

"What's it for, Tom?"

"They use it at the mine. Lots of it. It lifts silver from the ore."

"You've been there?"

"Six or seven times. They seem to need gallons of it."

But more than mercury was being loaded. Wooden crates containing machinery parts, barrels of lamp oil and tubs of grease, hempen cable wound on large drums, a stack of folded tarpaulins and an entire flatcar laden with cast-iron pipes. The cargo of the train now being readied would be escorted to the railhead by Colonel Sorderer, Tom Bryce and ex-Confederate guards.

Dawlish had been sent ashore to report on progress – *Sprightly's* captain was unable to conceal his impatience. He had negotiated hard with Turnbull, withholding promise of Sherwin's services until he was guaranteed transport as far as the railhead. The gunvessel's engineer and two of his artificers worked through the night with the railway's machinist, but the reboring had still gone slowly. Now the cylinder was ready and being remounted on the shunting locomotive. Only with that completed, which would not be before nightfall, could the various wagons be coupled. One only was already in place, a flatcar pushed by sweating labourers and secured ahead of the large tank-locomotive that would take the train beyond Colima. The flatcar was already walled to shoulder-height with sandbags, loop-holed in places, a small redoubt on wheels.

"It looks like it came under fire before now, Tom." Dawlish noticed that sand had leaked from small holes in several of the weather-worn bags.

"Still the safest place to be." Bryce shrugged. "I've seen worse."

He'd been a sergeant in a cavalry unit, the 28th Texan, he'd said, was proud of having been at Mansfield and at Pleasant Hill, names that meant nothing to Dawlish.

"Couldn't stomach the idea of surrender afterwards. We bled too much for that," he said.

Sorderer, the regiment's colonel, clearly felt the same. Many, similarly unwilling to accept defeat, had followed him south to Mexico. Described by Tom, with some awe, as 'a brave commander and a true gentleman,' he had created *El Pacífico's* sixty-strong guard force. Plutus had contracted for another dozen for duty at the *Glorioso* mine.

When Dawlish returned to *Sprightly*, Weatherby was unhappy that the train could not be ready to depart before midday on the morrow. His own preparations were in hand. Temporary command of the gunvessel to be transferred to Ashton, her first officer. Grove and eight of his marines to provide an escort on the rail journey. Dawlish, valuable for his French as much as for his Spanish, to act as interpreter.

All that remained was to board the train and get underway. Disguise it as he might, Weatherby clearly loathed this assignment and wanted it to be over, back at sea again, out of the riding boots he'd bought for Dawlish and himself from ex-Confederates. The mission was ill-defined and the circumstances that would determine solutions unclear.

With so little known about what was happening in the vast country into which they would advance next day, it did not auger well.

*

The train left Manzanillo early the next afternoon under command of Colonel Sorderer, a spare grim-faced taciturn man of forty. There must be no ambiguity about his position, he'd told Weatherby. *Sprightly's* three officers and dozen marines were passengers, carried on sufferance. His own word would be absolute and, if they didn't like it, they were welcome to get off at any time.

"We must humour the fellow," Weatherby told Dawlish and Grove. "But any problems should be referred to me."

The track, single, was level for the first thirty miles, running south-east-through a narrow strip of flat land between the ocean and the hills. There were passing-points every ten miles, Dawlish learned, hundred-yard sections of double track where one train could pull in to allow another to pass.

The only passenger coach – reserved for Sorderer and the three men he called his officers, and offering grudged accommodation to Weatherby, Grove and Dawlish – was coupled directly behind the locomotive. The windows were covered outside with inch-thick wooden boards and the glass had been removed. Each was loop-holed in two places. The boxcars with mine-supplies were coupled behind, followed by two flatcars carrying crates and piping, and a brake van that Bryce called a 'caboose'. At the rear was another sandbag-protected flatcar, like that ahead of the engine.

Even on this section, speed never exceeded ten miles an hour. Dawlish recognised that the often-uneven track, rather than the power of the locomotive, was the restriction. Riding in the aftermost redoubt-flatcar with Grove and his marines, he sensed something like a holiday spirit among them. Tom Bryce, calling himself a lieutenant, despite his rank of sergeant in the late war to the north, commanded a dozen guards. Relations with the marines were already warm – tobacco exchanged, laughter at each other's accents and pronunciations, comparison of weapons, jokes about uniforms. The marines, as always, were immaculately turned out but each of the guards, though largely civilian-dressed, had some remnant of Confederate uniform. Ragged and faded grey tunics with yellow piping and battered kepis with cracked leather bills – most items still retaining badges of rank or unit – were all worn with an air of self-reliant pride. For all their shabbiness, these men exuded a defiant air of being unconquered.

Dawlish felt embarrassed that the British Enfield muzzle-loaders looked antiquated when seen side by side with the breech-loading

Lorenz rifles that the ex-Confederates had brought south with them. Even more surprising was Bryce's Henry.

"You've never seen a repeater before?" He sounded incredulous as he shook an astonishing fifteen rounds from the magazine in the stock and ejected another from the breech. Then he handed it to Dawlish.

"Took it from a Yankee. So too, some of the other boys. You can load 'em on a Sunday and fire all week," he said. "Ammunition's hard to come by, though."

"It's accurate?"

"Good to two hundred, at the least, maybe three. Fit to knock the ears off a squirrel."

They were passing cultivated fields, white clad figures with hoes crouched in labour there, never looking up to see the train pass. Did they know – or care – that an emperor reigned in Chapultepec, Dawlish wondered. Would their lives be any better if the French left or if the Juaristas replaced them? He remembered the tenants on his properties in Shropshire. Inherited from his beloved uncle, the six small farms, managed by an agent, brought in little. Most of that – and it never was enough – was spent on upkeep, leaving him only a pittance hardly enough to pay for his uniforms. Many of the tenants lived in squalor – a few must resent him – and their more enterprising sons had left for America or Australia. But for these Mexican labourers, there could be no escape. They could only endure.

"Land over there's granted to Colonel Charles M. Pettigrew, 9th Arkansas." Bryce was pointing to fields mottled with stunted maize, a low adobe shack beyond. "Not making much of a go of it neither. Reckon he'll move further south. Better openings for gentlemen there, work for fighting men."

"South? Where?"

"Peru or Colombia, Ecuador or Bolivia or Chile maybe, some damn place like that. Somebody's always fighting somebody else down there. An' we've heard talk of a Colonel Culbertson, writing back to Sorderer that he's looking to recruit likely men, raising a force."

"For whom?"

"God knows. Anybody, I guess. It don't matter none if it pays well."

"I heard talk of some of your people serving at sea," Dawlish said.

"On the *Quetzal*. You've heard of her? The Imperial ship? An Austrian captain with a fancy name and a couple of our people."

"You know their names? Lorance perhaps, or maybe Welborne?"

Men whom Dawlish had served with two years before, Confederate officers in temporary service, as he had been himself, for Denmark. He had wondered what had become of them. Bryce had much of Welborne about him, not just the same age, but the bitterness that underlay confidence and outward cheer.

"Welborne, you said? Lorance? No. Don't know 'em. Hardly ever had sight of the ship anyways. It's too busy chasing Yankees running guns an' supplies in for the Juaristas."

Four of Bryce's men were on their feet on either side at any time, scanning the landscape.

"Do you expect trouble so near the coast?" Dawlish asked.

"Unlikely. Always possible, though. Not the Juaristas, not yet. But bandits, far worse. And the further we go up the Armería valley, the more dangerous it gets."

The guards in the sandbagged car ahead of the locomotive must be even more on the alert, Dawlish thought, intent on sighting any obstruction on the track. Weatherby was up there with Sorderer and he wondered if the mood between them was thawing. It was hard to imagine *Sprightly's* captain in easy conversation with the reserved Sorderer, much less take directions from him.

The sun was setting when the train pulled into Ciudad de Armería. The name was deceptive – not a city and little more than a scattering of adobe buildings with a small church rising above them. *El Pacífico's* halt lay at the edge, a hundred yards separating it from the closest house. The train slowed and stopped while the halt's own guards drew back the *cheval-de-frise* that closed the gap through which the track passed. Once the train had puffed slowly through, they dragged the barrier back into position. The halt consisted of a water tower, several shacks, an open shed, a coal heap, a passing place and a platform for loading or unloading freight. Several small hand-cranked railcars stood on a siding. A thick cactus hedge ran around the perimeter. A slovenly Imperial Mexican sergeant and a dozen soldiers garrisoned it, supplemented by a half-dozen of Sorderer's men.

Dawlish saw that at places along the hedge there were U-shaped breastworks, walled with adobe, each large enough to shelter three or four men.

"Are those manned at night?" he asked Bryce.

"Just a look-out in each an' patrols along the fence."

"Have there been attacks?"

"Just a few shots." Bryce gestured to the scrub-covered slopes rising to the north towards the mountains beyond. "Somebody out there in the dark. Never came closer. Miles away by morning, I guess."

"They weren't followed?"

"No sense hunting needles in haystacks. Not our job. Sorderer says if Emperor Max's boys can't control the countryside, he's damned if he will."

Dawlish caught Grove's eye, saw the marine lieutenant was thinking the same as himself. Here, some seventy miles from Guzmán, the furthest large town still held by the French, Imperial authority extended to no more than a narrow strip to either side of the track.

*

The night's rest at the halt was passed as in an armed camp. The breastworks were indeed manned, two lookouts in each on this occasion. and Weatherby made it a point of honour that the marines should assume two of the four-hour watches, and he made rounds with a patrol himself. The halt was well managed – food supplies laid up, a cook and kitchen, cots for the guards in the adobe huts or in boxcars on a siding, adequate and well-maintained latrines. Other than a few women and children who came to sell fruit and eggs, and were allowed no further than the *cheval-de-frise*, there was no contact with the village.

Dawlish joined Grove and Bryce on a patrol at midnight, passing from one breastwork to the other, checking sentry alertness, ears strained for any sounds other than those of night insects. Only the soft warm darkness made the duty different to what he remembered from the cold wet misery in the Danish defences at Thyborøn that seemed an eternity before. He could sense Grove's nervousness – the marine lieutenant once confessed he envied his experience of combat, for he had none himself. Grove's fear of failing the inevitable test of leadership was obvious but unspoken. Dawlish felt it too, had never shaken it off since he had first seen action in China. He suspected he never would.

The night passed without incident. Cockcrows from the village announced too soon that dawn was breaking. The locomotive boiler had been kept warm and it took but a half-hour – during which the men breakfasted on cornbread and coffee – before steam enough was raised to depart. The previous day's mood of gaiety among guards and marines alike was gone, replaced by awareness of passage into a more dangerous world. Dawlish asked if he might join Weatherby in the sandbagged car in front of the engine and was permitted.

The *cheval-de-frise* ahead of the train was drawn back and it trundled through. It crossed a river – the Rio Armería, stony and dry but for a trickle at its middle – on a wooden trestle bridge and the track turned due north a few miles further on. From there it would run roughly parallel, sometimes close, sometimes more distant, to *El Camino Real*, the old Spanish track that led towards Guzmán and Guadalajara.

Ahead now was the gap in the hills that identified entrance to the Armería river's long, winding, climbing valley. The track would follow it to Colima, the last town it passed through before its construction had been suspended some ten miles beyond.

Then the hard travelling would begin.

*

The long slow climb from here to Colima would take two days, the track winding, often in tight curves, to decrease gradients. From the beginning, the locomotive was taxed almost to its limit and speed was often little more than walking pace. The line was an impressive achievement, not just the embankments and cuttings that must have demanded the labour of thousands, but occasional bridges, some simple structures across narrow gullies, others substantial trestles spanning twenty or thirty yards. London's Occidental and Pacific Railway Investment Company had invested heavily in *El Ferrocarril del Pacífico* and, although it carried minimal freight, money was still being spent on maintaining it. There must be high confidence in its earning power once the current chaos in Mexico ended.

But for now, it looked vulnerable, very vulnerable, as it snaked through the fertile but narrowing valley with ever higher hills to either side. There were villages here, all at a distance from the track, and tended fields bordered by luxuriant tropical growth, thick enough to hide a small army. A handful of men could rip up yards of track in a single night, could set fire to the creosoted timbers of the trestle bridges, could fade back into cover without fear of pursuit.

Dawlish said as much to Bryce on the next night's halt. It was half-way to Colima, little different to that at Ciudad de Armería.

"That'll come later," Bryce said. "Later, but it'll come."

"Bandits?" It was hard to see profit in it for them.

"No, Juaristas. They'll cut it if it suits them and then the French in Guzmán will be finished. Since they've given up Guadalajara, this line's their only way out of the country."

"So why aren't the Juaristas cutting it now?"

"Maybe they don't want to. Maybe they hope the French will see the light and know they can't hold Guzmán forever. Maybe the French commander's already thinking of high-tailing it down to Manzanillo without a fight and shipping home from there. Maybe Juarez's boys think they've bled enough themselves already an' happy to see the French let go in peace."

"And the emperor's supporters? They can't all leave."

"They'll just turn their coats and shout 'Viva Juarez!' until they're hoarse, and even then there'll still be a lot of scores to settle."

It rained heavily through the night, a warm downpour that brought misery to the sentries and ended before dawn. It left tendrils of mist boiling off the sodden ground as the sun climbed. The train was underway by seven, preceded now by four of Sorderer's guards on a hand-pumped railcar collected at Ciudad Armería. It was protected with sandbags, a smaller version of the flatcar ahead of the locomotive. Two heaved on the rocking beam, the others faced outwards. It moved with surprising speed and had already drawn a quarter-mile ahead of the train which, coaled and watered during darkness, lurched into motion in its wake.

Dawlish was in the leading flatcar with Weatherby. He sensed heightened alertness in the guards, recognised it in the intentness with which Sorderer scanned the green-clad flanking slopes through field glasses. The valley was funnelling towards what looked like a continuous wall with no obvious passage through.

"You're taking no chances, sir," Weatherby said to Sorderer. He had taken the glasses, was nodding towards the railcar that was now disappearing around a bend a half-mile ahead.

"I can't afford to take 'em. Can you, sir?"

Sorderer turned away, as unwilling now, as since first meeting, to respond to Weatherby's overtures of civility. Grey haired, grey beard closely cropped, face set in what seemed a permanent scowl of resentment, his Confederate uniform more complete, and less ragged, than any of his men's, he spoke only to growl commands. And yet those men worshipped him, Bryce had told Dawlish, whether they had ridden with him for three years and more or had joined him from other units when the war had ended.

"He'd rather roast in hell before he'd take the Yankee amnesty and oath of loyalty," Bryce had said. "The rest of us neither. He burned his house in Hempstead – north o' Galveston – before we left. Nothing would bring him back, he said. He'd been an attorney, but found he was a better soldier."

"Has he a family?"

"Died before the war on a visit to kin in New Orleans. Wife, three little ones. Yellow fever."

A gap was opening in the green-clad ridge ahead, a half-mile wide, not more, and beyond it yet higher hills and the promise of mountains further distant. There was no cultivation here and to the left of the track the night's rainfall was surging through the river's several rocky channels. Now the train was passing through, the incline slight, glimpses ahead of the valley widening again, a few fields of cultivation close to the line, scattered adobe shacks. Then, rough terrain again, scattered scrub coming close to the track. Ahead, dark shapes were circling, soaring high.

Dawlish pointed. "What are they?" he asked Bryce.

"Zopilotes, black vultures. Never good news."

One of the lookouts was suddenly calling and pointing. Not at the birds. Sorderer was swinging up his glasses to focus on the dot emerging from around a bend a half-mile ahead, shouting for everybody to drop, take cover, for word to be passed to the locomotive driver to stop. Brakes squealed, a shudder ran through the cars as they lunged forward on their couplings, before jerking to a halt.

Even at this distance, even with his naked eye, Dawlish could recognise that dot for what it was.

The railcar, racing back, its rocker beam flailing up and down, gathering speed with the incline as the line straightened.

And one man standing, waving, signalling alarm.

Trouble ahead.

Chapter 4

The guards' railcar that returned to report the obstacle ahead had approached no closer to it than a hundred yards – the sergeant in charge being cautious, and rightly so. Sorderer ordered Bryce to take a half-dozen men forward on foot. Dawlish was impressed by their stealthy advance, moving at either side of the track from one patch of cover to the next, flitting forward in ones and twos while the others waited their turn to leapfrog them. He stood watching with Weatherby across the sandbags on the flatcar, Sorderer by them.

Only the shrill of insects broke the silence and Dawlish's feeling of vulnerability was intensified by the nearness of the dense vegetation on the slope to the right. In Denmark he had seen men who raised their heads above parapets killed by a single rifle shot at longer ranges than this. Other than the lookouts, the other guards were heads-down behind the sandbags, watching through loopholes. Sorderer and Weatherby stood erect, heads and shoulders exposed, determined to give an example of calm resolution. While they did, Dawlish could not do otherwise. Fear was with him again for the first time in two years, the stomach-gnawing, throat-parching, terror that must always be disguised. It was worse during waiting than ever in violent action. But, as he had always managed before, he masked it. Just as, he suspected, the two impassive older officers by him were doing.

At last, a figure emerged on to the track, arms waving, beckoning forward.

"You want to join me, captain?" Sorderer asked Weatherby. He was already heaving himself across the parapet. "See what we've got to deal with?"

"Join me, Dawlish," Weatherby said.

They clambered across to the hand-pumped railcar and the guards on board began to heave on the rocker beam. It gathered momentum, moved fast up the track.

The barricade had been simple but effective, a few logs and small boulders placed where the track emerged from a sharp bend. The hand-pumped car that it derailed had come from the north and must have been running at speed down the incline. Its three occupants had seen it too late. Now it lay on its side at the bottom of a slope and their bodies – what was left of them – lay close by.

Bryce was waiting at the barricade.

"It's bad," he said. "Goddam animals. Goddam savages." He pointed down to the overturned railcar.

The bodies lay neatly in a row, shockingly white where not crusted with brown dried blood. Flies buzzed above them. Dawlish looked quickly away, had seen that they had been stripped and mutilated, wanted not to know more, knew the memory would haunt him anyway. Something far worse than zopilotes had been responsible.

Weatherby did not tear his gaze away. There was a tremble in his voice. "Could they have been alive when –"

"It wouldn't have been done if they weren't," Sorderer said. "It's not the first time we've seen the like."

Pieces of torn clothing were strewn about but there was no sign of boots or equipment. No weapons, packs, blankets or bandoliers. Only a single tin cup, trodden flat.

"Who are they?" Weatherby said.

"Not mine," Sorderer said. "They wouldn't have been so damn stupid."

A scrap of paper, creased and yellowed, had lodged against a bush. Dawlish picked it up, opened the single sheet. The handwriting was ill-formed, as if a child's, and the ink had run, from sweat perhaps, or tears. *'Mijn liefste man Dirk'* it began and ran on without punctuation until ending with *'je vrouw Marijke'* and three other names, *Joris, Lucas.* and *Lientje.*

"It's Flemish." He passed it to Weatherby.

"How do you know?"

"I was in Antwerp once. I recognise it. I think it's a letter from a wife. They had three children." He was forcing himself not to look towards the bodies, was fighting the urge to vomit.

"There's something else here." Bryce picked it up.

A stained wallet, a pitiful cheap thing, looted of whatever it had contained. Close by, they found torn halves of a faded sepia photograph. Fitted together, it showed an older man and woman seated, clothing rough but clean, pride on their round peasant faces, a young man in uniform standing between them.

"They're from the mine," Sorderer said. "Belgians, deserters probably. A few of 'em tried before but never made it this far. They must have reached Colima an' stole the railcar there."

"Belgians? Here?" Weatherby sounded incredulous.

"Empress Carlota's people. A couple o' thousand volunteered back home to be her bodyguard. Called it the Belgian Legion. They got more than they bargained for. Some of 'em are guarding the *Glorioso* mine now. The French won't trust them with anything else. They know every one of 'em would run if they had the chance."

"Who did this?"

Sorderer shrugged. "Bandits probably, Juaristas maybe. Does it matter? They're long gone by now. Just don't fall foul of 'em, captain." He turned, called to Bryce. "Get the train up here. We've got to press on."

"What about the bodies?" Weatherby's gaze kept returning to the remains, then jerking away again. "Are you just leaving them, Colonel Sorderer?"

"None o' my business. If you want to see to them, you're welcome, captain. But you'd need to be damn quick about it."

Grove's marines, cloths pulled across their faces against the stench, buried them with spades borrowed from the mine's supplies in one of the boxcars. One man weakened, rushed behind a bush, returned, shamefaced, traces of vomit on his uniform. Even though the Belgians were probably Roman Catholics, Weatherby said a few words from the funeral service over them.

Insects chirping, the midday sun merciless, uniforms soaked with hot sweat, steam drifting from the waiting locomotive. Pity. Sorrow for men never known in life. Dawlish felt a sense of desolation bordering on despair.

But Sorderer was satisfied. It all took less than fifteen minutes.

*

The train arrived in Colima in late afternoon. It was a substantial town, two large churches, two and three-storey buildings at its centre, humbler adobe dwellings on the outskirts. The track ran past at a half-mile separation. The halt – a substantial depot – had not just water and stored coal, but a maintenance shed with an inspection pit, several corrugated metal warehouses, a stone office building and adobe barrack huts. Loading platforms, a stiff-leg derrick, two dozen or more assorted wagons – one carrying a crane – lying on sidings showed that this had been the base for onward construction. Grass growing beneath the wagons was mute testimony that activity had stalled to the north. As at Ciudad de Armería, the perimeter was surrounded by a cactus hedge, reinforced in parts with sections of adobe wall as well as look-out positions.

They spent the night there, pulled out again at first light. Dawlish could sense the heightened alertness in the men around him. The inclines were steeper now and the track was snaking up a narrow, steep-sided, valley. The locomotive was straining at its limits and advancing at half of walking pace. Stops to build steam pressure were frequent.

There were green-clad mountains to the north-west and, towering beyond them,. the near perfect cone of a volcano, its steep slopes grey and bare, smoke drifting from the summit. Dawlish, fascinated, borrowed Weatherby's field glasses to examine it.

"*El Volcán de Colima.*" Tom Bryce was standing behind him. "They say it's dangerous, blows often. They fear it here."

"More than each other?" The mental image of the dishonoured bodies was strong.

"No. Less than that."

Whistle blasts from a mile distant warned the railhead garrison they were approaching. It was another armed camp, all but a small fort, the perimeter lined not just with a thick cactus hedge but, in places, sloped earthen walls some eight feet tall. A professional must have laid it out, for it was close to star-shaped, each outer face exposed to fire from another. Once inside, the firing steps on the walls' inner sides reminded Dawlish of the defences he had helped man in Denmark. A half-dozen field-artillery pieces – they looked like nine or twelve-pounders – stood on raised platforms behind embrasures, well-sited to sweep the ground beyond. All vegetation there had been burned away for three hundred yards. A cluster of low adobe structures stood in the interior, almost a village in itself. The rail track split into three parallel sidings, rusting wagons and passenger coaches along them. Another tank locomotive stood in an open-sided engine shed, a twin of that which had brought the train here. It looked fit for service. Behind it, a high coal heap. A large corral, partially roofed with thatch, occupied a corner of the compound, some three dozen horses resting in the shade. They looked high-quality and well-maintained, unmistakable as cavalry mounts.

The flag drooping from a staff above the highest building was Mexican Imperial but the garrison was French, the first such troops encountered. Despite their faded uniforms, the impression was of seasoned and competent men inured to hardship, without illusions.

Dawlish translated when Sorderer introduced Weatherby to the commander, a hard-eyed, leathery, major named Flandin. There were two line-infantry companies here, he said, a dragoon troop and artillerymen too. He made no attempt to introduce the Imperial officer, a young Mexican, who stood close by and snarled at him to keep silent when Dawlish began to speak. The only Imperial troops here, the major said, were supervising conscripted peasants. They were extending walls to fill the gaps still barred only with cactus.

"What about the mine? Ask him about the *Glorioso*, Dawlish!" Cut off from the conversation by his lack of French or Spanish, Weatherby was exasperated.

The French major shrugged when Dawlish asked the question and answered with obscene contempt.

"He says it's not his concern." Dawlish thought it better not to translate literally. "He's here to protect the line to Manzanillo, nothing else. The mine can look after itself, he says."

It was clear now what was happening, construction of a last-ditch defence. A rear-guard here could delay a Juarista thrust should the French fall back from Guzmán and towards the ocean. It was not a position to hold indefinitely, rather one needed to buy time to cover retreat along the track. It seemed an indication that a full French withdrawal might be imminent.

"But the mine —" Weatherby began. He must have come to the same conclusion.

"Where are the mules, major? The oxen?" Sorderer ignored Weatherby and addressed the Frenchman in Spanish. "You were sent a message damn near two weeks ago that we were coming with *Glorioso* supplies. You were to arrange with the mine to have mules and oxen waiting."

Another shrug. "France's army isn't here to do your bidding, monsieur. You can sort that out with the mine yourself." Flandin nodded towards Weatherby. "This English officer and his men. By whose authority are they here?"

Weatherby understood the tone if not the words and was bridling.

Dawlish forestalled him, spoke in French and advanced Weatherby a rank. "Captain Weatherby is to see your commander in Guzmán, major. It's a diplomatic matter, sensitive, important to your government as well as ours. He has a letter of introduction if you want to see it."

"You speak French well for an Englishman" Major Flandin's tone had changed.

"I lived in Pau when I was a boy. I loved it there. Good memories,"

"Aah, Pau. My grandfather came from close by. I never met him. He died at Austerlitz." Said with pride.

"A fine heritage," Dawlish said. He was hoping the major would not demand to see the worthless letter signed by Manzanillo's alcalde.

"It's important Captain Weatherby sees the *Glorioso* mine first. If you could assist, then –"

Sorderer was trying to break in now, in Spanish, but the Frenchman ignored him.

"We haven't fodder to feed the mine's animals for more than a day." Flandin spoke to Dawlish in French. "Especially when we didn't know exactly when this train would arrive. It's hard enough to keep our own horses fed. You can tell your superior that."

Dawlish translated. Weatherby was nodding calmly, playing up the role of one reasonable man understanding another. He sympathised with Flandin's concerns. He'd need to see the *Glorioso* before going on to Guzmán.

Sorderer broke in, began to swear at Flandin in Spanish. It would take another day, maybe two, for the haulage animals to reach here from the mine, he said, another two or three to move the supplies there. He was damned if he'd accept this lack of cooperation. He saw that nobody was listening and stamped away.

Flandin shrugged. "He'll be back. We'll be sharing a bottle tonight."

Dawlish mentioned the bodies.

"Probably *El Serpiente's* work. And it explains the pumped railcar that disappeared two nights ago." Flandin said. "Two of the Mexican guards are on charge for dereliction of duty for letting it happen. I'll have one of them shot as an example."

"Ask the major if we can borrow horses, Dawlish," Weatherby had been listening in impatient incomprehension. "Just for you and for me. Grove and his men can wait here."

The major was willing. "You can have an escort too. It's dangerous to move around without one." He looked up. The sun was still high. "It's twenty kilometres but you can be at the mine by nightfall if you start immediately."

They rode away ten minutes later with a dragoon sergeant, a stolid Breton called Morvan, and three troopers as guides and escort. Dawlish realised the major had not mentioned the Belgian troops at the mine.

Only one conclusion possible.

An encumbrance, not an asset.

*

The earthen track they followed climbed ever higher. The bare lower slopes of *El Volcán de Colima* rose a few miles to the north. No cultivation here, only sparse sun-baked scrub to either side. The French dragoons were taking no chances, halting at intervals, sending a scout ahead, advancing only when satisfied risk was minimal. They were heavily armed – short carbines in bucket holsters ahead of the saddles, revolvers and straight swords rather than sabres.

"Are there Juaristas around here?" Dawlish asked the sergeant.

"No. Not yet. But sometimes there's worse. *El Serpiente's* people."

"*El Serpiente?*" Dawlish had heard Major Flandin mention the name.

"Javier Belarra. A bandit. That's what they call him. Like a king in his areas north and south of here. He worked with us for a while and was useful for things our officers didn't want recorded. He knows we'll be gone soon so he'll do the same for Juaristas if it suits him. He might be working for them already."

"A cruel man?" Again, the memory of those bodies.

"It's a cruel country, monsieur. And a cruel world everywhere."

They encountered the first Belgians in late afternoon, a corporal's guard manning a trackside lookout-post on a ridge. They looked frightened as well as beaten, pride gone, faces stubbled and unwashed, ragged uniforms rank with sweat. Their little loopholed adobe shack was incapable of withstanding a fifteen-minute siege and they must know it. Empress Carlota's Legion might sound exotic, but the reality was squalid, even pathetic. The mine was a half-hour's ride ahead, the corporal said.

They heard it before they saw it, a dull monotonous thumping that must signal ore being crushed. They halted, looked down into a wide bowl bounded by low hills. Green higher up, the lower levels were denuded of growth, probably for firewood. Weatherby studied the scene through his glasses, then passed them to Dawlish.

He saw a scattering of adobe buildings there, small shacks too, a single large, white-painted, house. Pyramids of what must be ore lay behind a cluster of machinery of some sort and several large rusty metal sheds. Smoke rose from three tall thin metal chimneys stayed by cables. There was activity there, as busy as in a disturbed antheap, men moving between the equipment, small teams pushing laden trucks along a rail-track that emerged from a gash in the slope to the right. Animals wandered in the large corrals at the bowl's far side.

This was the British interest that had so concerned somebody in London, had prompted a telegram to San Francisco, had sent HMS *Sprightly* hastening to Manzanillo.

Time now for Weatherby to determine what measures were appropriate.

Dawlish did not envy him.

*

Major Baron André Damseaux – he stressed the 'Baron' when first met – impressed no better than his men seen either at the first look-out post or other positions closer to the mine. Guards there refused to take Weatherby and Dawlish to *El Glorioso*'s manager. Their orders were to bring all arrivals to the Baron. Now they were in the three-roomed adobe house that served as Damseaux's office and accommodation. His uniform was cleaner and less threadbare than his people's, but he had a listlessness about him, the air of a man going through the motions of command who wished only to be gone. He smelled of drink. He was surprised by the arrival of two British officers, was curious about the reason.

Damseaux had no English and Dawlish needed to interpret. The pleasantries over, they were sitting down.

"Did three of your men desert recently, major?" Weatherby said.

"Three days ago. How do you know?"

"We found them." Weatherby outlined the facts, not the details.

Damseaux covered his face with his hands and dropped his head. He shook it, as if in despair. Then he looked up again.

"There were two others before them." A quaver in his voice. "A month ago. We never knew what happened to them."

"How many men have you here, major?"

"Almost a hundred and fifty."

It didn't seem a lot for a perimeter so large and with a long road leading back to the railhead. And especially not with demoralised men. Damseaux must know it too, even if he didn't say so.

"Major Flandin said some brigand who calls himself *El Serpiente* might have killed the deserters. Is he a threat to you here?"

Damseaux brightened. "It's mainly talk. In the last month we've had supplies brought from the railway without incident. If he was a serious threat, he would have attacked then."

"There's equipment for the mine waiting at the railhead to be brought up here. We came up with it from Manzanillo. Were you aware?" Weatherby asked.

Damseaux swore. It was expected, but he'd received no warning of such an imminent arrival. Had he known, he would have had men and draught animals waiting to meet it.

"I'm usually the last to know such things." Said with resignation.

"But French support must be welcome if you need?"

"Oh yes. We can always rely on the French."

And, for all the weariness in Damseaux's voice, a hint of bitter sarcasm.

*

El Glorioso's manager introduced himself as Frank Atkinson. There could not be much love lost between him and Damseaux because he greeted him with cold formality. He too was angered by lack of information on expected arrival of the mine equipment. It would necessitate movement of mules, horses, oxen and wagons to the railhead. Damseaux excused himself and left to begin preparations for the escort.

Atkinson's office was on the ground floor of the large white house. It was wooden and looked as if it might have been brought in sections from Britain, with the mine machinery. It trembled with each new pound of the ore-crusher.

"I can offer you accommodation tonight, but we can't talk for long," he said when Damseaux had left. "I too need to get things organised now if we're to get the animals moving in the morning."

Weatherby understood.

"I imagine you're impressed by what you see, gentlemen?" Atkinson said. He was in his thirties, heavy, balding and bespectacled. Despite his stained and dusty working clothes, his accent was that of an educated man. "It's little more than scratching the surface so far, but profitable, no doubt of it. And this is only the beginning. There's more, much more. I've worked in Chile and Bolivia, but I've never seen anything half so good as this."

"How long have you been here?" Weatherby asked.

"From the start. Over two years." Spoken with pride. "Everything you see, I got going. And going's the way I want to keep it."

Dawlish found himself impressed. The man radiated energy and enthusiasm, seemed the sort that got things done.

"You're welcome here, gentlemen, very welcome," Atkinson said. "I didn't expect anybody so soon. And certainly not the Navy."

"You asked for support?" Weatherby looked embarrassed to admit he did not know.

"Two months ago. With things as they are, it takes a month or more to get a message through to the London office. Half the directors are in Parliament. They have influence. I expected they'd have had some diplomat sent to do a deal. They know which way the wind's blowing."

"How?" Again embarrassment.

"The French are realists. They know the game's up and they'll be gone before the year's out, with Emperor Max scurrying off behind them. Then Juarez will be president again and he'll need to reward his generals if they're not going to give him his marching orders also."

"Was the Plutus licence signed by the emperor?" Weatherby was remembering the speculations of the consul in San Francisco that Dawlish had reported.

Atkinson nodded. "Yes, more's the pity. It could make it easy to declare it invalid and re-grant it to some Juarista jefe. That's the danger."

"You said you'd hoped for somebody to come to make a deal, Mr. Atkinson." Weatherby spoke the word 'deal' as if it was unclean.

"Just an assurance from the Juaristas that Plutus would be glad to negotiate new terms." Atkinson smiled and winked. "Unofficial terms as well as official ones, if necessary. A guarantee that this mine won't be looted before the matter's settled. Together with a hint that Britain won't accept anything else than that lying down."

It was obvious now. Maximillian's pinchbeck empire was tottering, but Britain still recognised it as a de-facto government. It must still formally regard the Juaristas as rebels. No British diplomat could be seen to be treating with Juarez or his supporters.

Not yet.

But somebody in London, very senior in government, had decided that something must be done to mollify the Plutus directors.

That something could be what was so often used before. A reminder that Britain could deploy naval power along the Mexican coast, blockade harbours, halt the exports that must pay for Mexico's post-bellum reconstruction, force payment of debts owed to British bondholders, banks and traders. A single gunvessel was usually enough. *Sprightly* had done just that, earlier in the year, enforcing repayment of loans taken out by a spendthrift city government in another country further south.

And nobody better to convey that message than a naval officer, a man whose estimate of what constituted an appropriate measure could be disowned in the event of failure.

The door opened. A stout but not unhandsome woman stood there, clad, expensively, in the Mexican fashion. Her features told of part-Indian ancestry.

"*La comida está lista, Francisco,*" she said. "*Los caballeros deberían venir. De lo contrario, hará frío.*" A mere statement of fact, that the gentlemen must come. Otherwise, the food would be cold.

She left without introduction.

60

"My wife, Josefina," Atkinson said. "Not someone to argue with. You can eat now and there'll be beds for you here tonight." He looked at his watch. "Forgive me for leaving you now, I've a lot to do."

An old woman, morose, uninclined to speak, served the meal, an excellent one, and they saw nothing more of Señora Atkinson.

Dawlish had little rest that night.

The monotonous pounding of the crusher saw to that.

Chapter 5

Major Damseaux might have been dismissive of *El Serpiente* the day before, but he was taking no chances now. A third of his men, commanded by his deputy, a Captain van Maarkedal, would escort *El Glorioso's* draught animals to and from the railhead. Atkinson was still busy at the corrals, overseeing animal selection and harnessing, checking wagon wheels, was everywhere at once, encouraging here, reproving there in dialect-Spanish Dawlish could scarcely understand. He seemed popular with his workers, was dressed little better than they were and did not hesitate to assist them lifting a load or quietening a recalcitrant mule. He would have time for Weatherby and Dawlish once the haulage train had departed and until then they were free to explore the site.

They saw the mine's mouth – a drift, the Welsh foreman who accompanied them explained, a gently sloping tunnel reaching deep into the hillside. At any one time, day or night, over a hundred labourers were hacking ore in six other tunnels branching from it. A narrow rail-track ran from the drift entrance to the crusher and men were pushing wagons of excavated rock towards it. Weatherby declined the invitation to enter and expressed interest instead in seeing the machinery. The foreman was subjecting them to an involved and endless explanation of the use of mercury to extract silver from the crushed ore when Major Damseaux joined them.

"Your captain may like to see our defences," he said to Dawlish. "I'll be pleased to show him. Please translate for me."

Weatherby agreed. Dawlish sensed Damseaux had offered more from a hunger for company than any urge to enlighten them. It must be a nightmare being isolated here with troops, and maybe even officers, on whom he could not rely and with an English manager who seemed less than friendly.

In the circumstances, Damseaux had not done badly. Observation posts on the ridge crests above could provide advance warning of the approach of any major force. Their occupants had orders to fall back in such a case to the eight small redoubts around the perimeter, manned through the full twenty-four hours. These looked, to a naval officer's eye at least, well sited. Five were substantial structures, their sloped walls built of tailings from the silver extraction, but the remainder were little more than large rifle pits. Wooden *chevaux-de-frise* partly blocked the ground between and more were under construction. There was no artillery.

Nightly patrols ensured alertness, Damseaux said, and off-duty men, sleeping in a camp composed of adobe huts further back, could bring the redoubts to full manning within minutes. But there was something less than confidence in his voice. Not just awareness, Dawlish guessed, that his men were unreliable but that these defences might not be capable of repelling a bandit raid. And the Juaristas were organised armies now, well supplied from the United States, rather than individual guerrilla bands. If they came in force, this place could be overwhelmed in an hour.

They ate with Atkinson at midday. The first mule-strings were now leaving the camp, Belgians trudging on foot alongside them. Fearful though they might be of bandits – and Damseaux had circulated news of the fates of the recent deserters – their plod was that of men lacking alertness. Despite knowing the risks, Dawlish wondered how many might still attempt to escape on reaching the railhead.

At the table, Weatherby was reserved and formal.

"You suggest that I remind the nearest Juarista commander that British property is sacrosanct. Is that it, Mr. Atkinson?"

"A little more than that."

"How little more?"

"Confirmation that when the French are gone, and Damseaux's toy soldiers with them, Her Majesty's government will not object to the Juarez's republic renegotiating the *Glorioso* licence. On mutually favourable terms, of course. But not cancelling the licence, not confiscating what we have here already."

"And until then, Mr. Atkinson?"

"An informal undertaking that this mine will not be attacked. Doing so would be in nobody's interest."

"Can the Juaristas guarantee that? They can't speak for this *Serpiente* blackguard, can they?"

"Damseaux says he can see off any intrusion by *El Serpiente*. His troops are useful as escorts for my transports. But if you can obtain Juarista assurance that they'll offer the Belgians acceptable surrender terms, and free passage to the coast, there'll be no need for any resistance here nor damage to the mine."

"And where could Juarista leaders who're senior enough to agree to anything like this be reached, Mr. Atkinson?"

"Guadalajara."

It might as well be the moon. But Weatherby didn't reject the suggestion.

"Are the French to be informed about this?"

Atkinson shook his head. "Better not at the railhead, but at a more senior level. I doubt if they'd care much anyway. Their only concern is to get out. Giving up Guadalajara confirmed that."

Weatherby was silent, frowning, not meeting Atkinson's gaze. He must have spent the night brooding on the situation.

On *appropriate measures*.

He must be aware that doing nothing could not be an option. Plutus's directors and their political allies would not forgive Juarista cancellation of the licence, nor confiscation nor destruction of the mine. Some previous blunder might have exiled Weatherby to the Pacific Station backwater. He could not afford another. One false step would see his career ended. Yet success might bring advancement.

Atkinson could sense his unease and made to break it. He looked at his watch. "Today's ingot-casting should be completed," he said. "It'll be in the store by now. You might find it of interest. Will you join me?"

Situated north of the crusher, the store looked like a bomb-proof shelter such as Dawlish had seen at the Danish defences at Thyborøn. A mound of tailings covered its single windowless room, the entrance a thick iron-bound door, padlocked in five places. A rope, strung from posts, encircled it at a distance of ten yards.

"What's that?" Dawlish asked as one of two armed guards lifted it to let them pass under.

"The dead line," Atkinson said. "Only I, and my deputy, can pass."

"Nobody but a fool would try, mister," a guard said. Like the other, he wore a faded grey cap with a regimental badge, a last reminder of Confederate service. Sorderer's men, both carrying Henry repeaters.

"Paid by Plutus," Atkinson said. "And another dozen besides, Isn't that so, gentlemen?"

"That's damn right, sir!" One of them said. "Still with Capt'n Clayton, Fourth Texas Cavalry, just like old days up north."

"Dockwallopers for ever!" the other said. With pride.

Atkinson had brought keys. Once inside, he lit an oil lamp on a wooden table, a weighing scales and a ledger next to it and what looked like four dull grey bricks. Others like them lay in rows on two levels of wooden shelving on the walls.

"Almost two hundred by now." Atkinson gestured to them. "They'll be our first shipment. Just two months since we smelted the first ingot and we're doing better by the day."

"When did you start work here?" Weatherby asked.

"Twenty-six months ago."

The precision of the number indicated pride. And justifiably so, Dawlish thought. In that time, a workforce had been recruited, a drift dug, essential supplies and machinery imported and erected. All started when there had been confidence in the Imperial Government's permanence.

"Those are today's," Atkinson pointed to the ingots on the table. "We only reached three per day a week ago. Today it's four. We're hitting our stride, it'll be five, maybe six, by year's end."

Dawlish reached his hand out to touch them, then jerked it back.

"Careful," Atkinson said. "Those are still hot. Here – try these."

He took one from a shelf and handed it to Weatherby, then another to Dawlish. It was heavy, far heavier than it looked. It had been cast in a mould, the upper surface rough, the sides sloped and smooth. Its size seemed disproportionate to the effort and equipment needed to win it.

"It'll be about thirty-five pounds weight," Atkinson said. "Worth about eight hundred dollars as it is, more when further refined."

Dawlish was mentally calculating. Today's four ingots, worth three thousand, two-hundred dollars. Well over a million dollars, over a quarter-million sterling if this rate was sustained through a year. Income perhaps eighty percent after costs. *El Glorioso* was well named.

Weatherby must have been making the same calculations too. "You said this was just the start," he said to Atkinson. "How much larger could it be?"

"Twice at the least if we open a second drift and bring in more machinery. And there'll be even more, much more, after that, four or five new drifts. The whole mountain's laden with silver. But it'll need expertise. The Mexicans don't have it and Plutus does." He paused, let it sink in. "It's a British company, Commander Weatherby, listed in London. British shareholders and British dividends and some very influential people. And not ungenerous to any Mexican interests that could assist the process. All that's needed is —"

Weatherby held up his hand and stopped him. "Why haven't all these — what do you call them? Yes, ingots, been shipped already? They're surely a magnet for this *Serpiente* blackguard?"

"We're waiting for authorisation. They're Imperial property until we've paid the contracted royalty, ten percent, payable in weighed ingots. The French are managing the procedure and proving damn uncooperative about it." Atkinson paused. He was looking Weatherby straight in the eye. "Perhaps you might assist us with that, captain?"

Weatherby turned to Dawlish.

"We'll return to the railhead this afternoon," he said. "I've a few details to discuss with Mr. Atkinson first. Kindly find those French dragoons and have them ready to escort us."

A few details.

Settling the meaning of *appropriate*.

*

Three miles from the mine, they caught up with the column of wagons and animals trudging towards the railhead. The track was rough and progress slow. The night would have to be passed in bivouac, the Belgian escort-commander said. Neither he nor his men looked happy about it.

The ride was pleasant, with the air cool at this altitude but, as before, the dragoons were cautious. Dawlish noticed Weatherby's holster flap was open, as was his own, and his hand drifted back at intervals to the reassurance of his Adams revolver butt.

They reached the railhead at dusk. Alerted at their approach, Grove had drawn up his marines to salute them. Weatherby tipped the dragoons a silver peso each and went to thank Major Flandin – lacking a common language it was only a formality. He sent Dawlish back with Grove to the three-room shack allocated to them. It was spartan, but clean, and they had made the best of it. One of the marines brewed tea for them. He had secured goat's milk to colour it. Grove was eager to hear about the mine and Dawlish had just started when Weatherby arrived.

"Get your men rested," he told Grove. "If you set out at dawn you can reach the mine by evening. A hard march, but possible."

Weatherby must know that the twelve miles, much of it uphill, and in the heat of the day, would be a hell for the marines on foot, Dawlish thought. They'd had little exercise ashore for months, no practice for landing and firing the six-pounder field-gun carried for use on land, had done no marching. Feet would blister, men would flag, water in their canteens would hardly last the day. He saw from Grove's face that he was thinking the same.

"I'll arrange with Colonel Sorderer for two men who know the track to go with you," Weatherby said.

Grove looked bemused. "With respect, sir. Americans? Not French?"

"You're Royal Marines. You don't need a French escort, do you?"

"No, sir." Grove said. "Are we to guard the mine, sir?"

67

"You'll be there for only two or three days. Report to the manager on arrival. He's a Mr. Atkinson. He'll introduce you to the Belgian commander, a Major Damseaux. You'll give him your full cooperation if there's need for defending in case of attack, though that's unlikely."

"And then, sir?"

"On your way there tomorrow, about half-way, you'll meet a transport column coming from the mine. It's heading here with a Belgian escort. They may be nervous, so be damn careful approaching them. They'll be returning to the mine in a day or so with the equipment brought up from Manzanillo. After that, two or three wagons will be coming back here from the mine. You'll escort them. There'll be Belgians as well, as many as Damseaux can spare. But Mr. Atkinson has requested our support also."

The words unsaid, but the implication obvious.

Atkinson has as little confidence in the Belgians as the French have.

"May I ask what's to be escorted, sir?"

"Silver," Weatherby said.

The growing hoard in that bomb-proof shelter, its value increasing by some eight hundred sterling a day between now and its leaving *El Glorioso.*

A British interest incarnate.

*

Weatherby and Dawlish started north for Guzmán just after sunrise. Major Flandin had again lent horses and an escort – Sergeant Morvan and three troopers, as before. The decision to do so had not been Flandin's, Dawlish learned from a French officer of his own age with whom he'd fallen into conversation. Flandin had sent him to Guzmán with word of the British officers' arrival. The commander there had questioned him and sent him back with a message. They were to be brought directly to him, under escort. No other English to accompany them.

"Who's in command there?" Dawlish asked Flandin. The more Weatherby knew before meeting the commander, the better.

"Colonel Adolphe Durand.."

"A good soldier?"

"A soldier's soldier. He rose from the ranks, but nobody holds that against him." Praise indeed, since Flandin spoke with a refined accent. "He doesn't deny he was a cook's son. He was a sergeant in Algeria and commissioned in the field at Sevastopol. He was in Italy later, at Magenta and Solferino. Then here in Mexico."

"A dangerous man then?"

"The Juaristas fear him. He gives them good reason."

Guzmán was twenty miles ahead and they were following the broad *Camino Real*. It was climbing steeply through a broad valley, winding to ease the inclines. The gully-seamed cone of *El Volcán de Colima* lay eight or ten miles to the west and a twin, *El Nevado de Colima*, apparently dormant, just north of it, and more mountains further to the east. The land was green and, even at midday, the temperature comfortable. But the dragoons were even more vigilant than before, especially where the road ran through steep-walled defiles or crossed bridges over stream beds.

French posts, well protected with sandbags, were positioned at two or three-mile intervals and at each their progress was noted in a ledger. The only movement along this road was military, an infantry company plodding south to Colima, a string of wagons toiling up towards Guzmán. In places they encountered groups of Mexicans filling eroded sections under French supervision. The labourers looked up at the passing horsemen, bent again, faces impassive and yet still somehow conveying resentment. And patience. They must guess, and be comforted, that this was a road being readied for a retreat.

That same resentment was obvious in the few villages they passed through, women pulling children into their homes as they approached, men hurrying from view. In one, half the houses had been burned and browning stains on the pockmarked wall of the small church told of a savage reprisal.

"What happened here?" Dawlish felt revulsion as he asked Sergeant Morvan.

"*El Serpiente*, when he was still working with us. But it was necessary. The villagers had helped rebels here."

Toward midmorning they met three French troopers approaching at a fast trot. Two passed without stopping but the third reined-in to speak to Morvan. They were carrying news south to the railhead, he said, were warning everybody heading north for increased vigilance. There had been trouble four miles ahead, a guard post attacked. A small supply column had been encamped there for the night.

"Did they drive them off?" Morvan asked.

"No. The guards made a stand in their hut, but it was set on fire, and they were shot escaping from it. The rest had their throats slit, probably after they'd surrendered. And the animals too."

"*El Serpiente?*"

The trooper shook his head. "It must have been a bigger force than that." He turned away and urged his mount into a canter to catch up with his companions.

It could have been a Juarista unit, the first that had struck this far south, the sergeant told Dawlish. It must have bypassed Guzmán, was probably still moving, would camp one night somewhere far to the east or west. The terrain offered good cover. And then strike again somewhere far from here.

"This is the sort of war it's been," Morvan said. "That's what's been winning it for Juarez. We've held the towns but everything outside is theirs."

"Ask him how large a force," Weatherby said.

"He says probably sixty or so mounted men," Dawlish translated. "Sometimes a few pack-mules too. They reach far behind French garrisons and wreak havoc on their supply lines. And villagers help with food and information. They're afraid not to."

He had sensed venom in the sergeant's voice.

"It's worse than Algeria, he says. You can trust nobody."

They rode on, more alert than before.

Dawlish heard an internal voice reminding him that it was not his war, nor Weatherby's either. Not that it would matter to the Juaristas.

Nor to some representative of theirs with whom Weatherby was determined to bargain in Guadalajara.

He might be taking his interpretation of *appropriate* to extremes.

And they might both pay for it.

*

They reached the scene of the night's attack a half-hour later. A French dragoon-major, called Jouhaud, whom they met there, had ridden with two troops from Guzmán when the news reached it. An infantry company was force-marching behind but would not be here for two hours yet. He had the situation under control.

"But too late," he said. "They'd left nothing alive."

The post was the largest they had seen. Small sand-bag redoubts stood on either side of the road, one fifty yards from another. An adobe structure, set further back, had its roof burned and its walls fallen in. Behind it lay what must have been a site used for overnight camping by passing transport units, a large open space bordered by split-rail fencing and cactus hedging. Close-by, a pen for animals. Mules, oxen and a single horse littered it now, slumped in the blood that stained the soil around them, red slashes torn in their sides by birds that flapped from one to the other. In one corner, peasants were digging a long trench, dragoons standing over them with carbines.

Major Jouhaud followed Dawlish's gaze.

"They're from a *pueblito* over there." He pointed eastwards. "About a kilometre."

Even from a distance they looked cowed and were working with the clumsy haste of frightened men. A line of bodies lay behind them. Blankets, some bloody, had been thrown across them and the protruding feet were white and bare. Boots were valuable.

Dawlish felt sick. "How many?"

"Seven French. Nineteen Mexican Imperials." Jouhaud's tone conveyed both weariness and callousness. A man who had long passed beyond feeling, who valued survival only. "It shouldn't have happened, not if they'd kept good watch. And their arms and ammunition gone too. Like gold here."

Prompted by Weatherby, Dawlish asked about the villagers. Were they suspected?

"Not those." Jouhaud gestured towards the burial party. "We've questioned them. They're clean. But over there, those haven't been cooperative, not yet." He pointed towards a group huddled on their knees beneath a tree, hands tied behind their backs, closely guarded. "Somebody must have passed details of this place to the enemy. They probably didn't have much option. But we'll find out. We always do."

A bugle sounded from the north, a complicated call that announced a knot of horsemen cantering into sight, pennons fluttering from upraised lances. Even beneath a coating of dust their blue tunics and red breeches showed bright, a contrast to the dragoons' shabby uniforms. And a single rider out in front, more impressive still.

"That's Colonel Durand," Major Jouhaud said. "The man you've come to meet."

Chapter 6

Weatherby began to urge his mount forward. Major Jouhaud held up his hand to restrain him.

"Tell your superior to wait," he said to Dawlish. "The colonel has other business in mind for now."

Dawlish translated. Weatherby complied with ill grace. The major turned away and spurred towards Colonel Durand. Long, lean and lithe, he was swinging from his saddle, tossing the reins to a trooper, surveying the devastation. He could be no older than forty, judging by the wrinkleless sun-darkened skin stretched over a long cleanshaven face. He looked angry now – had good reason to be – but Dawlish suspected he was always angry, the sort of officer who was respected and feared but never loved by his men.

Major Jouhaud was making his report. They were too far off for Dawlish to hear what was said. Durand was listening with teeth clenched, mouth downturned, eyes narrowed, making only an occasional interjection. Now he was stalking toward the bodies laid along the trench, Jouhaud by him and still talking. The villagers who had been digging shrunk back and cowered before the levelled carbines of the troopers supervising them. Durand swept his sabre from its sheath, used its tip to flick back the blanket from the nearest corpse. Even from a distance, Dawlish could see the dark and bloody gash across the naked torso.

Durand let the blanket fall, sheathed his sabre, turned to Jouhaud, and gestured towards the bound prisoners kneeling beneath the tree. The major was explaining, the colonel listening with obvious impatience and at last shaking his head, saying something that made Jouhaud nod in agreement. Then Durand was striding towards the prisoners, opening the flap of his holster and pulling out the revolver within, the major following. One of the prisoners had noticed the movement, could not tear his gaze away, eyes locked in terror. Others were stirring, looking up, then quickly down, foreheads touching the ground, under the barked order of the sergeant of the detail guarding them.

"That blackguard's going to kill them." Mixed anger and disgust in Weatherby's low voice, awareness too that he could not intervene.

Dawlish had also recognised it and was watching in sick horror. A century seemed to pass before Durand reached the knot of kneeling men. He halted, studying them as a farmer's wife might select a chicken from her flock for a Sunday meal. They must all know what was to come and one was rocking back on his knees, raising his head, sobbing. Durand ignored him. The click as he cocked his pistol seemed louder than any shot and it brought silence.

"Bloody scoundrel!" Weatherby hissed to Dawlish. He pressed his mount two or three paces forward before he saw Major Jouhaud, standing behind Durand and, alerted by the movement, swing around. He was waving his hand across his face, forefinger upraised, shaking his head. The message was obvious.

Don't intervene.

And a sense of another message also.

You'll only make it worse.

Weatherby understood and was drawing rein. Dawlish saw he was trembling in anger, his fists clenched knuckle-white.

The colonel had selected his victim, one who now ground his face into the dust as if, ostrich-like, he might escape notice. The revolver muzzle was two feet from the back of his neck as it blasted. Durand must have done this before, for he had positioned himself to one side to avoid the fountaining blood. The body rolled over and dead silence followed.

If somebody has indeed passed information to the Juaristas, they'll be identified in minutes. If not by themselves, then by others. Poor wretches.

Durand returned to his horse, spoke to Jouhaud and jerked his head towards the prisoners, his meaning clear – don't delay. He swung back to his saddle. Jouhaud gestured towards Weatherby and Dawlish. Durand glared towards them but did not beckon them to come closer. Jouhaud still speaking, giving an impression of a man telling what his listener did not want to hear, but at last Durand nodded, said something. Without waiting for an answer, he wheeled his mount to face back the way he had come, his escort falling into place ahead and behind and breaking with him into a fast trot. He had been here for less than ten minutes.

"He'll scc you tomorrow in Guzmán." Jouhaud had come back to Weatherby and Dawlish. "You can keep your escort. You'll be accommodated overnight."

Dawlish could see Weatherby was seething with anger after he had translated. The slight was obvious.

"You'd better stay close behind him." Jouhaud said. "It's dangerous on this road." He turned to Sergeant Morvan, told him the same, and where to deliver his charges.

Time to be gone, to ride towards the dust raised by Durand and his escort.

Another pistol report sounded behind them.

One more example.

*

Four miles further on they encountered the infantry company marching south to reinforce Jouhaud. It was midday, the sun blazing in a cloudless sky, but the column was pressing on at a slow and steady rate that Dawlish guessed it could maintain all day. The troops reminded him of the French he had seen in China in '59 and '60, hard brutal men, confident in themselves and their officers, savagely reliable in battle and eager to loot and rape in its aftermath. The contrast with the listless Belgians at the mine was striking.

Guzmán came into view an hour later, looking similar, though larger, than Colima. Durand must have felt that he had made his point, had established his dominance, for he had sent back an aide to ask Weatherby to join him. The invitation might or might not have included Dawlish, but Weatherby brought him anyway. There were cold formalities, a handshake and a few neutral exchanges. Durand was abrupt in manner, and Weatherby still restraining his resentment, but Dawlish injected as much courtesy as he could into the translation of their exchanges. The heat and dust was not inducive to conversation anyway and they rode on in silence.

Three riders were cantering from the town to meet them, one out in front. They drew closer and Dawlish saw, from the red streak hanging down the horse's left side that the leader was riding side-saddle.

"A woman, by God," Weatherby said to Dawlish. "And a damn fine rider too."

She was urging her mount into a gallop, then riding past to one side of the track and sweeping around in a wide turn that brought her alongside Durand, before drawing in. Her blue jacket was frogged like his and a gold brooch studded with a single diamond lay on the left breast as if in imitation of his campaign ribbons. A dark veil, fastened to the brim of her plumed hat, hid her face. She raised her whip in greeting.

"Bonjour, mon colonel," she said. *"Le résultat était-il satisfaisant?"*

Her voice was sweet and Dawlish recognised a trace of the accent he had come to know when, as a boy, he lived with his dying uncle in Pau.

Durand did not return the greeting, just shook his head and growled something inaudible. She pretended not to notice.

"Les nouvelles sont mauvaises, Adolphe?" She had dropped her voice, was almost inaudible, had already guessed that the news was bad.

"Les nouvelles ne sont jamais bonnes dans ce pays maudit." Durand also spoke low, low enough that the troopers following could not hear. There was bitterness in his tone.

He's correct. There would probably never be good news in this accursed country.

The woman had noticed Weatherby and Dawlish for the first time.

"Ce sont donc les Anglais que vous attendiez, Adolphe?"

He must have told her that they were expected.

And as she spoke, and the Pau accent seemed stronger this time. Dawlish saw that she was looking past Weatherby and towards himself.

"Ask this fellow to introduce us to the lady," Weatherby said to Dawlish, who translated more diplomatically.

Durand ignored Weatherby and spoke directly to Dawlish.

"Tell her your names," he said.

"*Capitaine Frederick Weatherby de la Marine Royale de Sa Majesté Victoria et Sous-Lieutenant Nicholas Dawlish.*"

Weatherby was tipping his hat brim. "And the lady's name?" he said.

She must have guessed his meaning.

"*Sapin,*" she said. "*Madame Clothilde Sapin.*" And she looked away.

Dawlish suddenly felt sick.

Almost my sister.

She was speaking in a whisper to Durand. He was nodding before he turned to speak to the officer riding behind him.

"*Vous savez où amener les Anglais,*" he said. "*Je les veux dans mon bureau à huit heures demain,*"

No word of apology or explanation for Weatherby, just an instruction for him and Dawlish to be accommodated and brought to his office at eight next morning,

And then he was cantering towards Guzmán, the lady by his side, leaving the escort to trot on far behind.

"A damned murderous boor," Weatherby said.

But Dawlish, his mind in turmoil, didn't hear.

*

He was a twelve-year old boy again, on a slow morning walk – slower each day – to Pau's Parc Beaumont with his Uncle Ralph.

"Are you going to die, uncle?" he blurted out. He suspected and feared it, was screwing up his courage for days to ask directly.

It would be soon, his uncle said. There was nothing to be afraid of, it came to everybody in the end.

But Dawlish wept anyway and was embarrassed by his tears.

"You can do one thing for me, Nicholas," his uncle said. "I want you to care for Madame Sapin and for Clothilde too. Not to be with them all the time, but not to forget them. And to be as a son and as a brother to them whenever they need help. You'll do that for me?"

And he had promised.

77

It was easy to love the kind and dignified Madame Madeleine Sapin, whom he now, as a man, realised must have been his uncle's mistress rather than his housekeeper. It was easy too for her daughter Clothilde, a little older than him, to become like a sister.

He had kept contact, even after entering the Navy. His uncle left them generously cared for, investments for the mother, a '*dot*' – a dowery – for her daughter. Madam Sapin's letters, warm and affectionate, Clothilde's also, always reached him. And then, three years before, while he was still in the West Indies, they ended. Desperation prompted him to write to the minster of the Anglican church in Pau, to ask for information. The reply, one that displayed little Christian charity, reached him on his way to Denmark in '64. The 'person' he enquired about had died. There were stories that her daughter left Pau with an army officer. A married man and not her husband, the Reverend Augustus Lyall had underlined with pious relish. No name mentioned.

And now there was one.

Colonel Adolphe Durand.

*

Dawlish noticed little as they rode into Guzmán. Surprise, resentment and disgust churned within him. There could be no doubt that she had recognised him and didn't want to be recognised in return. His mind recoiled from the idea of Durand, this brute, this savage, ever having touched her.

It hurt most of all, that she had consented to this – he could not avoid the word – this betrayal of herself. The letter sent by the clergyman in Pau would have broken his uncle's heart, as it now broke his own. It was worse than he could ever have imagined.

"The place looks ready for a siege, Dawlish."

Weatherby's words roused him from his bitter reverie.

Artillery was just visible within the embrasures of the large redoubt dominating the approach from the south. Another like it lay further to the west and there were probably others like them on the northern and eastern edges of the town. Tumbled adobe huts and patches of scorched ground indicated clearance of fields of fire. Stakes painted like long barber's poles stood stark on the charred ground to mark ranges.

The impression of readiness continued in the streets – barricades with gaps the width of a cart and *cheval de fries* standing by one side to close them, loop-holed houses at corners, French foot patrols. The townspeople looked cowed and avoided eye contact. The Mexican Imperial troops encountered looked beaten already and too fearful of French retribution to escape by desertion out into the countryside.

The French tricolour, not the Imperial Mexican flag, flew above the governor's palace. Stone-built and massive, with the Spanish coat of arms still visible above the main door, fronted on the central plaza. High crenelated walls extended on either side. A gate to the right, well-guarded, gave entrance to what proved to be a large, enclosed space, a parade ground at the centre and buildings – barracks, stables, stores and magazine – closer to the walls.

Weatherby was less than pleased by their accommodation in what they were told was the officers' mess. Their two small rooms were little larger than monks' cells, and just as sparsely furnished, typical of what might be allocated to the most junior of lieutenants. The officer whom Durand directed to escort them was apologetic but unconvincing – they would understand space was limited in the circumstances, he said. He would dine with them this evening. In the meantime, they were welcome to stroll outside, but no further than fifty meters from the mess. Weatherby said, with bad grace, that they'd prefer to rest until dinner. The French officer shrugged and left them.

The dinner proved dismal, not for the food but the company. Their host clearly resented the duty. Enquires about the situation, however sensitively worded in Dawlish's translation, only brought abrupt replies that invited no further questions. Attempts at small talk died. Officers of various ranks were seated at other tables, but their mood too seemed sombre as they ate, drank and played cards – hard men who would not shrink from hard tasks.

The meal ended at last.

"Let's take a turn outside," Weatherby said to Dawlish. "And to hell with their damn fifty meters. You smoke, don't you?"

Dawlish did, though seldom, but he accepted a cheroot. Weatherby held a lucifer to light it before he lit his own. Darkness had fallen and the shadows were deep as they strolled around the compound without challenge. The rear of the governor's palace was more ornate than its frontage on the plaza. Steps at either end swept up in half circles to a wide balcony above. Dancing pinpricks of light indicated other smokers taking the night air and sentries were patrolling the parapets behind the crenelations. Twice they encountered guards conducting women in Mexican costumes, shawls drawn across their faces, from the gate towards the officer's mess.

"Damn lecherous fellows, these French," Weatherby said. "Always the same and half of 'em rotten with syphilis, I'll wager. Stay away from that sort of thing, Dawlish. Bad for any decent young man."

Dawlish barely heard him. Awareness that Clothilde must be close by, was perhaps in Durand's arms at this moment, tortured him. He knew that it would keep him from sleep, so when he turned to his room, lit by a single candle, he stripped off his boots and outer clothing and lay down on the bed's hard straw-filled mattress to read. He was halfway through a copy of *Les Misérables* that he had bought in San Francisco. He would have preferred it in French – he was determined to maintain proficiency – but a poor English translation was better than nothing. He forced himself to keep reading but failed to drive Clothilde from his mind.

He awoke with a start, was sure he had heard a knock on the door. The room was in darkness, the candle burned out, and he realised he must have drifted into sleep. Now came the sound of scratching and he thought immediately, with revulsion, of a rat. Groping in the pockets of the tunic folded by his bedside he found his box of lucifers and struck one. The sound stopped before the flame caught. He detected nothing in the dancing shadows and only the second match showed something white at the bottom of the door. It was a piece of folded paper, pushed through the gap beneath. He picked it up, opened it, had a glimpse of writing before the flame died. Heart thumping, he slid back the single bolt and looked out into the corridor. It was dimly lit but a lamp to the right showed a single figure shuffling into the shadows beyond. The creak of his opening door must have alarmed her – for it was a woman, in Mexican costume – and she turned.

Not Clothilde!

The lamp illuminated the wrinkled face of an old, stooped, Indian woman, a messenger only. She had seen him and before he could speak she held a finger to her lips, gesturing for silence. Then was gone.

He went back into the room, bolted the door, smoothed the paper, struck a lucifer. It needed only one to read the message.

Sous les escaliers à droite. Trois heures.

That the right was specified could only mean the steps to the balcony at the palace rear. And at three o'clock the sentries would be at the least alert.

There was no signature.

No need for one.

*

Only three lucifers remained by ten to three for he had checked his watch often in fear that he might be too early or too late. He wasn't sure if he wanted to see her, and less still what he could say to her. But, for whatever reason, she was taking a risk in summoning him and Durand was a dangerous man to defy. There was no option but to meet her.

Time at last to step into the corridor and pass down it as silently as he could. He had decided not to bring his pistol – should he be detected and stopped, it would be best to be unarmed. He reached the room where he had eaten, and the kitchen beyond, without encountering anybody. Out then into the shadows behind the mess and he flitted from the shadows of one building to the next, freezing at the sight of sentries. Still not challenged, he was circling the compound's interior anti-clockwise to avoid the main gate.

The worst was the last fifty yards. An open gap, bathed in the half-moon's silver light, extended from what must be stables toward the deep shadows along the palace's side. A sentry appeared at the corner of the balcony, paused, disappeared from sight again. Dawlish began a slow count and at sixty-seven the soldier was back, pausing, disappearing again. He returned at the count of seventy-one, turned back, was lost to sight once more.

Dawlish stepped from the shadow and forced himself to walk slowly across. If challenged, insomnia might just sound credible.

It felt like a journey of a thousand miles but he had reached the shadow beneath the balcony before he heard the sentry's footsteps returning. They stopped and, after a pause, receded.

He could see the twin stairways to the balcony now, open triangular spaces beneath as they swept upwards. The shadow of the nearer was deep and he edged into it.

"Nicholas."

She pronounced it in the French manner, as she always had, dropping the 's'. He could just make out her features, for she had cast a shawl across her head, but she seemed as lovely as she ever had.

"What are you doing here, Clothilde?"

He had agonised for hours over what to say, but the intensity of the disgust and bitterness in his voice surprised him.

"I have to live, Nicholas."

"Like this? With this —" he avoided in time the word that came to mind, "with this man?"

"You don't understand." Her voice was cold and held no hint of joy in seeing him.

"My uncle left money for your mother, for yourself."

"Do you know what it's like to be a bastard, Nicholas? Nobody in Pau believed my mother was a widow when she first came there with a baby. Nobody believed that story of a father killed in Algeria and they all guessed she was your uncle's mistress. We were children together, Nicholas, and we didn't understand."

A schoolfellow in the English school in Pau had once referred to her by the word she now used about herself. Dawlish had attacked him and two others who laughed about it. He'd taken a bad beating in return. When his Uncle Ralph heard, he praised him for his stance.

Those boys didn't matter, he'd said, but Madame Sapin and Clothilde did. He was proud of him.

"But you could have contacted me, Clothilde. My family would have helped, my sister Susan would have welcomed you and —"

Even as he spoke, he realised it would never have been practical, not in a dull English market town.

She was shaking her head in what seemed condescending pity. He saw she was dry eyed.

"You don't understand it, Nicholas, do you?" She might have been speaking to a child though was only a year his senior. "I didn't want to live as my mother did. And Durand will be a general, perhaps one day a marshal. He's spoken of that way and he's well regarded. He's proved his worth here in Mexico."

"By murdering in cold blood?"

"He's a soldier, Nicholas. It's his profession. He's good at it."

There was no hint of affection when she spoke of him. And she used his family name alone.

"I heard he was a married man."

She shrugged. "His wife won't live longer than another year. He'll marry me then. He promised it."

"Can you believe him?"

"He'll need a wife for appearances' sake when we get back to France. If he needs a mistress besides, he'll be discreet. I won't object."

"But if his wife doesn't die?"

"She's in an insane asylum and has consumption also. It's a miracle she survived so long."

Her cold calculation repelled him. Eight years ago, she had been a sister he loved. Now, this.

"Why did you call me here, Clothilde?" He wanted this to end.

"To tell you that I'm dead to you and you to me, Nicholas. To tell you never to mention to anyone that you know me. That if you see me. you'll look away and make no sign of recognition. That you'll never address as much as a single word to me."

"Clothilde —"

"Goodbye, Nicholas." She cut him off and extended no cheek to kiss, no hand to shake.

He would have accepted neither.

*

He found his way back to his room as he had come, unchallenged. Had tears come to him it might have been better, but they didn't. But gnawing emptiness did.

He too had grown up.

Chapter 7

Durand did not rise from his desk when they were ushered in to meet him next morning. No salute, no gesture of military courtesy, no handshake, no word of welcome, just a wave towards the single chair on the far side of the desk. Weatherby took it in silence and with a cold dignity that would have shamed any better man than this French colonel. They needed this brute's cooperation, he had told Dawlish over their meagre breakfast, and might have to endure a lot to get it. British interests counted for more than personal afront. Now he sat with pursed lips and waited. Dawlish stood by his right side, ready to translate.

The room was large, furnished with shabby remnants from the days of Spanish rule. Several oil portraits of earlier governors or viceroys survived between maps and documents pinned to boards around the walls. More maps strewed a large conference table. Despite the open windows, the day's heat was also growing.

Dawlish watched the immaculately uniformed colonel with cold loathing, disgust for his barbarism the previous day now mixed with outrage at Clothilde's corruption.

Three, four, long minutes passed, Durand scanning a document and at last signing it. Then he punched a bell on the desk and, without a word, handed it to a young captain who came scurrying in to take it. Only when the door was closed again did he lean back in his chair, his face half-amused, half-contemptuous.

"You say you're an English naval officer?" He made it sound as if he disbelieved it.

Dawlish translated. "He's trying to rile you, sir," he added.

"We're damned if we'll let him, Dawlish. Just tell him the cold facts."

But Durand looked unimpressed by the identity of Commander Frederick Weatherby, captain of Her Majesty's Ship *Sprightly*.

"What does *Sprightly* mean?" he said.

Dawlish told him.

The colonel shook his head as he might have when despairing of a child's naïvity. "You English," he said. "You still think it's all a game."

Weatherby's voice was calm. "Tell him, Dawlish, that agreeable as this meeting may be, we're here to see His Excellency the Imperial Mexican governor. And see him as soon as possible too. Say I have this." He produced the letter of introduction from Manzanillo's alcalde and pushed it across the table.

The colonel took it between finger and thumb as if it was unclean. He glanced at it for a moment, then tore it down the middle and dropped it in a waste basket by his side.

"There's no governor here, Imperial, excellent or otherwise," Something like triumph in Durand's tone. "He vanished a week ago after discovering his allegiance really lay with the Juarista cause. He may be with them in Guadalajara by now, though they have more likely shot him when he arrived. He could have left it too late to turn his coat." No pause for Dawlish to translate for Weatherby. "Several of his senior officials have disappeared also, but the remainder will hesitate to join them after two caught deserting yesterday are shot in the plaza at midday. You saw me sign the order just now. So you can tell your English ship-commander that if he has anything to say it's to me he'll say it."

"We have to deal with the blackguard, Dawlish," Weatherby said when he'd heard the translation. "Tell him I'm here to seek assurance about protection of British commercial interests. Nothing more. We've no axe to grind in the politics here. And don't antagonise him."

Though no friendlier than before, the discussion progressed with some smoothness, though little satisfaction, from that point on. As directed by Weatherby beforehand, Dawlish jotted the gist by pencil in a notebook. Durand did not object.

W: Could the colonel – on behalf of the Imperial Mexican government – continue protection of the assets and personnel of *El Ferrocarril del Pacífico?*

D: *Without doubt. All territory between here and the Pacific Coast under Imperial control – with French support. And remain so.*

W: But examples of hostile activity witnessed as recently as yesterday.

D: *Bandits or rebel forces have made a few raids. Effective measures in hand to deter them. El Ferrocarril's decision to employ American mercenary guards is wise.*

W: Is a withdrawal of Imperial and French forces to the coast in prospect?

D: *None of England's business. (Less polite in French).*

W: But haven't Juarista Forces occupied Guadalajara?

D (irritated): *Only because I & F forces have drawn back on Guzmán for tactical reasons. Temporary only. And none of W's business either.*

W: Apology if interest misinterpreted. As officer himself, finds D's reticence on this understandable.

D: *What else? Busy man.*

W. Another British interest. Plutus-owned *Glorioso* mine. Concern about delay of authorisation of silver export. Mine manager keen to pay ten-percent royalty, in silver, as soon as possible, then export.

D (Smiling): *Beyond my authority. Beyond ex-governor's too. Understands that Imperial government considering increase of royalty from ten percent to fifteen. Decision to be taken in Mexico City. Until then, export impossible.*

Dawlish saw Weatherby was taken aback. Few, if any, naval officers had much knowledge of commerce.

"Tell him *El Glorioso's* British owners have a licence from the Imperial Government. The terms must have been specified. Plutus made an enormous investment on that basis and hasn't yet received a penny in return. The terms can't be changed without joint agreement."

"Has your ship-commander a copy of the mining licence?" Durand said when Dawlish translated.

And no, Commander Weatherby had not.

Colonel Durand regretted he had none either. But even if he had, it would make no difference. Without orders from the Imperial Government, he could do nothing. It was impossible to say when they might be forthcoming. In the current state of unrest, communication with Mexico City was difficult, long and roundabout.

"But there's no need to be concerned about the mine's security, or the accumulated silver either," Durand said. "I've assigned Belgian troops to protect it. Tough veterans all and their commander's a devil of a fellow. It'll be safe until we receive orders from Mexico City."

Dawlish translated literally.

"Does he expect us to believe that?" Weatherby was fighting to control his indignation. "He must know we've been to the mine. And that Gove and his marines would guard the shipment to the railhead. No – don't translate that for him!" Weatherby lapsed into silence, a man realising he was out of his depth.

Durand, his face now a sneering mask, thanked Weatherby in exaggerated terms for his visit. If they departed immediately, he suggested, they could be back safely at the railhead before sundown. They'd be welcome to retain the dragoon escort and he wished them *bon voyage* in their warship.

"There's one more thing," Weatherby said.

No! A small voice howled in Dawlish's head. Don't say it. It can only make things worse, bring more humiliation. But Weatherby forged ahead.

"Tell him I wish to proceed onwards to Guadalajara. I need to discuss the security of the mine with the Juarista officials there."

For the first time, Durand flushed with anger when he heard the translation. "How's he going to get there? Walk? You've both come here like beggars, riding French horses and under French protection. Maybe he wants my men to escort you under a white flag to treat with the enemy? Are you stupid enough to think the rebel forces honour white flags?"

Though he remained calm, the answer angered Weatherby. All the more, Dawlish recognised, for being disrespected in the presence of a junior officer. And Durand did not relent and was on his feet now.

"Your ship-commander's insulting French arms." He spoke with cold fury. "He's insulting our ability to hold this country, the arrogant English *salopard*. Tell him he's lucky I'll let him have horses and escort back to the railhead. And be grateful that he won't be bound to his saddle." He sat down. "Now get out, both of you."

Dawlish made no attempt to translate in diplomatic terms. Durand had sat down again, was looking at some paper on his desk as if nobody else was present.

Weatherby stood up.

"Thank the colonel for his courtesy," he said. He was already moving towards the door.

The single word *merci* was enough, Dawlish decided.

He had never hated anybody with such intensity as at this moment.

Clothilde's master, Clothilde's choice.

*

The sky had clouded overnight and now, a mile south of Guzmán, the rain began. It fell in a steady torrent, running in streams at first off the sun-hardened track and then, mile by mile, turning it to liquid mud. The French dragoons wore capes across their shoulders. Weatherby and Dawlish had nothing to protect them and their clothing was saturated from the first minute. The temperature dropped several degrees, chilling them.

Dawlish had never felt more desolate.

It would have been better if Clothilde had died, he told himself. It was not her association with Durand that alone disgusted him. It was – he struggled to find the words – her hardness, her cynicism. He had carried the memory of the girl he had played with as happily and innocently as with his sister Susan. He remembered his late uncle's love for her and she for him. He'd learned his French from her even more than from her mother. He had retained an image of her as all that a girl should be – beautiful, clever, innocent, with the promise of dignified and fulfilled womanhood, a valued wife, a beloved mother. His uncle must have shared that hope and, confident in it, left her a dowry. A generous one, Dawlish knew. He was present when the will was read, when he learned that he himself was now owner of six farms.

"Dawlish!" Weatherby's shout interrupted his brooding.

The dragoon sent to scout a quarter-mile ahead was breaking through the grey curtain of rain and galloping back, waving. His fellows were swinging from their saddles, pulling carbines from their horses' bucket holsters, dragging the beasts into the scatterings of low scrub on a slope to the right of the track.

"Damn it, Dawlish! Get down!" Weatherby had slipped from his mount, grabbed the reins of Dawlish's beast as well as his own and was pulling them towards the scrub.

The dragoons' horses were already lying down in a small defensive circle, living barricades behind which their riders crouched, carbines at the ready. The position dominated the track. When they reached the circle, neither Weatherby nor Dawlish could induce their beasts to lie down. The sergeant, Morvan, swearing, managed it for them. He gestured to their holstered revolvers. They drew them and took cover.

The scout arrived, had thought he's seen figures scurrying between rocks further up the track. It might have been imagination – he was frank about that – but impossible to be certain in this rain.

It was better to take no chances, Morvan said. Better to wait here. If *El Serpiente's* men, or Juaristas, were close, they'd come to find them. Both were always eager to cut off small detachments, although this time they'd have a surprise in store.

And then the waiting, lying in wet misery, apprehension cancelling fatigue in Dawlish's exhausted, sleep-deprived body. The horses, well trained, stirred only slightly, incomprehension in their great noble eyes. He glanced towards Weatherby, received a forced smile in return, realised that he too was deep in his own wretchedness.

Appropriate measures.

Orders to take them in defence of British interests had brought Weatherby to Guzmán. Knowing he had achieved nothing by it, that he was wholly impotent to influence the matter, must rankle all the more in his awareness that failure would be harshly judged by far-off superiors. That he had received no specific instructions and been thrown back on his own judgement in a country of which he knew nothing, would not save him. If some previous blunder had indeed exiled Weatherby to Pacific Station obscurity, there could be no hope of redemption now.

Dawlish's heart went out to him. He had known Weatherby only as a good officer with three decades' service to his credit. He had seen him adroit in managing a minor diplomatic crisis at Nazareno earlier in the year and skilful in nursing the damaged *Sprightly* from Novo-Arkhangelsk to San Francisco, a dangerous storm notwithstanding. Weatherby was respected and popular with his officers and crew, treading a fine line between firm discipline and understanding of human frailty. He should have been a captain by now, should be commanding something larger than *Sprightly*. Success in Mexico could have cancelled some previous black mark and earned advancement.

And Weatherby knew it.

What might have been a half-hour passed. Dawlish, cold now in his sodden clothing, was grateful for the warmth of the rain-glistening flank of the horse that sheltered him. He wondered what decision Weatherby would take once – if – they got back to Manzanillo. It could be a direct return to Esquimalt, or heading to some port with a telegraph connection from where he could cable for further instructions – with Mexico in its present chaos, the closest might be in the United States. In either case it would be a confession of personal defeat, and Weatherby was a proud man. But for himself, Dawlish wished to be gone from Mexico and forget he ever had been there. The discovery of Clothilde's willing degradation was no less dispiriting than the cycle of atrocity and counter-atrocity inflicted on a helpless population by forces that cared nothing for them.

And then, at last, deliverance, if not from his depression but threat of attack. The dragoon sergeant was standing, shouting for them to rise, and drag up the horses. He was pointing towards the track below. A cavalry patrol was coming up from the south, plodding resolutely but unhurried through rain and mud, with no indication it might have seen recent action.

The scout's warning that Sergeant Morvan had taken so seriously had indeed been of a mirage. He was correct to do so, Dawlish thought. The bodies of those mutilated Belgian deserters had shown the price of underestimation.

Safe now to resume the ride to the railhead.

*

The rain ceased as suddenly as it had begun. The sky cleared and the sun boiled drifting vapour from the muddy track. Horses and clothing steamed. The ground hardened and the going was easier. They passed though the post where its garrison had been massacred two nights before. French infantry were manning it again and what had been a trench yesterday was now a long mound streaked with little gullies by the rain. Another like it, new, lay a little beyond. No sign of villagers or prisoners

They arrived at the railhead in late afternoon.

Grove came out meet them. Even before they had dismounted, he was addressing Weatherby.

"There's bad news, sir."

"About the silver? Did you bring it?"

Following the interview with Durand, that must be uppermost in Weatherby's mind.

Grove nodded. "We escorted it safely from the mine, sir. I would have loaded on the train, as you'd directed me, but Major Flandin seized it."

"You let him?"

"He had his men surround the wagons with bayonets drawn." Grove's tone was apologetic. "I protested. It got quite heated. Colonel Sorderer backed me – he'd expected also to escort the silver to Manzanillo. But Flandin was adamant. He said he has orders not to release the silver without instructions from Ciudad Guzmán. I didn't press it in the end." He paused, as if fearing rebuke.

"Very well, Mr. Grove. Bring me to Flandin." Weatherby turned to Dawlish. "You'll translate."

They met Sergeant Morvan of the escort leaving Flandin's office. He saluted and passed on.

"I'm damned if he hasn't carried a message from Durand," Weatherby said.

Flandin received them with courtesy and Weatherby was restrained, though persistent, in his protest. But orders just received from Guzmán confirmed previous instructions to impound the silver. Flandin understood there was no question of permanent seizure, just temporary delay until administrative concerns that he knew nothing about were resolved. Weatherby made a few further protests without great conviction but Dawlish saw that it was for form's sake alone. He was beaten. Flandin said that if Weatherby wanted to send a message to Atkinson, the *Glorioso's* manager, a French patrol would carry it. Weatherby accepted that, but not an invitation to dine. He wanted to depart for Manzanillo early next morning.

Dawlish, unwilling to see his captain's misery, avoided him that evening. Anxious to ignore the nagging memory of Clothilde, he busied himself in assisting Sorderer and the Confederates in preparations for leaving. The freight wagons were empty but for a few pieces of machinery from the mine being sent for repair at the railway workshop in Manzanillo. *El Ferrocarril del Pacífico* undertook such work at a price. The locomotive was coaled and the furnace fired for slow build-up to a full head of steam by morning. Both Grover and Tom Bryce prodded Dawlish for information about what had happened at Guzmán but he kept it to himself. They noticed his moroseness and gave up.

And then, another miserable night of broken sleep.

*

Departure at sunrise and passage down the line faster than on the way up. A hand-pumped railcar, protected by sandbags, once more scouted ahead under Tom Bryce's command. It was a dangerous duty, for in places it would have been difficult, even impossible, to retreat up the steep inclines should it come under attack.

"Nothing for it then but slam on the brakes, if we do." Bryce said when Dawlish remarked on that. "We'll have our Henry repeaters until you folks catch up with us. We've survived worse up north."

Leaving behind the smoking cone of *El Volcán de Colima* and through, without stopping, the town with which it shared its name by nine o'clock, dropping then through the Armería valley and past the point where the Belgians' defiled corpses had been found. But today the only sign of human presence was the sight of labourers in distant fields. They reached Ciudad de Armería an hour before sundown, covering in a single day what had taken three on the way up. They spent the night at the small armed camp there – no chances taken, the perimeter guarded and patrolled. Coal for the locomotive, food for the men and an unspoken but universal and palpable relief about being south of the most hazardous area. Departure early next morning.

And, at noon, a sight that brought joy.

The endless expanse of the calm blue Pacific.

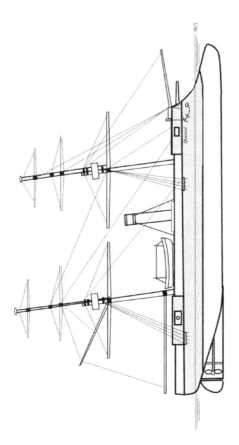

Builders: Arman Frères, Bordeaux, France
CSS *Stonewall* Class 1865
Construction: Wood on iron framing
Displacement: 1390 tons
Length: 186 feet overall
Beam: 33 feet
Draught: 14 feet

Machinery: 2 steam engines, 2 shafts
          1200 Horsepower
Speed: 10.5 Knots (max.)
Armament: 1 X 300 lb. rifled muzzle-loader
          2 X 70 lb. rifled muzzle-loader
Complement: 135
Armour: 4,5" – 5.5", shown as:

Mexican Imperial Ironclad:
Quetzal

Chapter 8

It was late afternoon, close to Manzanillo, passing the fields of stunted maize where Colonel Pettigrew, CSA, was failing to succeed as a farmer.

The hand-pumped railcar used for scouting had been left at Ciudad de Armería since, for now, Colonel Sorderer judged the coastal zone to be safer than further north. Depressed by Weatherby's morose brooding, no less than his own, Dawlish had chosen to ride with Bryce and his men in the sandbagged wagon ahead of the locomotive. The mood there was light and at intervals somebody broke into a song and the others joined in, accompanied by a twanging jew's harp. It was easy to like the spirit of these beaten but undefeated men.

The train was swinging into the last bend before the town. Dawlish was on his feet, looking over the sandbag parapet, eager for sight of *Sprightly* again. There was something clean and honourable about her and the world she represented – his world – at variance with the moral squalor that had disheartened him in recent days.

And now the curve of the bay was revealed, but his eyes locked, not on *Sprightly,* but on the larger vessel moored further in. He had never seen anything like it before.

"Tom! May I borrow your field glasses?"

Bryce joined him, followed his gaze.

"Must be the *Quetzal,*" he said. "Beautiful, ain't she?"

Dawlish had heard her spoken of as a gunboat, although that was a term too frequently used by landsmen for any type of warship. But this was larger and more menacing – and unprecedented. It was impossible to classify her.

He took the glasses, locked the vessel in the lenses. She might be little longer than *Sprightly* but the profile could not be more different. Twin masts, with a ludicrously tall funnel rising between them amidships, the freeboard high and God only knew what armament was hidden behind her bulwarks. But it was the sloping ram that drew most attention, extending down at almost forty-five degrees from the top of the forecastle. What might be the muzzle of a large-calibre gun jutted through a port below the bowsprit. Dawlish swept the glasses back along the hull. Its white paint was streaked with rust and he fancied that he detected a pronounced tumblehome.

"Where was she built?" he asked Bryce.

"Darned if I know. In Europe somewhere, I guess. Austria maybe – ain't that where Emperor Max hails from?"

"How long has she been here?"

"Eight or ten months, patrolling up and down the coast, scaring off Yankee ships runnin' in supplies to Juarez and his people. Never saw sight of her previously though. I was upcountry when she came into 'zanillo before."

"But you'd heard there were Confederates in the crew?"

Bryce nodded. "Why don't you join me in town tonight? We might run into them. It's sure likely some will be drinking."

Weatherby would need to make a courtesy visit tomorrow – this was an Imperial ship in an Imperial port – but he'd welcome as much information as he could get before going aboard.

"I'll join you, Tom," Dawlish said.

After the nightmare journey to and from Guzmán, Weatherby would not grudge him an evening's shore leave.

*

It was impossible to know how much Weatherby had told Ashton in his quarters after arrival on *Sprightly*. The first lieutenant would have had little to report – the vessel had swung at anchor without incident – but the meeting was a short one. Dawlish found it difficult to imagine Weatherby sharing the full details of his humiliation, easy to envisage orders for quick departure. But it hardly mattered. Grove's marines had stories to tell of the mine, the silver and its seizure by the French. Dawlish, when pressed by Sanderson, the second lieutenant, about what happened in Guzmán, had avoided answering. It was a confidential matter, he said, Weatherby's responsibility. But from

Sanderson he learned the *Quetzal* arrived the previous day and that Ashton had gone across to explain *Sprightly's* presence. He returned quickly and, though he did not elaborate, it sounded as if he hadn't been well received. *Quetzal's* captain spoke English with only the slightest accent, he said.

Tom Bryce was waiting at the wharf when a ship's boat landed Dawlish there – Weatherby approved his going ashore. It was a relief to have washed and changed into clean clothing.

"There's a cantina called *La Galina* that most of our Confed boys favour. We'll try there first." Bryce winked. "Girls there too, if you're so inclined. Guaranteed clean, all of 'em."

Dawlish shook his head.

But no worse in their ways than Clothilde.

The town's streets were narrow, lit only by lights from open windows. Women sat in doorways, gossiping in the soft darkness. Children still played and men smoked in small groups. It seemed peaceful, but Dawlish saw Bryce was carrying a holstered pistol and paused at deeper shadows before advancing. He should have come armed himself, he thought. The memory was suddenly vivid of that *Sprightly* seaman knifed in a Novo-Arkhangelsk tavern.

La Galina proved less threatening, a large single storey building set in a low-walled garden. Most clients seemed to be drinking quietly at lamplit tables outside. Several who had been guards on the train greeted Bryce and Dawlish with invitations to join them. Differences of rank didn't seem to count for these men, all brothers alike in exile.

Bryce shook his head. "Any o' folks from the *Quetzal* about?"

"In there." A wave toward the building. "Two of 'em. With the colonel."

Groups of three and four were sitting at tables in the large dim room within, most playing cards and ignoring the bored-looking Mexican women by their sides. Nobody turned from their play as Bryce and Dawlish entered. It hardly seemed a temple of exotic sin. In a far corner, Sorderer, facing the door, was with two others, their backs turned. He stood up on seeing the newcomers and beckoned.

Dawlish recognised Travis Welborne before his full face turned to him. They had sat together for long cold and wet hours in the turret of the ironclad *Odin*, the renamed Confederate *Galveston,* in temporary service with the Danish Navy, two years before. They had been close, had relied on each other in battle. And Welborne had taken Dawlish's place as turret commander when *Galveston* sailed away, under Confederate colours, to raid Union shipping on the world's wide oceans.

"Dawlish, Nick Dawlish!" Welborne had grasped his hand, was smiling, as joyful as if reunited with a brother. Dawlish felt a surge of affection – and concern. Though they were both of an age, Welborne's face now seemed a decade older. He must have had it hard in the two years since.

The other officer, a stranger, had also risen and was extending his hand.

"Lieutenant Jesse Rogers, sir. Late CSS *Galveston.* And US Navy 'til the war. Annapolis, Class of '54. Honoured to meet a friend of Travis."

He must have joined after Dawlish left her, another Confederate officer who had slipped through the Union blockade and made it to some neutral port *Galveston* visited. Dark and heavily bearded, he might be little over thirty but was already greying. Dawlish saw him wince slightly when he shook his hand and noticed then he was carrying one shoulder higher than the other.

"How are you two gentlemen acquainted?" Sorderer was speaking to Dawlish and Welborne.

Dawlish hesitated. He had undertaken never to admit that he and other British officers had volunteered for Danish service. A certain royal personage wanted to forget he had ever supported such a venture. But Welborne was governed by no such promise. He broke in and summarised *Galveston's* service as the Danish *Odin* with pride.

"Damned if I'd known anything of this," Sorderer said when Welborne finished. "We heard little of anything in the last year o' war. Too busy fighting for our lives."

"And for honour," Rogers said. "Southern honour."

Sorderer called for drinks.

Dawlish felt uneasy. "I trust you gentleman understand that the Danish affair is still a sensitive matter in Britain," he said. "Mention of it could end my career. "I'd appreciate if –"

"We'd never heard about it," Sorderer said. "You can take it for granted, lieutenant. You'll never hear it mentioned. Not by us."

The others nodded assent.

"What became of *Galveston*?" Dawlish felt relieved now. "And of Captain Lorance?" He had last seen them in the remote Orkney anchorage of Scapa Flow and heard nothing of either since.

"Lorance sank her." All elation gone from Welborne's voice. "We'd heard of Lee's and Johnson's and Kirby-Smith's surrenders when we put in to Rio de Janeiro. The Yankees weren't going to have her. Lorance and a dozen like Rogers and myself, we blew her bottom out. *Galveston* went down with her ensign flying."

Regret and pity surged through Dawlish. He had given that ship so much and Lorance was one of the best men he'd ever known.

A long silence then that Sorderer broke. "Never surrendered to the Goddamn Yankees? Us neither. Couldn't stomach it."

"What happened after the Orkneys?" Dawlish said.

"We'd less than a year to hit back against the Union, though we didn't know it. But we hurt the Yankees, hurt 'em badly where they most cared about, in their pockets." Pride now in Welborne's tone. "Lorance said it was too late to break their blockade on our ports so we went after Union merchantmen. A dozen or so off the Cape of Good Hope, even more off Brazil. We hadn't men enough for prize crews, so we burned the lot. Didn't kill nobody though – Lorance was proud of that. He kept 'em on board until we'd taken some small ship worth nothing and sent them ashore in it. Did it twice, into Recife and another time into Freetown."

It had been the pattern established by other Confederate raiders, as far distant as the East Indies.

"I'd served in *Florida*." Rogers sounded bitter. "She'd managed much the same as *Galveston*. I got away when the Yankees boarded her in harbour in Bahia. A neutral port! Violation of Brazilian sovereignty!

Even Brazil's emperor protested. Not that it mattered a damn to the Yankees. Not a gentleman among them."

He'd made his way to Rio afterwards, had been there when *Galveston* docked to hear the devastating news of the surrenders. "I came near to putting a bullet in my head then," he said.

"Me too." Welborne breathed it half-aloud.

Dawlish understood. He remembered the vehemence of Welborne's resentment of the Union. It was something Lorance never shared. A pre-war naval officer himself, and with a family tradition of opposing slavery, only loyalty to his home-state of Virginia committed him to Confederate service. Reluctant though that decision was, his dedication thereafter had been unstinting. He was a superb professional and a man above hate.

"I volunteered to help scuttle *Galveston*," Rogers said. "There was some satisfaction in that. We'd saved a boat for getting back to Rio. And afterwards we mostly split up and went our ways."

"And Captain Lorance?" Dawlish said.

"Went back to Virginia. Said the issue was decided, once and for all, that we'd have to swallow it. Nation needed rebuilding, he said. Since Lee had decided the same, it was good enough for him."

Dawlish was not surprised. He turned to Welborne. "Did he try to convince you also of that, Travis?"

"He tried. But I've lost too much. A brother dead at Shiloh. Another's leg taken off at Vicksburg. Our plantation burned by Union locusts – seeing it killed my father. Thank God my mother died before the war." Welborne paused. "I'd no falling out with Lorance. He was an honourable man and he'd thought hard about it. But me – I'd rather starve than swear a loyalty oath to the so-called re-United States."

Sorderer and Rogers were nodding. Dawlish sensed their desolation and waited before speaking.

"How did you end up aboard this Imperial ship?" he said to Welborne. "Or you either, Lieutenant Rogers?"

"Hunger." Rogers was first to answer.

"We were still in Rio when *Quetzal* put in," Welborne said. "She was heading for the Mexican Pacific Coast, passing round the Horn.

Built at Bordeaux, France, and bought out of Emperor Max's own pocket, we've heard tell, and her captain a crony of his from when they'd served together in the Austrian Navy."

"Kapitän Baron August von Berchtold-Ampringen." Rogers rolled off the name with contempt. "He'd resigned from the Austrian Navy to join what was to be Mexico's. Some navy – 'cept *Quetzal*, nothing bigger than a schooner! And Berchtold had driven the ironclad so damn hard and so damn badly since they'd left Bordeaux that half her crew jumped ship in Rio and two officers and her surgeon – Austrians– walked off also. So he was glad to take us when we presented ourselves."

"Rogers as first officer, myself second," Welborne said. "The third's a Mexican, a young fellow called Ignacio Vázquez, younger than you or me, Nick, and he don't speak English. He'd been sent to France for experience in her navy – I can't say he learned much – and he'd joined *Quetzal* at Bordeaux."

"We had to recruit an almost full new crew," Rogers said "Seamen from everywhere – British, French, Swedes, even a Greek – but few of 'em with naval experience. More of them disappeared when we arrived here but we made up for them with Mexicans and a few Chileans. We picked up a new surgeon in Valparaiso."

"An ironclad, you said?" Dawlish had guessed as much but had not been close enough to see her armour.

"Best anywhere," Rogers said.

And then the full story.

She and her sister had been built in France, allegedly for the Egyptian Government, but funded – like *Galveston* – by the Confederacy. After Lee's surrender, Union forces took possession of the first, CSS *Stonewall,* in port at Havana. But the second, *Manassas,* was incomplete then, though already armed, and still at Bordeaux. The new Emperor of Mexico bought her from the shipyard and renamed her *Quetzal.*

"Berchtold was in such a hurry getting here that there was no time for training before we departed Rio." Welborne was shaking his head.

"Nearly turned turtle off the Horn. But we're getting her fighting fit at last – and no thanks to Berchtold for that."

Rogers, a qualified naval professional, and Welborn, who'd proved an excellent gunnery officer when in Danish service, would have been well placed to forge the ironclad and her crew into a dangerous weapon.

Unwilling to join in criticism of a senior officer, even if of another navy, Dawlish said, "Has *Quetzal* seen action?"

"No. Nothing worthwhile," Rogers said. "We're under orders not to engage American traders, even if they're laden to the gills with Juarista supplies. Looks like Max's French friends don't want to antagonise the US of A any more than they've done already, and they're the ones who matter. Berchtold insisted on bombarding two villages held by Juarista sympathisers and sunk a few fishing boats. A waste of munitions, nothing more. Made him feel good though."

"What does *Quetzal* carry?" Dawlish said. "I've never seen anything like her."

"Better see for yourself, Mr. Dawlish," Rogers said. "You'll be impressed. Once your captain has paid his respects, you'll be welcome. Berchtold's very stiff about protocol."

Dawlish flicked his watch open. Time to get back to *Sprightly* before Weatherby retired. He stood up, excused himself and shook hands all around. Tom Bryce didn't.

"You wouldn't be tempted to stay on yourself?" He winked. "Satisfaction guaranteed."

"I've business in *Sprightly*," Dawlish said.

"Then I'll walk with you to the wharf," Welborne said. "We can catch up on a few things, *Galveston* and such."

Back through the streets that were now all but deserted. Welborne wasn't interested in discussing memories.

"A word o' warning, Nick," he said. "You'd better advise your captain to handle Berchtold carefully."

"Protocol?"

"That's the least of it. The man's crazy, getting worse by the day. Resigned his Austrian commission and came here looking for battle and glory. Now he's found his hands tied – want's action and success and can't have 'em. It's eating into him all the worse since he heard about Lissa."

The news had reached San Francisco before *Sprightly* left. It had been a crushing Austrian victory – Austria's only one – in a six-week war that she had never expected. When Prussia, her ally in the Danish war two years before, had declared war on her, the new Kingdom of Italy had taken the opportunity to strike at her also. And in mid-July, off the Adriatic port of Lissa, the Austrian navy had smashed the Italian fleet – literally, since ramming had proved the deciding tactic.

"It's better your captain doesn't mention it," Welborne said. "No congratulations, no admiration, nothing."

"But the Austrians won," Dawlish said. "Superbly, worthy of Nelson. You've seen reports, have you?"

"Some American newspapers reached us. Looks like them Italians never had a chance once the Austrians drove at them hell for leather. But it broke Bechtold's heart that he'd missed it and it was two days before he left his cabin. He'd have been there, captaining his own ship if he hadn't resigned. Seems he'd been a friend of the Austrian admiral responsible. Can't recollect his name."

"Tegetthoff," Dawlish said.

"That's it! And now Tegetthoff's a hero and Bechtold's commanding a one-ship squadron that's ordered to avoid action lest it's upset the Yankees. He's no fool. He's guessed that the French will be gone soon and Emperor Max won't last a week after. Berchtold wants some chance of glory before that happens. Even if it kills him."

They had reached the wharf. *Sprightly*'s boat was waiting.

Dawlish had a lot to tell his captain.

*

Weatherby, alone, and in formal uniform, crossed to *Quetzal* next morning. Dawlish noticed that he was not wearing the Crimean and Chinese campaign medals he normally wore on such occasions – he was taking no chance of reminding Berchtold that hard fighting had eluded him. He returned two hours later and called Dawlish to his quarters.

"I'm grateful for your advice," he said. "I approached him as I'd approach a full admiral. He loved it. He seems to know half Britain's aristocracy – his aunt's married to a Lord Leverstoke and he's hunted with the Quorn and the Beaufort. Safe subjects and no mention of Lissa, so we got on well. And it appears he's put in here for machinery repairs. The railway workshop has the facilities he needs. He's complaining about how long they're taking."

"Did you learn how she's armed, sir?"

"You're itching to see her, aren't you, Dawlish? Well, you deserve it. I'll send you across with some message this afternoon, thanks for the meeting, compliments, that sort of thing. I suspect one of your Confederate friends can show you around."

"Thank you, sir."

*

Quetzal proved even more powerful than Dawlish expected, not just for her guns but protection.

"Two turrets, but neither of 'em like *Galveston's*." Welborn said.

They were standing by the funnel, looking first forward and then aft. Dawlish saw now that the high forecastle hid a circular iron drum, as wide as the ship herself.

"Five and a half-inches thick," Welborne said.

"Hand cranked?" Rotating *Galveston's* turret had needed brute human strength.

"No need. It's fixed but with ports on both beams and one directly ahead. Rogers says it's more like a citadel than a turret. With a ten-inch three-hundred pounder inside. And there, abaft the mainmast –" he pointed aft towards another curved iron wall, "two seventy-pounders, each with a wide arc to starboard or to port. Same armour thickness as for'ard. You want to look inside? Yes? Then follow me."

There was no access from the deck – it was necessary to go below to reach the interior through the trunking that dropped from it to the magazine. Dawlish saw now that this was no circular drum but two separate iron walls, one forward one aft, and open spaces between on either beam. Here were the ports through which the port and starboard seventy-pounders could fire, each on an inclined-slide pivot-mount, tackles in place to haul them to bear. Judging by the half-circle brass roller paths beneath the mounting's rears, each weapon could sweep wide arcs ahead of and abaft the beam.

Now to the forward citadel, also fixed and dominated by the single huge three-hundred pounder, pivot-mounted like the smaller weapons aft. Three ports, one on either side and one for direct fire ahead from above the ram.

"Is the hull armoured too?" Dawlish asked.

"Four and a half-inches along the waterline. And something better still – twin engines and twin screws. Run one of 'em ahead, the other astern, and she'll turn on a dime."

Nothing in the entire Pacific that could challenge this brute with any hope of victory, Dawlish thought. Emperor Maximilian had bought himself a killer. Berchtold must have dreamed of winning glory in her.

And now she was swinging uselessly at anchor while American vessels ran in supplies to the Juaristas.

No wonder that Berchtold was seething on the brink of madness.

Chapter 9

Ten days passed and Weatherby made no announcement about departure. He was seldom seen outside his quarters, and his orders were transmitted through Ashton, who in turn directed an intensive maintenance effort. Much was essential – inspection and repair of standing and running rigging, cleaning of furnace and boiler, tightening of glands and packings, trimming of the coal bunkers. But when this was completed – holystoning decks that had been holystoned to perfection the day before, and surfaces painted that didn't need it and repolishing brass that was already gleaming – it could only evoke resentment not just in the crew but in the officers also. Boat-pulling races and a tug-of-war ashore, and cutlass and bayonet drill – under Dawlish's direction, for he took a pride in his own skill – combatted the boredom but couldn't do so indefinitely.

Dawlish recognised it might be himself alone who understood Weatherby's indecision. His own fluency in French, and to a lesser extent, in Spanish, had brought him into closer contact with his captain than his rank could otherwise occasion. On the fruitless journey to Guzmán he sensed Weatherby's hope his protection of British interests in the face of chaos would cancel some earlier black mark on his record. Weatherby had done his best and his best had not been good enough. He was delaying departure, Dawlish suspected, in the hope that some new crisis might require his intervention. But he could not wait forever.

The crew was allowed ashore in small groups only, accompanied by a marine sergeant and two of his men, all armed. It was not however danger that Dawlish sensed lying over the town when he brought Grove with him one night to meet Tom Bryce at *La Galina*. It was fear.

"The alcalde's snuck off to God knows where," Tom said. "If your captain needs anything approved. then he'd better get it done now before the other officials follow and forget they ever swore an oath to Emperor Max. The teniente commanding the fort –"

"Robles?" Dawlish remembered the shabby young officer who'd met him on first arrival. He'd looked beaten already.

"That's right, Robles. He's gone too. A sergeant's in command of the fort now but he'll disappear any day. Everybody else is keeping their heads down. All of 'em know the game's up for Max. The French know it too, and they'll go soon, and when they do the wrath of God's going to fall on anybody who declared for him. The Juaristas have a lot of accounts to settle."

And yet Durand, in Guzmán, had conveyed no impression of intention to depart, Dawlish thought. The town was well fortified and he looked like a man who would not yield easily.

But it won't be my concern anymore.

He wanted only to be gone.

And forget Clothilde forever.

*

The open boat crept into Manzanillo's bay, urged on by a weak breeze and a ragged brown lug-sail. It headed towards the wharf initially but *Sprightly's* sluggishly stirring white ensign must have drawn attention, for it altered course towards her. It drew alongside and Dawlish, officer of the watch, looked down to see a small clinker-built ship's lifeboat. It contained one man only. Emaciated, his trousers and flannel shirt – all he wore – hung loose. He had no hat and his face was burned red. His voice was a croak when he called up. Only with difficulty did Dawlish realise that he was begging in English to come on board.

He fell on trying to catch the rope thrown to him and was unable to rise. His craft was drifting away and it took *Sprightly's* duty boat to bring it back and two seamen to lift him to the deck.

"Sit him down there." Dawlish pointed to a mooring bitt. It was necessary to hold him upright. "And bring water."

Gripping the pewter mug with both hands, the man drained it in a single slurp, then retched and held it out for more. He babbled what might be thanks but proved incoherent when questioned. Dawlish had

108

him brought below to the care of the sick berth attendant – *Sprightly* did not carry a surgeon – and went to inform Ashton.

"Where's he come from?" the first lieutenant asked.

"He looks like a shipwreck survivor. He could be English or American – he's hard to understand. There was nothing in the boat, no food, no water. Nobody else either. He must've made a hasty escape, whatever he came off. Days ago, I'd say, considering his state."

"Will he survive?"

"He's far gone with sunstroke, sir," Dawlish said. "He's starving but I don't know how much food he should have." He'd heard of men like him killed by being fed too much too soon. "I suggest he needs a surgeon, sir. *Quetzal* has one."

"No need to say he's not of *Sprightly*. I imagine Captain Berchtold wouldn't refuse."

And he didn't.

*

It was a day before the survivor was strong enough to talk. Even then it was for five minutes only. *Quetzal's* Chilean surgeon – who had stayed with him through the night – forbade longer. Weatherby and Ashton were present, Dawlish also since he was the only one who could communicate in Spanish with the surgeon.

The survivor's name was Jem Redshaw. Second mate. *Jenny Dixon.*

Each word was an effort.

"British?" Weatherby asked.

"Glasgow registered."

"What happened? Storm? Fire?"

"Taken."

"Taken?"

"Seetanecho."

Redshaw's head dropped back on his pillow. The surgeon turned to Weatherby and held a finger to his lips. No more for now.

"What's Seetanecho?" Weatherby said when Ashton and Dawlish followed him to the chartroom. "Any of you hear of it? An island? A town? A port? No? Me neither."

Whatever it was, it must not be far from here or Redshaw couldn't have survived without water. They pored over a chart of this part of the Mexican coast.

"No Seetanecho," Weatherby said at last. "Maybe it's a person? A privateer perhaps? Some local pirate?"

But Dawlish was still searching,

"This could be it." He pointed. "Zihuantanejo." The Spanish pronunciation bore just enough resemblance to Redshaw's effort.

It looked like a small town, little more than a dot some two hundred miles to the south-east. It lay at the head of a small bay, its narrow entrance flanked by peninsulas.

It was a possibility, no more. And *Sprightly* carried no register of British merchant shipping so it was impossible to identify a *Jenny Dixon*. But it sounded a plausible name – some owner's wife or daughter – for any British trader. There was nothing more to be done for now.

They spoke to Redshaw again in late afternoon. He seemed stronger.

"What did you mean by your ship being taken?" Weatherby asked.

"We was boarded, sir. By Mexicans. Mexican Rebels. We was told Seetanecho was safe. It bloody well wasn't. They let us anchor, all friendly like 'an –" He paused, saw he had their attention. "Would there be a drink, sir? Rum maybe? Whisky if you have it?"

"That can wait. Was anybody killed?"

"Not while I was on board."

"But you escaped?"

"I was lucky. Hid in the chain locker when I saw what was up. I think all the others was locked in the hold, Enoch Ridley – he's *Jenny's* captain – an' Sandy McCafferty, first mate, an' the rest. We'd dropped our boat just before that and it was still moored alongside. I'd stayed hid an' I lowered meself into it in the dark. Nobody noticed."

"What was the *Jenny Dixon* doing there?"

"Delivering supplies for the government. Loaded at San Pedro."

"Which San Pedro? There's dozens of 'em."

"In California, sir." Redshaw suddenly looked evasive. "Nothing illegal. All above board, sir."

"Supplies for what government?"

The question was reasonable. For the United States, Benito Juarez was still president of Mexico. American arms were pouring in to support his forces.

"For the Mexican government, you said, Mr. Redshaw. Which one? Imperial or Juarista?"

"I don't know nothing about politics, sir. It was just for the government we was told." Redshaw was looking towards the surgeon as if hoping he'd intervene. "I'm tired, sir. Can I rest a bit?"

Weatherby ignored him.

"Were you carrying arms? Guns? Ammunition?"

"Everything was all in crates, sir. To be landed at Seetanecho. Didn't see inside 'em meself. I don't know nothin' more. That was the captain's business."

Redshaw groaned and dropped back on his pillow.

It might have been genuine and the surgeon was taking no chances.

Give him a few more hours rest.

But no rum, no whisky.

Not yet.

*

"You have American friends in *Quetzal*, Dawlish," Weatherby said when they left the sick bay. "Send a message across. Invite them to meet you at – where's the place you've been before?"

"*La Galina*, sir."

"Good. A social meeting. But find out if they know anything about this *Jenny Dixon*."

"It's better I meet just one of them," Dawlish said. "Welborne, second officer. We're more of an age." No mention of prior service together. The months spent under Danish colours were recorded in his personal file at the Admiralty as recovery at home from illness.

A seaman went across with an innocuous note for Welborne and returned with an acceptance. They'd meet at the wharf.

"So you've a hankering tonight for *La Galina's* ladies, Nick?" Welborne clapped him on the shoulder when he landed.

"Just for different company."

La Galina was no livelier than when he'd been there before. Dawlish waved away a girl who approached them, was mortified then to realise that she was the owner's daughter, just come to take orders. Welborne covered his embarrassment and asked for tequila for both. Dawlish loathed the drink but this was no time to object.

They sat in the corner where they'd been before.

After a few minutes' casual conversation, Dawlish said, "Do you know anything of a vessel called *Jenny Dixon?*"

"How in hell did you hear of her, Nick?"

"Just tell me, Travis. It may be useful to both our captains. We've one of her crew on board. He's half-dead and he's being damn cautious about what he'll tell us. It's he for whom *Quetzal's* surgeon's caring."

Welborne hesitated, then said, "We've been on the lookout for her for the last three weeks. We'd assumed an American ship must have detained her. Where's she now?"

Dawlish told him.

"It figures. She was headed there," Welborne said. "But the place was still held by an Imperial garrison."

"It isn't now. The *Jenny* was boarded by Juaristas a few days ago. She's probably still there."

"It'll kill Berchtold," Welborne said. "It'll eat him up. If we hadn't put in here for repairs, we could've saved her."

"It might still be possible." Dawlish suspected Weatherby must already be brooding on the chances for success.

A British interest needing rescue. Compensation for failure ashore.

"What was the *Jenny* carrying, Travis? Arms? She's come from San Pedro in California. I thought that the US is supplying only the Juaristas, not Imperial forces."

Welborne laughed. "If there's money in it, there's always a deal to be done and always customs men to turn a blind eye. The Union's awash with weaponry it no longer needs and ready to sell to anybody with hard cash. Emperor Max will have paid through some middleman."

And it would have raised no suspicion if the cargo was to be shipped in a British-registered vessel, Dawlish realised. The consignment papers would probably have listed Siam or China or Japan as the destination, or any of a dozen other countries hungry for bargain arms. If the captain of a U.S. Navy ship encountered the *Jenny*, he would have hesitated to detain or search her. It was such an incident that had brought the Union to the brink of war with Britain five years before.

"Why was the *Jenny* heading to Zihuantanejo?" Dawlish said.

"Because the French have abandoned everything inland from there for fifty miles north and south along the coast. They withdrew east, towards the Puebla and Vera Cruz. They'll have taken their artillery and everything else worth a damn with them."

"But there were still Imperial forces left at Zihuantanejo?"

"There were, poor devils. They were cut off there, hard pressed. And many of their commanders must have seen the writing on the wall. It wouldn't surprise me if whoever was holding Zihuantanejo just turned his coat and handed the place over to the Juaristas. A smart man in the circumstances, if he did."

Dawlish had picked up on a single word.

"Artillery, you said, Travis. Was that what *Jenny Dixon* was bringing for the Imperial forces? Artillery?"

Welborne nodded. "The French didn't rate the Imperials much and never supplied them with decent artillery. Now Emperor Max and his cronies are stupid enough to think that a dozen pieces – ten-pounder Parrotts, or the like – would enable them to hold Zihuantanejo."

But the loss of the artillery isn't the issue. For Weatherby it's looting and detention of a British vessel. And for Berchtold an opportunity to strike hard against the Juaristas whether it makes any difference to the war or not. For both, recovering this ship would be a chance of glory. Perhaps their last.

Dawlish saw that Welborne must be thinking the same.

"Has *Quetzal* ever visited Zihuantanejo?" he asked.

"No. I guess Bechtold never thought it was important. But we stood eight miles off there for two weeks to watch for the *Jenny's* arrival and help her as necessary to deliver her cargo. Then we'd problems in our engine room. Berchtold decided to put in here for repairs. He was confident by then that the *Jenny* wasn't coming, that probably the Union Navy had detained her."

It had been a stupid judgement, Dawlish thought, made worse by acceptance of the slow rate of repairs in the railway workshops. Weatherby would have cruised weeks back and forth under sail alone off Zihuantanejo, even with his machinery ailing.

"So you know nothing about Zihuantanejo as an anchorage, do you?" Dawlish said. "Soundings? Hidden reefs or rocks on the approach? Defences?"

Weatherby would have investigated all that for every likely anchorage along the coast had he been assigned a duty like Berchtold's,

Welborne shook his head. "No more than's on the chart, an' I guess it's the same you're using yourselves. An' nothing about defences neither. Can't imagine the Imperials having much to defend with anyways."

"We've had this conversation as friends, Travis." Dawlish felt a slight flush of shame for exploiting old camaraderie. "I'd appreciate if you keep it confidential."

"Do you think I'll swallow that, Nick?" Welborne seemed amused. "You came her to pump me – don't take offence. I'd have done the same. And you'll be repeating every word to your captain when you get back to your ship. Why the hell shouldn't I do the same?"

"Because Weatherby will be coming across to *Quetzal* tomorrow morning. He'll have a proposal that your Baron Berchtold will jump on." Dawlish knew he had no authorisation to make any such suggestion and was gambling he'd not enrage his captain. The young Nelson would have done the same, he told himself. "If Weatherby hasn't done so before noon, then you'll be welcome to report everything I've said."

"You're sharp, Nick, I'll give you that." Welborne was silent, toyed with his glass, was thinking. At last he said, "I guess that the old days in *Odin* count for something. So yes, I'll hold off 'til noon."

But memories hadn't decided Welborne, Dawlish saw. He too had recognised Weatherby would have a more practical proposal than any that Berchtold might dream up.

With only the outline of that bay on the chart to go by.

And a plan ready before noon on the morrow.

Chapter 10

The sun had dropped below the western horizon when *Sprightly's* whaler drew away from her. The sea was calm, and the gunvessel was loitering twelve miles south of Zihuantanejo, hidden, even in daylight, from any observer on the coast. She was alone because *Quetzal*, her departure delayed by completion of her engine repair, was not expected to join for another day.

The whaler was running shoreward under sail, headed for the coastline west of the entrance to the bay. Dawlish had studied if from *Sprightly's* foretop that afternoon, cliffs rising behind narrow beaches and the ground beyond sloping up to green-clad hills. Now, in darkness lightened only slightly by a crescent moon, it was impossible to discern anything but the outline of the mountains further inland, black against a star-studded sky.

Dawlish was sitting in the sternsheets with Grove and Vázquez, *Quetzal's* third officer. Other than the whaler's crew, the only others on board were two marines. Command of this reconnaissance would have fallen to more senior officers, Sanderson or even Ashton, had either spoken Spanish or if Vázquez spoke English. Finding the location where the *Jenny's* crew was held would demand the Mexican officer entering the town and mingling with the inhabitants, addressing them in an accent that would not arouse suspicion. But making contact with the crew, if they could be found, would demand English.

"Watch the fellow closely," Weatherby had said. "Captain Berchtold thinks highly of him but half of Mexico seems to be turning their coats nowadays."

"Vázquez won't, sir," Dawlish said. "Not after what happened to his family."

He'd met the young Mexican after Weatherby and Berchtold agreed their plan. He talked with him on the passage from Manzanilla, eager to improve his own Spanish in advance of what he guessed would be an ordeal ahead. Neither he nor Vázquez would be wearing uniform, even though, if captured, it might offer some protection. He could not free himself of the memory of those mutilated Belgian corpses. His stomach was knotted with fear and he hoped it wasn't obvious. Four years before, serving in HMS *Foyle*, he'd been entrusted with a reconnaissance ashore on the coast of Colombia. Half-frightened, half-delighted, by the responsibility, he was flattered that his captain had sufficient trust in him. But it was a reconnaissance from a distance only, without need to venture into a hostile town. He'd seen extensive action since, didn't fail in Danish service. He often flinched but always justified trust. Yet those recollections did not comfort him now.

Scarcely twenty, Vázquez was of the wealthy Mexican caste that welcomed the French and their puppet emperor. An ancestor arrived with Cortez, he claimed, and the family possessed large landholdings in Coahuila ever since. Mines brought even greater riches than ranching.

"No drop of Indian blood in all those years." Pride in Vázquez's voice, something of arrogance too.

In the years of civil war and turmoil before the French intervention, his father had been a finance-minister, one uncle a general, another a bishop and cousins held no-less prestigious posts. All were committed enemies of the Liberals led by Juarez. Vázquez almost spat when he mentioned his name – he was a Zapotec, an Indian peon, with ideas above his station. The Vázquez family aligned with the French when they drove Juarez from office. They welcomed the invaders' catspaw emperor and received posts in the new Imperial government. In expectation of heading a future Mexican Navy, the young Ignacio was sent to France to learn his profession in her navy.

But the family had backed the wrong horse, as they must surely know by now. Juarez's own forces, strongest in the north, had occupied and confiscated the Vázquez lands and mines, had shot an uncle and three cousins and burned their homes. With French withdrawal now all but a certainty, there'd be no recovery of former wealth. Juarista retribution was always merciless. The options would be death or flight abroad. Dawlish wondered why Ignacio Vázquez had not stayed in France. There was nothing for him here.

Nothing but a brief opportunity for revenge.

And perhaps that was why he was by Dawlish's side now.

The *Jenny Dixon* was British but wrestling her back from the hated Juaristas might bring Vázquez some small measure of satisfaction.

*

The whaler dropped sail a mile off the cliffs, the bay to starboard cut off from view by a small headland, then pulled forwards under oars. Faint moonlight identified the slight line of foam along the shoreline. Dawlish had moved to the bow and was straining to identify a landing place. Three possibilities disappointed on closer inspection – ideal beaches but backed by vertical and probably unscalable cliffs. The whaler was paralleling the shore north-westwards and Dawlish fretted that each new stroke meant a longer distance to cover overland towards Zihuantanejo town.

And, at last, a crescent beach in a small rock-flanked cove and a notch in the cliff-line that might offer an easy climb.

The whaler grounded and two seamen dropped overboard to drag the bows further up the sand. Even then, Dawlish and the landing party found themselves in knee-deep water. One of the marines stumbled and fell forward. He regained his feet easily but the pack he carried – with essential supplies, including food – was saturated.

The party came ashore, Dawlish and Vázquez, Grove and the two marines. Dawlish was in overall command – his commission being two months older than Grove's. Heavy loads, enough for three nights ashore. Enfield rifles for all and Adams revolvers for the three officers. The whaler disappeared into the darkness. It would return on each of the next three nights – if all went well, then the party would meet it for evacuation on the second, but the possibilities of quick retreat or delayed escape earlier or later than that could not be discounted.

They began their climb. It was steep and in places necessary for one man to lift another on his shoulders to reach a ledge above. Boots loosened scree and each tiny avalanche seemed loud enough to rouse anybody closer than a mile. It took a half-hour, would have needed twenty minutes without the packs and rifles. Standing at last on the crest, Dawlish saw the outline of rounded hills ahead. No winking lights betrayed human habitation and the only sound was of night insects and the short bleating of a distant goat.

Pocket compass in hand, Grove led them in line-ahead north-eastward towards the top of the highest hill. Thick scrub covered the parched ground, necessitating detours around the densest thickets. They crossed a single narrow pathway only, droppings indicating goatherds might use it.

The hill to the right still hid Zihuantanejo's bay from sight when Grover raised his arm and gestured for the others to drop.

"You smell that?" he asked Dawlish in a whisper.

A sniff. The faintest trace of woodsmoke.

"You go forward. See what you can find," Dawlish felt his own fear stronger now. "Be damned stealthy about it. I'll hold the rest back here."

"I'll leave my rifle," Grove said. "If I have to, I can crawl easier without it."

He moved away at a crouch and was lost in the brush. Dawlish retained the others in the shadows, Enfields loaded but uncocked.

The night was full of insects' chatter and ten anxious minutes passed before Grove reappeared.

"D'ye see that ridge?" He pointed to the right of their line of advance. It was only slightly higher than where they now were. "The bay's beyond. But there's what might be a camp on the far side. Lights there and a fire. Some movement too."

"How far?"

"About a half-mile from here."

"Show me," Dawlish said.

He padded behind Grove to the ridgeline, each catch of a sleeve against a thornbush, each dry twig crunching underfoot, seeming loud as thunder. They dropped just sort of the crest, went forward on hands and knees.

And there was the almost circular bay, the moon reflected in its mirror-still waters, the dark unlit mass that must be the *Jenny Dixon* at its centre. On the shoreline to its left, a scattering of pinpoints of light identified the town. This ridge must be two or three hundred feet higher. But it was down along the steep slope that dropped to the water that Grove was pointing. There was some structure halfway down there. At its centre a fire was burning and at intervals figures blocked the flames for an instant as they moved to and fro. Three smaller lights too, lanterns perhaps.

Dawlish was cursing himself now that he had not brought a nightglass. He studied the structure as best he could. It must have a purpose. He looked across the bay and saw the peninsula on its far side. To the right was the open sea.

The structure must be another of those small Spanish forts like that at Manzanillo. Situated as it was, it commanded the entrance to the bay. Looking closer, he fancied the fire might be a brazier at the centre of a square courtyard, the faint flicker of its flames reflected on the inner walls. It might be as toothless as its Manzanillo counterpart but that it was occupied at all was ominous. Capturing this small but strategically placed harbour was a triumph for the Juaristas. They must be doing all they could to secure their hold. And the *Jenny Dixon* had carried artillery – only field guns, but artillery nonetheless and potentially lethal to an unarmoured vessel like *Sprightly*.

Dawlish nudged Grove, who was lying by his side, and jerked his head. Time to return to the others and resume the climb towards the hilltop. He felt a thrill of satisfaction. Discovery of the fort was the reconnaissance's first success.

But only if he could return to *Sprightly*.

And what would face him in the coming day terrified him.

*

It was still three hours to dawn when they reached the summit. The brush was thick there, offering ideal cover for Grove and the marines who must spend this day, and maybe the next, in hiding. But the greatest advantage was an even better view over the harbour. The fort, only identifiable now by a weak shimmer of light above it, would be visible in daylight. Grove's task was to observe it, identify what armament it might or might not carry and make a sketch of it and any other defences visible.

Dawlish and Vázquez lay down, blankets clasped around their faces to keep off insects, heads pillowed against their packs while the marines kept watch. Sleep came with difficulty to Dawlish. Death, very unpleasant death, might lie ahead and he must risk it without a weapon and in reliance on an in-name-only naval officer, inexperienced and perhaps dangerously arrogant, whom he'd met just days before. It was no comfort to remind himself that the young Nelson would have relished a mission like this. He thrust away thoughts of his family – they might never know what became of him – and of discovery of Clothilde's selling of herself. But, at last, he drifted into unquiet slumber.

The sun was not yet up but the eastern sky was lightening when Grove awoke him, as directed. His joints were aching and a drink of water – there could be no cooking fire here – was little stimulation. He forced himself to eat a dry biscuit and encouraged Vázquez to do likewise. The young Mexican shook his head. He looked as if the full enormity of the undertaking had dawned on him for the first time.

From the cover of the brush, Dawlish studied the town. It had not yet come alive. Perhaps two miles distant, it was larger than he expected, three streets running toward the beach and intersecting two others parallel to it further back. A square lay at the centre and fronting it was the only building higher than a single storey. The belfry tower at one side marked it as a church. A few of the houses had tiled roofs but the majority looked to be of whitewashed and thatched adobe. Small huts lay along the foreshore, many with fishing craft lying on the beach before them. A broad track ran inland from the town and snaked up towards the mountains beyond.

What looked like a large raft was tethered to the *Jenny Dixon's* side. That must have been how the cargo had been brought ashore. Landing it across the beach would have demand a brutal effort, for there was no wharf, but impressed labour would have been unwise to challenge Juarista orders. The *Jenny* herself, a large barque, gave an impression of good maintenance. She was riding high and a few figures were moving about. Two boats – they could be *Jenny's* own – were stroking towards her from the beach, packed with men.

The bay, at its widest, was about a mile and a half across, bounded on the far side by a hilly peninsula. The entrance to the bay could not be wider than a half-mile and the fort, just visible from Dawlish's viewpoint, dominated it. Try as he might, he could not identify any guns mounted there. In his absence, it would be up to Grove to get closer to clear that doubt.

Dawlish opened his pack and pulled out the grimy clothing, once white, for which an amazed labourer in Manzanillo had accepted a peso. It had not been washed since, deliberately, and smelled of sour sweat. That was all to the good, would make it more convincing, he told himself as, with revulsion, he pulled on the cotton shirt and trousers. His bare feet looked too white, so he rubbed dust into them. Crude sandals and a crushed broad-brimmed straw hat completed the transformation. He'd trimmed back his beard to stubble in recent days – most poor Mexicans seemed to have moustaches only.

But I can't change my features, I've nothing of the Indian look of the poor and *neither has Vázquez. We'll need our broad brims and, if possible, stand with the sun behind us if challenged.*

The young Mexican was also changed and seemed repelled by what he had become. A handshake with Grove and a hint of pity in the glances of the marines as Dawlish, leading, and Vázquez, following, set off, northwards, down the hill. Neither were armed and they carried about three pesos each in total, mixes of full coins and centavos. The brush was thicker here than on the seaward side and the going slower. Goats bleated somewhere close. Halfway down, they encountered a man-wide track. Droppings – fresh – and tufts of goat hair on thorn bushes indicated that a herd had passed recently.

Dawlish hesitated, then decided to follow the track. It might lead downward at some point and speed their progress, even if it meant an encounter with a goat herder. They turned right. The track was winding, following a contour, and in places the brush was open enough to give glimpses of the town. It was still far below them, but little over a mile distant.

122

"*Estás caminando demasiado rápido, Nicolás,*" Vázquez said. "*Peones caminan lentamente. Pero pueden hacerlo todo el día.*"

Lesson learned. They had been walking too quickly. Labourers walked slowly but could keep it up all day if they had to. Vázquez must have seen this since childhood. His tone conveyed little sympathy. Dawlish had seen it too on the journey to and from Guzmán, the shuffling misery of the humble and the powerless who owned nothing but their lives.

Onwards for ten minutes and then a branch in the path, one following the contour, the other, which they took, dropping away to the left. Ten minutes more brought them to a broad track at the base of the hill, a scattering of huts along it. They turned right. The town lay a mile ahead. By now, their clothes were dusty and wet with sweat. Nobody seemed surprised or suspicious as they passed, not men and children working in vegetable patches nor women washing clothing and hanging it to dry. Once, two dogs ran out, barking, but retreated when Vázquez bent to pick up a stone.

Even at their slow pace, they overtook an oxcart drawn by two animals, maize cobs piled high between fences on either side. The driver, a bent old man, walked alongside with a goad. The wheels were solid disks of wood. The axle squealed with each revolution. The sight depressed Dawlish – the straining beasts, the primitive vehicle, the man's defeated, resigned, plod.

It would be for Vázquez to ask any necessary questions in the town. Dawlish, distrusting his own accent, would confine himself to nods, head-shaking and a few brief words or phrases. But Vázquez's accent might jar just as much. Here was an opportunity to test it without great risk.

And, in a worst case, not enter the town, a small cowardly, wheedling, inner voice reminded him. Retreat was still possible.

"*Habla con él, Ignacio,*" Dawlish hissed "*Deséale buenos días, quéjate del calor. Cualquier cosa.*" Talk to him, wish him good day, complain about the heat. Anything.

Vázquez nodded. He must have the same fear. But when they drew level with the cart he called out, "*Hola, amigo! Que dia! Hace calor!*"

He had prepared well. His accent was different to his normal, educated, one and something closer to what was heard at Manzanillo. It might not be identical to that here, but it must be close enough not to arouse suspicion for the driver answered with *"Siempre lo mismo,"* – always the same.

They left the cart behind and were close to the town outskirts now. A barrier lay across the track, a single pole laid on piles of adobe bricks, two blue-uniformed men with white crossbelts on guard. But this not what would hold back any serious intruder. A small earthen redoubt lay behind it on the left. Its larger counterpart on the right was positioned fifty yards up a slope. Both were embrasured – for a single cannon on the left and for two on the right. It was impossible to see if guns were already mounted. Higher on the rightward slope, a score of labourers was digging under supervision of uniformed soldiers, most likely an entrenchment for riflemen. Any enemy approach from the west would be subject to small-arms and artillery fire. Judging by what he'd seen of earthworks in Denmark, Dawlish recognised the work of an experienced military engineer. The Juaristas knew the value of Zihuantanejo as a point of import and were here to stay.

Nothing for it now but to trudge on towards the barrier. They'd practiced their story and agreed names – Nicolás Magón and Ignacio Cárdenas – and more besides. But it was a story, Dawlish knew, that could break down after a few minutes' interrogation, even if no violence was involved. His mouth was dry, his heart thumping and Vázquez must be no less frightened.

Up to the barrier now, a sentry waving them to come around it. His uniform was threadbare and faded but it was a uniform. Emperor Maximilian might label Juarez a rebel, and his armies brigands, but the uniform showed that the Juaristas here had been part of the usurped republican government's forces, and were still loyal to it.

Vázquez edged around the barrier and Dawlish followed. Both had bowed their heads and cringed slightly in a show of fearful respect. They were peons, all their lives at the mercy of any more powerful man.

Where did they come from? If anything, the soldier's tone was bored, the question a formality.

From La Majahua. Vázquez gestured westwards.

It was a name Dawlish had found on a chart, a coastal village, some fifteen miles distant.

The soldier accepted it without suspicion. And what had they come to do in Zihuantanejo?

His grandmother was sick, very sick, Vázquez said. The tremor of fear in his voice was useful now. He rubbed the back of his hands across his eyes. She might. . . he was afraid she was dying. He'd come with his cousin Nicolás to buy medicine. They'd brought money, as much as they could borrow. They hoped they had enough.

"*Es mi abuelita tambien,*" Dawlish mumbled and wiped his eyes. She was his grandmother also. He expected the soldier to ask for their money, but he didn't. He too probably had a grandmother.

Instead, he waved them through and wished them well.

Chapter 11

They entered the town along one of the streets paralleling the beach that Dawlish had observed from the hilltop. It was flanked here by well-maintained adobe houses and storm drains ran along either side. A few larger houses, some stone-built, must be residences of local merchants or officials. Further on, a few stalls were selling vegetables and fish. They passed several women, well dressed in local style, followed by barefoot girls in rough cotton dresses carrying the day's food purchases in baskets. A man in civilian clothing – black-suited, white shirted, a gold watch chain strung across his waistcoat – rode past with a menial trotting behind and carrying a leather briefcase. His glance passed over Dawlish and Vázquez but did not linger. Vázquez stepped even further to the side, bowed his head, swept off his hat and held it before him with both hands as if in homage. Dawlish followed suit. Vázquez must be accustomed to seeing such deference shown to his own family in earlier days. The rider ignored them and passed on. He might be some petty notable, or a lawyer, or a merchant – all that mattered was that, if he noticed them at all, he dismissed them as peons who knew their places. Some in this town had already reconciled themselves to Juarista authority and were determined to do well under it.

They stood aside again when they saw troops approaching, two four-man ranks, not in step but still with an air of discipline. Three or four dozen civilians followed, struggling to keep up, some with rough picks or shovels. They were of all ages and looked frightened. All they had in common was they looked poor. Some were barefoot. Two more ranks of soldiers at the rear, their bayonets fixed, and a mounted sergeant with a drawn sabre was ranging back and forth along the column to deter desertion by the conscripted labour.

This was a hazard Dawlish had not anticipated. Vázquez and he had striven to make themselves look like these unwilling men. Now they too ran the risk of impressment and the chances of escaping from these experienced Juarista troops would be minimal.

They were close to the centre now, affluent-seeming houses on this main thoroughfare but obvious poverty and squalor in the narrow alleyways to either side. The day's heat was still growing and they were parched.

"Let's search for a cantina, Ignacio." Dawlish felt sufficiently confident now that they would not stand out. "Very cheap and poor. Maybe we can hear something useful there."

They found one down an alley, an open-fronted adobe shack with a few benches and tables within. Two men slouched in silence at one, empty glasses before them. A large middle-aged woman emerged from the back, wiping her hands on her apron. She welcomed them and Vázquez answered. The day was hot, he said. They wanted to drink something.

She waved them to a table. "*De donde vinisteis?*" She had noticed the dust on their clothing and was asking from where they'd come. More worryingly, she might also have noticed some strangeness in Vázquez's accent.

From La Majahua, he told her. Before she could press him further, he asked how much it would cost to drink here. There was Pulque and Tequila, she said, three centavos the glass. Vázquez shook his head. They could not afford that. Just water would be enough. They were poor men. They settled for *agua fresca*, lime-flavoured water, two glasses for a centavo. Vázquez made a play of producing the single coin and parting from it was if it was his last.

The urge to swallow in a single gulp and ask for more was strong but the impression of poverty must be maintained. The owner must have seen their careful husbanding and understood the cause. She came back with a jug and refilled their glasses.

"*Sin precio,*" she said. No charge.

"*Que Dios y su madre la bendigan, señora,*" Vazquez said.

But no, she said. Neither God nor his mother were welcome here anymore. She looked towards the two silent men at the other table and dropped her voice. Juarez and his people hated God. They'd shot the priest – a good, kind man – last week and closed the church, burned pictures and a crucifix, stolen vessels. They had their own uses for it now. But God would punish them.

Under the table, Dawlish nudged Vázquez's knee with his and shook his head slightly.

Don't press her. This talk is dangerous.

He'd heard resentment of the clergy's wealth and abuse of power had fuelled religious persecution – of the innocent no less than the guilty – in Juarista-controlled areas.

And that mention of unspecified new use for the church was worth investigation. Four years before, in a small revolution-racked port in Colombia, he'd seen one used as a prison.

Vázquez had taken the hint and was telling now, with suitable emotion, about their *abuelita*. And yes, the hostess knew of somebody who could help. No, not a *médico*, not a doctor for the rich, but – she spoke in a whisper – Madre Yesenia. Some said she was *una bruja*, a witch but no, she was just a good woman who knew about plants and herbs and cures.

They left with complicated instructions for finding Madre Yesenia on the far side of the town. It was valuable information, useful cover for their movements if they were challenged. Vázquez might have minimal competence in naval matters but he was proving his worth as a scout.

*

They found their way to the central plaza through a succession of lanes and alleyways. The urge to look back to see if they were being followed was strong but Dawlish resisted it. The cantina's hostess had sounded suspicious, maybe even frightened, of the two silent men drinking there. In a land tortured by civil war, distrust and caution could well mean survival. Safest to maintain the fiction of two peons from a distant village on a quest to save their beloved grandmother.

The church would have seemed small elsewhere but here it dominated the tiny plaza, as it might have done for two centuries or more. A single large door lay at the centre of its frontage. There must be windows back along the sides but there were none here. The belfry tower rose to the right, a green, white and red flag drooping from it. To the left, was a long blank wall, enclosing what could be a priest's residence and garden. And all solidly built, even if the whitewash was stained and flaking, a structure many like it had furnished improvised fortresses in countless wars and revolutions.

And ideal as a prison.

Sentries in Juarista uniforms stood on either side of the door. Two more paced back and forth along the frontage, bayonets fixed. The plaza must have once throbbed with the bustle of the town's market but now it was deserted but for a few stalls, and fewer customers. Even women with children stayed ten yards or more from the sentries when they passed them.

Yet we must get close.

Dawlish whispered his intention to Vázquez.

"It's dangerous, Nicolás." But he must have sensed Dawlish would do it anyway and said, "Yes. But let me choose when."

They paid a centavo each for pieces of fried fish and hovered, munching them, by a stall, viewing the customers, mostly women, moving through the tiny market. They spotted several candidates, but none were leaving in the direction they needed.

And then, at last, Vázquez nodded slightly towards a vastly pregnant woman, poorly dressed. She was steadying a basket on her head with one hand and holding a small child's with her other. Both were barefoot. Looking weary, her gait slow and ponderous, she must be near her time. She was starting diagonally across the plaza, the church on her right.

They let her advance about twenty yards and about to follow when she reeled a little and put down the basket unhandily.

Vázquez hurried towards her, Dawlish following. She was trying to lift the basket again. The child, two years old at most, looked bewildered.

"*No se preocupe, señora,*" Vázquez said. "*Ayudaremos.*" He gestured to Dawlish to pick up the basket – five cobs of corn and a few small fish

– and began helping the woman to her feet. Her face was streaming sweat and her thanks came in gasps.

Dawlish felt panic rising in himself. Could this be the start of childbirth labour? He knew nothing of the process, only that it was an ordeal that too often killed. He felt powerless. Should he run back to the stalls and fetch some older women to help?

But Vázquez had raised her to her feet, urging her to rest on his arm. Where did she live? She pointed towards the corner of the plaza. Just a little beyond there. Dawlish carried the basket and led the child by the hand. He asked what his name was. Pablito, he said. His unquestioning trust was touching.

Progress slow, slow enough not to arouse suspicion in the guards. Past the church's great iron-studded door. Dawlish could hear nothing from beyond it, but that meant little. Any prisoners there would probably be slumped in despairing torpor. Now they were passing the blank wall. Along all twenty yards of its length, large and irregular brown splotches and spatters stood out against the faded whitewash at chest and head and shoulder level. Dark patches on the ground before, dry now, their origin unmistakable. The Juaristas were as merciless – and as thorough – in their retribution as the French.

Five slow minutes brought them to the lane in which the woman lived. Neighbouring women came to fuss around and help her into her shack. Her husband had been impressed for work that morning but with luck might be released that night – it was often so. Señora Dolores would be in good hands here, a wrinkle-faced old woman said – she herself had helped deliver fifty or more children. Most survived, most mothers also. And yes, she knew of Madre Yesenia. She was *una bruja*, she said, a dangerous woman, someone to be avoided.

They left and worked their way around the back of the church and its walled compound, snatching glances from beneath their hat brims. There were soldiers on guard here also. There must be a parapet below the top of the inner side for a sentry looked down from above the single door in it. There were windows, probably unglazed, high on the church's sidewalls though it was hard to see through from ground level. Another door at the back of the belfry. *Jenny Dixon's* entire crew could well be imprisoned there but, if so, it was impossible to imagine making contact.

Dawlish felt his spirits sink. So much had been risked for nothing. *But we've come this far safely . . .*

There might yet be something to see of value.

*

They followed the track that led from the plaza to the beach. Houses gave away to a scattering of fishermen's shacks. There was activity out at the *Jenny Dixon* now, a boom abaft the foremast swinging out loads from inside her hold and lowering them to the raft alongside, where three or four dozen white-clad figures – they looked like conscripted labour – were stacking crates. The pulling boats Dawlish had seen from the hilltop were tied alongside, presumably ready to tow the raft shoreward. They must have made at least one trip already, for a small mountain of wooden boxes with rope-handles lay above the water's edge. Under direction from a platoon of soldiers, labourers were loading them on bullock carts or pack-donkeys. The dimensions of the longer crates indicated rifles inside. The smaller, stencilled in black with the letters U.S. probably contained ammunition. No sign of cannon – they must have been landed already.

Better to move away from the soldiers. Dawlish looked towards the fort. It must be a hundred feet above the water, maybe more, a difficult target for bombardment from the sea, and its elevation meant a range advantage for whatever was mounted there. A track snaked and hair-pinned along the hill towards it from the westward end of the beach. From somewhere near the hilltop, Grove might even now be observing the fort's interior, looking for artillery, preparing a sketch.

The sun was at its zenith and they were again thirsty. A smell of roasting fish drew them to an open-sided stall, roofed with thatch, boats drawn up on the sand to either side. A few customers, seemingly fishermen by their clothing, were sitting on benches at rough tables and a woman was cooking over a bed of charcoal. It offered the chance of food, drink and the comfort of shade while watching the *Jenny*.

They attracted no attention when they sat down. The others there were silent, some even drowsy, fishermen already fatigued by their morning's labour of hauling bots up the beach and sorting the night's catch. Five centavos each bought charred fish, bowls of spicy bean stew, doughy pancakes that Vázquez called tortillas and watery corn beer.

Dawlish found his own head dropping towards the table after he ate and had to shake himself to stay awake. There was no respite of unloading out at the *Jenny* and he was resolved to see what more was being brought ashore before he would leave.

But leave for where? There might other places than the church where the *Jenny's* crew was held but the story of the search for Madre Yesenia might not always be believed. Every moment in this town held the risk of capture. Darkness was hours away and he wanted its cover for getting back to the hilltop.

Yet, even so, the air was still and hot and he was tired. Another five minutes' rest here could not increase the danger.

"Nicolás!" Vázquez was nudging him – he must have drowsed off with his forehead touching the table.

Shocked into wakefulness, he realised that the other customers were on their feet, calling and gesturing towards the *Jenny*.

"*Qué pasó?*" He had the presence of mind to use Spanish when he asked Vázquez what had happened.

"*Un accidente!*" One of the fishermen had overheard and answered before rushing to the foreshore with the others.

There was commotion on the raft. A cable must have snapped and a load had crashed down from the boom, Vázquez said. A hubbub of anger reached them from across the water. It died suddenly at the sound of two pistol shots – order restored. The white-clad labourers on the raft edged in silence to its sides as soldiers cleared a space in the middle. Two men – officers or sergeants perhaps – crouched over a heap that might be a crate's debris. Or bodies.

The cantina was deserted now, the customers gathered on the foreshore to watch, arguing about what could have happened, explaining to newcomers who were coming running from the town. Dawlish and Vázquez joined them. Not doing so might arouse suspicion.

Figures were dropping into the pulling boat alongside the raft, an air of order about them, a crew taking its places. Then something – it took four to carry it – was being lowered into it. And then another, and another, unmistakable now as bodies. Three men, walking wounded, were helped down after them. The boat pushed off and stroked towards the landing point on the beach. The crowd surged there to watch. Around the pile of landed crates the soldiers had set a cordon and were pushing the shuffling crowd back even as more joined from behind. Dawlish found himself jostled towards the front and separated from Vázquez, who was now over to his right.

They could hear the sounds of pain even before the boat's bows crunched on the beach. The first body lifted out was dead, blood soaking its white shirt but the two that followed, though limp, cried in agony as they were manhandled down and laid on the sand. From their poor clothing, they looked like the conscripted labourers seen earlier. A path was being cleared through the crowd for a man in a dark well-cut suit to come through. He held a leather bag.

"*Es médico!*" a man shouted by Dawlish's side. Somebody had been sensible enough to rush for a doctor.

The other injured men were landed also. One's arm was hanging loose and the others were limping. The onlookers were pushing forward in shocked fascination as the doctor kneeled by the worst-wounded men.

And now a sergeant was barking, sending two soldiers to open another laneway through the throng. The clamour died and Dawlish sensed fear around him. An officer came stalking through, two younger ones behind. His uniform was creased and dusty but a single band of gold braid encircled his kepi. The sergeant looked frightened as he saluted. The officer cast a single glance over the wounded and pointed toward the *Jenny*. Then he demanded – Dawlish could just make out his words – why work had stopped. One of the boat's crew was stammering an explanation, but the officer cut him off. He turned to the sergeant, gestured to the crowd and shouted an order.

Dawlish was unable to distinguish the words, but the crowd had. It was already breaking up, scurrying away along the foreshore or back towards the town and a few dropping to hide behind beached fishing boats. Too late, he realised that replacements were needed for the casualties. He turned to run, tripped, was on his knees, was trying to rise when hands grabbed him from behind and dragged him to his feet.

Deep in his brain, the cold small voice of reason told him not to struggle, not to argue, only to submit. Now he, like a half-dozen others, was being frogmarched towards the boat. He looked around. The beach was all but deserted and he could see no sign of Vázquez.

Urged on by the threat of rifle butts, the new captives scrambled into the boat and crouched between the thwarts. The crew took their places at the oars and backed water. Five minutes later the boat nudged against the raft.

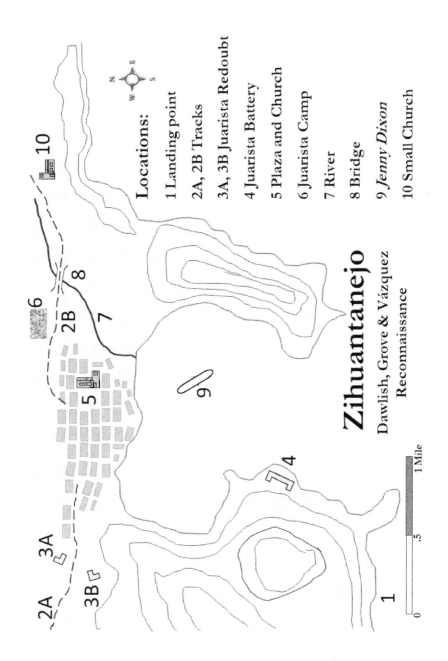

Zihuantanejo

Dawlish, Grove & Vázquez
Reconnaissance

Locations:

1 Landing point
2A, 2B Tracks
3A, 3B Juarista Redoubt
4 Juarista Battery
5 Plaza and Church
6 Juarista Camp
7 River
8 Bridge
9 *Jenny Dixon*
10 Small Church

Chapter 12

Repairs were complete and *Jenny's* boom was in service again. The next load was rising from the hold, swinging out across the bulwarks and lowering towards the raft as Dawlish and the other new conscripts boarded. A sergeant directed them to stand with waiting labourers as the net containing a half-dozen long crates touched the deck.

Now the heaviest work began, lifting the crates from the net, four-man teams dragging them to join a row of others like them at one end of the raft. There must be a dozen rifles at the least in each, Dawlish thought. Ammunition boxes were stacked beyond them and at least thirty wooden barrels rested on chocks. But no sign of the artillery that Welborne had mentioned – it must all be ashore already.

Dawlish was frightened. One wrong word, one small deviation from the role of cowed and unresisting worker, could be fatal. It was welcome that the supervising soldiers shouted for silence at the first hint of chatter by the captives. And yet he saw nobody beaten. Clearly exhausted older men were told to rest under an awning and there were occasional breaks in which to slurp water from buckets. The Juaristas were hard taskmasters, but he sensed that for the poor of Mexico they were less feared than the French. He flung himself into the work, carried and dragged more than his share, cringed in respectful submission each time an overseer approached. And all the time his mind was churning possibilities for escape, but all depended on being ashore. Until then, every man here, Juarista or captive alike, was a threat.

Another net-load landed, and another. On the bulwark above, one hand gripping a shroud for steadiness, a supervisor was shouting orders for lifting from the hold, for swinging the boom out over the raft, for the slow lowering. The hook was attached to a travelling block with five sheaves. It was well-oiled, Dawlish saw, and the inch-thick cable reeved through it was running freely.

A professional job.

And unlikely that any resident of Zihuantanejo, or any officer of Juarez's army would have such expertise . . .

And though the orders being shouted above were in Spanish, the accent was different to what he'd yet encountered in Mexico . . .

He dared not look up, lest his features be recognised as unusual, and once he thought he heard brief swearing in English. Heart-thumping, dry-mouthed, he reined in his curiosity, waited until he added another box of ammunition to the stack. His fellow labourers laid theirs down too and were straightening up, turning away. He was sure in that instant nobody would take notice of him and, as he also straightened his back and turned, glanced up for an instant.

But it was long enough.

Dark trousers. A stained and sweat-soaked grey vest. No jacket. A peaked nautical cap. A round face sun-burned red. Ginger hair and beard. Dawlish had seen dozens like him in ports around the world, mates or bosuns of British merchantmen. He was from the *Jenny Dixon,* no doubt of it. He could be the first mate, Sandy McCafferty, whom Redshaw had mentioned. And there might be others.

A brief respite before the next netload swung out, dropped slowly, settled on the raft. The hook was disconnected and raised a few feet, the net drawn back, the crates and boxes manhandled off it. The hook was dropped again – a little too much, Dawlish saw – for it was lying on the net, not suspended, and the cable was loose in the sheaves.

He saw what could come of it.

Now linked to the hook, the net rose again when the order came to hoist. One moment it was flat on the deck and then rising into a cone prior to lifting free.

And then it stopped, stopped dead. The loose cable had slipped off one of the sheaves and jammed between it and the block.

"Ned! The bloody line's wedged!" The words in English, the accent Scottish, called by the man on the bulwark to some figure hidden by it. "I don't trust none of these bloody dagos to know what to do. Get down there and free the bloody thing."

Dawlish drew back, heart pounding. Was this an opportunity?

Ned was coming down a Jacob's ladder. He was young and agile, his upper torso naked, a sweat rag tied about his throat, his head sheltered by a frayed straw hat. When he turned on reaching the raft, Dawlish saw one eye blackened and the cheek below bruised purple.

Not a willing helper . . .

Ned bent over the block and began to inch the cable free with his fingers. Questions were racing through Dawlish's brain as he watched – were there others of the crew up there? Some or all? Were they detained on board overnight or brought ashore? Could he find some way of communicating with this Ned?

A shout from one of the soldiers reminded Dawlish he should be lugging an ammunition box towards the stack. He bowed his head and grabbed one, sick with the realisation he'd let his pose slip, that his curiosity could have been noticed. When he returned for another box, he drew near the seaman and risked a single glimpse. Ned had freed the cable, was pulling it tight around the sheaves, then holding the block vertical.

"It's clear!" he shouted up to McCafferty on the bulwark. "Hoist away!"

He held the block vertical until the cable tautened and the net soared up.

"Don't bloody-well stand there all day!" the Scots voice above called down. "Get up here, Ned! One more load does it!"

He was six feet from Dawlish, close enough that even a loud whisper might have reached him. The urge was strong – and dangerous. There were too many around to risk it. Wiser to remain compliant and anonymous.

The next netful was indeed the last. Some twenty men – they must have been working in the hold – came down the Jacob's ladder. The majority were Mexican labourers, but McCafferty and Ned and four others were clearly British. Three looked like Malays – not unusual aboard a British merchantman. Urged by a soldier at the head of the ladder, the Scotsman was the last man down. They joined the other labourers, now confined to one end of the raft by a hedge of bayonets.

The ship's boat was manned, the oars double-banked, and the raft's slow tow to the beach commenced.

Dawlish understood why the load had been concentrated at one end of the raft, sinking it lower to match the beach's slope. The boat slipped its tow, the raft's higher end some twenty yards from the water's edge. Barked orders urged the labourers to drop overboard along each side. Dawlish stripped off his sandals, thrust them inside his shirt, then lowered himself into waist-deep water. Then he and the others were pushing the raft forward until it grounded.

Still guarded by a cordon of troops, the pile of crates already at the landing place had diminished, but the oxcarts and mule teams that carried them away were back, waiting for the raft's arrival. Impressed labourers, exhausted by the day's toil, were waiting too.

And now the worst labour of all began, dragging the crates up the raft's incline, manhandling them on to the beach and then the muscle-straining agony of loading them on carts or mules. The sun was almost down by now and many were tottering from fatigue. *Jenny's* crewmen were not spared. Dawlish edged his way close enough to hear their futile swearing, hoping for a whispered exchange, but each time he fancied a guard was too near. The question nagged him that whether he was being rightly cautious, or if his nerve had failed him.

The sun had dropped and light was dying in the western sky. The last of the carts and mules plodded away towards the town, leaving the remaining stacks of landed boxes to be removed the next day. The cordon opened, just enough for the labourers to pass through one by one. It was finished for today, Dawlish heard others around him say as they shuffled into line. With luck they might escape impressment on the morrow. A few spoke of slipping out into the countryside beyond under cover of darkness. But no, others told them. The price would be high if caught. Remember the two executed earlier in the week?

Dawlish was close to the opening now, guards with bayonets on either side. From far back he heard English voices – even if he could not make out the words, the rhythm of the monotonous swearing was unmistakable. There was just enough light to see they were separated from the others into a small, guarded group. He felt a flush of hope –

they might not be released like the labourers but conducted back to wherever the remainder of the crew was held. If so, he might be able to follow them, dangerous as it would be without Vázquez with him to parry unwelcome questions.

His turn at last, shuffling towards a rough table, lit by a single lantern. By his black suit and white shirt, the man sitting there looked like a civilian clerk, a ledger before him with a metal cashbox by its side. Two soldiers guarded him. One growled to Dawlish to remove his hat and show respect for the Señor. He held it before him with both hands – they were bleeding, officer's hands unused to physical labour. Head bowed, he approached the table.

"*Nombre?*" The clerk didn't look up.

"*Nicolás Magón, señor.*" Dawlish's voice a mumble.

The clerk added it to a long list in the ledger. "*Puedes escribir?*"

Dawlish shook his head. He couldn't write.

One of the soldiers pushed a pen into his hand and guided it to make an "X" behind his name. The clerk reached into the cashbox and gave him a twenty-five centavo coin.

The honour of the Juarista cause had been upheld. The battle was for the poor. No labour without just recompense.

And Dawlish could walk out free into the soft darkness.

*

His knees were weak, his hands trembling, but not from fatigue. The fear of the last seven hours had sapped his spirit. This was the most insidious enemy of all, he realised, and he must collect himself if he would survive.

And not just survive, the familiar cold voice within reminded him. *Prevail. Finish the mission.*

The labourers already released had hurried off into the town with their quarter-pesos and the remainder were following them in twos and threes. He was alone. He trudged fifty yards along the waterline and found deep shadow behind a drawn-up fishing boat from which to watch. *Jenny's* men were still within the cordon and must be marched out soon.

Ten minutes passed. Dawlish's lacerated hands ached and he was hungry, yet calmer now. The clerk closed his ledger, stood up, was readying to leave.

"*Nicolás!*" A voice hissing behind him.

A moment later, Vázquez was crouched by his side. He had gone back to the town, he told Dawlish in whispers, and watched the raft from afar, moving constantly to avoid suspicion, ready to fall back on the story of his search for Madre Yesenia if questioned.

He didn't desert me. He could have been halfway to safety with Grove by now. But he had stayed.

The clerk had left, his path lighted by a soldier with a lantern. Barked orders inside the cordon, movement of dark shadows as of men being marshalled, somebody shouting in English, "About bloody time, mate!" More orders, more protests, but at last a small knot was emerging through the cordon, troops with fixed bayonets on either side and several following behind. The *Jenny* contingent was on the move.

It had all been worthwhile, Dawlish realised, his patience, his silence his cringing compliance, his bleeding hands and aching muscles. It had earned a chance of finding the crew's place of detention.

He crouched in the shadows with Vázquez until the captives had disappeared among the huts on the town outskirts. Then they stood up and followed, forcing themselves not to hurry. From somewhere ahead, a single voice, a poor singing one, and weary, but with a hint of defiance about it, was launching into a song.

I've just come back from Australia,
As you can clearly see,
Sent out for the benefit of me health,
Very kind treatment for me.

Dawlish recognised it. The tune an easy one, he'd caught snatches of it on the lower deck and heard its chorus echoing from taverns and roaring from penny gaffs. And not the sort of song which his sister Susan would sing to her own piano accompaniment.

"*Cállate la boca!*" A guard was yelling for silence.

And now another voice was joining in, and then two or three more.

> *They thought a tenner would do me good,*
> *As well as I could be,*
> *But they gave me a ticket of leave,*
> *Which was the ticket for me.*

"*Cierra la boca! Cállate*" Other guards shouting too, but the singing continued, futile yet somehow splendid in its defiance. Then a sharp cry – it was easy to imagine a rifle butt pounded into a singer's stomach – and a brief silence before the voices, fewer this time, took up the tune again. It happened twice more before the singing died.

There were some at least of the *Jenny's* crew who had fight in them. And they deserved better than this.

Dawlish and Vázquez were in the town now, heading up the broad street leading to the plaza, avoiding the shadows – furtiveness at this point could only raise suspicion – and looking little different to most others. The only light came from candles or lanterns at windows or on the few stalls still doing business. People were moving on the street and chatting at doorways, children still playing and men drinking, and some arguing, in a cantina. The escort and its prisoners ahead had almost reached the plaza, were moving at a now-silent plod. They seemed to have evoked no curiosity – their morning and evening passage to and from the beach must be an established routine.

At the corner of the plaza now but the group was heading, not towards the church, but a narrower street dead ahead on the opposite side. Dawlish and Vázquez waited until they were lost from sight around a bend, then hurried after. The street was short and it petered out, became a track, on each side small adobe houses or squalid shacks separated by vegetable patches. The bend straightened. In the moonlight – the only light other than flickers from the huts – the escorted group was about a hundred yards ahead. Stealth essential now, with little civilian movement in which to blend.

Further on, the track branched, leading on the left to what looked like a small camp, rough huts laid out in two rows, cooking fires, dark outlines of what might be small redoubts, a spindly lookout tower, voices, an impression of recent improvised construction. But the escort was taking the other branch and Dawlish and Vázquez followed, holding to whatever shadows were cast by trackside growth.

Now two lanterns winking ahead and the escort was moving towards them, slowing, answering a challenge. Then a greeting and the lanterns showed guards pulling a pole aside to allow passage.

Dawlish looked to Vázquez. Both shook their heads. Too dangerous to risk, nothing for it but to move into the brush at one side to work their way around the barrier. They did so with infinite caution, fearful of the slightest crunch of dry growth underfoot. Then a low gurgling ahead, unmistakable as a stream. They advanced to its bank, saw it was some fifteen yards wide, swirls and eddies on the surface. Vegetation trailed in it on the opposite side. To the left the lanterns were visible again and, in their feeble light, the silhouette of a wooden bridge.

No option now but to attempt the stream. Dawlish pulled off his sandals – he dared not lose them. He went first, the gravel beneath painful to his soles. The water was to his knees until he was halfway, then deepened without warning to his waist. He almost fell, for the current was strong and tearing at him. He glanced towards the bridge and froze. There was a soldier there, a matchlight flaring to illuminate his face and then dying to leave the pinpoint of a glowing cigar. A long minute passed, an eternity, as pinpoint waxed and waned and waxed again. It seemed impossible the soldier had not seen Dawlish but he was intent on nothing but his smoke. And then a call from the other guard drew him away.

Dawlish went on – the stream was growing shallower again. He gained the opposite bank and crouched in the foliage there. Now Vázquez's turn, his crossing without incident. They pushed on straight, under cover, for another hundred yards before turning left to find the track. It was curved at this point and gave no sight of the bridge.

Five minutes more. A few shacks, mostly unlit, vegetable plots, a small field of maize, and then low scrub on either side, always enough shadows for their steady advance.

They rounded a bend, saw lights two hundred yards ahead, some of them moving, against a dark outline of a building, larger than a shack. Voices now and the smell of woodsmoke. They moved into the scrub to the right, went forward at a crouch, flitting from one deep shadow to another. The voices were louder, relaxed, some even jovial. The smell of woodsmoke was blended with that of cooking food. From further to the right, Dawlish fancied he could hear waves breaking on a shore. It could not be on the beach of Zihuantanejo's bay – the pursuit of the escorted group had been roughly north-eastwards. This shore must be beyond the far side of the eastern peninsula bounding the bay.

The scrub was thinning, the ground open ahead. Dawlish gestured to Vázquez to stay put, then crept ahead himself. He found deep shadow at the edge of the brush, dropped and wriggled into its cover.

The building he had seen was a small church, not grandiose like that in the town plaza but low and squat and probably of adobe. A poor church for poor people. If it had windows – and he could discern none – they must be tiny. No belfry, just a cross at the apex of the roof above the narrow door. A low wall to one side enclosed what might be a graveyard. Three shacks close by, a few lanterns, and what looked like a canvas tent. In the dancing light of a cooking fire, he saw uniformed men. How many? Not more than a dozen, judging by the size of the escort that brought the prisoners back and forth daily and allowing for a few more to guard those not selected for work.

He had no doubt now that this was where *Jenny's* crew was held. The delay imposed by crossing the stream had meant that they had already arrived here about a quarter-hour before him. They must be well under lock and key by now. His hope of making any contact with them was gone. All he could do was discover more about this site.

It took well over an hour. Vázquez joined him and they circled the church, observing from the scrub. Remote from the town, the location might indicate an intention to keep the crew as a bargaining counter or for ransom.

But it was close to the shore . . .

They were back at roughly the point where they had started the circuit and it was time to work back towards the stream and wade across again. They would drink from it, the only opportunity for water if the remainder of the night went as Dawlish intended.

Six hours of darkness remained. They would work around the northern side of the town, go to ground at the first sight of danger, move again only when sure the chance of challenge was past. It would be essential to give the check point on the far side of the town, a wide berth, so too the defences under construction and then cross the track they guarded a mile at least further to the west.

With luck they could be by dawn at the base of the hill on top of which Grove and his marines were keeping watch.

Hungry, thirsty, exhausted, drying clothing chafing and feet rubbed raw by unaccustomed sandals, there was no option but to keep moving.

Memory of the pockmarks and stains on the wall in the plaza were incentive enough.

*

They reached Grove's still-undetected location on the hilltop just after dawn. Food, water and a few hours' sleep refreshed. Then, until nightfall, Dawlish took turns observing the bay, the town and the fort, jotting sketch-maps in a notebook. *Jenny's* boom still swung cargo on to the raft. The conscripted labour was there again, some of *Jenny's* crew probably again among them. The barque had been here for upwards of ten days, so the total quantity of arms she carried must have been enormous. It was no coincidence that the Juaristas had taken Zihuantanejo shortly before her arrival. Some sympathiser in San Pedro must have learned of her cargo before departure and passed the word on. Given United States support for the Juarista cause; it might even have been through official channels. *Jenny* sailed unsuspectingly into a newly captured port, now a point of entry for supplies and a base for strengthened thrusts against the French and Imperial forces to the east.

Down in the fort, the barrels and mountings of the old Spanish-era cannon were thrown in a heap. Five large modern field guns – ten pounders, maybe even twelve, Grove estimated – nestled in embrasures. Their arcs commanded not just the narrow entrance of the bay but the approach outside it. Slopes of earth and rubble had been heaped behind each embrasure to catch the guns' recoils. Loading, training and elevation exercises occupied much of the day. The crews might not have been artillerymen until recently, but now some professional gunner was forging them into an effective team.

Dawlish's party remained concealed all day on the hilltop. The sun was merciless and their water canteens were now but quarter-full. Only the strictest discipline – a mouthful every three hours – kept thirst at bay. But, at last, blessed sundown came. They waited an hour, then began the cautious descent towards the beach where they had landed.

Sprightly's whaler was waiting.

An hour later they were back on board and a dark profile a mile further to the west confirmed that *Quetzal* had arrived.

Far enough offshore to be unobservable from land.

Chapter 13

Sprightly steamed five miles eastward after darkness fell before swinging north toward the coast, hidden from the view of Zihuantanejo's fort by the peninsula on the eastern side of the bay. Her cutter had been swung out on davits on one side, a whaler directly behind and a second whaler was ready for launching on the other. The men they would carry were waiting to board.

Few of *Sprightly's* crew has seen action previously. Dawlish could sense the unspoken fear around him. His own might be worst of all, he thought, fear of failure, that his decisions or hesitations – and yes, possibly his cowardice – might cause the deaths of the men he'd command. This night would involve the sort of exploit he had thrilled to read of as a youth, the cutting-outs ambitious young officers had carried off so often, so successfully and with such aplomb, in Nelson's day. Now the reality was on him, he wondered if they too had been consumed beforehand by the same fear. He glanced across the deck, saw Grove by the cutter and whaler with his dozen marines and eleven bluejackets, and wondered if he too was feeling it.

Jem Redshaw was standing with Dawlish, probably fearing more than any other this night. Loyalty to his ship and captain had brought him here. Lacking all military training, he had nevertheless volunteered to join Dawlish's party.

"I know *Jenny* better than my own missus," he'd said.

And because of that, his role would be vital tonight.

Dawlish's reconnaissance, and especially the unexpected presence of the guns in the old fort, demanded refinement of the plan developed by Weatherby and Berchtold before leaving Manzanillo. The first part was now commencing and *Sprightly's* three pulling boats, laden with men and weapons, would play roles as significant of those of the ironclad and gunvessel.

A faint glimmer hovered above *Sprightly's* funnel as she reduced revolutions and crawled towards the land's dark outline, then turned again, to port, to parallel the coast at a mile's separation. The hilly ridgeline of the peninsula that closed Zihuantanejo Bay's eastern side lay like a black wall ahead. *Sprightly* slowed and hove-to a mile off the landward base of the peninsula. Somewhere close to the north, cut off from view by low scrub-clad ridges, must be the adobe church in which *Jenny's* crew was locked. It was time to drop Grove's landing party. Within minutes, the cutter and whaler that carried them were lost in the darkness as they stroked towards the shore.

Sprightly crept southwards now, parallel to the peninsula. Dawlish's party – a dozen seamen, and Jem Redshaw too – had transferred to the remaining whaler, ready to drop. The gunvessel hove-to about halfway down the peninsula and Weatherby watched in silence from the bridge as the whaler settled in the water.

His fear must be greater than my own. He's risking his reputation and his career as well as his life. Grove and I are taking almost half his crew with us. Those left are mostly in the engine room. He'll have hardly enough to man the guns . . .

Dawlish's whaler pulled towards the shore and *Sprightly* turned away to rendezvous with *Quetzal* as stealthily as she had come. He was sitting in the sternsheets with Redshaw, armed only with cutlass and pistol. The seamen had Enfield rifles, loaded but uncocked, under orders to use them only on Dawlish's word. It was their cutlasses that could decide the nights work in silence. Redshaw alone was unarmed – he'd be a danger to himself, he'd said, and a seaman had been instructed to keep close to him throughout.

Steep cliffs plunged into the water all the way to the peninsula's tip. The whaler nudged as close in as Dawlish dared, to take advantage of any shadows. On slowly now, the slight creak of the greased rowlocks smothered by the sound of water lapping on the jagged shore.

Then rounding the tip, the bay's mouth coming into view, so too the dark mass of the hills on the opposite side. Dawlish searched for the fort but found no glows of light to identify it. It was an hour past midnight and all there, other than a few bored sentries, must be asleep. Any lanterns burning in the courtyard were hidden by the walls.

On further, hugging the peninsula's inner shoreline, as steep as that on its far side. Weak moonlight showed the bay as calm. Dots of light were swinging into view from west to east as the town revealed itself. Before it lay *Jenny Dixon's* dark silhouette. No sign of life there, none either of the raft being moored alongside. It must have been left part-way up the beach at the end of the last unloading.

The only protection against observation from the fort or town was to remain close inshore, the whaler's and her crew's profiles indistinguishable against the peninsula's black mass. The rowers were pulling gently, halting when a seaman stationed in the bows spotted isolated rocks, backing water, giving a wide berth as they advanced again. And still silence from the north-east. Grove's force must be close to its objectives now and still undetected.

Moored by a single anchor, *Jenny Dixon's* heading was towards the south-east, her port flank exposed to the town. The raft had been secured to this side during her offloading and Dawlish remembered Ned, the bruised British seaman, dropping down to it by a Jacob's ladder. With luck, that might still be there.

The barque was a cable's length off the whaler's port bow and it was time to break away from the peninsula's dark silhouette. Slow, gentle stokes now across the calm intervening water – even in tonight's weak moonlight it seemed to shimmer as bright as at noonday. It seemed impossible nobody might see the whaler from the town as it glided on. The seaman crouched at the bow – a young foretopman, Joe Rawlins, much admired for his agility and strength – was holding a grapnel attached to a coil of rope, waiting for his moment. There would be no spoken orders.

Closer and closer to *Jenny*, then passing beneath her bowsprit, then paralleling her port side. No sound of movement on board, no lights either. The town lay directly ahead but still no alarm raised. Lightened of her cargo, riding high in the water, the barque's black flank was like a cliff.

And no Jacob's ladder hung down it.

That it had been hauled up after the conscripted workers went ashore at sunset indicated somebody remained aboard.

Oars shipped in dead silence and the whaler nudged against the barque's side. Rawlins was on his feet, steadying himself against the

149

boat's gentle rocking, swinging the grapnel in a circle at the rope's end, four, five times to give it momentum, then hurling it upwards. It disappeared over the bulwark, hit the deck beyond with a thump that should have alerted any reliable sentry. Rawlins was drawing on the line and a faint scraping told of the grapnel moving over the planking to find some hold. Then the rope taughtened and held. Secured by wraps around the foremost thwart, it anchored the whaler to the barque. Rawlins, armed only with a cutlass thrust through his belt, was climbing it already, hand by hand and his bare feet – all the seamen's were bare – finding silent purchase on the wooden flank. He reached the bulwark top and flopped over. Another man was following, a third awaiting his turn.

Anxious seconds, waiting for a weary sentry's challenge, for a cry of alarm, for a weapon's discharge. None came, nothing but the gasps of Rawlins and the two now with him as they heaved the rolled-up Jacob's ladder to the bulwark-top. It balanced there for an instant, then uncoiled, whipping outward like an alarmed snake before it pounded against *Jenny's* flank.

Dawlish was first up, then followed by all but one man left in the whaler to guard it. As instructed, the bluejackets were fanning out forward and aft along the deck, securing the deckhouse abaft the foremast, the hatches, the companionway and deckhouse aft.

All done in silence and within three minutes of the whaler drawing alongside. Two uniformed sentries, caught drowsy and awakening too late in terrified surprise, were being bound and gagged with sleeves torn from their shirts.

"There may be others below." Jem Redshaw was by Dawlish's side. "If they're anywhere, they'll be in the officers' accommodation aft."

Dawlish, revolver at the ready, was first down the companionway, two seamen behind and Redshaw following with a lantern. Each door kicked open was a terror in itself, even though all proved empty, not just of people but anything movable.

"I've damn well lost all I have," Redshaw was trembling with anger. "Near two hundred dollars and eighty-six gold sovereigns in my trunk. An' the photograph of my Anna and the kids. Set in a silver frame it was." He gestured to an empty closet, its door wrenched off. "Every stitch I had an' not a boot left to my name."

Back on deck, the bluejackets had taken cover behind the bulwarks, rifles at the ready. Silence reigned. Dawlish looked towards the town. All calm there – the boarding had not been observed. Nobody in the fort noticed either.

It had gone better than he could have hoped. *Jenny Dixon* was his.

But she was trapped inside the harbour by guns that could tear her apart in minutes and too large to sail her with his small crew if she wasn't, too heavy to tow with the whaler.

Nothing to do but wait.

And hold her against any threat.

*

Dawlish had expected, indeed longed for, the flash that lit the north-eastern sky for a second only, and the low rumble that followed. The peace of the last hour had ended and Grove's landing force was in action. Only later would Dawlish hear its story from the lips of the young marine lieutenant himself.

*

Hampered by the low light, it took longer than planned to find a landing place. Grove decided however that it was close enough to the 'X' on the sketch map Dawlish made after his reconnaissance and which indicated the closest point on the coast from the adobe church incarcerating *Jenny's* crew.

The cutter and the whaler ran on to a small beach backed with bluffs rather than steep cliffs. Dragged just enough up the sand to allow fast relaunching, two rifle-armed seamen would remain with the boats to guard them.

Grove, with two marines, went ahead to find an easy route up the bluff. His sergeant, Swanley, stayed with the men at the beach to allocate loads and check weapons. The ascent proved easy. A low scrub-clad ridge lay a few hundred yards beyond. No lights there. Grove sent one of his marines back to guide the remaining force and went ahead with the other towards the ridge.

The scrub was sparse and they reached the crest line without difficulty. The slope ahead dropped gently for what might be a quarter-mile towards a valley bounded by the dark curtain of mountains to the north. Grove had brought a small telescope. The danger of sun-flashes on a lens had precluded one on the previous reconnaissance but tonight it was invaluable and represented no such hazard.

Over to his left – he estimated as some two miles – Grove could discern the moonlit waters of Zihuantanejo's bay. *Jenny's* dark outline nestled at its centre and he wondered if Dawlish had already boarded her. A few lights burned in the town and quiet seemed to reign there. Shifting his scrutiny to the right, he saw a large cluster of lights and a few weak fires. That must be the Juarista camp that Dawlish had identified and it constituted the greatest threat to success of this landing.

By Dawlish's reckoning, the adobe church was about a mile north-east of the bay. It must be somewhere to his right but Grove could not see it. Another, lower, ridge or thick foliage might be blocking it from sight. He would have to gamble on that, for time was slipping away. Remaining on the crest, he sent the marine back to guide the others.

When they arrived, Grove led them in single file behind him on a handheld compass bearing of north-east by north. The brush grew thicker as they descended in silence and with orders relayed back along the line, man-to-following-man, by hand signals. Now the ground was rising again. There was indeed another low ridge ahead, as Grove had surmised, though at an angle to the first.

He halted the party just below the crest and went forward with Sergeant Swanley to take cover there.

Success!

There, further to his left than anticipated, and some eight hundred yards distant, was the greyish outline of the church against the darker land behind. The only lights were the faint glow of dying cooking fires and a single lantern.

"That's where they are." He gestured and handed the telescope to Swanley. "There, to the left of the church, do you see that wall?"

"Aye, sir." The sergeant nodded. Freeing *Jenny's* crew would be his responsibility.

"That's the graveyard. Work your way around to its rear with your marines. No nearer than a hundred yards and stay in cover as you do." It was the plan developed with Dawlish's advice and Swanley had already been instructed. But now, with action and the chance of failure close, it was best to repeat it. "Cross over into the graveyard only when those lights are blocked by the church and there's no sentry in sight. And dead silence, mind. Stay in cover until you hear my signal."

"And if there's none, sir?" Swanley said.

"If I'm not back in an hour, go ahead without me." Grove found himself speaking with detachment, as if of some other man, and of that man's death. His fear had weakened, was replaced by rational caution. "No shooting if you can help it, then get the prisoners to the beach. Leave the seamen on the ridge here. They've orders to cover your retreat. I'll join you at the beach if I can."

Grove didn't wait to see Swanley's group's departure.

He had business of his own.

*

Grove and his six marines were advancing westwards, through the scrub that Dawlish had identified south of the track that led to the town. The night was loud with insects, drowning any crackle of twigs snapping underfoot. Frogs' croaking, low at first but louder with each step forward, indicated the stream must be close ahead.

He turned to Dermody, the marine following him. "Wait here, all of you."

The growth was thick and shadows deep, making his onward progress slow. It took long minutes to reach the stream. He looked to the right. There was a bend there and he could not see the bridge. He moved upstream along the bank, holding to the shade. Around the bend then and the bridge came into view a hundred yards beyond. It was as Dawlish had described, a flat span linking high banks and supported by spindly supports about a quarter-way across from either side. He had seen enough and returned to his men. All good shots, though none had ever fired in anger. Four to give cover, two to accompany him to the bridge.

"Corporal Shaw, Johnson, Gallagher and you, Wilkes!" He spoke in a whisper and gestured northwards. "The track's that way. Move up along it under cover until you see the bridge. There's probably a guard there, maybe two. Don't alarm them and don't show yourselves. When we come back, we may be running, so hold your fire 'til we're with you."

He didn't wait to see them disappear, just jerked his head to the two remaining marines, Prescott and Dermody. Both were carrying packs in addition to their rifles. He led him back as he'd returned from the river, ignoring the fear that now haunted him again. The most dangerous task of the night lay ahead and he would not delegate it. Should Swanley's action at the church trigger gunfire, success of Grove's action would delay arrival there of aroused forces from that Juarista camp which Dawlish had seen somewhere on the far side of the stream.

At the bank now and sheltering in the brush. The bridge stood out in dark outline against the grey water. The near darkness would be both a help and a hindrance for what would come. All three advanced upstream some fifty yards, hugging the shadows inward of the water's edge, then paused. There was a sentry on the bridge, plodding wearily across, turning, returning with unwilling steps, a resented duty that must seem pointless to him. No sign of a second man, though there had to be one – he must be somewhere on the far side, perhaps dozing.

"It's time," Grove whispered.

Both men had been instructed beforehand and knew what to do. Dermody slipped off his pack, opened it and hung it around Grove's neck so that he could reach inside with both hands. Prescott did the same with his own and left his rifle with Dermody, who dropped and crawled to the edge of the brush. He had two loaded rifles now, and when the sentry had passed from sight, cocked them with clicks that sounded like gunshots.

Crouching, still under cover, Grove and Prescott moved forward until they were four or five yards downstream of the bridge. Oblivious of their presence, the bored sentry's steps sounded on the planks almost above them. Grove saw that the two closest bridge supports looked no thicker than telegraph poles. The current swirled in eddies around them but it was impossible to judge the depth.

The sentry's back was turned as he plodded again towards the other side, unaware Dermody would be holding him in his sights. Grove left Prescott behind and moved under the bridge itself. He waited until the returning sentry's steps sounded above him and only began to lower himself into the water, as they receded.

He found himself immersed to his thighs. The supports were no more than four yards away and the bottom shelved only slightly as he waded towards that on the upstream side. The current plucked at him and it was hard to maintain his balance. He was halfway when he heard the steps returning and froze until the sentry turned and went back. A few paces more through the water brought him to the support. He clutched it and waited until the footsteps had once more come and gone. Then, from the open pack on his chest, he drew out a five-pound bag of black powder, wrapped in waterproofed canvas, and a coil of quarter-inch coir rope. It took three passages of the sentry, each halting work, before the parcel was lashed to the support, placed so the length of wax-sealed slow fuse emerging was at the top.

Grove remained clinging to the support. When the sentry was crossing towards the far bank again, he jerked his head to Prescott. It was the marine's turn to drop into the water and wade to the downstream support. He had a charge to bind to it and he did so within four minutes.

"Go!" Grove hissed.

Prescott heaved himself up on to the bank and disappeared into the scrub. He was to join Dermody in keeping the bridge under rifle-aim.

Grove had never felt more alone, more vulnerable. His hands were shaking as he drew a clasp knife from his pack and cut off the end of the waxed fuse. Now the worst part of all. He pulled out a box of lucifer matches, selected one and struck it. The rasp sounded deafening to him. The flame flared and died. Now another and this time the wooden end had taken fire. He laid it gently alongside the fuse tip, held it there. The flame was close to his fingers before he saw the fuse's first spark.

Six minutes – in theory. Several tests on *Sprightly* had determined the length chosen but they also showed variations of thirty seconds more or less.

He forced himself to be slow as he waded towards the downstream support – a stumble now would be disastrous. Footsteps were approaching on the planking but he did not pause this time. A minute and a half must have passed and Hell was brewing at his back. If necessary, Dermody and Prescott would deal with the sentry. He reached the support, clung to it, cut the tip off the fuse – it was timed for four minutes. He stuck three matches in turn but his trembling hands could not hold them close enough to the fuse for it to catch. He fought the urge to abandon the effort – one charge was already in place and that must surely be enough – but forced himself to try one last lucifer. This time, the fuse sputtered.

No need for silence now. He was up on the bank, crashing through the brush towards Dermody and Prescott, shouting at them to retreat to join the others. From behind him he heard a voice calling *"Quien pasa? Quien pasa?"* He had lost all sense of time, had pounded what might be forty yards, when curiosity, irrational but irresistible, drew him towards the stream so he would see what he had achieved. At the bank he took cover and saw two figures on the bridge, one pointing toward the brush he had run through.

And then a detonation, a ball of flame, and then a second, almost simultaneous, set off perhaps by the first. The bridge was illuminated as the boom washed over Grove and for an instant it seemed to stand intact. Then, as the red glow faded, all to the right of the supports close to the opposite bank was swinging downwards from them, like a dropping drawbridge, disintegrating as it hit the water.

Grove's spirit soared. Fear had not stopped him.

There was a barrier now to any Juarista advance from the nearby camp. Not an impassable one, for men and horses could wade across, but enough to buy time for Swanley's force, back at the adobe church.

Grove headed what he guessed was north-eastwards through the scrub to find the track. No crackling of rifles from the direction of the church. Swanley would have launched his force into action as the explosion lit the sky – that was the signal. The silence indicated he'd taken any guards still awake, and any sleeping, by surprise, and settled the business with bayonet and rifle-butt alone. Keys might have been found by now, or handed over under threat, and *Jenny's* crew liberated.

A challenge halted Grove just short of the track – his marines were in cover there. Two hundred yards to the left, a thread of black smoke was still drifting skywards and thinning. Fast orders now, a dash along the sides of the track to the stream, quick deployment to kneel in cover on the banks to either side of what had been the approach to the bridge, Grove with three men on the right, the remainder to the left.

Five minutes passed. Continuing silence told that Swanley might by now have started the retreat to the beach. And then, coming nearer, the sound of pounding hooves, horsemen from the camp arriving to investigate the explosion. They swung into sight from around a bend, a half-dozen of them. They should have dismounted and crept forward through the shadows, but were flushed with the stupid over-confidence that betrayed so many cavalrymen through the ages. They were still coming on and less than twenty yards from the far bridge-end when Grove called the order to fire. Six rifles blasted and he himself loosed with his pistol. Two horses were down, their riders struggling to drag themselves free, and a third's saddle was emptied. A rider at the rear managed to halt, wheel about, race back around the bend as he had come.

"Reload!"

Marines bobbing to their feet, biting cartridges, pouring powder down Enfield barrels, spitting in balls, ramming, dropping again.

"Fire!"

Rounds tore into the jumble of men and horses.

No need for more. The volleys had served notice the eastern bank was defended, by how many men would be hard to guess. Any more dangerous advance from the camp would now be slow and cautious. When it did come, outflanking the bridge by wading upstream and downstream of it, the Juaristas would find nothing.

"Fall back!" Grove called.

Triumph, no less than relief, lent wings to their feet.

*

There were three bodies outside the adobe church, one with its throat slashed, the others killed by bayonet. Pounding on the door from within, and shouts in Spanish to be let out, confirmed it held different prisoners now. The nearby shacks were deserted but a few items of upturned furniture indicated the occupiers had been surprised in slumber. Several rifles, their stocks smashed by swinging them on to the ground by their muzzles, lay on a smouldering cooking fire. No sign of Swanley or his people. Their attack had been fast and efficient. There no need to blow in the church door. Willing or not, somebody had handed over the keys.

Rifle shots sounded from the direction of the stream, probably Juaristas from the camp firing at shadows. Fast up the scrub-clad slopes – Grove and his marines were panting but not slowing – and a challenge met them at the last crest from the bluejackets that formed Swanley's rearguard.

"Got 'em all?" Grove's chest was heaving as he drew breath,

"Every last one, sir."

And ten minutes later the cutter and whaler were pulling out to sea, laden with *Jenny's* crew. Most seemed bemused and had still not taken in the reality of their liberation. Her captain, Enoch Ridley, a white-haired, white-bearded old man, was sitting by Grove in the cutter's sternsheets, embarrassed by his tears of thanks. He owned a quarter-share in *Jenny Dixon*, he said, and losing her would have

158

beggared him. After his rescue from the church he was sure the Navy could accomplish anything and that the barque would be his again within the day. Grove refrained from telling that her recovery was still in the balance.

Still touch and go.

Chapter 14

The flash and rumble that told Dawlish of the bridge's destruction had died. Now lights were appearing in the town, some static, some dancing in the darkness as alarm-driven feet hurried to investigate. Confused shouting carried across the water and a bell began to toll. Further off, a bugle was calling. He glanced towards the fort. There were lights moving there too. Ten minutes later came the brief and distant crash of rifle fire, and the silence that followed, confirming that Grove had repulsed the earliest effort to investigate. He must by now be withdrawing towards the adobe church.

No sign of concern in the town yet about *Jennie Dixon,* but the light of dawn would reveal the whaler alongside. It was still hours away but he had to be prepared. He forced from his mind the awareness that though the barque's high bulwarks would protect against small arms, they could offer no defence against artillery should any be brought to bear. He had himself and a dozen bluejackets to defend her. Three men placed under cover at bow and stern, two on either flank and one each on fore and mizzen tops. Twenty-five rounds in each man's pouch. Two-rope-handled ammunition boxes had been lugged on board and already opened. Jem Redshaw, with the two axes brought from *Sprightly,* was at the forecastle, close to the capstan.

Three hours passed, the alarm in the town diminishing. Dawlish visited each group in turn and had no need to exhort for greater vigilance. Every man was aware of the enormity of his vulnerability.

The sky was brightening in the east, the inland mountain crests black against it. Dawlish scanned the still-dark southern horizon, eager for the first sign of deliverance and finding none. He looked eastwards again, saw the dawn's shell-pink fade and the sky lighten, the land and the town and the bay reveal themselves, and the sun itself soar as an incandescent ball from beyond the mountain curtain. He turned to the south again. There, framed by the peninsulas bounding the bay, he saw two long trails of smoke rising above the horizon.

Though still hull-down, *Sprightly* and *Quetzal* were on the way.

*

Jenny Dixon had lain stationary through the hours of darkness but now, as the sun soared higher, a weak sea breeze was weathercocking her about so that her bows now pointed towards the bay's mouth. The town was coming alive but there were few uniforms visible – all attention must still be focussed over to the north-east in the area of Grove's activity. With luck, he and his people, with *Jenny's* crew, would be safely out to sea by now and waiting for rescue.

Dawlish was crouching in cover by the bowsprit, holding the approaching *Sprightly* and *Quetzal* in his glass. They were hull-up by now. growing larger by the second, the ironclad leading, the gunvessel off her starboard quarter, yards bare, smoke rolling from their funnels. It seemed impossible no look-out in the fort had seen them yet. Two more minutes passed before a cannon-blast ruptured the morning calm. He watched for the splash of a falling shot and saw none. The fort had fired a blank for alarm alone. The range was still too great for hitting and whoever had command was astute enough to be conserving precious munitions. A small group was gathered on a rampart top and a sun-flash showed one at least was viewing the advance by telescope.

"Mr. Dawlish, sir!" A seamen left at the stern had come forward. "A boat's coming from the beach."

"Uniforms?"

"Aye, sir."

Dawlish rushed aft with the man, saw that there were indeed Juarista troops on the foreshore, others emerging at the double from the town. A single boat, perhaps a dozen men in it, was already a hundred yards from the beach and pulling towards *Jenny*. Two fishing boats were being dragged into the water and uniformed men, all rifle-armed, were hoisting themselves into them. Alerted by the fort's alarm, somebody, at last, had noticed the whaler by the barque's side and understood its significance.

He wanted them to be nearer, for the range to be almost point-blank and only then unleash a volley on the approaching boat.

"Heads below the bulwark!" he shouted. A call then towards the men at the bows, "Rowlands! Jeffries! Fuller! Join me aft!"

Six men under cover at the stern now, two on each flank. The seamen in the crosstrees were already holding the approaching boat in their sights.

"Wait for my word, lads! Then up and choose your targets. And hold until my word. Rapid fire then until I order cease!"

He was standing on a mooring bit, face and body hidden to eye-level by a bulwark and holding the nearing boat in his lens. Six men pulling – they looked like civilians, maybe fishermen – and eight or ten uniformed troops standing between then. Two more were steadying a third upright at the bows and his rifle was raised. What might be an officer – his uniform was less shabby than the others and more ornate – was standing in the sternsheets and trying to hold his balance.

Dawlish saw his face – cleanshaven, near his own age – and tore his gaze away. He looked not unlike Ignacio Vázquez and at any other time and place all three might have met in friendship in some cantina.

But that young man's a fool. He has no idea of who or what's on board this ship. He must have commandeered the first boat he found at the beach, crammed it with every man he could and only now is wondering what to do next.

For the boat was slowing, a hundred yards distant now and almost directly astern of the barque. It was starting to edge over to come alongside on the port side. The young officer was hailing but his words were indistinct. He waited for a reply, got none, and called again.

Dawlish did not want to remember the agony of indecision on that face. He snapped his glass closed.

Harden your heart . . .

The boat was pulling ahead again, was eighty yards off the port quarter . . .

"Up!" Dawlish shouted. "Find your targets!"

Heads and shoulders above the bulwark now, elbows rested on it, rifles steadied, three endless seconds to allow aiming.

A single shot, the Juarista in the boat's bows firing uselessly . . .

"Fire!" Dawlish yelled.

Six rifles at *Jenny's* stern blasting as one, another from the mizzen top an instant later. Dawlish resisted the urge to join them – it would be futile with his revolver.

Several already downed in the boat, the oars breaking stroke and trailing, a single rifle replying, men diving for illusory cover, others crouching and attempting to aim.

"Rapid fire!"

Dropping below the bulwark-top now, fast reloading, up again, a ragged volley this time.

And carnage in the boat. It was drifting and bodies lay heaped in it – there was movement, but no attempts to fire back – and three men were in the water, hanging to the gunwales.

Another lash of fire, bodies jerking, chunks of timber torn from the hull, somebody lurching to his feet and falling back.

Enough.

"Cease firing!"

Several seamen didn't hear and Dawlish had to shout again before the last rifle fell silent. He looked at the shattered boat and its cargo of butchery, was sickened, and quickly looked away. Caught by some faint air, it was drifting away to port leaving struggling bodies and smashed oars behind. Somebody, maybe more than one, was still alive within it and the sound of agony – sobbing, pleading, choking, knife-sharp, unforgettable – carried towards the barque across the still water.

The two other boats were falling back. At three or four hundred yards, the chance of hitting them would be as futile as any fire they might themselves bring to bear. The brief battle's noise had drawn spectators to the beach and yet more troops were arriving.

Dawlish sent the men who'd come from the bows forward again. He followed, running, eager for sight of *Quetzal* and *Sprightly*, longing for them to open fire and draw attention from the trapped barque.

Then a report, unmistakable as artillery, washing overhead.

The fort!

He reached the prow in time to see a column of white spray collapsing, safely distant off the port bow. Held in his glass's lens, he saw smoke drifting from the nearest of the embrasures, followed by a flash and a billowing cloud from the next seawards of it. The sound reached him just before a short plume of foam ploughed the surface just beyond the first's dispersing froth. Either round would have wrought destruction on *Jenny*, might even have brought down a mast had it struck but . . .

Hope coursed within him. The weapons in the fort were incapable of bearing on the barque. The embrasures had been sited long since by some Spanish engineer to command the approach and mouth of Zihuantanejo's bay, not its interior. Another lash of flame and rolling smoke, and another round throwing up another harmless fountain.

Jenny Dixon was trapped but, for now, remained invulnerable.

Quetzal and *Sprightly* were still forging on, now little over a mile beyond the bay's mouth. The ten-inch three-hundred pounder protruding from below the ironclad's bowsprit could outrange the field guns in the fort and it must open at any moment.

A long minute passed and its silence – no rifles, no artillery – was ominous with the promise of the thunder yet to come. *Sprightly* was swinging to starboard, as planned, reducing speed, starting a slow circle that would hold her beyond the bay's mouth, well out of the fort's reach – for now. And *Quetzal* was also edging to starboard, away from the course that had been carrying her towards the centre of the bay. Directing the quartermaster on her open bridge, Berchtold must be relishing this longed-for moment, this chance of glory. In the armoured citadel in her bows, the enormous gun would be loaded with bursting shell, Rogers and his crew alert for the order to open fire. Close to the stern, enclosed by iron walls, Welborne would be in command of the seventy pounders on either beam. Their time would come, but not yet.

The fort shattered the silence, a single weapon only, a shot at extreme range that plunged harmlessly two cables short of *Quetzal* and far off in aim. However competent an artilleryman the Juarista commander might be, he could have no experience of firing on a moving target. *Quetzal* had slowed, must be at half-revolutions now and she was edging over to port in a broad turn, then breaking from it to drive straight towards the fort. Closer and closer – the bow-on view and the ten-inch muzzle yawning above the wave washing over the ram must be a terrifying sight for the gunners at the embrasures.

A long spear of flame and rolling black smoke reached beneath *Quetzal's* bowsprit. The boom reached Dawlish's ears just before the shell impacted on the steep slope well below, and to the right, of the fort's bastion. A flash, earth and foliage thrown high, grey smoke dispersing to reveal a crater punched in the surrounding scrub.

Failure.

Rogers' men must be working like demons to reload, sponging the barrel, ramming powder bags, swinging the next shell across by an overhead hoist, thrusting it home. *Quetzal's* course was unchanged, still bow-on to the fort, the range closing.

Two guns blasted simultaneously from the embrasures, a third a second later. All shots fell short, but nearer, much nearer, than before, one almost directly ahead of the ironclad, the others off the port bow.

Dawlish saw the ten-inch's barrel running out again. The ironclad's bows edged ever so slightly over, held the new course for seconds only, then straightened. *Quetzal's* main weapon was being locked on a fixed heading for direct fire ahead and Berchtold was using the ship herself to aim it. Nothing remained to Rogers but to judge elevation.

The fort fired first, all five guns, almost as one. Skidding plumes as the rounds hit the water in a ragged line across *Quetzal's* path. Placed high as the fort was on the hillside, its weapons must be at maximum depression. No hit sustained, but the white rips of foam about her must have un-nerved the ironclad's quartermaster, for her bows were swinging slightly over at the very moment her ten-inch roared.

And failure again, nothing but a smoking crater some fifty yards to the left, and below, the stone bastion.

Quetzal was turning away into a broad circle that would carry her seawards and then back for further bombardment. When the fort lay off her starboard beam, flame stabbed from a seventy-pounder in the stern citadel. The shell landed about twenty feet below the bastion and did no more damage than shower earth on the gunners sheltering there. The ironclad was gathering speed but three or four minutes would pass before she could open fire again. And all the time, off the eastern peninsula bounding the bay, *Sprightly* was circling in safety. Entering the bay would mean her running directly past the embrasures' artillery. With her wooden hull lacking *Quetzal's* armour, a hit by a single bursting shell could-inflict serious damage.

The slow dance of the circling ships was almost mesmerising, but a seaman had arrived from the stern to draw Dawlish's attention from it.

"There's something happening in the town, sir." A tremor in his voice. "Guns I think."

Fear clutching at his heart, Dawlish hurried aft with him. Caught in his glass, the reality proved even worse. A field gun and limber had reached the beach and uniformed men were swarming around them, unhitching the mules that had drawn it. He remembered the cannon nestling in the redoubts flanking the track west of the town when he and Vázquez had entered on their reconnaissance. From there, the good roadway he had walked down, and the town streets, would have given fast passage to the shore for wheeled artillery. Now the mules were being led aside and willing hands swinging the gun's trail around to lay it on *Jenny*. The limber was open and men were carrying charges and balls from it. At this separation, rifle-fire from the barque's defenders would have no chance of silencing it.

Dawlish had thought of this possibility before but forced it from his mind. He could do nothing to prevent it and banked on rescue by *Sprightly* before it materialised. But *Quetzal's* heavy cannon had failed so far to silence the fort and guarantee the gunvessel safe entry to the bay. Over the bulwark top, Dawlish could see mules dragging another gun and limber from the town to the beach. He turned, leaned out and looked seaward along the barque's side. *Sprightly* was still circling and *Quetzal* still coming about to attack again.

A report from shoreward drove him aft again. He saw a streak of white foam dispersing twenty yards to starboard, all but parallel to the barque's axis.

A damn good opening shot. And a better is inevitable.

"Go forward!" he shouted. "Take cover! Lie down!" Then up to the two men in the tops, "You too! On deck! Now!"

He waited until all others had dashed to the bows to find shelter ahead of the forward deckhouse, then followed and crouched behind a mooring bit. Jem Redshaw was sheltering nearby, still with the axes. His eyes were closed and he was gathered in a ball, his shoulders shaking.

Another blast from the beach but no impact on the ship. Seconds later, a report announced the newly arrived second gun was now in action. It missed.

An eternity of dead silence, unspoken fear on any faces he could see, despair at inability to strike back, recognition of what must surely come, the agony of waiting.

Now the first hit, a detonation on the after-deckhouse that threw out a fan of splinters. Twenty seconds later another, somewhere against the port flank.

Dear God! Not on the waterline!

Sound lashed from seaward, unmistakable as *Quetzal's* ten inch. Dawlish forced himself to break cover, ran to the bulwark and saw smoke dispersing around the ironclad's bow. Lighter smoke was drifting from an impact on the hillside to the right of the fort. A low flickering showed the bone-dry brush had ignited.

Quetzal was almost stationary, with just enough forward speed to allow her to remain bow-on to her target. Rogers must be driving his gun crew like slaves to reload quickly, for the huge cannon vomited again, this time gouging a crater directly below the centre of the bastion. Thirty feet higher and it might have collapsed it. One of the guns there opened in futile defiance, dropping a shell well short of the ironclad.

Another shudder throbbed through *Jenny's* hull as a shell smashed high on her port flank, tearing a gap in the bulwark and showering splinters. Dawlish dared to rise and look. The second artillery piece on the beach was better positioned than the first, which was almost directly astern of the barque. A hundred yards rightward, it could lay fire on the full length of the vessel's flank.

Now *Jenny's* agony began. The gunners on the beach had fallen into a rhythm, one or the other firing each minute. Two rounds in every three were hitting. The Juarista gun directly astern was still hurling explosive shells but the other had switched to solid ball. Successive detonations scoured the aftership and what remained of the deckhouse there was smouldering. Thump after thump along the port side told of roundshot biting but, other than at two further gaps beaten through the bulwarks, it was impossible to judge where, and how high, above the waterline. Dawlish tried to reassure himself that wooden ships had survived worse pounding in Nelson's day, but explosive shells were rare then. Under the repeated impacts on her flank, the barque was swinging anticlockwise on her mooring to expose her full length to both cannon on the beach.

"Fire, sir! Fire!"

Terror in a seaman's voice as he pointed towards flames licking, and strengthening, from debris at the stern.

I should have rigged hoses to the pumps when we first boarded. Stupidity, my stupidity! No option now but to send men aft to do what they can.

"Rawlins!" he called. That man had done well in the boarding and could be relied on.

"Aye, sir."

"Take three men with you. Heave overboard as much of that burning timber as you can. If it spreads, we're finished."

Trepidation on the men's faces as they went aft, but they did go. Dawlish looked towards the bay's mouth. *Quetzal* was still crawling forward, close enough now that shells from the fort were falling only tens of yards before her. Distracted by *Jenny's* battering, he had no idea how often she might have fired, but though the bastion appeared intact, a blaze was spreading up the hillside to its right and another growing on the slope below the nearer embrasures. He saw another tongue of flame lancing from *Quetzal's* bows and, a moment later, a detonation against the bastion's furthest end. Even if it had not entered through an embrasure to burst within, the shock must distract the gunners for precious seconds.

And Weatherby, in *Sprightly*, must have seen this too, must be grasping the moment, for the gunvessel was curving out from her lazy circling. Smoke billowed from her funnel – more anthracite being shovelled into her furnace – and a white wave was building at her bow as she gathered speed. She was racing towards the entrance to the bay, nearing the zone commanded by the fort, magnificent, glorious at this moment.

Dawlish glanced aft. Rawlins and his helpers were using unburned timbers from the shattered deckhouse to lever blazing debris toward the nearest gap smashed in the bulwark. Shocks – they seemed continuous – reverberated through *Jenny's* hull as ball after ball smashed into her port flank. Only God could know how much damage had already been inflicted.

And now the worst hit of all, a fiery detonation high on the mizzen and the gaff wrenching free to crash down onto the burning wreckage beneath, though the mast itself still stood. By some miracle, Rawlins and his people seemed to have avoided injury and Dawlish sent two more men – the most he could afford to lose – to join them.

Quetzal's blast drew his attention. She was close in now, range almost point blank for her and a patch of foam, close off her starboard beam, confirmed one cannon in the fort had come near to hitting her. Her round exploded close to the bastion top – another distraction for the gunners there. Then she was pulling away, speeding up, and arcing over towards the approaching *Sprightly*.

The cannon firing solid shot from the beach had raised its elevation, reaching for *Jenny's* masts and yards. Three balls – racing black dots – flew high and harmlessly above the topmasts but then came a break in the steady firing rhythm and the sickening recognition that the weapon's barrel was being dropped a few degrees. When the feared report did come, the ball ripped away half of the mainmast's port shrouds and sped on to drop far over to starboard. The fire at the stern was raging and growing, its heat driving back Rawlins and his men. Somewhere beyond it, another shell struck – the poop must be a shambles.

But *Sprightly* was ploughing on with a bone in her teeth, well in reach of the fort's artillery. Unmolested by *Quetzal*, they must be swinging trails around, raising elevations, sponging, loading, ramming, aiming. If the commander there was wise, he would make no attempt to track the speeding gunvessel but instead lay all his weapons directly across the bay's entrance and blast her as she passed.

Two cables off *Sprightly's* port quarter, *Quetzal* was still arcing over to pull into a course parallel to hers. Both vessels drove on – still no fire from the fort. The inferno of burning scrub was spreading and a grey haze from it drifting above the bay.

Dawlish disguised despair, telling himself that, if she could survive another five minutes, the *Jenny* might yet be saved. But the fire aft was unabated – even deck planking was burning now – and solid shot had brought down the mainmast's lowest yard. The mizzen's tarred shrouds were blazing and it could not stand much longer. But *Sprightly* was coming and he must be prepared for her.

Jem Redshaw was trembling when Dawlish dragged him to his feet.

"Stand by the capstan with that axe!" he shouted. To a seaman he said, "You! Take that other axe. I'll want the cable cut, but wait for my word!"

He called Rawlins and his men forward, concentrated them and all the others at the bows.

"You see *Sprightly* coming? She hasn't deserted us. We must be ready for her!"

Responsibilities allocated – Rawlins, the most agile, to catch the heaving line, two to back him, others to haul in the heavy towing cable and make it fast. Only then hack through the anchor cable.

Sprightly was at the mouth of the bay now and *Quetzal* had drawn level on her port side, shielding her from the fort. The ironclad's ten-inch could not be brought to bear but the seventy-pounder in the after citadel could. It fired now. The shell's flight seemed to last forever before it exploded on the slope below the bastion and hurled up a cone of soil and brush. Again, no damage done, but enough to give the gunners pause.

A minute passed. Ironclad and gunvessel were nearing the narrowest section of the bay's mouth. *Quetzal's* seventy-pounder opened again even as flame rippled from the fort's embrasures – three weapons in quick succession, the others seconds later. Splashes showed four shells dropping just ahead of the racing vessels but the fifth struck *Quetzal's* armoured side abaft the funnel. A flash, smoke, but no apparent damage – the shell could have done serious injury to the wooden gunvessel but the ironclad was driving on unchecked.

Sprightly and *Quetzal* had run the gauntlet unharmed and the fort's guns could not train back far enough through the embrasures to reach them. But *Jenny's* ordeal was not ended – another yard was down and the mizzen, its port shroud wholly burned away, was toppling. It fell to starboard and shattered where it hit the bulwark, the upper part disappearing from sight. The gunvessel was running straight towards her, and the ironclad edged over to pass on her starboard side. Both bow-waves were dropping, showing them slowing.

A muzzle flash below *Quetzal's* bowsprit and rolling smoke and a ten-inch shell screaming past *Jenny* towards the beach. Dawlish did not see the impact but heard the blast. He had eyes only for *Sprightly*. Foam was churning at her stern as her screw reversed but she was still gliding onwards, slower by the second, towards the barque's starboard flank. Weatherby was at the bridge wing, speaking trumpet in hand.

"I can't bring her too close," he yelled. "Are you ready?"

"Ready, sir!"

"Sanderson's aft with the towing cable! Ready to receive?"

"Aye!"

Rawlins was standing on the bulwark to the side of *Jenny's* bowsprit, arms free, two men holding his legs for steadiness. *Sprightly's* bows had curved to port and were level with *Jenny's* burning stern before her forward momentum died. She was stationary for an instant before the threshing screw began to draw her astern. Now Dawlish saw the cable party by *Sprightly's* stern, a seaman held up on the bulwark with a lead on a sounding line. Lieutenant Sanderson stood behind with men ready to ease the heavy towing line overboard.

Sprightly's screw stilled and she was slipping astern at half-walking pace. The separation between her stern and *Jenny's* bow was closing. Twenty yards, fifteen, closer still . . .

Another discharge from *Quetzal,* a sound of an explosion on the beach. Dawlish realised neither shell nor shot had battered the barque since the ironclad's previous blast. One or other of the Juarista cannon might have been eliminated and perhaps the second's crew had fled. It didn't matter which. Both weapons were silent.

"Ready, Joe!" The man with the casting line on *Sprightly* was shouting to Rawlins and swinging the lead in a circle.

"Ready!"

The lead was breaking from its rotation, soaring across towards Rawlins, and he was reaching for it. He failed to catch but it cleared the bulwark and thumped down on the deck behind him. Three men pounced on it and the line behind. Time then to draw the heaving line in, and the thicker line at its end, one strong enough to bear the weight of the tow cable to follow. It came across, dripping, and was passed aft to the capstan and made fast. Dawlish checked, yelled across that he was ready for towing, heard Weatherby shouting through his trumpet that he would steam dead-slow ahead to take up the slack.

Now Jem Redshaw and the seaman with the second axe were chopping alternately at the anchor cable. Fibres flew with each blow. It was half-severed when Dawlish saw what remained was stretching and thinning.

"Get back" he shouted just before it parted with a sharp crack and whipped like an angered cobra as the end raced towards the hawsehole and disappeared. He sensed *Jenny* dropping astern, then holding, then crawling forward under tow towards the entrance of the bay.

Quetzal should have been turning away to run parallel to *Sprightly* and shield her and *Jenny* as they crawled out past the fort, but she was stationary, bow-on towards the beach, flinging shells well beyond the deserted shoreline and which burst in the town.

Sheer, futile, bloody murder of innocents.

Dawlish glimpsed Berchtold on the ironclad's bridge, a telescope to his eye, his uniform immaculate, gold braid gleaming, his very stance theatrical, an artist's image of a commander resolute in the heat of battle. Smoke was rising from somewhere in the town.

Perhaps from that poor cantina where the kindly woman owner had refilled my glass without charge and told how to find a bruja.

Berchtold was enjoying this moment of vindictive, self-imagined, glory, some recompense for his loss of his Austrian career. In the forward citadel, Rogers and his gunners must be exhausted by now, smashing round after indiscriminate round into the town when instead they should be readying for the run out from the bay, *Quetzal* shielding *Sprightly* as she had on the way in.

Sprightly had attained walking speed and Weatherby was risking no higher lest the tow part. Yet, slow as she was moving, it was enough to blow back the flames at *Jenny's* stern and prevent their spread forward. It would take long minutes before the two vessels would reach the arc commanded by the fort to creep shieldless before its guns.

Quetzal fired again, wasting another shell and yet more precious time. Berchtold was still posing on her exposed bridge.

We're going to die because of that man.

Weatherby had had enough. He was on the starboard bridgewing, his anger and frustration as obvious as the self-regard of Berchtold's pose, and *Sprightly's* steam-whistle was screaming, once, twice, to draw attention. The Austrian gave no impression of having heard and didn't turn. The whistle screamed again, without break this time, until at last Berchtold looked back as if at some trivial annoyance. Weatherby was waving to him, but he made no acknowledgment. Yet a minute later, foam was churning at *Quetzal's* stern and she was drawing back from the shoreline, then lurching forward again to surge about in a tight turn to head seawards.

The brush on the slope below the fort was blazing and the air was shimmering in front and above the bastion. But the Juarista gunners were holding their nerve and a single weapon opened from an embrasure to throw up a white splash two cables off *Sprightly's* port bow, close to the eastern peninsula. Even though the embrasured guns could not yet be brought to bear, they had all the range needed to dismember gunvessel and barque alike when they passed.

Quetzal was racing to catch up now, the ten-inch's muzzle protruding from the bow port angling over to bear on the nearer end of the bastion, still four cables distant and half-obscured by smoke drifting from the burning hillside. It would be an impossible shot, but Berchtold ordered it anyway and it fell well short.

Sprightly was close to the danger zone and another round had dropped a hundred yards before her bow. The ironclad was swinging over now, straightening, dropping speed to match the gunvessel's, drawing level with her at a half-cable's separation.

A shield at last.

Berchtold, at his port bridge wing, lifted his cap and bowed. Weatherby just raised his cap. Then the Austrian walked to the opposite bridge wing and did the same towards the fort. An actor playing a hero in a melodrama could not have done it better.

Now the slow passage through the fort's cannonade, its fury concentrated on *Quetzal* – all the more perhaps because of the hated Imperial ensign at her staff. Most shells fell without striking, for even at this low speed, a moving target would challenge any gunner trained only for land warfare.

But three did hit.

Two that could do no more than scorch *Quetzal's* armoured flank.

And a third that exploded low on her foremast. It didn't bring it down, but a fragment smashed Berchtold into a bloody heap and left the helmsman by him untouched.

More fire, no further hits and only a last few shells falling far astern.

All three ships passed out into the open sea.

Dawlish felt mixed joy and relief and exhaustion wash through him.

He knew he had done well. He hadn't failed his men or his captain. Or himself. There was still brutal hours' work to be done to save this stricken *Jenny*. But that didn't matter.

He would live.

Thank God.

Chapter 15

And now began the long battle to save the *Jenny Dixon*.

The fire at her stern was still burning, though less fiercely than before, when *Sprightly*, hove-to five miles offshore, cast off the tow and came alongside forward. Weatherby had a party standing by her pump, hands ready on its levers. Sanderson crossed with a dozen men and ran a canvas hose aft – that had been Dawlish's first request, for *Jenny's*, like every other moveable object on board, had been looted at Zihuantanejo. It stiffened as the pumping began but the stream emitted seemed puny compared with the flames. A rolled hose was passed across. Jem Redshaw directed its connection to *Jenny's* own pumps and the boarding crew began heaving on their levers. Weak as both jets were, they proved enough to keep the flames in check and even-drive them back to allow smouldering debris to be pushed overboard.

Grove's cutter and whaler approached, under sail, in mid-morning. Both were low in the water, solid- packed with men, evidence of the liberation of *Jenny's* crew.

"That's Cap'n Ridley," Redshaw pointed to the old man with Grove in the whaler's sternsheets, his eyes locked in mute misery on the burning ship. Both boats drew alongside *Sprightly*.

"More hands for the pumps," Sanderson said to Dawlish.

"If I might suggest, sir," Dawlish said, "perhaps they shouldn't be sent across. They don't know yet that they've nothing but the clothes on their backs. Once they realise they're paupers, they won't put their backs into it."

Sanderson paused, then said. "You're correct. I'll send a man across to speak to Weatherby about it."

But Captain Ridley was allowed across.

And what he saw broke his heart.

*

Quetzal was also loitering nearby, efforts in hand to clear wreckage on the bridge. Rogers, in command now, sent Welborne over in a boat to *Sprightly* with a message for Weatherby. Before going back, he crossed to the *Jenny* to view the damage. The fire was well under control by now.

"You'll do damn well out of this, Nick," he said to Dawlish.

"How?" The question had taken him aback.

"Prize money. You'll have your share."

"But Captain Ridley has her again. The steering isn't damaged. Jury-rigged, she'll make Manzanillo for repair."

"You're green, Nick. D'ye think Rogers will accept that? You may have boarded her but *Sprightly* could never have towed her out without *Quetzal's* covering. Fair's fair, Nick, fifty-fifty, down the middle."

Dawlish glanced forward, saw Redshaw sitting on a hatchway with Captain Ridley, his arm around his shoulder as he might comfort a child. Ridley was slumped, elbows on his knees, hands covering his eyes. He looked smaller than when he'd stepped aboard, a man aged twenty years in as single hour.

"He has trouble enough." Dawlish nodded his head towards him. The idea of profiting from his misery repelled him. "He doesn't deserve any more."

"He'll have it whether he likes it or not. Jesse Rogers won't be giving up on this and he's damn well right. The law's the law and if this *Jenny* ain't a prize then she's salvage. There's money in it either way. You'll take your own share gladly enough if it comes to you."

"I won't want it."

"Do you think Ridley's lost more than we have, Rogers and myself? We've lost our whole country." Welborne's voice was cold. "Four years of war and nothing to show for it 'less we bend the knee and swear allegiance to the Yankees."

"But —"

Welborne cut him off. "We took this ship fair and square and we earned our share of her. Charity begins at home."

Dawlish could sense bitterness, no less than anger. There could be no rational discussion and he did not want to lose a friend, an old shipmate. He'd always refrained from asking if his family were slaveowners lest, if they were, it might change his perception of him. He changed the subject.

"What about Captain Berchtold?"

"Born unlucky. His name must have been on that shell. Nobody else was even scratched." No regret in Welborne's voice. "Rogers is doing the decent thing about him before sundown. The Kapitän Baron's parcelled up real neat already. Your Cap'n Weatherby's agreed to come over to say a few words before we drop him. Then we'll be setting course for 'zanillo."

Berchtold had seemed vain and arrogant on the only occasion Dawlish had seen him close. He'd been vicious as well as stupid when he'd shelled innocents in Zihuantanejo. To begin with, there'd been nothing dishonourable in his hunger for glory but resentment at missing Lissa must have unhinged him. Somebody would mourn perhaps, but few, if any, in *Quetzal*. His family might raise a flattering memorial near his ancestors' tombs in some ancient Austrian church. But it was a poor memory to leave behind.

May I not be so remembered.

Welborne left and, soon afterwards, Weatherby came across to see progress. The fire was doused by now and little remained of it but a smouldering and steaming heap. The after deckhouse and some thirty feet of the deck planking abaft it were burned away, yet the hull-framing beneath, though charred, looked intact.

"Damn well done, Dawlish," Weatherby said. "This, and the boarding too. Grove also, fine young fellows both of you." There was an air of confidence in his voice that had been absent since his rebuff in Guzmán by Colonel Durand. Pride too. He had gambled and he had succeeded.

Appropriate action to protect British interests.

As that telegram at San Francisco had demanded.

Though not with a gunrunning trader in mind, red ensign or not.

Dawlish hesitated before asking the question that troubled him. For Captain Ridley's sake he feared the answer.

"Will the *Jenny* count as a prize, sir?"

Weatherby's face hardened. "I'd have expected better of you than that, Dawlish. Is that all you've been thinking of?"

The accusation stung. "No, sir, but –"

"She damn well isn't a prize, though maybe some unprincipled lawyer could make a case of it." Weatherby's voice softened. "You're a young man, Dawlish. Wealth's important, but never sell your soul for it."

Stand your ground. I want this decent man's respect.

"The idea hadn't entered my head. I was surprised when Lieutenant Welborne from *Quetzal* –"

"Did he raise the subject? Was it perhaps just speculation?"

"He was emphatic, sir. From the way he talked, I presumed he'd carried you a message from Mr. Rogers about it so I thought that –"

"It's the first I hear of it, Dawlish! What more did he say?"

"That salvage might be claimed if she wasn't judged a prize."

"More bloody nonsense! Rogers – I suppose I'll have to call him Captain Rogers now – is clearly misinformed about the legalities." Weatherby paused, as if embarrassed by his outburst against another officer, albeit a foreign one, in the presence of a junior. "A sense of delicacy probably stopped him mentioning the idea with me until after poor Berchtold's buried. I'll explain matters to him then. And one more thing, Dawlish. Not a word of prize money or salvage to anybody else."

An hour before sundown, a long white-canvas parcel slipped from beneath an Imperial Mexican ensign along an inclined plank and plunged into the water alongside *Quetzal's* flank.

And even as *Sprightly's* gig was still stroking back with Weatherby, foam was churning beneath the ironclad's counter. She gathered speed and swung her bows west-north-west.

Towards Manzanillo.

*

Sleep was brief and uncomfortable, for *Jenny Dixon's* crew most of all, when they returned to their stripped ship with the few spare hammocks, blankets and cooking utensils *Sprightly* could spare and realised nothing of their own remained. Work began again just after sunrise, fashioning a jury rig under the direction of *Sprightly's* Lieutenant Ashton while Captain Ridley, nominally responsible, looked on, still stunned and almost comatose. *Sprightly's* carpenter did what he could for patching rents in the barque's sides – none, luckily, close to the waterline. The euphoria brought by liberation had faded among *Jenny's* crew. There were no more defiant penny-gaff songs and they were shocked by the brutality of their penury. None recognised Dawlish as the ragged labourer who'd worked a day alongside them and he did not wish to embarrass them by recalling their humiliation.

Jenny lacked a mizzenmast now and both the mainmast's yards lay on the deck amid a tangle of cordage and canvas. It took hours to clear them. The mainyard was splintered beyond immediate repair but the topyard remained almost undamaged. But enough remained to fashion a rig that would allow slow and unhandy progress. Battle-damaged vessels suffering far worse in Nelson's era had made port safely. And that was what *Jenny* must now do, under sail. *Sprightly* could not spare the coal to tow her.

The work continued well into darkness. Another full day would be needed, with daylight essential for setting standing and running rigging. Before he turned in, Dawlish found himself summoned to Weatherby's cabin, was invited to sit, was offered a glass of wine.

"Would you be confident to bring the *Jenny* to Manzanillo?" Weatherby said.

Seize the moment. Ones like this seldom come in peacetime.

"Yes, sir."

"I wouldn't have asked if I'd thought otherwise." Weatherby smiled. "Captain Ridley will be in nominal command but in the state he's in, he's unlikely to interfere, so it'll be up to you. You'll have to be tactful with the poor old fellow but I'll trust you for that. I doubt if the crew will be worth much either but you'll have a dozen of *Sprightly's* men to support you."

"Thank you, sir."

"Then make a list of anything else you need. Ashton will see that it's passed across during the night. *Sprightly* will be leaving for Manzanillo at first light."

Better still. Not just confidence that I can sail her there but trust I can complete the jury rigging first.

But not easy, he knew. Failure would threaten on every mile of sluggish progress, but he'd cope with each problem as it came. What mattered was that, sooner or later, a report would arrive at an Admiralty desk in Whitehall and mention this. And, with luck, somebody would remember his name.

"I'll see you in Manzanillo in three or four days then. Slow and steady'll do it. That'll be all, Mr. Dawlish."

Dawlish stood to leave but Weatherby must have sensed his hesitation.

"Is there something else?"

Junior officers didn't query captains but, in the circumstances, Dawlish thought he could risk it without suggesting insubordination. The question had been nagging him.

"Did Captain Rogers mention *Jenny* being a prize, when you met him, sir?"

Weatherby reacted as a captain should. "None of your damn business, Dawlish!" But then his irritation faded. "No, he didn't say a word, or anything about salvage either. I didn't press him. So don't hang about, you've work to do."

"Thank you, sir."

But, when he reached the door, Weatherby called him back.

"I believe every word you've told me, Dawlish. You're an honourable young man. That's why it worries me."

And that must be why *Sprightly* would head for Manzanillo at dawn.

Weatherby trusts me and he's most certainly not trusting Rogers.

*

Sprightly entered Manzanillo's bay just before sunset four days later. Her passage had been slow but uneventful. The storm Dawlish had feared might materialise never did and, even with her improvised rig, *Jenny Dixon* ghosted on light airs, never exceeding four knots, a scorched and tattered red ensign flapping on a halyard. Captain Ridley had not shaken himself from his torpor and Jem Redshaw, first mate again, showed no reluctance to defer to Dawlish. He, like the rest of the barque's crew, was haunted by fears of an uncertain future.

"What's going to become of us at Manzanillo?" he asked and Dawlish could not answer, not even on the twentieth time of asking.

"We haven't a penny between us, and its not a port where we're likely to pick up another ship. Besides, if we're sticking with the *Jenny*, where's the money to pay for repairs?" Redshaw' words were flooding from him now. "An' need repairs, she damn well will. This bloody rig might get us to Manzanillo but I wouldn't trust it no further. There isn't a British consul there to help us, is there? No! I bloodywell didn't think there would be! An' Mexico'll be a bloodbath when the Juaristas win. They're damn well sure they will, and they're right, they'll have a score to settle with us and …"

Pity Redshaw as he did, Dawlish hardly heard him. By now the litany had become a familiar extended whine. A man who escaped alone in an open boat, and a crew that maintained cheerful defiance as captive forced labour, were defeated now. They did just short of what they were asked and without the presence of *Sprightly's* men on board it might have taken as long again to make port.

Sprightly and *Quetzal* were anchored at Manzanillo as if they had never left. No wisps of smoke drifted from their funnels. Neither boiler was fired, not even enough to maintain harbour pressure. Only one conclusion possible.

Neither intended departing soon.

*

When Dawlish made his report, Weatherby said, "Well done", and nothing more. That he treated *Jenny's* safe return as unexceptionable was a compliment. He had expected nothing else.

Dawlish sensed the increased confidence Weatherby radiated when last seen was still with him. So too did Ashton and Sanderson, who'd been asked to join them. Probably *Sprightly's* entire crew did also. Success in action, especially without casualties, had that effect.

"We'll do what we can for the poor wretches for now." Weatherby had listened without interrupting to Dawlish's account of the *Jenny's* crew's despair. "We'll feed 'em, and they'll have all the slops we can spare. But we need to get them and their ship out of here as fast as we can. They're liabilities, especially as things are at present."

Dawlish understood. He'd seen how *Sprightly's* stores had been depleted to get the barque this far.

"There's a small boatyard here and it's got timber stocks – we checked – and the railway's workshop can handle metal fittings," Weatherby said. "Our chippy's well capable of supervising the *Jenny's* repairs – he'll enjoy it in fact and it'll keep her crew out of mischief. But it's going to take money, more than I can advance against guarantees, more than *Sprightly* carries."

Weatherby was right to be concerned. Royal Navy captains were subject to ferocious analysis of their expenditures. *Sprightly* was too small to warrant a paymaster, but careless, though honest, accounting mistakes or bad decisions made in good faith could wreck careers. He glanced towards Ashton.

"We need coal," the first lieutenant said. "We devoured it on that little venture to Zihuantanejo. *El Ferrocarril del Pacífico* has it in quantity, anthracite, best quality Welsh, but her manager, Turnbull, is driving a hard bargain. We can only accept it."

Yet the prospect didn't seem to dishearten Weatherby. If anything, he seemed to relish it.

"As I see it, the Imperial Government has an obligation," he said. "It commissioned the *Jenny* to carry a cargo and sent her into harm's way. Captain Ridley fulfilled his part of the bargain. The late Captain Berchtold recognised that, and the obligation to save her. He was an honourable man and if he were alive now there wouldn't be a problem. The Imperial government, or the French on its behalf, is holding back *Glorioso* silver pending resolution of those nonsensical wranglings about royalty payments. The government has silver enough to pay for *Jenny's* repairs. We'll need to ensure it does."

Weatherby's going to grab another opportunity for appropriate action to defend British interests.

"We're not going to resolve it tonight," Weatherby said. "But there's something you may be able to help with tomorrow, Dawlish. Because Rogers isn't on board *Quetzal*. We're sure of that."

"As I visited Turnbull yesterday, a train was pulling out," Ashton said. "An engine with a sandbagged flatcar ahead and a single passenger coach behind and another flatcar with ex-Confederate guards. Turnbull made light of it when I asked. Rogers chartered it, he said, and was on it and going to report the Zihuantanejo affair to the Imperial authorities. Whether that meant Guzmán, Turnbull didn't know. But Rogers was certainly going as far as the railhead."

"There's probably more to it than that," Weatherby said. "Especially considering what you, Dawlish, heard talk of prize money or salvage. Your friend Welborne's been left in charge of *Quetzal*. Go across tomorrow and chat with him, casually, old friends yarning about what happened at Zihuantanejo. But be subtle, find out all you can about what Rogers is up to. See me before you go. I've a few other things to discuss but they can wait 'til morning. You look like you need a good night's sleep. Have that first."

*

Dawlish, washed and comfortable in the fresh clothing he had longed for since Zihuantanejo, was pulled across to *Quetzal* at noon next day. He had been spotted and Welborne met him at the entry port, smartly uniformed, linen immaculate. The deck was well-holystoned, the brasses gleaming, and a spotless canvas awning shaded the aftership. Even if his full command was temporary, Welborne was glorying in it. He invited Dawlish aft to the captain's saloon, offered brandy but, when declined, called for coffee instead. They sat back on richly upholstered chairs. Dawlish accepted a cigar from a silver box.

"Better quarters than in the old *Galveston*, ain't they, Nick?"

There had been only rusty bare surfaces on that ironclad, rushed to sea before completion to avoid seizure by the British government. The winter they served in her when she was the Danish *Odin* was been cold and comfortless.

Even when we weren't being shot at. And all for nothing. Only to be told I must forget it ever happened and accept posting to the Pacific Station until memories fade.

The town lay framed in the great windows at the transom. On the wooden-panelled bulkheads to either side were large paintings of a snowy mountain scene, the same castle seen from different viewpoints. They looked old.

"Berchtold's." Welborne had followed Dawlish's glance. "His ancestors owned that place for nine or ten generations. He never stopped reminding us. I guess we'll have to do our best to get the pictures back to his family when all this is over."

"How do you think it's going to be over, Travis?"

Welborne shrugged.

"It won't be long before the French pull out. We'll go with them. If Emperor Max wants to stay and take his chances with the Juaristas, there's nothing *Quetzal* can do to help him."

"What'll happen to her? Do you expect the French will take *Quetzal* over?"

Welborne shook his head. "She was bought with Max's personal money. I guess his family will want her back. We'll sail her to Austria and 'spect we'll be rewarded for it." He laughed. "They might even give us commissions. Or maybe make us Counts or Dukes or Lords or whatever they call 'em over there."

"Duke Jesse and Count Travis," Dawlish said. "You won't want to acknowledge your humble old shipmate Nick then."

"But money at the least." The lightness was gone from Welborne's tone. "We'll have earned it. Rogers is determined to be a damn sight more aggressive hunting down Juarista supply ships than Berchtold ever was, whether or not they have Yankee Navy protection."

"Prizes?"

"You're milking me now, Nick. I don't like it."

It felt as if the temperature had dropped five degrees in the warm cabin. And the sense of a friendship close to ending.

"*Jenny Dixon*," Dawlish said. "Rogers has his eye on her, hasn't he?"

"Your Captain Weatherby can talk to Rogers about that when he gets back."

"From Guzmán?"

"Yes. Guzmán." Welborne's tone was icy.

We've both grown up since Denmark. Just two years.

"If Weatherby sent you to find out, you're welcome to let him know that Rogers doesn't need his permission to go to nearest town with Imperial government presence. Just tell him Rogers' gone to report Berchtold's death and get confirmation of himself as *Quetzal's* captain."

A silence. An awareness, probably mutual, that a Rubicon had been crossed. Welborne broke it.

"Another cigar, Nick?" He reached out the silver box. "Genuine Havanas. Here, take a few for later."

"No, Travis. But thank you.". It was hard to say, and what had to follow was harder still. "Weatherby did send me with a message for Rogers. Informal and no need to have it on paper. Just a reminder that *Jenny Dixon's* flying a British flag and under British protection, *Sprightly's* protection. A dozen marines are on board to resist any unauthorised attempt to board her."

Dawlish stood to go.

"They were good days in *Odin*, Nick," Welborne said. "Hard at times, but good days."

"They were, Travis. Good days."

And neither made a movement to shake hands as Dawlish left.

185

Chapter 16

Dawlish reported his conversation with Welborne to Weatherby next morning. He was listened to without interruption. The one question asked at the end came as a surprise.

"Do you remember what Atkinson said about the value of a silver ingot when we were at *El Glorioso*?"

"About eight hundred dollars, sir."

"What I remembered too. Two hundred sterling."

That was the end of the interview, but Dawlish was sent for again late that evening. The scuttles in Weatherby's quarters were open but, even so, the air was still warm and heavy. He was in his shirtsleeves.

"No need for formality, Dawlish. You can take off your tunic if you wish. We've work to do."

Papers lay on his writing desk and more were arranged in what appeared to be in some order on his cot. Three closely printed books lay open there also.

Weatherby followed Dawlish's glance. "*Maritime Law* and *Admiralty Regulations* and *Acts of Parliament* and all of 'em damn well conflicting and confusing when it comes to our particular problem."

"Our problem, sir?" There seemed so many of them.

"*Jenny's* repairs. I'm depending on my own common sense to get 'em paid for."

Weatherby reached out a paper he'd picked up from his desk. It was in his own hand, clearly a draft letter, probably the result of earlier attempts and, even now, there were sentences crossed out and other wording inserted. No addressee, but the first few lines told that it could be for one recipient only.

"Is this for Colonel Durand, sir?"

"Just read it. We can put in the flowery greetings later."

Dawlish had tried, without success. to forget Clothilde but now the mention of her lover's – her master's – name brought a stab of misery. He read the draft's first paragraph.

"You're assuming the powers of a British consul, sir?"

"That's right, Dawlish. *Jenny's* British-registered. If there was a consul here, he'd have to handle the mess. There isn't, so I'm claiming the necessary authority."

He's sticking his neck out, gambling again. An action that would be approved afterwards only if it proved successful.

But there was something more audacious still. A proposal that, in view of a delay by the Imperial Mexican Government in release of silver mined by a British company, Plutus Mining Limited, a small portion be transferred to the acting British consul at Manzanillo under full assurance of subsequent reimbursement of outstanding royalties by Her Majesty's Government.

"Practical and simple, isn't it?" Weatherby sounded pleased. "It'll pay for *Jenny's* repair. The Admiralty can recover the costs from her owners afterwards. The Treasury will have to sort out that royalty business with Plutus and they in turn will settle with the Imperial Government."

It didn't sound simple. Lawyers spent years and earned fortunes arguing disputes about agreements that might appear practical to those outside the profession. Dawlish had heard his father state this countless times. But sub-lieutenants didn't lecture captains, especially when they were pleased with themselves.

"How much silver would be involved?" Dawlish said.

"Twenty ingots should be enough – no, let's make it twenty-five, five thousand sterling's worth. *Jenny's* repairs can't cost more than half that and we'll have something left in hand for unexpected expenses. They'd be weighed in the presence of a representative of each party and the outcome accepted and signed for. The value can be finalised later by reference to the market price per ounce on some specific date. We can let the bookkeepers back in Europe settle that in their own good time. We should be able to have the ingots in a week or less."

It might seem to Weatherby like an ethical and practical solution but he isn't entitled to make any such bargain. And Durand would laugh at the very idea.

"Your father's an attorney, isn't he, Dawlish?"

"A solicitor, sir." The other word implied lower social and professional standing.

"Much the same. You must know something about phrasing legal documents. I mean the 'heretofores' and 'asforesaids' and 'notwithstandings' and suchlike."

"I don't know much, sir. Almost nothing."

He'd never wanted to know. It was a relief that his elder brother had been given no choice but to follow in his father's footsteps. And feel trapped and unhappy as a consequence.

"You must have picked up something, Dawlish."

"I copied a few documents for him, sir, when I was last at home. That was all."

Even if recast in proper legal terms by an expert solicitor, this proposal would still sound bizarre. Success at Zihuantanejo has gone to Weatherby's head.

"We're in the country of the blind here, Dawlish, and you're the one-eyed man. You can redraft it better than I can – just a few impressive legal phrases here and there. Take this. It could help."

It was a thin volume with *'Admiralty Court Act, 1861'* on the spine.

"I can't make much head nor tail of it myself," Weatherby said, "but you might find something to make use of. But however you redraft the letter, don't change the substance of the terms. Just make it sound impressive."

"But Colonel Durand doesn't speak English, sir. We didn't meet any of his people who did."

"No problem about that, Dawlish. You're damn fluent in French, aren't you? The only man on board who is. When I'm satisfied with the English draft, you can translate it." He smiled. "And put in all the flattering expressions of respect to start and end with that Frenchmen like."

Cold fear was rising in Dawlish. He wanted to be gone from Mexico and from its cruelties and its horrors.

And from Clothilde.

"How will the letter be delivered, sir?"

But he had already guessed the answer.

"By you, Dawlish! No better man!"

His fluency in French, and growing competence in Spanish, were curses, Dawlish told himself. They had brought this misery on him. It was long after midnight now and he was working in his own narrow cabin. The few modifications he made to Weatherby's draft, modifying sentence-structure and inserting a few half-remembered legal phrases, passed muster, even impressed. Now he was translating the English into French. He'd have to bring four copies with him to Durand, two in English and two in French, already signed by Weatherby himself, and with instructions to return with Durand's signature on one of each. That would constitute a legally valid agreement, Weatherby had decided.

Three hours of effort had yielded several pages of restarts and modifications and rephrasing, always trying to imagine how it would appear to Durand. The thought of that man reading his work repelled him and worse still …

He tried to tear his mind away but failed.

He'd have to go to Guzmán and the possibility of a chance encounter with Clothilde filled him with disgust.

Sweat dropped from his forehead onto the paper, blotting the letters. The translation was as good by now as it ever could be, he decided. All that remained was to make a final version, containing all the changes. But it could wait a little. Ten minutes away from this stifling cabin would make no difference.

He went on deck, was saluted by a marine sentry and walked aft. The town lay as quiet in the moonlight as Zihuantanejo had been when he boarded the *Jenny* there. He lit a cigar, a humbler one than Welborne offered him what seemed an aeon ago, and leaned on the toprail. The prospect of travelling again to Guzmán still nagged him, the more so since the errand was a futile, even farcical, one.

And yet …

Weatherby was no fool, whether at sea or on land. It was he, not Berchtold, who had created the plan for recovering *Jenny Dixon* and her crew, mainly by convincing the Austrian it was his own idea. He'd carried it out, coldbloodedly, without loss. In the last year, he'd been successful in managing challenges at Nazareno and Novo-Arkhangelsk which had diplomatic and political complications. He was a good seaman and a good leader. His only failure while Dawlish had been in *Sprightly* was to secure Juarista assurances about the future of the *Glorioso* mining concession, and that was only because Durand had the power to block his onward travel.

British interests. Appropriate action.

The *Jenny Dixon* was an interest, and to save her now, he needed the *Glorioso* silver. And releasing even part of that silver would be a first step towards contesting the royalty increase and . . .

Weatherby wasn't giving up.

The chance of success might be slim, but what had he to lose?

Weatherby was competent and courageous, but his career was already in the doldrums. Something in his past – and probably unrelated to his professional capability – had seen him shunted to the Pacific Station. He was abstemious, though not a teetotaller, so it was unlikely to have been some inebriated blunder. He might have offended somebody in high places, or there could have been a woman involved. But success on this ill-defined venture to Mexico might well cancel whatever was held against him. *Jenny's* deliverance had been a first step to that. He needed a second.

And for that, Dawlish must go to Guzmán.

It might be a fool's errand, and for him distasteful, but he'd do his best. He owed that to a man whom he admired.

He cast the cigar butt overboard and turned back to complete fair copies of the translation.

*

Dawlish would travel to the railhead north of Colima in the same way Rogers had done a few days earlier. A locomotive, a single passenger car, and sandbagged flatcars at either end, protected by a dozen ex-Confederate guards.

"I considered sending a few marines with you, Dawlish," Weatherby had said. "But I thought Durand might consider it provocative. But you're friendly with those Confederate chaps. Damn fine fellows from what I've seen of 'em. And the French don't take exception to them. They can provide a guard to the railhead. I'll ask Turnbull to see to it."

For their services, as for the anthracite that *Sprightly* needed, the manager of *El Ferrocarril del Pacífico* demanded a high price. Weatherby could look forward later to close querying by Admiralty administrators.

The lightly loaded train would make quick time. It would arrive at Ciudad de Armería by nightfall, perhaps even reach the fortified halt between there and Colima. The railhead might be reached late the following day. When Dawlish had previously been up the track, the gruelling inclines that slowed the train carrying cargo for the mine to a crawl. The climb would be faster and easier now. The only obstacle to making such time was if Rogers' train was met on its way back to Manzanillo. There were just seven passing places along the entire route. Given the inclines, the train climbing from the coast would have to reverse to the nearest passed. A whole day could be lost.

"What about *El Serpiente* and his savages?" Dawlish asked Tom Bryce, who would command the guards.

"No problem from 'em recently. I've been up and down the track twice in the last three weeks without trouble. Rumours in the villages are that *El Serpiente* moved his band further north. And that he's wholly hand in glove with the Juaristas now to cut off Guzmán." He paused, looked concerned. "Where are you going once you've reached the railhead? *El Glorioso?*"

"No. Guzmán."

"How?"

"The French at the railhead will lend me a horse and escort." Dawlish tried to sound confident that they would. He had doubts. "It's official business. They'll help."

"Just pray they don't, Nick. It could be bad further north."

*

The locomotive had built steam through the early hours and the safety valve was close to lifting. Weatherby came to see the departure and for a last word with Dawlish.

"A sensitive matter, something best not put on paper. A warning for Durand – you can sugar-coat it as best you can but leave him in no doubt. The fellow will try to intimidate you. He'll probably ridicule your rank. But stick to your guns even if he threatens to have you frog-marched out."

He'd laugh about it to Clothilde afterwards. She might even see it.

"Mention the importance Her Majesty's government places on good relations with France. That the loan of the ingots would foster them further and that I'll ensure the credit for the friendly gesture goes to him. He'll have heard how the Prussians smashed Austria in a few weeks this summer. They're Europe's greatest land power now and France must know it'll be next in their sights. With that in view, good French relations with Britain will be worth gold, much less silver. He'll understand. He'll sign."

Careers are built on gambles like this, Dawlish tried to reassure himself. *If it succeeds, I'll share the glory. Nelson never held back.*

And a small, cold, inner voice reminded him that for every Nelson there must have been dozens of other officers, all now forgotten, who'd gambled and lost.

But the die was cast. Nothing for it now but play out the game.

*

Speed was as high as anticipated, limited only by the need to slow on tight curves. At a halt halfway to Armería – a passing-point, a water tower and little more, protected by an Imperial sergeant and a dozen soldiers – another train stood stationary on the section of double track there, taking on water.

"It's Rogers," Bryce said. "Coming back to Manzanillo."

The train was longer than when it left. An extra, decrepit, passenger car, had been attached. Dawlish guessed it was from those he'd previously seen idle at the railhead.

But what surprised him was the crowd. French troops in ragged uniforms were in the majority, many of them hobbling on crutches, a few one-legged, others with bandaged arms or heads. Two officers were marginally better clad, though one had lost an arm. There were civilians too, glad to be released from the heat in the enclosed cars, if only for an hour. All seemed dazed. Mexican men, who looked like minor officials, sweating in black suits and trying to keep their dignity. Women in European dress, bedraggled by heat and exhaustion, most French by their looks but a few Mexican. Several children ran about but the majority were too bewildered or too tired to play and stayed close to their mothers. Upwards of a hundred people in all.

Dawlish's train had no need to replenish water and he did not want to expose himself to questions from Rogers, so he wanted to move on quickly. But this crowd – it looked like the beginning of an evacuation – demanded explanation.

"Find Rogers," he said to Bryce. "And apologise for me. He winked. "I'm feverish and can't leave the train. I'm lying down. Ask him what's happening. Be fast about it. I want to be underway in ten minutes."

Rogers must see through the diplomatic lie. Bryce would probably tell him the truth anyway, one Confederate to another, but it didn't matter as long as he returned with clarification.

Dawlish remained, sweltering, in his own passenger car, studying the scene through the loopholes in the barricaded windows. It depressed him to see the listless children, the mothers comforting them, the maimed men, the ruined lives. An air of defeat and futility overlay it all.

And then his heart stopped. In the shadow of one of the coaches, two women – ladies, by the dresses that looked expensive even at a distance – were seated on small folding stools. One was stoutly built but the other slim and graceful. They were half- turned away from Dawlish and their wide-brimmed straw hats, the younger's adorned with ostrich feathers, hid their faces. A wicker picnic hamper lay on the ground between them and a servant in Mexican attire was attending a small silver spirit-stove, brewing what must be coffee. They sat as if holding themselves apart from the surroundings, straight-backed, ignoring the heat and dust and as elegant in their manners as if entertaining in their own parlours.

Clothilde!

The anger and regret he had tried to forget was back again, but more painful, more bitter than before. So too memories of Pau, of the happy, innocent, months together, of her gentle mother, of his uncle's love for the girl he regarded as a daughter. Hurt as it did, he could not tear his gaze away.

The maidservant was rising from the stove, handing them cups and saucers from the hamper, then bending again to raise a coffee pot. She served the heavier woman first but the other, when she reached out her saucer, turned her head.

And she was not Clothilde.

But that did not ease the pain. He realised then that her degradation would torture him for years, perhaps forever. And she was still in Guzmán. He might have to endure the agony of meeting her there with Durand, have to bow to her as to a stranger, have to repress his disgust at her cold calculation.

It was a relief when Tom Bryce returned.

"They're being sent down to wait for a ship," he said. "Durand wants them out of Guzmán."

Useless mouths. The cruel but accurate term that, throughout history, described the wounded, the ailing and the dependents. Everybody unable to participate in active defence but consuming essential supplies.

"What ship?" Dawlish said.

"French. Even Rogers was surprised to hear it."

"When's it expected?"

"He doesn't know. Not for a while he thinks. The French commander in Guzmán – Durand, isn't it? – was tight about it. There are a few officers and Imperial officials on the train. They've orders to find accommodation for these people in Manzanillo."

"More coming?"

"Rogers doesn't know that either. But he thinks it's likely. The Juaristas are closing in on Guzmán. Maybe Durand's preparing for a siege. Or it could be he wants to skedaddle before it's too late. Either way he won't want to be saddled with sick or weak or wounded."

"Did Rogers let anything slip about *Quetzal?*"

"Only that's he's confirmed as captain. He's damn proud of it."

More questions than answers.

Time to press on to Armería.

*

They arrived an hour before sundown, with time enough in hand to press on to the next halt up the line. But Dawlish decided against it. Better to spend the night inside the cactus fence and with the protection of the ex-Confederate guards stationed here.

Sleep didn't come until the early hours and, even then, it was restless. Memories of Clothilde, and fear of meeting her, were a torment. Watered and coaled, the train pulled out again at dawn and the climb towards Colima commenced. Though lightly loaded, progress was slower than expected, not least because of frequent stops to scan the track ahead for signs of blockage. The memory of the Belgian bodies found on this sector were still fresh, regardless of any information that *El Serpiente's* force had moved north.

El Volcán de Colima's lazily drifting smoke was in sight but the day's delays were such that Colima itself could not be reached before sundown. The night had to be spent at another passing-point, one lacking the protection of even a cactus fence or dispirited Imperial troops. The hours of darkness, spent in nervous watch, seemed endless. But dawn did come in the end and at eleven next morning the train pulled into Colima, took on water and advanced to the railhead without incident.

After this, Dawlish would be dependent on French cooperation alone.

Chapter 17

Major Flandin, in command at the railhead, was surprised by Dawlish's arrival. He was cordial and didn't question his reason for going to Guzmán nor did he refuse the request for loan of a horse and for an escort. It was official business. That was enough.

"It must be tomorrow, though," he said. "Most of the dragoons are on patrol. They're out every day, protecting everything that moves between here and Guzmán. And you, Lieutenant Dawlish, you'll join me for dinner."

Dawlish was allocated the same spartan accommodation as before. Bryce would remain in the train and wait until Dawlish's return in two or three days' time.

Much had changed within the small fortress. There seemed to be fewer troops than before but a new cluster of tenting and adobe shacks, with foul-smelling latrines too close to them, had sprung up inside the perimeter. The mix of their occupants was the same as seen around Rogers' stationary train, useless mouths with an air of exhausted bewilderment and fear. They'd arrived last evening from Guzmán and were waiting for a train to Manzanillo, a French dragoon lieutenant named Nadaud told Dawlish. They'd have to wait longer, he said. An important person was coming from Guzmán tomorrow and would have priority. There'd be a lot of baggage. A locomotive was being readied at Colima and would arrive that evening with a specially prepared passenger car. It would need a heavy guard, French, not Confederate, when it departed for Manzanillo. There were few enough here already, Nadaud said, and the railhead defences would be weakened. It was the first time Dawlish had heard of French troops being used like this.

Flandin proved a good host that evening and Dawlish didn't need to probe. The Frenchman volunteered that a well-entrenched outpost north of Guzmán had been surrounded, bombarded and stormed. The Juaristas had withdrawn but, before leaving, bayonetted, every man not killed in the fighting. It was the first time they'd concentrated so much artillery in this area, an indication heavier forces were advancing on Guzmán from Guadalajara. In the circumstances, it was reasonable, Flandin said, to move wounded and dependents down to Manzanillo. A Colonel Macquart would take command there.

Dawlish mentioned that he'd heard of a French ship being due at the port. Was an evacuation in prospect? Flandin wouldn't be drawn. It would be better to raise the matter with Colonel Durand. He also evaded answering Dawlish's question about the security of the road, *El Camino Real*, between the railhead and Guzmán. There'd been a few more attacks along it, he said, but all minor and easily repulsed. Probably *El Serpiente's* brigands. But it necessitated patrolling the track more intensively than before, especially with so many vulnerable people being brought here. Dawlish would encounter some tomorrow when he was riding to Guzmán.

Flandin was clearly unwilling to pursue the matter further and he asked Dawlish about Zihuantanejo – he'd heard something of it from Rogers when he passed through. Dawlish realised he'd taken a glass too many of Flandin's wine and was being less than modest about his own part. Feeling guilty, he compensated by giving full credit to Grover for his achievement ashore. But the tale, and afterwards shared reminiscences about Pau and its society, passed the evening pleasantly. Only as he left did he ask, as if casually, if the mine's accumulated silver was still here.

And it was.

Under armed guard.

*

A full troop of dragoons set out on *El Camino* for Guzmán at first light. It was better that Dawlish should follow an hour later, Flandin had said. Anybody without business on the road would have been cleared off it by then. Dawlish's escort was formed of the same dragoon sergeant, Morvan, and the same three dragoons, with whom he had ridden before. None seemed either pleased or sorry to see him.

The first two posts passed were more heavily protected with sandbags than before. The next was new, situated at a stone bridge over a dry stream. A few houses that stood close by had been tumbled to yield adobe bricks for the fortification and their tiny vegetable patches were overgrown. All three posts were more heavily manned than any seen previously. The necessary infantry could only have come from the railhead garrison – it was unlikely Guzmán could spare them. *El Camino Real* was obviously considered under serious threat.

It became even more noticeable when they passed through two small villages previously inhabited. A new post was established at one and both were not only deserted but their wretched adobe shacks had been levelled.

Half-way now and nothing had yet been seen coming from Guzmán. Dawlish fought to stay alert for signs of danger, as the escort was doing, but gloom was weighing on him. He dreaded what would probably be a difficult meeting with Durand, though he'd do his best. The chance of seeing Clothilde worried him even more.

The sun was still climbing and growing hotter by the hour. On long sections, the brush to either side had been deliberately burned back for-fifty yards or more to deny cover to attackers. From beyond the blackened ground came the loud shrill of crickets and grasshoppers. The next post would be that where the massacre of its occupants had occurred, and where Dawlish had seen Colonel Durand inflict such indiscriminate retribution. Now it was fortified again, Morvan said, a good place to eat and rest before continuing.

It was still a mile ahead when a single shot rang out from somewhere behind and the trooper just ahead of Dawlish fell against the side of his horse's neck. The startled beast dashed forward, dislodging the body from the saddle and dragging it, head bouncing on the track, before the stirrup-leather tore free. The riderless horse was galloping away as the next shots, four or five, came in quick succession. Dawlish looked back and saw horsemen, eight or ten, spilling from the brush at one side of the track, as many again from the other, clouds of black ash churning about their hooves.

Sergeant Morvan swung his mount around, had taken in the onslaught, was reaching for his sabre and shouting to the others to gallop for their lives. Dawlish followed and, as he passed the fallen rider's body, saw that it lay broken, face up, eyes locked open and staring sightless towards the burning sun. Morvan was drumming behind him and the two other dragoons were already far ahead. The urge to glance back was overwhelming as well as stupid, but Dawlish yielded and saw the riders behind had reached the track and were pounding up it, those further back hidden in swirling dust. Morvan yelled to keep going, not look back, that the guard post ahead was near.

Now another ripple of fire ahead, one of the horses collapsing with flailing hooves, its dragoon pitching forward over its head, then trying to rise, before a volley from the brush to either side cut him down. The horseman close behind was still driving his mount onwards, skirting the fallen horse and rider. Shots crackled but he was through, unscathed, and disappearing around a bend seconds later.

The chasing hooves sounded like thunder to Dawlish and he too had no option but to urge his mount ever faster, though it was already at its limits. He only had his pistol, useless in these circumstances. A hundred yards ahead, a figure was darting from the brush, reaching the middle of the track, dropping to one knee, raising a rifle. Fifty yards now and Dawlish could see he wasn't wearing Juarista uniform. A huge sombrero shadowed his face and bandoliers crisscrossed his chest.

The other rifles had fallen silent – this man must be respected, even renowned, and entitled to claim this moment of insane bravado. The track was narrow, and there was little room to weave, but the rifleman's muzzle followed every slight deviation in the onward rush. The range was almost point-blank, but he was still holding fire, a demonstration of cold, deadly, courage that would be remembered for years. But Dawlish still drove on, his only hope the other's nerve would fail as he drew closer.

Then movement to Dawlish's left, Sergeant Morvan drawing level, then five strides ahead and holding there, sabre held up diagonally across his body for a downward slice to his right. The rifleman was swinging his weapon towards him and firing.

And missing.

Morvan bore down on the man, now leaping to the right. Horse and rider shaved past and the sabre stroke that should have bitten deep between neck and shoulder met only air. The escape brought the rifleman blundering into Dawlish's path.

An instant then to pull the horse's head over, to see terror on a scarred and moustachioed upturned face. Dawlish felt his right boot smashing into the man's shoulder, spinning him, throwing him down.

Rifle-fire crackled again. Figures – they seemed like dozens – were emerging from the brush and firing from the open. The thunder of hooves from behind seemed even closer than before. Dawlish crouched over his mount's neck and Morvan was twenty yards ahead, his pace unchecked. Now the rifles were falling silent – the bulk of that force must have been passed – but there was no let-up in the mounted pursuit. The only shots now sounded like the riders behind letting loose with pistols with little chance of a hit.

A bend ahead passed between higher ground on either side. As Dawlish and Morvan rounded it the sound of pursuit dulled by a fraction but did not let up. Beyond the turn, the track lay dead straight, and the post's sandbag redoubt was clearly visible. But there was movement ahead, more horsemen, eight or ten of them, halted on the track. Some were pulling carbines from bucket holsters, swinging from their saddles and disappearing into the brush at a crouch. Two men remained mounted, were taking the reins of the riderless horses and were dragging them into cover further back.

French dragoons!

They were lost to sight in the brush before the beat of following hooves strengthened again – the pursuing horsemen had also rounded the bend. Morvan was past the point where the dragoons had disappeared into cover. He was not slowing and he made no acknowledgment that he had seen them. Instead, he tore on, Dawlish following, leading the unwitting horsemen behind into the ambush.

The hoofbeats were louder again, growing closer. The riders could see the post ahead and Dawlish and Morvan racing towards it. Pistol-shots sounded, as futile as before, but evidence of determination to bring them down before reaching safety. Dawlish, heart thumping, mouth dry with fear, pounded on – he must be close to, or past, the hidden dragoons.

And, suddenly, a voice shooting somewhere behind and to his left. *"Tirez!"*

Then the fusillade, not individual shots but the simultaneous blast of disciplined professionals. And another, and another.

Dawlish didn't draw rein, not for another fifty yards, but then wheeled around and saw a horse and rider lying motionless on the track behind. Another beast was trying to rise, screaming in agony as it fell back, its rider crumpled before it. A cloud of dust beyond told of the erstwhile pursuers now in retreat.

Morvan had halted and was trotting back. Two men were emerging from the brush. The first was the lieutenant, Nadaud, with whom Dawlish had spoken at the railhead the previous day. He must be in command of the troop that left there early this morning. Following him was the dragoon from Dawlish's escort who'd survived the ambush's first fury and escaped up the track.

"How many?" Nadaud addressed Morvan.

"The fifteen or sixteen you've seen. But more, a lot more, I think, under cover."

"You're lucky Bechard reached us." Nadaud gestured towards the dragoon who'd ridden ahead. "Five minutes later and they'd have had you. We'd halted at the post and were about to continue for Guzmán."

Nadaud sent Bechard to summon the dragoons still in cover and bring the horses. It was essential to get back to the post's defences.

Dawlish followed Nadaud and Morvan to the first downed horse, its head bloody, already dead. Its rider lay alongside, unwounded but no less dead, head twisted at an impossible angle, neck broken. Civilian peasant clothing, bandoliers, boots of soft, untanned, leather. Not a Juarista regular. His holster held a revolver Morvan identified as a *Lefaucheux* – French issue.

The other wounded animal, was trying to rise on a smashed foreleg and falling back, its cries heart-piercing. Dawlish could not bear to listen. He drew his pistol, forced himself to come close enough to feel its terror, and aimed for the point where diagonals from each ear to the opposite eye crossed, then fired into it. The great body shuddered and slumped, quivered one last time and was still. Only now did Dawlish hear its rider's moans. He'd thought him dead but the man was clutching his bloodied stomach, a dark pool on the ground beneath. Lost in his despair and agony, he didn't seem to notice Dawlish's presence.

He can't live. Can I deny him the mercy I gave his horse?

Nadaud saved him from the dilemma.

"You see those boots?" He pointed. They were proper riding boots, the same as he wore himself. "And that revolver? Another *Lefaucheux*." He pulled it from its holster and called Morvan. "Hold him up, sergeant."

Dragged by the hair to a half-sitting position, the wounded man was gasping, eyes open in terror as well as pain.

"Where did you get your boots, amigo?" Nadaud asked in Spanish. "And this?" He raised the *Lefaucheux*.

The prisoner didn't answer.

Nadaud stood back for space enough to kick him hard in the crutch. He ignored the scream, bent close to his face.

"You took them from a Frenchman, didn't you? Was he dead yet or did you and your amigos take your time to finish him?"

The man was trying to shake his head in denial but Marvan held it tight by the hair.

"How many of you?"

A gasp that might have been *ochenta*, eighty.

"That's a lot. You're sure?"

A gurgle. "*Más o menos.*"

"Who's leading?"

A gasping mumble.

"Again. Who?" Pistol raised to whip across the face.

This time the answer was just understandable.

"Belarra." A moan. "Javier Belarra."

Dawlish had heard it once before, remembered who he was.

El Serpiente.

Who'd served the French until recently. The boots and revolver might have been acquired through barter, even donation.

"Stand aside, sergeant." Nadaud cocked the revolver.

Dawlish stood and walked away. He heard the shot and didn't look back.

They'd have given us even less mercy.

Now a fast canter towards the post.

Brief rifle-fire crackled from behind. The *ochenta* – there might well be that many – had reached the high ground there and were shooting. The range was too long and there were no casualties.

But notice had been given that, for now, the road back to the railhead was impassable.

*

This post, about halfway between the railhead and Guzmán, had been reconstructed since Dawlish last saw it in the aftermath of the previous attack on it. A third sand-bag redoubt, a hundred yards beyond, now supplemented those at either side of the track. Well-sited for mutual support, it also commanded the head of a shallow ravine gouged into the slope to the left and disappeared into brush at its lower end sixty or eighty yards below. Two miles westwards, the ground rose again towards the bare slopes of *El Volcán*.

The perimeter was surrounded by cactus fencing or shallow trenches filled with thorn brush. The ground outside was burned back for a hundred yards, in places more. Two new adobe buildings had replaced the one destroyed in the earlier raid. The stock-pen was almost empty but for a few mules and cavalry remounts. There was a new well and watering troughs by its side. The low mound over the long grave where the earlier defenders were buried was already mottled with weeds.

"It's too dangerous to press on towards Guzmán," Nadaud told Dawlish. The French regular sergeant who commanded the post concurred. All his men, French and Imperial infantry alike, had been in the redoubts, awaiting attack, since the first sounds of the ambush.

"If Belarra has men south of here, then he probably has them to the north as well," he said. "But they'll hesitate to attack the column coming from Guzmán. It'll have a powerful escort."

"When's it due?" Dawlish asked.

"Late afternoon. It's slow, it will have wagons with it. It will have to stay here overnight. If it meets serious resistance, it'll turn back. Those are always the orders."

Nadaud told the infantry sergeant to stand down half of the men in the redoubts – he wanted them alert for night duty. In the darkness, *El Serpiente's* people might well come closer.

The dragoons were unsaddling their horses and leading them to watering. They'd done well, had earned it. He owed his life to them, Dawlish thought as he walked with Nadaud to one of the adobe huts to eat there. When he lifted a cup of coffee his hand was shaking. Excitement had sustained him during the dash for safety and joy of deliverance engulfed him immediately after. But that was gone now and realisation of how close he'd come to death – very unpleasant death, if he'd been captured –replaced it.

It's not my fight. I'd have died for nothing.

Dawlish sensed Nadaud was more worried than he admitted. They lapsed into silence.

Until Belarra, *El Serpiente,* chose to withdraw, the track back to the railhead was blocked. It would take infantry, with artillery support, to dislodge him and the railhead garrison could scarcely spare either.

"But he'll go," Nadaud said. "There'll be a few shots in the night to give cover for his withdrawal, so we'll keep our heads down. With luck you can be in Guzmán tomorrow and –"

He didn't finish the sentence. Gunfire, this time from the north.

Not rifle-fire alone but the deeper boom of artillery. And *El Serpiente* had none.

The column en route from Guzmán was under attack.

Juarista attack.

Chapter 18

The sound was similar to that of the light field gun *Sprightly* carried for use by landing parties. Dawlish said as much.

"American six-pounder," Nadaud said. "We've seen them before. The Yankees are supplying them to Juarez. Easy to transport. They might even have brought them in pieces with mules."

They could hear now there were two of them, firing twenty or thirty seconds apart, then a minute's pause, then the same sequence. And the rifle-fire was coming in volleys, a degree of discipline about it that had been absent in *El Serpiente's* fusillades.

The post-commander was shouting for the troops who had so recently been sent to rest before night-duty to join those already in the redoubts. Nadaud was allocating half of his troop to supplement them and directing the others to resaddle.

It was easy – and horrific – to imagine what must be happening up the track. Juarista artillery and supporting infantry hidden in ambush and allowing the column moving southwards to pass unscathed. A second force, perhaps supplemented by some of Belarra's brigands, in hiding two or three hundred yards further south. Only when trapped, unsuspecting, between the two enemy forces, would fire open on the slow-moving French column.

Then six-pounder shells dropping on the track at the column's rear, explosive to panic the horses, shrapnel to lash their riders. The first ripples of rifle-fire from cover, riders spilling from their saddles, mounts collapsing. An onward dash towards illusory safety, wagons slewing, an attempt to form a rear guard perhaps, and a few confused souls frozen in shocked disbelief. *Dear God! Let there not be women and children there!* And then the leaders of the flight plunging into the fire of the other ambush just beyond. The six-pounders would be shifting aim, ever so slightly, raining destruction on what was left of the column.

And so it must have been, for the fire petered out within ten minutes, individual shots at the last, all too likely the cold execution of survivors.

Dawlish joined Nadaud.

"They're sealing off Guzmán," the dragoon lieutenant looked shocked. "We had reports they were bring up more artillery, heavier, maybe twelve pounders, more infantry."

"What about the column? You told me somebody important was coming with it. Who are they??"

"I don't know. The Juaristas probably know better than we do. They've supporters everywhere." Nadaud began to move away, hesitated, and came back. "I'm taking a few men up the *Camino* in case any survivors from the column have slipped through. With Belarra's *salauds* to our south, this post's undermanned already." He looked hard at Dawlish.

Silence. The unasked question hung in it. Would Dawlish join the defence? Every man would be needed.

It's not my fight. Not Britain's either.

And the memory of those tortured bodies of those Belgian deserters returned unbidden.

French or Imperial or British, El Serpiente's devils won't distinguish.

"Give me a rifle," Dawlish said. He already had his revolver.

To put in my mouth if it comes to the worst.

*

Nadaud rode north with a half-dozen men. Dawlish stationed himself in the most northerly of the redoubts and found both surprise and acceptance from its occupants. At irregular intervals, a flurry of individual rifle-shots rang out from the densely vegetated ridge to the south, the brigands there serving notice they were still in place. The range was too great for accuracy. Other than a few rips in sandbags and small earth-fountains erupting from the walls of the adobe buildings, no harm was done. A half-hour passed – no sound of shooting. Nadaud must still be advancing up *El Camino* with infinite care.

Then, from the north, what might have been the roll of very distant thunder. It faded, was back, was growing again, was dying to nothing, was returning, was settling down to a steady rumble.

Dawlish recognised it, had known and been terrified by it at much closer range when he'd served in Denmark. It was the sound of heavy artillery bringing down fire on defended positions, on earthworks or entrenchments, prelude to direct assault. This was not the fire of the six-pounders that had smashed into the column on *El Camino*. It could only herald an attack on one or more of Guzmán's outer defensive redoubts.

And perhaps the beginning of a siege.

Then rifle-fire rattling from the north, close, very close. All eyes shifted to the point where *El Camino* disappeared around a bend. A plume of dust was rising above the brush, drawing closer.

A single wagon burst into sight, drawn by two horses, its driver somehow keeping his seat and lashing with a long whip as it swayed and skidded in the turn. Three riders behind – not Nadaud's dragoons, but two in plain blue uniforms and the other wearing the blue and red colours of Durand's guards. All crouched over their mounts' necks, at the gallop. They were on the straight run to the post now, dust swirling behind them. At any moment Dawlish expected to see Nadaud and his men pounding around the bend but instead heard a small volley of carbine-fire, the same unmistakable bark that had saved him during his own flight hours earlier. A pause, another volley, another again, then silence. Only when the wagon and its foam-lathered horses were shuddering to a halt past the redoubt did Nadaud and his men emerge into sight, slowing to a canter, their pursuers driven to flight.

The three other riders were drawing rein. Dawlish went with the post-commander to meet them. The two blue-uniformed riders took no notice they neared and were helping the third dismount.

A swirl of red, not breeches but a long skirt, though she had been riding astride.

Her face was covered by a veil but even before she swept it away Dawlish knew who it could only be.

Clothilde.

207

She recognised him immediately, but looked past without acknowledgement. The same message she'd given him in Guzmán.

I'm dead to you and you to me.

*

Nadaud invited Clothilde into shade at the huts. Dawlish stood to one side, torn between the desire for retreat and the shame of standing his ground.

She ignored them both, was concentrated on telling the two riders who had arrived with her, privates both, to find canvas to shield the baggage in the wagon. The cover had been lost during the flight and the valises, hat boxes and leather travelling cases would suffer from the intense sunlight, she said. Then she turned to Nadaud – no word of thanks for having rescued her from close pursuit a quarter hour before – and demanded fresh horses be provided immediately for the wagon, and an escort to bring her to the railhead. She'd no intention of spending the night at this wretched post.

Nadaud told her there were brigands lying in ambush south of here, close enough to have opened desultory fire on this post at intervals. And this English officer – he gestured to Dawlish though Clothilde didn't turn her head – had had a narrow escape from them, just this morning. Two others hadn't. That was maybe so, she said, but couldn't a single messenger get through somehow to the railhead? No doubt there were troops enough there to collect her in safety?

And, all the while, Dawlish saw Nadaud, seasoned and ruthless though he was, had a note of pleading in his explanations. He knew who she was, and feared her for that. He persisted with patience, took no offence at her scornful dismissals of difficulties. At last, with bad grace, she consented to wait in the nearer adobe hut. Nadaud led her and jerked his head to Dawlish to join them. His expression told that he wanted somebody to divert her ire.

Yet, for all Clothilde's selfish arrogance, for all the repulsion Dawlish felt, it was impossible not to admire her. That she'd recently survived a massacre had not shaken her. The artillery shells had fallen on the column as if from nowhere and amid the chaos she had raced ahead without a backward glance, her only concern the preservation of the wagon laden with her baggage.

What had happened to the remainder of her escort, Nadaud asked. The troop of dragoons? The company of plodding Imperial infantry?

She shrugged. They'd been unlucky, that was all.

Dawlish spoke and knew that, if he did not, remembrance of silent acceptance of her treatment of himself and Nadaud would haunt and humiliate him forever. Why was she traveling to Manzanillo, he asked. Was it unsafe to remain in Guzmán, was it the beginning of an evacuation?

"I remember you. I saw you with your commander when he came to Guzmán. You were his translator, weren't you?" She made it sound as if he'd been a lackey. "You speak French well enough for an Englishman," she said. "And as for –"

He cut her off. "I learned it in Pau, madame," he said. "I stayed there for a few months with my uncle when I was a boy."

No flicker of emotion on her face when she spoke.

"As to why I'm going to Manzanillo, I can also ask you, lieutenant – that's your rank, is it not? – why you're going to Guzmán? Your answer will be the same as mine. That you've business there. And that it's none of mine."

She turned to Nadaud. "Have somebody brew coffee for me. And send someone to fetch a small valise from the wagon – white kid leather with a monogram, CS in gold. Carefully. I don't want it scratched. And there must be a room where I can rest. If there isn't a bed there, get one. And warm water for washing."

From the north, artillery still rumbled, heavier now, probing Guzmán's defences. Clothilde must have heard it too, but she made no remark.

"Is there some woman here who can assist me?" she demanded.

"You didn't bring a maid, madame?" Dawlish said.

"She was on a mule. She wasn't fast enough to keep pace with me when the gunfire started."

No hint of concern or regret.

Nadaud was apologising that there were no women here but if –

He froze.

A report from the south, the unmistakable sound of a six-pounder, such as had opened the earlier attack on the column, but nearer. Dawlish was counting, one, two, three seconds . . .

And then the explosion somewhere outside.

The maximum range's about fourteen hundred yards!

Some shell fragment must have pounded against the wall's exterior, not penetrating, but shaking a choking cloud of adobe-dust off its inner surface.

"Stay here!" Dawlish yelled at Clothilde and then rushed with Nadaud to the door. He could already hear horses panicking in the stock pen, men shouting. Blinking in the sunlight, their eyes locked onto the scrub-clad ridge to the south. And yes! Some two hundred yards to the left of the *Camino*, birds were wheeling in alarm and grey smoke was dispersing above the scrub.

Too far distant to reach with rifle-fire.

"Juarista regulars." A tremor in Nadaud's voice. "God knows how many of them. Maybe just a single gun…"

But there could be more than just one fast-moving six or eight mule team with weapons carried in sections to reinforce *El Serpiente*. With two or three in place to the south, this position could be pulverised within an hour.

Derisive cheering now from the ridge, cross-bandoliered figures showing themselves and shaking weapons. There must be others closer, still under cover.

A small crater close to the mound above the graves, still smoking, showed where the shell had fallen. No damage done but the blast had stripped leaves from a nearby tree. Terrified horses were milling around in the pen – one down however. No human bodies though and anybody not inside a redoubt when the shell had fallen was in one now. They offered some protection against any but one dropping directly into them.

Nadaud looked back towards the adobe huts – a hit on either would collapse it – and shouted to Dawlish.

"Get that woman out. And in there!" He pointed to the nearest earthwork, that sited at the head of the ravine.

Dawlish ran back, saw Clothilde just inside the door, looking out, not cowering. He grabbed her by the arm,

"Hurry! They'll fire again at any moment."

Red skirt hitched high – he saw riding boots beneath – she ran with him towards the redoubt, rounded the sandbagged barrier outside the entrance and gained the interior. The space was roughly hexagonal, eight yards across at its maximum, and the walls, loop-holed and sloped, were some eight feet high, firesteps in place to allow shooting across the parapets.

There were a dozen and a half there, Imperial and French infantry of the post's garrison and eight dragoons, Sergeant Morvan among them. He'd taken command of the redoubt, he said. A rifle at every loophole, and the dragoons with carbines crouching on the firesteps.

"Sit there!" Dawlish forced Clothilde down on a low stack of ammunition boxes, two buckets of water, with a dipper, by its side. She didn't protest but was fumbling under her skirt. He looked away in embarrassment, but others did not. When he glanced back – feeling guilty as he did – he saw a small two-barrelled pistol in her hand. It must be a Derringer, he thought, the name notorious since one had killed the American president the previous year. She must have foreseen the possibility of capture and carried the weapon inside a boot top. Like himself, she was determined not to be taken alive. She caught his glance and, for the first time, smiled.

He nodded and felt stronger admiration. She had resolution and, if frightened, as she must be, was hiding it. There might indeed have been some truth in her mother's story of a father killed in Algeria. Courage was often inherited.

Another report, Dawlish counting again, four seconds that lasted four centuries, and then the blast somewhere outside. No fragments plunging into the redoubt, probably not into the others either, for there was no shouting and the horses' shrill whinnying sounded more of terror than of pain.

Dawlish heaved himself up to look across the parapet, saw smoke drifting above the same area of brush as before.

How long since the previous shot? Three minutes? Certainly not less. The fire must then be from a single weapon, for if there had been another, they would be opening in sequence, dropping a shell each minute.

Scant comfort though.

Almost three hours of daylight left, time enough for even a single six-pounder to wreak havoc.

And, yet after that second shell, Dawlish sensed fear lessen a fraction in those around him. Relief flickered on faces that had burrowed into to the wall in expectation of the next shell. Now it had fallen, they knew they were unscathed and there was hope the sandbags would continue to protect them.

Cheering again from the ridge. Dawlish and Morvan looked over the parapet, saw Nadaud doing the same from the redoubt to the right. Shouted assurances of no casualties. But the horses were frantic in the pen, their cries and terror piteous. Another beast was down and yet another dashed about, flank torn by a shell fragment.

Two minutes passed – more than enough to load a six-pounder, but the gunners must be taking their time to adjust their aim. Mule-carried shells and charges would be in short supply, too precious to drop anywhere other than into a redoubt's interior.

Now the next shell, again a miss, but when Dawlish looked again, it had been close enough to blast a small crater close to Nadaud's redoubt. There could be two minutes at least until the next . . .

But it didn't come.

Not yet.

For rifles were sounding from the brush beyond the blackened cordon of burned ground. Not volleys but individual shots, spaced and most likely carefully aimed. Dawlish raised his head for seconds only, saw thinning smoke above the scrub at two, three, four locations – no men in sight – and then ducked down again.

Sergeant Morvan had moved toward the entrance, was crouched by the barrier there, and now yelled, fury in his voice.

"The horses! They're aiming for the horses!"

Dawlish joined him, feeling anger and horror. It was hard to kill a horse with small arms fire, their bulk large and the vital organs deep within. But they could suffer.

And they were suffering now, trapped, plunging, kicking, screaming, beating themselves against the high rails, one trying to jump, failing to clear the upmost rail, falling and thrashing, then trampled by others' pounding hooves.

The pen's gate was a twenty-second sprint away and five more would swing the gate open . . .

"We can release them!" Dawlish shouted at Morvan.

The dragoon sergeant blocked his path.

"They'll scatter and jump those!" He pointed to the trenches filled with thorn brush. "We won't get them back. And we can't get away without them."

"But –"

"It's a hard world, lieutenant, for beasts no less than men." In the voice more regret, more emotion, than could have been expected from that grim Breton peasant sergeant.

Terrible as it was, the logic was unarguable.

A few minutes longer – two more horses down on broken legs, others rushing in brief spurts, blood streaming bright on a dapple grey and dark on a bay, a mule kicking and biting in their midst, a hell unleashed on innocents, a torment for any who loved such noble creatures.

Then silence.

Sudden realisation that it was not just the rifles but that the six-pounder had been quiet for far longer.

Now, from the south, slightly muffled by the intervening ridge, rifle-fire was crackling again. It rose and fell, rose again, now sporadic, now with some degree of discipline.

Only one explanation possible.

Something was moving north along *El Camino* towards this position and under fire.

Dawlish turned to Clothilde.

213

"Stay! You'll be safe here." He saw for the first time what might have been a trace of fear. "I'm coming back!"

Dawlish? pushed past Morvan and dashed to Nadaud's redoubt. He found him on the firestep, surveying the ridge through binoculars.

Nadaud handed him the glasses.

"Look there," he said. "On the crest."

Just below it, where the scrub thinned, a knot of uniformed men was heaving on the wheel-spokes of a small artillery piece and others ahead were lashing the mules that were drawing it up the slope.

"Juaristas," Nadaud said. "They must have outflanked us to the east."

"And Belarra's people?"

"Across the crest already. We're not their concern, not for now. They rushed across at the first sound of fire from their lookouts on the far side of the ridge."

"Relief from the railhead?"

"Almost certainly," Nadaud said. "The sound of cannon attacking us must have reached Major Flandin. He's sending a force north to find what's happening."

"How strong could it be?"

"Too few to get through. Flandin's already short of infantry for manning the railhead's earthworks. And almost all dragoon units are somewhere along this track."

"And they'll retreat?"

Nadaud shook his head. "Any force Flandin sends will have orders to hold its ground if fired on. They'll be in cover in brush by now, around where you were ambushed."

The six-pounder was silhouetted on the crest, then slipping from view, onto the opposite slope. Within minutes, Flandin's relief force would have more than rifle-fire to keep them pinned in cover.

"And you intend to hold here?"

Nadaud shook his head. "Suicide. They'll be attacking here again once they realise Flandin's force isn't budging. But that won't be yet. We've time, a half-hour at the least. If they don't before sunset, there's a chance".

Two hours away. . .

"So, are we breaking out, Lieutenant Nadaud?"

"Not all together. We've lost too many horses for that and most of the infantry here can't ride anyway."

A boom from the direction of the ridge. A plume of smoke billowed up beyond the crest. Flandin's relief force was under fire.

"So who's being left behind?" The idea appalled Dawlish.

"Nobody."

Nadaud told him his plan.

It was desperate.

Chapter 19

The sky was cloudless and the waning crescent above gave light enough for any movement in the open to be visible from two hundred yards away or more. But so far, as the path led south-westwards, skirting the lower slopes of *El Volcán*, it was flanked by brush and the greatest danger of detection came from sound. One braying mule – and there were four, though no horses – could be enough.

And yet, Dawlish tried to reassure himself, the chance of encountering the enemy was slight. The Juarista six-pounder with *El Serpiente's* people, by now six or eight miles distant, was still firing at intervals, proof the troops sent by Major Flandin were still holding their ground, as was the enemy on the ridge. While that contest of wills continued, it was providing a diversion to cover escape.

The two dozen Imperials and French infantry from the post's garrison made up most of this retreating party but there were nine dragoons also for whom there had been no ridable mounts. Even on foot, they were proving invaluable, reconnoitring ahead as they would have done on horseback, identifying paths that avoided any signs of small-plot residence. Sergeant Morvan was in overall command of the group.

Lieutenant Nadaud had not planned on Dawlish being with this party. He'd offered him a mount with the dragoons who were to break out from the post towards the east, then swing south-west to the railhead, giving *El Serpiente's* position a wide berth. The remainder of the garrison must leave on foot. The ravine that ran up close to the post could give cover for gaining the scrub beyond. After that, the objective would be the Glorioso mine and its defences. Pressing hard, they might reach it by sunrise. There had been no intention of bringing mules.

Dawlish had volunteered to go with the foot-party. He'd be useful for dealing with the British mine management, he had said, but he didn't mention the real reason lest it sound sanctimonious. It would shame him to escape with Nadaud on a mount better deserved by a dragoon private. He was an officer, even if not a French one, and care for subordinates was a sacred duty.

But now there were the mules, three heavily laden, one ridden, slowing progress because urging them too vigorously might trigger loud protest. Getting them down the ravine in silence had been a nightmare and it succeeded only because they been unladen, their loads carried down by men and placed on them afterwards.

It was Clothilde who inflicted this extra burden and Dawlish was present when she did. Nadaud had intended her to ride out with him and his troopers – she was a good horsewoman. She accepted without thanks, then asked about her baggage. Most was still piled in the wagon it had come in.

"We can't take it all, madame," he said. "Just your most precious things. All you can carry on the horse I give you."

"There'll be other riders. They can each take some." Not a suggestion, a demand.

"We may run into an ambush, madame. We may need to fight or to run. We can't be encumbered. For your safety too, madame –"

"Do you expect to reach the railhead safely, lieutenant? Do you think it's likely?"

"Yes, madame. We've a good chance of it."

"And when Colonel Durand reaches there, or when he summons you to Guzmán, as he will when the road is cleared, what will you tell him? That you've left my possessions for those bandits to loot before they retreat?"

"But, madame –"

"Are you sure you want to answer to Colonel Durand, Lieutenant Nadaud?" Cold fury in her voice, determination to have her way at whatever cost. "Some would say you're deserting your post. The colonel has had men shot for less."

Nadaud was trying to explain again but with less conviction. Dawlish sensed he would yield, despite his proposals being pragmatic. Clothilde – pampered, entitled and indulged, by Durand – could not and would not see it.

217

And yet . . .

A memory was back, one that had haunted him since he'd first heard of her disappearance from Pau. That pledge he'd made as a boy to his dying uncle, that he'd care for Clothilde and her mother. A promise as binding now as it had been then. He couldn't remain silent.

"There's another way, Madame Sapin," he said. "Safer but slower. You might not be able to bring everything, but you could bring most. There are four unwounded mules in the pen."

"They couldn't keep up," Nadaud said. "Not with the horses —"

"Let this Englishmen speak," Clothilde snapped.

He felt again that he was nothing to her, only a tool to be used and discarded when no longer needed.

"I'm joining the group heading on foot to the *Glorioso* mine," he said. "It's ten or twelve miles from here, not easy going to get there, but less likely than Lieutenant Nadaud's riders to encounter brigands. The mine's well defended – I've been there before and seen it is. You'd be safe there and could go on to the railhead when the danger's past."

"I don't intend to walk," Clothilde said.

"You needn't. You'd have a mule to ride, and three more to carry as much of your baggage as they can. It'll be a well-armed group, about thirty men." He paused. "I'll protect you as I'd protect my own sister."

She ignored him and turned to Nadaud.

"Is this feasible?" she said.

Nadaud shrugged. "Probably. But it'll slow the whole group down." He looked towards Dawlish. "Are you sure you want to do this, lieutenant?"

I don't. But I owe it to my uncle, to her mother.

"Yes."

And that was why this column was now threading its cautious way along winding goat-paths. It was forced to retrace its steps and take another track sometimes when dragoon scouts returned with reports of habitation ahead or of the present path deviating from the south-westward line of advance. Occasional open patches in the brush necessitated flitting across in three or four-man groups and the mules being brought over one by one. For this, even Clothilde dismounted, as she also did on the steeper inclines.

Dawlish stayed close, helped her mount and dismount, but she addressed no word to him and he stayed silent. But she never complained of discomfort, painful though it must be to perch side-saddle – the saddle being a folded blanket – on the bony haunches of the mule led by a French private. The monogramed white leather valise never left her clutch and three other mules followed with their incongruous burdens of extravagance.

The march was ever slower and fatigue a growing torment, a break of five minutes each hour, water-rationed to a single swig from a canteen and the discipline mercilessly imposed by Morvan. But hour-by-hour, the irregular barks and flashes of that Juarista six-pounder were further and further to the north-east, and the volcano's perfect cone and its drifting plume fell back northwards.

During the darkness, the low rumble of artillery from the north, from Guzmán, subsided but, as the eastern sky brightened into pink, began again. The fortified city's defences were under determined attack. Clothilde must have heard the distant thunder too but, if it frightened her, she didn't show it. Her confidence in Durand's ability to blunt the Juarista offensive might be total.

Or perhaps she didn't care about the outcome anyway.

Not as long as she could still cradle that monogrammed valise.

Clothilde! Clothilde! We were innocents together, sister and brother. I adored you. What are you now?

But the was another question, one more terrifying still.

What have you made of yourself?

*

They could not be more than a few miles from the mine when dawn broke. The night's march had been slow, its sinuous progress doubling what a crow would have flown. Soon after dawn, two dragoons returned from those sent to scout ahead and brought a terrified youth with them. He'd been found with a herd of goats. When he cringed before Morvan, eyes bulging with fear, twisting his sombrero in his hands, Dawlish saw he had every expectation of being murdered.

Could he lead them to the mine?

He was nodding, gabbling. *Sí señor, sí, sí,* he knew the way, most certainly, *sin duda,* he knew it. He pointed to a ridge to the south. The mine – they called it *El Glorioso,* and his uncle worked there, he said – was beyond there and, *sí señor, sí,* he'd lead them to it. Morvan was pressing his pistol's muzzle under the boy's chin and telling him that he'd be the first to die if he played them false.

French, Imperial or Juarista, it makes no difference. Millions like this wretch will still count for nothing, however it all ends.

Dawlish glanced back. Clothilde was watching with impatience and no trace of sympathy or pity. He felt ashamed to hang back from intervening – he could see the youth needed no such intimidation to gain his subservience – but now, so close to the mine, he was unwilling to confront Morvan.

And yet, distasteful as it was, finding the youth proved a boon. The column moved faster now, despite fatigue, guided along the merest traces of paths that otherwise would not have been noticed. Exhaustion grew as the sun soared and heat increased and insects shrilled. Dawlish found it an effort not to drift off into something like a trance, aware only of the need to put one foot in front of another. That was dangerous, the more so since every man in the column was perhaps feeling the same and their alertness falling. The sound of bombardment at Guzmán was low, muffled by the shoulder of the volcano that was now between them, but it was never cut off completely. Clothilde had left just in time.

The Juarista six-pounder on the ridge above *El Camino* was silent now, its meagre stock of shells probably consumed. It might already have withdrawn but *El Serpiente's* men hadn't, for brief rattles of small-arms fire were just audible at intervals and the French force sent up from the railhead must still be probing north. Just before ten, heavy cannon fire sounded, maybe a twelve pounder Flandin could ill-afford to spare from the defences at the railhead but had sent north anyway. Its firing rhythm was steady, maintained for a dozen shots, then a pause, and then the same again. Explosive shell must be dropping on the slope where the brigands remained in cover, sending small iron balls and casing fragments ripping through the brush. After the first salvo, *El Serpiente* would almost certainly have withdrawn his people back over the ridge, and some might have made the decision for themselves before that. The rifle-fire had died and the officer whom Flandin had sent must now be deciding whether push on up *El Camino* with the small force available and risk another ambush.

By eleven, the crest of the ridge the boy had indicated as hiding the mine was less than a mile ahead. Morvan halted the column and selected a dragoon to go forward with him. Then he approached Dawlish.

"If there are Belgians up there. I can talk to them," he said. "But there may be Americans too. And I can't speak English."

"I'll join you if you let the boy go free."

Morvan made no objection.

Dawlish's heart was pounding, his mouth dry, as they slipped into the brush at the left of the track. Whether the mine's lookouts were Belgians or ex-Confederates, nobody would take chances after hearing the distant gunfire of the last twenty-four hours. Progress was slow, visibility ahead never more than four or five yards, but vegetation thinned as the incline steepened closer to the crest. Then, at last, the growth petered out so only bare rocky soil lay ahead, pocked with small shrubs and thirty or forty yards wide. They sheltered in the last cover they could find at the edge. The ridge was curved here, convex towards them, and it was impossible to see for more than two hundred yards to either side. But the crestline was sloping up to the left. The highest point – and any observation outpost would need height – must be in that direction.

They moved leftwards at a crouch, flitting from cover to cover, edging forward to get a clear view of the crest, then retreating into the scrub again. Five minutes passed. Morvan had crawled to a safe viewpoint, was hissing, beckoning the other dragoon and Dawlish to join him. They crept forward. Morvan pointed to a low hummock on the skyline, almost directly ahead. It could be a random litter of rocks, or it could be a small zareba.

Time to break silence, for the sergeant to call out in French to identify himself, to be questioned in the same language, though differently accented. His answers must have satisfied, for he was told to advance with arms upraised. A ragamuffin figure in the remains of what must have once been an elaborate uniform rose above the rocks and searched him while another held his rifle on him. Both were Belgian privates. More questions, then Morvan turned and told the dragoon to go back to the waiting column and bring it here.

Dawlish came forward and looked down into the great bowl that contained the mine, its workings and the small redoubts around the perimeter. Smoke was drifting from the chimneys above the metal sheds and a low, regular, thump told of the ore crusher still in operation.

Nothing had changed since Dawlish saw it last except that, as the manager, Frank Atkinson, hoped, it might by now perhaps be producing yet more silver per day.

A British interest.

And a refuge, however temporary.

＊

The column plodded down towards the mine and was met by a mounted Belgian officer whom Dawlish recognised from his previous visit as Captain van Maarkedal, the deputy commander. He listened with no obvious sympathy to Sergeant Morvan's summary of events. The arrivals were welcome to stay one night here, but no longer. The railhead garrison was just a day's march away. They must leave for there tomorrow.

"I'd like to speak to Major Damseaux." Dawlish had stood back until now.

"You're that Englishman who was here before, aren't you?" van Maarkedal said. "What are you doing with these people?"

"A British concern. An official one. Like this mine."

222

"And that woman?" van Maarkedal's tone was hostile as he stared at Clothilde.

"A lady in distress," Dawlish said.

She had kept her seat on the mule during the steep descent and now was sitting straight-backed, somehow still elegant in her uniform-like riding habit. She had drawn her veil across her face and was ignoring van Maarkedal.

"Is Major Damseaux here?" Dawlish said.

"The baron?" van Maarkedal made it sound like a gibe. "He rode to the railhead this morning. He wanted to know what's happening in the north, towards Guzmán. We've heard gunfire since yesterday."

He's concerned about a French retreat, fears being abandoned. Probably with good reason. The Belgian Legion will be the last of Durand's concerns.

"When does he return?"

"Before sunset."

"And Mr. Atkinson?"

van Maarkedal shrugged. "Maybe in his office. Maybe at his house." He turned to Morvan. "Follow me with your people, sergeant. I'll see they have a meal and somewhere to rest."

They left and Dawlish turned to Clothilde. "I'll bring you to the mine-manager's home, madame." Dawlish pointed towards the large white wooden house.

"Who's the baron I heard that man mention?" she said.

"The commander here. A Belgian officer, a Major Damseaux. Of Empress Carlota's Legion. I understand he's a baron."

"Is he?" A note of surprise in Clothilde's voice. "Really a baron?"

"So I believe, madame." Dawlish had found something sad about Damseaux stressing it when he'd first met him. He'd seemed broken in spirit, clinging to the title as a last assurance of worth.

Dawlish took the mule's leading rope, told the men with the three baggage mules to follow, then brought her to Atkinson's house. One of the servants spotted them from the verandah and disappeared inside. By the time Dawlish was helping Clothilde dismount at the steps leading to it, Atkinson's wife, Señora Josefina, had emerged. As when he'd seen her before, her dress was Mexican and rich. She waited a moment, unsmilingly eyeing Clothilde, before inviting them up.

Dawlish made the introduction. Madame Sapin – Señora Atkinson. Clothilde didn't raise her veil as etiquette demanded and the señora had noticed it. After the formal words, neither woman spoke.

"Madame Sapin is fatigued." Dawlish broke the uncomfortable silence. "She needs a place to rest. Could you perhaps –"

Señora Josefina didn't let him finish. She turned to a maid standing behind. "Take this woman to a guest room."

No '*madame*', no '*señora*', just a woman, a '*mujer*'. No flicker of emotion on her impassive Indian features as she said it.

"I want a woman to assist me," Clothilde said in Spanish. "And warm water for washing. Clean sheets on the bed. And have my baggage brought to my room." She gestured to the mules.

The señora's response might have been less insulting had it been angry. She just turned from Clothilde in silence.

"Do what this woman wants," she said to the maid.

And walked back inside without another word.

*

Dawlish didn't wait for Atkinson to arrive and went to find him. He met him halfway to the office and insisted going there to discuss developments rather than accept the offer of immediate rest. He'd be grateful to accept accommodation later at the house. Atkinson probed why he'd been on the way to Guzmán but Dawlish evaded answering. He'd been sent on minor official business. Atkinson didn't seem convinced and was concerned by news of the attacks along *El Camino Real*.

"Those light guns you mention, lieutenant. Could they destroy the sheds or crusher or anything else here?" he said.

They could, if the Juaristas brought one or more six-pounders and sufficient munitions to anywhere on the surrounding ridges. They could devastate everything except the mine drift itself without ever coming into rifle-range. But Dawlish didn't want to say it.

"I don't think they'd want to do that, Mr. Atkinson," he said. "It's worth too much to wreck anything they'd need if they capture it later."

"I've heard of civilians being sent down to Manzanillo, lieutenant. Are the French withdrawing?"

"Not yet, I think." But there was no way of sugaring the pill. Atkinson deserved a straight answer. "But they will, in less than a month or so, I think. Guzmán's under attack. Even if it repulses the Juaristas this time, it can't keep doing so."

Long silence until Atkinson said, "I knew it had to come."

"Is there any agreement yet about the royalty matter?"

"No. All the silver mined is still stocked at the railhead. We send a shipment there about twice a month. The last was ten days ago. It needs a strong escort and sometimes Major Flandin can't always help, so we must wait 'til he can."

"Have you achieved five ingots a day?"

"Sometimes even six. We'll keep producing. French or Juarista, they'll need the revenue. And they'll need Plutus, no matter what." But there was a hint in Atkinson's voice that might be of a man trying to convince himself.

Dawlish changed the subject. He'd brought a French lady here, he said, a friend – with decency, he could use no other word – of Colonel Durand's. Señora Atkinson had already kindly offered her hospitality.

"A friend of Durand's?" Atkinson said. "Capital! We can dine together this evening. I'll send to have a proper meal prepared. Damseaux should be back from the railhead by then. He'll be delighted to join us. We hunger for company here."

He brought Dawlish back to his house, was pleased on getting there that Madame Sapin was being well cared for, was solicitous that Dawlish, hungry and exhausted, had food and drink and rest. His clothing would be washed, dried and ironed, ready when he woke.

All welcome, very welcome.

*

225

Dawlish had requested he be woken when Damseaux arrived back from the railhead. It was an hour to sundown and he went to the major's quarters to see him. He looked weary and disappointed – he'd heard from Major Flandin of the action to the north on *El Camino*. Over that of his sweat, the smell of brandy was stronger than before. Damseaux had been seeking solace.

"Is there any word of withdrawal from the railhead, sir?" Dawlish said.

"Nothing. But two trains full of French families and wounded set off this morning for Manzanillo. They were full beyond capacity."

One of them could only be the train that bought me from the coast. Until it returns, I'm stranded.

"van Maarkedal told me you'd brought a woman with you."

The hint of cold anger in Damseaux's tone was surprising.

"Madame Sapin," Dawlish said. "A friend of Colonel Durand's."

"I thought as much. Atkinson's invited me to dine with him and you tonight. Will that woman be present?"

"I don't know. She might be too fatigued."

Damseaux's expression had hardened. He waited a full half-minute before speaking.

"Atkinson's invited me already. I've accepted. I can't refuse now."

No longer just anger in his voice.

It could be sheer hatred.

*

Atkinson greeted them at the door and led them to a comfortable parlour, a double door, open, leading to a dining room beyond. Dawlish counted four places laid on the round table there. No sign of Señora Josefina. A barefoot manservant entered and brought bottles and glasses on a silver tray. Dawlish accepted wine – from California, he learned – but the others favoured brandy. The conversation was difficult, with long silences, for both Damseaux and Atkinson looked preoccupied, worried by Dawlish's news.

And then the parlour door opened and the manservant was bowing and ushering in Clothilde.

She had looked beautiful as a schoolgirl but now she was magnificent, wearing a low-cut evening dress of light-grey silk, her arms bare almost to the shoulder. She must have attended to her own hair, for there was nobody here who could have readied it like this. She wore no other jewellery than pendant diamond earrings and a simple golden necklace supporting a pearl and diamond cluster. The French Empress Eugénie could look no more stunning at a Tuileries ball than Clothilde did at this instant in these modest surroundings. The white leather valise and three humble mules had carried this luxury here, and probably more besides.

Dawlish stood back, unwilling to endure her cold denial. But he sensed Atkinson and Damseaux had been struck by surprise greater even than his.

Clothilde was advancing, smiling, as sweetly and innocently as Dawlish remembered when she'd approached his uncle for some small indulgence – and always got it. For one instant, he detected a flash of calculation as she looked towards the two other men and identified, by his threadbare uniform, which must be Damseaux. Then she was no longer meeting their gaze and dropping into a graceful curtsy.

"Monsieur le baron Damseaux," she said. Her voice was low and admiring, almost breathless. She might be an abbess meeting an archbishop. "We've never met, but I've heard your name. An old and honourable one."

And Damseaux had bowed, was reaching out his hand, taking hers, kissing it, then raising her.

"*Votre serviteur, madame.*" The hatred, the anger, had gone from his voice." *Votre très humble serviteur.*"

Her humble servant.

And it sounded like no empty formality.

He meant it, a man instantly conquered.

Poor fool.

Chapter 20

It was Atkinson's house but Damseaux ignored the etiquette that fact demanded. He took Clothilde's hand in his with elegant courtesy, conducting her to the table and seating her to his right. Dawlish hung back so Atkinson would sit on her other side for he wanted no conversation with her. He didn't need to worry. She was concerned with Damseaux only, and he with her. Atkinson's French was only passable and he seemed relieved that Dawlish kept him busy in English with a stream of questions about the mine and its machinery.

Across the table, Clothilde, perfect in her manners, fetchingly modest in demeanour, was listening in rapt attention to Damseaux when he spoke. Dawlish, feigning interest in Atkinson's enthusing over the finer points of ore-crushing, heard only snippets that were half-drowned by the steady thumping of the machine itself.

Clothilde knew of the Belgian Legion, she said, was impressed by the chivalry that brought its volunteers to guard Empress Carlota in Mexico. The loyalty that induced them to leave ceremonial duties at Chapultepec and risk death in the field in the Emperor's service was beyond praise.

Damseaux, a modest hero, made light of it. Soldiering was a tradition in his family, he said, service a duty. It had been, for generations.

Clothilde was enthralled. It must seem like a sacred trust, she said.

He'd been drinking steadily but his speech was still clear. His mother had instructed him in that duty of honour when he was a boy. She'd been French, he said, a lady-in-waiting who accompanied the Empress Carlota's mother to Belgium to wed King Leopold and then married a baron of old Burgundian nobility. She'd died young.

Clothilde dropped her eyes and dabbed them with a lace handkerchief plucked from her bosom. Such memories were golden and she too had known great tragedy. But then, as if too moved to pursue the matter further, she enquired about the Imperial Court at

Chapultepec. Did Empress Carlota indeed import her gowns from the House of Worth in Paris? She'd heard she rode beautifully and was a splendid figure on horseback. Was that true? Did His Majesty, Emperor Maximilian, indeed waltz better than any man at court, as many said? And, she said shyly, perhaps Monsieur le Baron was being too loyal when he confirmed that *l'empereur* did. Perhaps he himself was no less well accomplished? He demurred. He hadn't waltzed since his wife died. The memories were too painful.

He stopped, was almost maudlin.

And then she pounced.

Dawlish caught the quick gleam of calculation in her eye as she reached out timidly and touched Damseaux's hand, then withdrew it quickly and looked away as if in confusion. He too looked confused – genuinely so, Dawlish thought.

"One must endure, madame," he said. "We owe that to the dead."

Clothilde nodded sadly.

"So much death." Her voice was low. "So much in this unhappy Mexico." She paused, then sighed and looked away. "It was tragedy that brought me here." She took her handkerchief from her bosom again and – despite his melancholy – Damseaux stared in admiration. "It was greater tragedy that I was forced to stay until –" Her voice, low now, was almost breaking, and she didn't finish the sentence.

She dabbed her eyes again and choked back a small sob before continuing. "One can't undo the past. A woman's life can be so very hard. And men can be such deceivers. As you said, Monsieur le Baron, one can but endure. One must." She looked away as if embarrassed that she'd said too much.

Even Atkinson noticed, had broken off in the middle of a long explanation of the use of mercury at the mine, was looking uncomfortable. Dawlish, disgusted, didn't want to look at her lest he see again that gleam of calculation, perhaps even of challenge or invitation to join in her charade.

But Damseaux was oblivious of their presence. She had laid her left hand on the table and he was reaching for it and –

Sounds of gunfire, just audible above the thumping of the cruncher, a brief ripple, then another.

Atkinson sprung to his feet, face suddenly pale.

Individual shots now.

Dawlish too was on his feet, was pulling out the pistol that had never left him. He was a stranger here, had no status, was looking to Damseaux for orders.

Which didn't come.

Damseaux had risen, was swaying slightly, was looking bewildered.

But Clothilde had grasped him by the arm.

"For God's sake, Monsieur le Baron, save a helpless woman! I beg you! You can guess what would happen to me if –"

And for all that her words were begging, her tone was the most resolute here at this moment.

Damseaux prized her fingers from his arm. "Trust me, madame," he said. "Depend on me!" She was looking up to him with great pleading eyes. He fumbled with his holster and drew his pistol. "Stay with this lady, Mr. Atkinson," he said. His pronunciation was slightly slurred. "Quench the lights! Let nobody leave this house!" To Dawlish he said, "Follow me!"

He stumbled slightly as they reached the verandah. Dawlish had to steady him on the steps down. The smell of brandy was strong.

The distant gunfire was intense and unrelenting now. Suddenly, a bugle sounded close-by. Half-clad Belgian legionnaires, roused from sleep, were stumbling from the adobe barracks with their weapons. Lanterns danced and sergeants were bellowing at latecomers, hustling them into sections. Above the corrugated roofs of the machinery sheds, Dawlish saw tiny stabs of light winking against the darkness of the ridge beyond, one cluster to the south and the other south-west, rifle fire from attackers and defenders indistinguishable. Damseaux had seen it too, seemed dazed and was silent. Then Captain van Maarkedal came running. His tunic was unbuttoned but he was armed with both revolver and sword. And he didn't look drunk or dazed.

"It's Redoubts 3 and 4," he said to Damseaux. "I've called out everybody who's resting. Half of them to reinforce 3 and 4 and the remainder to 5 and 6. If 5 and 6 don't come under attack then it may be able to work behind the attackers from them."

"Yes, yes, captain." Damseaux's head must be clearing, though slowly, and he was nodding. "The right decision, admirable. Yes, that's correct. You'll reinforce 3 and 4. I'll take the remainder to 5 and 6. Work around behind them, that's the idea."

van Maarkedal shook his head. "That's not wise, monsieur. You're needed here in overall command. Lieutenant Ansleme can handle defence at 3 and 4. I'll head for 5 and 6. If there's an opportunity, I'll counterattack. If not, it's better to stay inside the defences."

"Don't question my orders, van Maarkedal!" Damseaux had sobered enough to recognise insubordination. "And what about the French who're here?"

"I've sent them to Number 1 to secure the track to the railhead." van Maarkedal was surly now. "Their sergeant, Morvan, seems to know his business. Are you content with that, *mon baron major*?"

Damseaux nodded.

Before they left, van Maarkedal, ignoring his commander, said to Dawlish, "Find Atkinson. Tell him to silence that damned crusher. We need as much quiet as possible."

Dawlish headed back towards the white house, now unlit. Shots still crackled to the south and south-west but they were sparse – most probably sniping and return fire through redoubt loopholes at imagined movements. The sound of the crusher died – Atkinson must have come to the same conclusion as van Maarkedal. Dawlish found him standing by it with the Welsh foreman. He was carrying a shotgun and looked frightened.

"I didn't expect this," he said. "I didn't think they'd want to destroy the mine. You didn't think it either, Lieutenant Dawlish." It sounded like a reproach. "Do you know what Damseaux's doing about it?"

Dawlish was about to tell him when a grizzled man in a patched Confederate uniform hurried up, eight men similarly-clad following, all armed with Henry repeaters. Atkinson addressed him as Captain

Clayton. He'd doubled the guard at the silver store, he said, four men now. He was holding back these others until he knew more.

"What's Damseaux doing?" he said.

"Reinforcing the redoubts under attack," Dawlish said. "Number 3 and Number 4. Do you know the numbering?"

"I'm a soldier, son," Clayton said. "Damn sure I know. What reinforcements?"

"He sent half the men who were resting to 3 and 4. He's himself taking what's left to 5 and 6."

"What's he doin' for reserves?"

"There aren't any, sir. But the other redoubts are manned normally."

"Goddam idiot!" Clayton said. "So all he has will be over there." He gestured towards the distant rattle of gunfire, louder since the crusher had fallen silent. "What if it's nothing but a feint? If this isn't the main attack. What if it's coming from the north?"

"Can you reinforce one of the redoubts there?" Atkinson was hesitant, a civilian suggesting to a professional.

"We could try," Clayton said, "But we'd stand a damn good chance of being gunned down by the Belgians holding them. They'll be trigger happy, shoot at anythin' that moves."

Suddenly, close by, five shots, identical reports, barely a second apart. Then silence.

"It's a Henry!" Clayton shouted.

It could only be from a guard at the silver store.

A British interest.

∗

Clayton didn't approach the silver store directly but sent three of his men to skirt around it to the right, as many again to the left. They would take whatever cover they could and hold fire. One man, a skilled tracker apparently, would crawl closer and report back what he found.

"You've a weapon there." Clayton nodded towards Dawlish's pistol. "Care to join me, son?"

"I'll take your orders, sir."

Atkinson was about to speak but Clayton forestalled him.

"Better stay behind the crusher, sir. That shotgun o' yours ain't worth a damn just now."

Silence since those five Henry shots, broken only by the irregular fusillade continuing on the ridge to the south. Damseaux's and van Maarkedal's reinforcements must be creeping up there.

Dawlish flitted from cover to cover with Clayton and his two men, taking it in turns to seek refuge behind sheds and tailings heaps. The silver store, still unseen, lay directly ahead.

And still no alarm. Whoever was at the store must be hoping the brief burst of repeater fire would have been dismissed as rifles blasting to the south. Five minutes passed and Clayton's group was crouched behind the long slope of a tailings heap. He gestured to one of his men, sent him crawling to the crest. He was back a minute later.

He'd seen the store – it was fifty yards beyond the base of the tailings' forward slope. Two dark figures were busy with something at the door. No sign of Confederate guards. Clayton sent him back to the crest to observe.

Soon after, movement on the slope to the right. A low hiss, then another. No challenge from Clayton – this was trust, Dawlish realised, absolute trust of his people, built in shared skirmishes and perhaps on battlefields. The man approached slowly, was the tracker sent to investigate more closely. He huddled with Clayton and Dawlish overheard the whispers.

"I found Dick Brooks, rear o' the store. Throat cut. They'd taken his Henry."

"The other boys?"

The tracker shook his head. "Couldn't see 'em. Probably the same as Dick. Whoever's done it must have moved in silent, like snakes. God knows which of our boys got off them shots before they finished him."

"Did you see the door? There are two fellas doing God knows what there."

The man shook his head.

"An' round the rear?"

"One. I was damn lucky he didn't step on me when I found Dick. An' one on each side too. In the shadows."

"That makes five," Clayton said. "Get back to the others. Tell 'em to wait 'til they hear our shooting."

The tracker disappeared as he had come.

Clayton crawled to the tailings' crest to join the observer already there. An eternity passed, enough to let the tracker join his fellows to the right of the store.

The firing on the southern ridge erupted again, concentrated volleys, once more trailing off into individual shots. The Belgian reinforcements must have reached the redoubts there by now, were probably blasting blindly into the darkness. Clayton had been right – the attack on the redoubts was indeed a feint, intended to draw attention from the infiltrators who had passed, undetected, between the northern defences. The silver, as much as five men might carry, was the goal. With so many labourers working at the mine, it would have been easy to contact one back at his village and induce him to describe the store's location.

Clayton, revolver in hand, gestured to Dawlish and the guard with him to come forward, lie down just below the crest and sight on the store's door. When he'd fire, all others would shoot too and cut down whoever was there.

Dawlish had just raised his head above the crest, could see the store, saw two dark figures scuttling from its doorway to crouch some three yards to either side of it. Then sparks were racing in a sinuous path from one of them towards the door. Just as they reached it, Clayton fired into the air and the Henry-armed guards blasted, three, four, five rounds each that might or might not have found their marks.

Then the explosion, flashing at the doorway, then engulfing it in rolling black smoke. Dawlish ducked below the crest – he hadn't fired his pistol – and heard Henrys unleashing a murderous leaden storm from left and right of the store's sides. Clayton was calling for him and two guards to advance. They scrambled to their feet, dashed down the far side of the tailings slope. The attacker who set off the charge was crumpled in a heap but muzzle flashes told of the second man blazing back with a Henry taken from a murdered guard. Location identified, he was cut down by the guard to Dawlish's right.

And then it was over, the Henrys silent, all guards converging on the store, finding two living, badly wounded, and three dead. Their peasant clothing, their bandoliers, their boots of soft, untanned, leather left no doubt as to what they were. But Clayton confirmed it anyway. He ignored the wretch lying on his back – blood bubbling weakly from his mouth, eyes locked open and dulling by the second. The other wounded man was trying to rise, hands clasped around his thigh and blood spurting between his fingers. Clayton's kick in his chest laid him sprawling, then he planted his boot upon his neck. He pointed his pistol directly at his face.

"Who're you with? You've this one chance to talk." He lifted his boot.

Face contorted in pain, the man attempted to spit at him.

"Last chance, amigo," Clayton said. "With Gabarra?"

"With *El Serpiente.*" Spoken with pride.

Then Clayton stood back and fired. He turned to the nearest of the guards and jerked his head towards the man drowning in his own blood.

"Finish him."

Better than the end inflicted on those Belgian deserters.

Dawlish looked away.

And realised the shooting to the south had died.

*

Atkinson was shaken when Dawlish found him behind the crusher.

"The silver?" he asked.

"All there. The door was blown in but there'd been no time for any to be taken. The guards' throats were cut. By El Serpiente's brutes, all dead now."

Clayton appeared. That he'd lost four men was bitter.

"Dick Brooks was with me at Glorietta. Nat Brodie's brother was killed at Fort Bisland. Leland an' Culter joined in '64, just boys. Leland

235

damn nearly died at Bayou Bourbeux but he came back anyway." Clayton had been merciless minutes before. Now there was a quaver in his voice. "Throats slit like hogs. They'd got careless. They were tired of it all. We all are. It was bad up north 'gainst the Yankees but a damn cleaner war than here."

The Welsh foreman arrived, half-carrying an exhausted Belgian private. He'd found him collapsed near the boiler-sheds.

"I think he turned tail from up there." He motioned towards the southern ridge where silence now reigned.

Dawlish questioned the private in French. Between his accent and his laboured breathing, he was hard to understand.

But he hadn't run away. He'd come for help.

"Le baron a été blessé." Each word an effort. *"Gravement blessé."*

Damseaux had been wounded. Seriously.

Still gasping for breath and the word *'brancard'* was just understandable.

"He needs a stretcher," Dawlish said.

There was one in the boiler sheds, according to the foreman, medical supplies also. They'd handled injuries here several times. Clayton volunteered to bring it with his men. The foreman would carry a bag with bandages.

Atkinson invited Dawlish to return with him to his house. The ladies would need assurance that the danger was passed. Lamps were burning there already. For a moment, Dawlish considered not joining him, then decided that he must.

But the thought of meeting Clothilde repelled him.

*

But he had to meet her when they brought Damseaux to the house. He was lying on the stretcher, barely conscious, face drained, tunic saturated red on the right side. Clayton was holding a pad of blood-soaked bandages against the wound – it seemed to be just below the rib-cage – and keeping pace with the men carrying the stretcher. The foreman, panting, followed.

van Maarkedal had come ahead to make arrangements for receiving him. "*C'était une décision stupide*," he told Dawlish. When the attackers had withdrawn it was too dangerous to follow. Darkness and brush were on their side. He'd told Damseaux as much but he didn't want to listen. Because of that, a corporal and a private were dead and he was wounded.

Clothilde was waiting on the verandah, lantern in hand. She had changed into a simple dark dress and wore a white apron she must have borrowed from the kitchen. Señora Josefina stood behind her, face impassive. She made no move to follow Clothilde when she hurried down the steps to meet the stretcher.

And then Clothilde's lamp, held high, was illuminating Damseaux's pallid face, and her own too. He recognised her, tried to speak, but the effort was too much and he gasped in pain. She reached for his hand and drew it to her lips. "*Courage!*" she whispered. "*Courage, mon pauvre baron!*" She held his hand as the stretcher was manoeuvred up the steps – each one drew a stifled groan from him – and into what had been a dining room just two hours earlier. Now the table was cleared. A ewer of steaming water, and a bowl, and a heap of fresh towels lay on a sideboard behind it and a white enamel bucket below. Señora Josefina had disappeared.

They lifted him onto the table. Clothilde raised his head, ever so gently, and slid a pillow beneath it.

Clayton withdrew the sodden bandage pad, dropped it in the bucket and the foreman handed him another. He peered into the wound.

"The ball's still in there, I think" he said. "It can't remain."

For a brief instant, Dawlish saw torn flesh, blood, clothing in saturated shreds around it. Clothilde had seen it too and she hadn't flinched, just continued pressing Damseaux's hand, holding his gaze and mopping his forehead with a lace handkerchief.

"Any of you gentlemen able to get it out?" Clayton said. Nobody offered. He shrugged. "I've done it before. Can't promise anything though. Give him whisky first, brandy if you have it."

And afterwards, three minutes of agony while Clayton probed with a narrow-nosed pliers fetched from the workshops. It still bore a sheen of engine oil but he wiped it on his sleeve before he began. Dawlish and van Maarkedal held Damseaux down by the shoulders, Atkinson by the feet. Clothilde rolled a table napkin tightly for him to bite on. Her eyes never left his, even when his spine arched from the table as Clayton prodded.

He located the ball, touching metal on his third attempt. There was bleeding each time he withdrew the pliers, the foreman staunching the flow with bandage pads.

"No bone broken. And he ain't stomach nor gut-shot neither." Clayton was wiping his brow with the back of his hand, leaving a red streak, as he steeled himself for the worst step of all.

Now the agony, Damseaux almost impossible to hold down as Clayton worked the pliers' jaws around the ball

And gripped, pulled, then dropped it on the table.

"*Merci d'être Dieu,*" Clothilde whispered. "*Merci à sa sainte mère.*"

Damseaux was gasping. The foreman covered the wound with a fresh pad.

"There's a lot o' dirt in there," Clayton said. "Bits of uniform, sand too maybe. I've seen wounds like this mortify, kill in days." He looked to Dawlish. "Ask that French lady if she has a tweezer."

She went to fetch it. Dawlish had seen his sister use one like it when tending to her eyebrows. Clayton reached out but she didn't give it.

"Tell him this takes a woman's touch" she said to Dawlish, then looked down, met Damseaux's eyes. "Forgive me, *mon pauvre baron*. I'll be as gentle as I can."

And she was, lifting each bloody shred of fabric, each fibre, each grain of dirt, from the raw flesh. Her hands were red, her white apron smeared where she wiped them, working a minute at a time, resting as much in between while the foreman staunched the bleeding. Damseaux was quiet now, lost in his own world of pain, groaning weakly only when she pinched wrongly,

It lasted fifteen meticulous minutes until at last she said to Dawlish, "Tell them to bandage now. I've done my best."

Damseaux didn't hear her.

He was drifting into something between sleep and delirium.

Chapter 21

Damseaux survived the night – a bed had been made up for him in the parlour and Clothilde never left his side. He was feverish, half-delirious, by morning.

There were bodies to be buried, *El Serpiente's* men dumped in a pit dug in a tailings heap, the Belgian corporal and private, together, with more dignity. There were no coffins, just blankets wrapped around them. As many of their comrades who could be spared from the redoubts were paraded. van Maarkedal, to whom command had devolved, read from a prayerbook and a firing party loosed a volley over the grave.

The four ex-Confederates were buried in a trench. Clayton led a prayer and remembered them. *They had fought the good fight, had finished the race, had kept the faith. In their death they were not divided: they were swifter than eagles, they were stronger than lions.* One of their younger comrades was weeping openly. Then another volley.

Dawlish was impressed that Sergeant Morvan, without bidding, had paraded his men to offer respect. Within an hour they were to begin their march to the railhead. Dawlish was to accompany them and travel on to Manzanillo. Since Clothilde had been headed there before the attack on the column, it would be safest for her to join the party. He wondered if she would.

He had lain awake for what had remained of the night, haunted by awareness that his mission had come to nothing. He had failed to reach Durand in Guzmán and failed to secure the release of silver needed for *Jenny Dixon's* repair. It was through no fault of his own, but failure nonetheless. It would bring him no blame – Weatherby was a just man – but success would have earned commendation. And commendation was essential for a young officer with high ambitions but no family influence who'd been sent to the Pacific Station to avoid embarrassment to certain people in very high places. He could not accept defeat easily, he decided – Nelson wouldn't have. Alternative courses churned in his brain and in the end only one had merit. For that he would need Atkinson's connivance and Clayton's support. Little time remained for convincing them.

Dawlish turned from the graves – before final filling, rocks were being laid on the bodies to deter disturbance by predators. The sight depressed him, the futility of the insane venture that had brought those simple men here, the misery inflicted on an impoverished people by all sides, the ubiquity of death. The crusher was silent and what normally was an antheap devoid of activity. The attack had struck fear into the workers and many might never return.

He went to the house and found Clothilde sleeping on a chair drawn close to the bed where Damseaux. had lapsed into sleep of a sort. The clean nightshirt he now wore was wet with sweat and great beads of it stood out on his forehead.

Dawlish's attention switched to Clothilde and, for an instant sadness, regret and the remains of love flushed through him. There had been happiness in Pau, even though his uncle had been facing death with Stoic resignation. They'd been sister and brother together, innocents both, and he'd made a sacred promise that he'd care for her. He hesitated to awaken her.

But she must have sensed his presence, for she opened her eyes and recognised him immediately.

"Lieutenant Dawlish." Said in a whisper. "You startled me."

He told her why he'd come, that Morvan would be leaving within the hour for the railhead, that he himself would escort her that far, that her baggage must be loaded soon on the mules that had brought it.

Damseaux must have heard something, for he too was stirring, passing an arm across his face and mumbling something. Clothilde noticed and she was at once wiping his brow, then taking his hand and holding it. He looked up at her, his few words just distinguishable before he drew her hand to his lips.

Merci. Merci, Madame.

She was looking Dawlish full in the face, spoke loud enough for Damseaux to hear.

241

"You're asking me to leave, lieutenant." Reproof in her tone. "You're suggesting I abandon this brave man in his hour of need. No, lieutenant! A thousand times no! He needs a woman's nursing." She looked down at Damseaux and met his gaze. "My place is here."

Dawlish realised she wanted him to answer, that he should emphasise the danger of her remaining here, that Atkinson would ensure that Damseaux would have the best care possible should she leave. And she would refuse, would cast contempt on his proposal in near-theatrical terms while the sick man listened and admired.

He turned away, resisting the urge to ask, in Damseaux's hearing, what message she'd want sent to Durand when the road to Guzmán was again open. But to do so seemed too mean, too squalid. He walked to the door in silence. That flush of affection he had felt when he'd see her sleeping was gone.

Forever.

*

He found Atkinson in his office and told him why he'd been on the road to Guzmán. Before further detailing, he produced an English version of the document he'd helped Weatherby to finalise.

"Durand would never have accepted this." Atkinson had read it through three times, asking for clarification during the last.

"Would you have been content if he had?"

"Yes. It's excellent in theory. But that's irrelevant. Durand's determined to control every ingot produced. He has us in a vice. Plutus sank a fortune and hasn't raised a penny profit yet. There isn't a damn thing we can do about it."

"How many ingots here at present?"

Atkinson calculated silently, then said, "We sent a load to the railhead ten days ago. Forty-seven more cast since."

Over thirty-five thousand dollars, some nine thousand sterling.

"They could easily have been lost last night," Dawlish said. "The Belgians are worn out. There's no guarantee *El Serpiente* won't be back, maybe with a Juarista artillery piece in support." He paused, let the

242

words sink in. "The French can't even keep the road from the railhead to Guzmán open. Guzmán itself is under siege. Right now this mine is the least of their concerns."

Atkinson was silent. He looked older, more worn.

Dawlish waited, sensed despair.

"There could be a solution," he said at last. "A partial one but Plutus would surely welcome it. Commander Weatherby would support it."

I'm gambling now.

"Tell me."

Atkinson didn't interrupt but, when he'd heard all, brought Dawlish back over the plan, step-by-step, querying the practicality of each. He made a few suggestions, emphasising they didn't imply endorsement. And then he asked Dawlish to repeat it, start to finish.

"You said Weatherby would agree. But you haven't been able to discuss it with him."

"It's close enough to what he intended," Dawlish said. "He'll support it."

But only if the plan succeeds.

"You say you want Clayton and two of his men, lieutenant. What if he's not willing?"

"Without them, it's impossible. But give him the choice. Let's talk to him. He must have taken greater risks in the last five years."

Then back and forth for another ten minutes.

Until Atkinson said, "I'll send for Clayton."

*

Sergeant Morvan insisted on taking with him the four mules that carried Madame Sapin's baggage. If she was determined to remain here, and wanted to come later to the railhead, she could send for them. He needed the beasts for carrying any men who might suffer heatstroke on the march. It was already late in the morning when they left the mine and the pace would have to be ferocious, through merciless noonday and afternoon sun, if they were to reach the railhead in daylight.

243

Atkinson lent Dawlish a horse, and Clayton had a mount of his own –
he'd ridden south from Texas on her, he said – but all others were on
foot. By the time they reached the railhead, both had dismounted and
were leading their animals with two exhausted men on each. It was
dark now and the distant booming from Guzmán, infrequent all day,
had died completely.

Major Flandin was as welcoming as before. Nadaud and his troop
had reached the railhead safely. Both accepted that Madame Sapin had
chosen to remain, for now, at the mine. Flandin was surprised to see
Clayton. There were matters to be arranged with Weatherby in his
consular capacity at Manzanillo, Dawlish explained. Clayton was
coming as Atkinson's representative.

"You'll have a long wait," Flandin said. "There are no trains here. I
sent all evacuees from Guzmán to Manzanillo. One is returning as
soon as possible, in two or three days, I hope."

Dawlish had already heard much the same from Tom Bryce,
who'd stayed behind to wait and met him and Clayton on arrival.

"Two days, Major Flandin? We can't delay that long," Dawlish
said. "It's sensitive business, about the mine licence and the royalties
matter."

Flandin shrugged. "Are you ready for a long walk then,
lieutenant?"

Dawlish shook his head and translated for Clayton.

And, as rehearsed, Clayton looked thoughtful for a moment. Then,
as if suddenly inspired, said in English, "There's more than one way of
skinning a cat. Is there a pump-railcar we can borrow?"

Dawlish feigned incredulity. "Too dangerous." He wasn't sure how
much Flandin might understand. But all that mattered was that he'd
hear an argument between them.

"The gradient's downhill most of the way," Clayton said. "We'd
move fast. And easy going near the coast, level enough. With you an'
me, Tom Bryce and two of my boys pumping we could make it."

Dawlish was shaking his head, as if dismissing the idea. They'd
never make it. Clayton urged again.

"What's he saying?" Flandin asked. "Translate for me."

"It's hardly worth it," Dawlish told him. "It's not practical."

"Translate anyway. Every word."

The idea intrigued Flandin. Soon the discussion was between him and Clayton, with Dawlish acting as translator only. Flandin called for a bottle and glasses. Two old soldiers together. Soon, reminiscences. Each had taken greater risks than now proposed, in Algeria, along the Mississippi. It was indeed practical. With sandbag protection, and all carrying Henrys – Dawlish was welcome to borrow one – they needn't fear *El Serpiente* or any other goddamn bandit. His people were all further north anyway. There were at least two sandbagged railcars here already, ready for use. Leaving at dawn, with the long inclines before them in their favour, they should be at Ciudad de Armería by evening and spend the night there.

Dawlish took convincing.

He asked to see a map. Flandin sent for one. Made and signed by a British surveyor in *Ferrocarril del Pacífico* employ, it was more a diagram than a map, the track shown in parallel strips, with distances, inclines, halts and passing-points marked. Further discussion, another bottle called for.

And at last, Dawlish yielded.

With apparent reluctance.

*

There were few preparations necessary other than to grease the car's bearings and load a keg of water, basic provisions and a box of ammunition. The car was already walled to waist-hight with sandbags.

Flandin came to see them off, shook hands and apologised that he could not spare any men as escort. All were needed here. No sounds of artillery had sounded from Guzmán this morning. It might mean the Juaristas had withdrawn, he said. If so, the next effort must be to reopen a passage along *El Camino*. It was likely then that Durand would send everybody at Guzmán incapable of lifting a rifle to Manzanillo.

A push from bystanders got the car moving and, even on the mile-long level section south of the railhead, it took only occasional pumping of the rocking beam to keep it moving at the speed of a cantering horse. The incline began thereafter and the track was weaving a sinuous path. No pumping needed now – the weight of the sandbags, load and five men saw to that. Speed gathered and on the tighter bends it was necessary to apply the brake.

Dawlish standing at the front, scanning the track ahead with Clayton by his side, feared they might have arrived this far too soon. If so, it might be necessary to stop short of Colima and start a brutal return up the track, four of them straining on the pumping beam to fight against the incline. Each blind bend brought hope that what they sought might lie beyond it and each, when rounded, disappointed.

Into another bend, and the track straightening, brush to either side.

And a single man standing between the rails two hundred yards ahead and waving a white rag above his head.

Relief.

Rendezvous successful.

*

Six of the guards whom Clayton left behind at the mine had reached here with seven of its mules. The twelve rope-handled and padlocked wooden boxes they'd carried lay hidden behind brush on the right side of the track. Stencilled PMC – Plutus Mining Company – in black letters, each box was wrapped around with braided brass wire, the ends joined by a large lead seal with the letters, PMC, in cursive script, enclosed within an octagon.

The mules looked exhausted, the men too. They'd left the mine early the previous afternoon and, led by a local guide, had pushed on through the hours of darkness, arriving here only a half-hour before. With four ingots per box, the total weight came to almost three quarters of a ton. It took five minutes to load the boxes behind the sandbags.

"Here are the lock keys." The sergeant who led the pack train handed them to Dawlish. "And Mr. Atkinson sent this too."

246

A large manilla envelope, two handwritten sheets within, the wording agreed the day before with Atkinson, and signed by him. It drew heavily on the proposal that Dawlish had been carrying to Durand at Guzmán.

That in view of the state of unrest pertaining in the vicinity of the Glorioso mine, and the recent attack on it, repelled with significant loss of life, forty-seven thirty-five-pound silver ingots were being entrusted to the representative of Her Majesty's consul at Manzanillo, who will deal with accredited Mexican Imperial Government representatives to agree matters related to payment of royalties on said silver.

Dawlish signed both copies, handed one back to the sergeant to give to Atkinson as a receipt, then mounted the railcar. Clayton and his men were already aboard.

With the extra weight there was no need for a push. Releasing the brake was sufficient to send the vehicle rolling down the track.

*

They reached Colima within the hour and had difficulty braking the loaded vehicle even though the track-section there was level. The French lieutenant in command of the small French garrison didn't query the pass-document Major Flandin had signed, nor did anybody suspect what lay behind the car's sandbagged breastwork. There had been no reports of bandit activity recently, the lieutenant said, and the track ahead was safe.

The incline was slighter now, constant but for a few level sections where pumping was needed to maintain momentum. Curves, even the wide ones, were frightening however since the greater weight had increased speed substantially. It was necessary to slow on the tighter bends and Dawlish kept to himself the concern that the brake bands on the axels might burn out long before the level ground closer to the ocean.

But his greater fear, one which he shared with Clayton, was meeting the upcoming train of which Flandin had spoken. The chance of encountering it at one of the ten-mile separated passing-points was negligible. On its own, less the sandbags, the car could be lifted from the track. But the silver would make that more difficult. There would be no option other than to unload the sandbags and silver, hide the boxes, lift off the car, then transfer everything back again once the train had moved on. The search ahead with field glasses was no longer just for dangers of attack but the slightest trace of a steam plume in the distance. They paused five minutes at each of the passing-places reached, climbed as high as possible on the ground on either side to get the best view of the widening Armería valley. Only when reassured – and assurance could never be total – did they set off again.

And so the long day passed, sun beating down, lassitude an enemy, thirst assuaged by the water keg, brief periods of pumping, sightings of villages and peasants working in distant fields. Small posts where Imperial troops had guarded bridges a few weeks before were abandoned now. Their occupants must have seen the trains of French refugees from Guzmán pass and made their own decisions. Some would have cast off their uniforms and returned to their villages while others fled to the Juaristas with their weapons. All must have realised that the end was near for the French occupation and the Mexican Imperial puppet government. It was not yet too late to cut ties to them before the Juaristas came to settle scores.

They reached the last passing-point before Ciudad de Armería just after five o'clock. Two hours to darkness and ten miles to go. It was achievable. One last sighting down the valley from a nearby bluff and, this time, Dawlish spotted a faint white wisp in the far distance.

He handed the field-glasses to Clayton. "What do you think?"

Guzmán's studied it, then said, "It's the train. They won't go beyond Armería, not this late. They'll stay the night there. It'll be better that we be there already to greet them."

Under an hour later, they braked to a halt fifty yards short of the *cheval-de-frise* that blocked the gap in the cactus perimeter hedge through which the track entered. Shouted exchanges and then they were inside. No sign yet of the upcoming train. This post had been largely manned by Imperial troops before, and only a few ex-Confederates. Now there were no Imperials to be seen. Seasoned-looking French had taken their place.

Clayton and Bryce knew the remaining ex-Confederates, old comrades all, by name. None queried the reason for this unorthodox passage to the coast and accommodation was gladly allocated in one of the adobe buildings. The railcar remained parked on the siding and didn't look out of place next to two others standing there. The upcoming train would have the main track to itself, next to the coal heaps and water tower. It pulled in, at a crawl, as the last light was fading in the west, three flatcars and four empty passenger coaches, the crew and six ex-Confederate guards.

Over a meagre dinner, news exchanged. That the mine had been attacked and valued friends killed there, that Guzmán was under threat, might well be evacuated, that this train might be ascending this track for the last time, would return laden with refugees. Macquart, the old and sick French colonel who now in command of Manzanillo, had established his administration in the offices of the already-fled alcalde. The refugees were occupying requisitioned accommodation – residents had been given an hour to leave – and food-prices were soaring. Two suspected Juarista spies had been stood against the church wall and shot by the French. And *Quetzal* had left port two days before.

The mood was sombre. All recognised there was no future here for ex-Confederates, not when Washington was supporting the Juarista cause. They'd lost one homeland, had hoped to find another here, were now in a worse situation than the French refugees, who at least stood a good chance of their own government arranging evacuation by sea. Dawlish heard several men swear they'd never crawl back to Yankee servitude – would rather starve – but the vehemence of their declarations hinted at consideration of it. Clayton said nothing, but Tom Bryce was determined to go south, to Nicaragua, Colombia, Ecuador, Peru, anywhere but Texas.

The perimeter was patrolled through the night but Clayton placed one of his men, out of sight, inside the railcar lest a sentry peer inside. A precaution only, for it was unlikely to attract attention, and it didn't.

In the morning, while the locomotive was still raising steam, the car began its roll towards the coast.

And Dawlish was wondering how Weatherby would receive him. He'd exceeded his authority, was risking career and reputation, might trigger a breach in Anglo-French relations.

But he was delivering forty-seven ingots, not the twenty-five for which he'd been sent. That might count for something. – or damn him.

Chapter 22

The railcar rolled into Manzanillo late in the afternoon. Aided by inclines, progress had been rapid in the morning. Closer to the coast, the land levelled and constant pumping was needed to maintain speed. They took it in turns, Clayton and Dawlish included.

Three miles from Manzanillo they encountered a guard post manned by French troops, not Mexican Imperials. A hundred or more local labourers had begun construction of a substantial redoubt close to the track. Another was underway on slightly higher ground a quarter mile to the north. Evacuated earlier from Guzmán, the French looked spent already, weakened by fever and three years endless campaigning. Production of Flandin's pass was enough to be waved through without search.

Manzanillo came in sight – *Sprightly* and *Jenny Dixon* lying at tranquil anchor, *Quetzal* gone. French tricolours flew above several buildings, the Imperial flag over the *alcaldía* alone. Just outside the town, uniformed survey parties, with theodolites and level staffs, were setting out what must be two further redoubts.

Like those up the track, too big for defence by infantry alone. There'll be embrasured artillery here. I've never seen any in this town before. The nearest pieces are at the railhead. These redoubts aren't being built to save Manzanillo. Only to secure it long enough until ships arrive for evacuation.

Clayton's men mounted guard on the railcar when it halted in the *Ferrocarril del Pacífico's* sidings while Dawlish headed towards the wharf. The town felt different now – fewer Mexicans, more French, not just invalid troops drinking in cheap cantinas but women with children haggling shrilly with stallholders over the price of food. There was an air of passive desperation, uncertainty and fear. Nobody wanted to be here, perhaps least of all the remaining Mexicans whose housing had been requisitioned. Makeshift shacks and lean-tos were providing shelter for those who could not find it with already overburdened relatives.

Dawlish left Clayton and his people guarding the loaded railcar. *Sprightly's* whaler, laden with baskets of vegetables and fruit, was pulling away from the wharf when he arrived. He called it back to take him across. He had phrased and rephased his report to Weatherby in his mind. However, now the meeting was minutes away, he could remember little of the logically structured explanation prepared.

On board, it proved worse that Weatherby made no comment, neither as he listened nor when Dawlish finished. He just sent for Lieutenant Ashton.

"Mr. Dawlish has brought some items back with him. I want them taken aboard after midnight when the town's quiet. Twelve boxes and each'll take two seamen to carry each – that's it, Dawlish, twelve, isn't it? Good. And Mr. Ashton, have Grove bring a dozen marines to escort them, all armed, bayonets fixed. Dawlish will show you where to find the items."

"If we're challenged by a French patrol, sir, what are we to say?"

"You can't speak the language, can you, Mr Ashton?"

"Not a word, sir."

"I'll have Dawlish write something. Telling 'em it's a matter of Her Majesty's consular business, protected diplomatically." Weatherby turned to Dawlish. "Draft something impressive to that effect. I'll sign and Mr. Ashton can show it if he must. The French here are such dispirited poor devils that they haven't the appetite for trouble. They'll accept it."

*

Weatherby neither approved nor disapproved Dawlish's action when he called for him next morning. That could bode either good or ill. The silver was aboard – a French patrol had indeed been impressed by the document he had drafted – and stacked under marine guard in the paint locker. The boxes remained unopened, the seals intact.

"Full uniform," Weatherby already looked impressive but Dawlish was in working rig. "You'd better get changed. Best bib and tucker. I've sent to inform Colonel Macquart I'm visiting him at eleven. You'll translate."

"Who's Colonel Macquart, sir?"

"State governor, garrison commander, town governor, acting alcalde and a man who's dying slowly on his feet. He'd been in Guzmán and arrived a few days ago. Not a bad fellow, though it's been damned difficult communicating with him. The bloody French never seem to learn more than a word or two of English."

Dawlish changed and returned. There was a half-hour before they'd need to leave, Weatherby said. He wanted to hear more about the pressure on the French, the closure of *El Camino Real*, the assault on Guzmán, the attack on the mine.

"Durand's command's cut off from the rest of the French. He knows, like all of them, their game's up in Mexico," Weatherby said when Dawlish finished. "Evacuation's the only sensible alternative. But the question's when?"

And Dawlish couldn't help doing what he'd vowed not to do.

Think of Clothilde.

Would Durand help her escape now she'd thrown her lot in with that poor fool Damseaux? The Belgian already had a title and status in his country,. while Durand had only prospects. If Damseaux survived, he'd see it as due to her patient nursing. But if he didn't . . .

I'm not my sister's keeper.

But a persistent internal voice could not be silenced.

I made a promise to my uncle.

*

Colonel Macquart's right eye was covered by a black patch. He was reading a document with the aid of a large magnifying glass, head cocked to one side, when they entered. He looked old enough to have served with the first Napoleon. Even in this land of intense sun, his skin was waxy pale and his hands were trembling. His right had a ring finger and thumb only. He didn't stand up to welcome them. Weatherby took a chair in front of the desk without being invited and motioned to Dawlish to do the same. He introduced him as his translator.

"Tell your superior to be quick," Macquart's voice was weary, lacking cordiality. "Tell him I'm a busy man."

"Tell him I'm one too. That we'll keep it short," Weatherby said when Dawlish translated. "Tell him I'm here as Her Majesty's consul as well as *Sprightly's* captain."

Yet, after that, the exchanges went better than expected.

Lieutenant Dawlish – Weatherby omitted the 'sub' – had been en route to carry important documentation to Colonel Durand in Guzmán. Colonel Macquart was welcome to see the document in question.

Weatherby reached into his briefcase and produced his own copy, in French, of the proposal. He pushed it across the desk and Macquart accepted. He'd read it later, he said.

Weatherby said there could be no doubt Durand – who had impressed as a pragmatic man – would have agreed to the proposal. It was in the interests of all parties. He trusted Colonel Macquart would recognise their merit also.

Dawlish had run into an ambush north of the railhead and been rescued through the heroism of French cavalry. He'd participated in the defence of a post that had come under attack and been essential to the safe retreat of part of its garrison. He'd also appointed himself guardian of a lady – a friend of Colonel Durand's – perhaps Colonel Macquart might have met her, a Madame Sapin?

And yes, the colonel did know her, though he pursed his lips and made no comment. His demeanour indicated he was little interested, that the challenges here in Manzanillo were oppressing, perhaps overwhelming, him.

Dawlish's linguistic skills had assured safe arrival at the *Glorioso* mine, Weatherby said. It had come under attack shortly afterwards by a large brigand group. Perhaps the colonel might have heard of its leader, a barbaric scoundrel who called himself *El Serpiente*? Dawlish played an important role in the defence. The attack was repulsed but the threat now appeared greater in view of the losses suffered by its defenders.

Seizure of silver had been *El Serpiente's* objective and Dawlish had taken decisive measures to get it back to Manzanillo. Unorthodox measures, Weatherby admitted, but pragmatic and in the spirit of the proposal which was being carried to Colonel Durand. The silver was of importance to both Imperial and British interests. That was what he'd come to discuss.

Weatherby passed across the receipt Dawlish had signed for reception of forty-seven silver ingots from *El Glorioso's* manager.

The mention of silver awakened Macquart 's interest. Where was it now? And how much?

Aboard HMS *Sprightly* in sealed boxes. Dawlish did a rough mental calculation. About seven hundred kilograms, he told Macquart.

Of course, exact weight should be determined in the presence of Imperial officials, Weatherby emphasised. He understood that in the current circumstances, Colonel Macquart filled that role. The boxes must remain sealed until then. Thereafter an agreement would be reached on the proportions of the silver to be held in trust by both Colonel Macquart and Her Majesty's consul, Weatherby himself.

And all this in accordance with the proposal being carried to Colonel Durand when blockage of *El Camino Real* made it impossible to deliver. Colonel Macquart would no doubt need time to consider it? If so, Weatherby would be pleased to return whenever convenient.

Macquart indeed needed time. They left him peering at the documents through his magnifier, another responsibility to crush him.

"He'll bite," Weatherby said as they walked back to the wharf. He paused, then added. "By the way, Dawlish, bloody well done."

No more said, but it was enough.

*

They met Macquart again that afternoon and, after a few minor changes to the proposal, gained his general assent.

"It's the line of least resistance for the poor wretch," Weatherby said afterwards. "His life isn't worth a month's purchase and he's got cares enough already without risking a diplomatic incident."

That night, together with Sherwin, *Sprightly's* commissioned engineer, they visited the railway workshops. The manager, Turnbull, confirmed he had weighing scales of high accuracy, a set of standard weights also. He'd have no objection to them being used.

They returned to Macquart next morning and agreed a procedure for opening the sealed boxes and weighing ingots, all to be watched over by himself and Weatherby with two witnesses they would nominate. Details of each numbered ingot must be agreed and recorded. Thereafter, Macquart should choose twenty-two of the forty-seven ingots and the remaining twenty-five, the number requested in the proposal to Durand would be returned to *Sprightly,*. A document, drafted jointly by Dawlish and a French officer with a legal background, would then be submitted to Macquart and Weatherby for comment, finalisation and their signatures.

Easy, compared with what happened in the previous week. Tonight, I'll sleep soundly.

*

Dawlish had arranged to meet Tom Bryce at *La Galina* the following evening. It was crowded. Almost all the customers were French officers, mostly little better than invalids, but there were a few ex-Confederates too. There was no intermingling and an impression of armed truce rather than of common interest. Bryce was sitting in a corner with Captain Clayton and Colonel Sorderer. None of them was smiling.

"These gentlemen told me you'd got the silver out," Sorderer said. "Think the French will let you keep it?"

"It's in hand." Dawlish didn't want to say more.

Sorderer questioned him about the ambush on *El Camino*, the retreat to the mine and the attack on it. It grieved him, he said. He'd known all the Confederates killed there.

"We all came south together," Bryce said. "Band of brothers."

"Is it worth keepin' the rest of my folks at the *Glorioso*?" Sorderer said. "We don't want to lose more."

It was Weatherby who should be asked, not him, Dawlish thought, but he knew Sorderer could never bring himself to do so. The mine was a British interest that had needed all the protection it could get, but it seemed hard now to sacrifice stateless men – or the Belgians for that matter – to delay the inevitable.

"The French won't hold Guzmán much longer." Dawlish had decided that it was better not to answer directly. "They'll retreat to the railhead and maybe hold it as long as they can."

"I've heard the like from their people up there," Bryce said. "Officers, some of 'em. An' my guess is they won't try to hold the railhead no more. They'll take their stand at Colima. Easier to defend."

"Either way, a Juarista force could take the mine within a day," Dawlish said. "And they'll want it intact. No damage."

No need to say more. Sorderer could draw his own conclusion.

"We don't owe the *Glorioso* nothing," Clayton said.

Dawlish wondered if Damseaux's deputy, Captain van Maarkedal, was thinking the same at the mine. With his superior incapacitated, maybe dying, the decision whether to defend it would be his.

And Clothilde? Who'd care about her?

"Clayton tells me you and your captain visited Turnbull at the railroad yard, a couple o' nights ago, Mr. Dawlish." Sorderer said. "Did he say anything about guarding the line?"

Dawlish shook his head.

"Maybe he should have. Colonel Macquart ordered him to end the *Ferrocarril's* contract with us," Sorderer said. "No more of our guards on the trains, none along the track neither. French troops taking over from the end of the week."

Turnbull should have told Weatherby this. So too Macquart.

"Paid only to Saturday." Bryce sounded bitter.

"What will you do then?" Dawlish said.

"Get the hell out before the Juaristas arrive," Clayton said. "If we can, that is. Not just us an' our boys but gentlemen like old Colonel Pettigrew who've tried to cultivate the land."

Sorderer and Bryce were nodding. It seemed to Dawlish too cruel to ask how they hoped to leave or where they'd go. Young men like

Tom Bryce might find mercenary work in countries rent by civil war further south but Sorderer and Clayton, and others like them, were too old for that. And they'd need a ship.

Dawlish sat with them for another ten minutes. They were drinking heavily and joylessly now. He excused himself.

Weatherby would need to know all this.

*

The weighing had a certain ceremonial air – Macquart with one of his officers as witness, Weatherby with Ashton as his. Sherwin and the *Ferrocarril* mechanic, Bill Kemp, handled the weights and scales, closely watched by another French officer. Dawlish recorded each step – acceptance of reference weights, unlocking of the padlocks, breaking of the box seals, numbering the ingots individually by stamping them, then weighing on a balance-scales normally used for exact measurement of alloy-components before melting in a cupola. The entire weighting procedure was repeated a second time before Weatherby, Macquart and witnesses all signed. The variations between the individual ingots were minor – less than half of one percent – but important for Macquart's selection of twenty-two. Then a bottle of wine was produced, toasts drunk to the monarchs of Mexico, France and Great Britain, statements made of mutual regard, wishes for eternal national friendship and final handshakes.

An hour later, twenty-five ingots were heading to *Sprightly*, under marine guard.

At the wharf, Weatherby spoke to Sherwin.

"Could you melt an ingot?"

"We've a forge on the ship, sir," Sherwin said, "but I can't guarantee we'd reach the temperature needed."

"I thought as much. But you get on well with that fellow, Kemp, at the *Pacífico* workshops? Could he do it?"

"He has a cupola, sir, needs it for bronze for bearings. He'll be able."

258

"Could he recast it into smaller pieces, Mr. Sherwin? An ounce each, maybe even half-that. Could he do that accurately?"

"He'd need to make moulds, sir. But yes, it must be possible."

"Go, have a word with him then. If he can do it, I'll arrange the matter with Mr. Turnbull."

Dawlish, standing by, was calculating.

One ingot, weight thirty-five pounds, value two-hundred sterling. An ounce worth about seven shillings.

Weatherby was creating his own currency.

Another gamble.

*

Jenny Dixon's repairs began two days later on the promise of payment in silver. Three ingots, two of them melted into ounce bars, had been signed for by her Captain Ridley, as a loan from Her Majesty's consul. He'd have to make his own terms with Manzanillo's only boatyard and the *Ferrocarril* workshop. Weatherby would release further ingots if and when justified.

All but destitute, most of *Jenny's* crew had taken labouring work on construction of the new French redoubts. They had toiled as virtual slaves for the Juaristas and were now doing the same for the Juaristas' enemy for pittances. They were glad to return to their ship – now moved closer in to the boatyard. *Sprightly's* carpenter oversaw the work and estimated it would take two weeks to get her seaworthy.

Dawlish was coming off the forenoon watch a day later when he saw a thin ribbon of steam two or three miles to the east. It could only be the return of the train he had encountered at Armería on its way up to the railhead when he'd been heading for the coast. It must be heavily laden, for it was crawling. He wondered if Clothilde might be on board. It should mean nothing to him, he knew, but even so he yielded and sought permission to go ashore.

He was at the *Ferrocarril* sidings by the time it crept in. The three passenger coaches looked packed and there were soldiers, in French uniforms, on the roofs. The three flatcars were laden with artillery –

twelve-pounders, as best as he could judge. Crates and barrels were stacked among them, improvised awnings giving shade to the gunners. travelling on board.

Dawlish watched as the coaches disgorged a torrent of misery. A few shabbily clothed Frenchwomen, soldiers' wives, but most were Mexicans in traditional dress, carrying bundles and dragging children, while older siblings carried younger. Most must be the families of Imperial soldiers now terrified of Juarista vengeance. Many of the troops were walking wounded or sick. When a stretcher was carried past, Dawlish caught the smell of gangrene that he'd come to loathe in Denmark.

He waited until the last of the passengers emerged. No sight of Clothilde – though it was hard to imagine her in such company. He approached a French lieutenant with a bandage around his head and was limping with a stick, who said he'd come from Guzmán. It had repelled a Juarista attack and inflicted losses, he said. He'd been wounded at an outer redoubt. But the attack seemed aimed only at probing the strength of the defences. There were reports of heavier Juarista forces moving towards Guzmán from the north. *El Camino* had been reopened. Human and animal remains found where the retreating column had been ambushed – the column from which Clothilde escaped – showed that the massacre was savage and total.

At the flatcars, Dawlish recognised a French captain he'd seen at the railhead. He and his gunners were unwounded and had come to man the redoubts under construction here. The artillery had been taken from the railhead defence works, almost half of what was there. They'd be replaced by weapons coming south from Guzmán.

No doubt now – Durand was about to leave the city and fall back on the railhead.

And was there news from the *Glorioso* mine? Any word of the Belgians there? Dawlish could not bring himself to mention Madame Sapin.

The artillery officer shrugged. He'd heard nothing.

Dawlish walked back through the thinning crowd. He saw Sorderer and Clayton talking to the train guards. There was an air of sullen despair about them, of awareness that their employment by *El Ferrocarril* was at an end, of recognition they had no future here. But Dawlish had no care for them. He was still searching for Clothilde and not finding her.

And unsure of what he would have said or done if he had.

Chapter 23

Once more it was as in the time when *Sprightly* had swung at anchor before news arrived of the Juarista capture of the *Jenny Dixon*. As then, Weatherby remained mostly in his quarters and shared nothing of his intentions with his officers. Moored in a tranquil bay, endlessly maintaining that which was maintained to perfection already, *Sprightly's* monotony, broken only by drills, landings of the field gun, boat races and tugs of-war ashore, had cast gloom and growing resentment over the crew.

It made it worse that they could no longer go ashore in Manzanillo town. Four trains had brought more French, no longer invalids and dependents, but combat-ready troops – artillerymen and infantry withdrawn from Guzmán to man the new redoubts. Brawls in cantinas and brothels between *Sprightly's* seamen and French veterans had caused too many broken heads. They might not speak each other's languages but catcalls about Trafalgar and Waterloo, accompanied by obscene gestures, were easily understood. Consequently, shore leave was now confined to an isolated cluster of adobe shacks along the beach a mile outside town. Enterprising Mexicans improvised cantinas there and women arrived to sell themselves. Marine guards patrolled the perimeter, and *Sprightly's* cutter brought the last revellers back by midnight.

Weatherby was however hungry for information. He sent Dawlish ashore daily to meet French officers, ostensibly on routine administrative matters of mutual concern. If there weren't any, he went anyway, building contacts and trust. It helped not just that he spoke fluent French but that he'd experienced the cutting of *El Camino Real* and already met some of the officers who'd come from the railhead. All spoke of the imminence of final withdrawal from Guzmán. And from Weatherby's queries, Dawlish deduced he had only one concern now, the *Glorioso*.

A British interest, less defensible by the day.

Saving it would restore, and perhaps advance, Weatherby's career. Losing it would mean court-martial for seizure of the silver under a legal fiction and ignominy thereafter. But, for now, he was holding his nerve.

While seeking in solitude a solution which might not exist.

*

A friendly French officer mentioned to Dawlish that another train was due from the railhead the following day. As was his practice now, he went to see it. Timing, as always, was unpredictable. It might be a day long wait. He went to the *Ferrocarril* workshop, watching repairs and drinking coffee with Bill Kemp, the mechanic. By midday, no train, so he invited Bill to join him for lunch at a cantina that gave a good view of the sidings. They sat outside in the shade of a thatched roof. Two French majors were there already with a formally dressed civilian who looked Mexican, most likely one of the few remaining Imperial officials.

Dawlish had come to enjoy Mexican food and Bill Kemp was good company. An hour passed pleasantly – the other customers were still here –- before the sound came of regular marching. That was unusual – there was normally little sense of organisation about the French's reception and unloading of trains. It worked, somehow, only because grizzled sergeants made it work.

But now an infantry platoon came into view, in step. To shouted commands, it formed into line, then took up position along each side of the tracks facing outward, five yards between each man and bayonets fixed. The French majors and the Mexican civilian had stood outside the cantina to watch. The captain commanding the platoon came across and saluted smartly. Dawlish could just hear him report the train being seen in the distance. It should arrive in fifteen minutes. Then he noticed Dawlish's uniform and nodded towards him.

"Should he be here, sir?" His words were scarcely audible.

One of the majors shrugged. "It makes no difference," he said. "We'll be informing the English later anyway."

They sat down in the shade again. A train-whistle shrieked, still far off. Now more troops were arriving, six men and three mule-hauled wagons with them.

"How many trains are up the line at present?" Dawlish asked.

"Two," Kemp said. "Mainly to bring flatcars and open wagons to the sidings at Colima."

Building up reserves for fast evacuation. Even without locomotives, and with men enough to push, they could coast long distances down the inclines.

But the train that finally drew in surprised. Two sandbagged railcars, manned by French infantry, coupled to the front of the locomotive, a single passenger coach and one high-sided open wagon behind, then two more sandbagged cars. No train that had gone up or down before had carried so much protection. It crept to a halt between the two lines of outward facing troops, some of whom changed position to enclose the mule-wagons that now came forward. The French officers and Mexican official left the cantina and were met by what must be the train commander. Handshakes, apparent congratulations, smiles of satisfaction.

The unarmed soldiers hinged down the side of the wagon to reveal a stack of wooden boxes, unmistakable for what they were by their rope handles and black PMC stencilling. The unloading commenced, slowed by the need for the French officers and an Imperial official tugging at the closed padlocks, scrutinising each leaden PMC seal.

Now accepted, a number daubed in red paint by a French Sergeant, recorded in a ledger, each box was then lugged across and lifted on to a mule-wagon. Dawlish was counting also and reached thirty. A hundred and twenty ingots. That must be about half of all stored at the railhead.

He waited until the closely escorted wagons lurched away and followed toward the old fort, over which the French tricolour flew. The gates closed behind them.

Now to inform Weatherby back in *Sprightly*.

But he was too late. As he approached, a boat crewed by French soldiers was pulling away from her. An invitation from Colonel Macquart for Weatherby to view the boxes had already been delivered.

*

The silver was stored in what had been a magazine. The examination of the seals and counting of boxes in the presence of Weatherby and Macquart had something of the same ritualistic formality as when those which Dawlish had brought were recorded. But there was one difference – under Colonel Durand's instruction, Macquart was not to allow opening or weighing.

"Tell the old fellow it's not acceptable," Weatherby said to Dawlish. "We were open about the whole business before and expect no less now."

Macquart seemed embarrassed when he explained that Colonel Durand had sent strict instructions. He could not disobey them, Commander Weatherby would understand that. But the silver would be in safe keeping. He'd be willing for men from *Sprightly* to stand guard with his own troops.

"Thank him," Weatherby said. "He's an honourable old chap and I'm glad to accept the offer. But when's the rest of the silver due?"

Only when rail transport was available, Macquart said. In the present circumstances there was heavy demands on it. Colonel Durand was unwilling to risk sending all in a single shipment lest there be an ambush somewhere along the rail line. Macquart then handed Weatherby a sealed envelope addressed to him by Durand himself.

Weatherby didn't speak as they returned to *Sprightly*. He asked Dawlish to join him in his quarters, where he opened Durand's envelope. It contained a single sheet, headed with the Imperial crest.

"Translate for me, Mr. Dawlish."

He did, and the content shocked him. But Weatherby listened without emotion and asked to hear it again, slowly, stopping after each paragraph so he could make notes.

It opened on a conciliatory note, accepting, though with reluctance, that a junior British officer had brought silver ingots to Manzanillo. Durand acquiesced in the agreement thar Weatherby had reached with Macquart about its division and future determination of its exact value.

"Damn generous of the blackguard not to demand your head, Dawlish," Weatherby said. "And he might have been gracious about thanking you for rescuing that woman of his. He didn't mention her. Maybe she's still nursing poor Damseaux at the mine."

It hurt to hear Clothilde spoken of like this. Dawlish had never mentioned he'd known her before and didn't intend to ever. But that didn't lessen the pain.

My uncle loved her as a daughter and made me promise . . .

But it was the mine that concerned Weatherby. In the current state of military operations, Durand wrote, it was impossible to guarantee the security of *El Glorioso*. The Belgian force stationed there would protect production, and transport to the railhead, as long as possible, but military necessity might demand its withdrawal in the near future. And, except for a few non-committal references to mutual respect, cooperation and goodwill, nothing else.

"He doesn't mention Damseaux," Weatherby said. "If he's dead, he'd surely have remarked on it. How fit do you think the poor fellow could be by now?"

"Still not well, sir. The wound was serious." Dawlish refrained from adding he suspected Damseaux had been drinking heavily for some time. His incapacitation might indeed prove beneficial for the mine's defence. "But his deputy, Captain van Maarkedal, seems capable enough." He paused before saying, "Captain Clayton mentioned to me that he's considering pulling out the few of his own people he still has there under Plutus contract."

"Would this van Maarkedal be able to make a stand?"

A big question for a junior officer but one that only I can answer. I've been there, seen the situation.

Dawlish didn't reply immediately, was grateful Weatherby gave him time to think.

"I don't know how far van Maarkedal can trust his men," he said at last. "They want to be gone, they're sick of Mexico. They might just see off another bandit attack, but will run up the white flag when the

266

Juaristas appear in force. God knows what might happen to them and to Mr. Atkinson and his staff then."

Weatherby made no comment. He turned away, was gazing through the scuttle at the bay's calm expense and *Jenny Dixon,* now almost fully restored.

Five minutes passed in silence.

"You're on good terms with some of the French officers, aren't you Dawlish?" Weatherby said. "Good! Wring them for every scrap of information you can and report back to me."

Dawlish left him.

A man alone, burdened with command, faced with impossible decisions, accepting them willingly And never expecting sympathy.

The sort of man I hope to be one day.

*

Dawlish learned little more in the next two days than he'd heard before from his French acquaintances. All were apprehensive – it didn't bode well that expected trains had not arrived. But on the third day, alerted by steam-whistles announcing approaches, he had himself pulled ashore. Two trains had drawn in on separate sidings, one with three passenger coaches, the other with four. Troops were already lowering wounded from them, some with improvised crutches, were others on stretchers. Foul streaks of blood and human waste had leaked below the doors and filthy bandages looked as if they hadn't been changed for days. Stretcher-cases were being loaded into mule-drawn wagons and those who could walk or hobble sank to the ground to await their turn. It would be long in coming, for the stream of stretchers seemed unending. The last turn of all would be for the lengthening row of bodies with upturned faces covered by blankets.

It was hard not to retreat from this tableau of misery, from the weak moans, the occasional screams, the vacant stares, the stench of death and gangrene in the baking midday heat, the sight of overwhelmed military surgeons and their orderlies doing their inadequate best to prioritise removal. Colonel Macquart, with two senior officers, was listening to a major, with one arm in a sling, who'd arrived by train. Their solemn faces indicated shocked surprise.

Dawlish, watching, lost count at two hundred and forty still-living, and two coaches had not yet disgorged their tragic cargos. Even from the seemingly most mobile of the walking wounded he hesitated to ask what had happened.

Over at the water tower, he spotted Turnbull and Kerr filling buckets and sending *Ferrocarril* workers to carry them to the wounded. Dawlish felt suddenly ashamed of being a passive witness and went across. Turnbull nodded and said nothing, just handed him a tin mug and jerked his head towards two full buckets. He joined the workers passing between the wounded, handing mugfuls to those capable of holding, raising them to the lips of those who couldn't. He felt the same sense of despair and helplessness that he'd experienced in China and Denmark, when he'd been confronted by suffering on this scale. But he choked back his revulsion, spoke words of comfort that he knew could give none, passed from one man to the next until both buckets were emptied. It seemed so inadequate. He turned back towards the water tower for refills.

"Lieutenant Dawlish!" The words slurred but the voice vaguely familiar.

He turned to see the dragoon lieutenant, Nadaud, limping towards him with the aid of a crutch. The right leg of his riding breeches had been cut away above the knee. Below it, a stained bandage wrapped the entire calf. One side of his face was dark with dried blood. Dawlish advanced to meet him and saw that an ear-to-chin gash across his left cheek had been pulled together by five or six knotted stitches.

"You're wounded!" A stupid thing to say, but the words slipped out.

Nadaud nodded, looked about to collapse.

"There!" Dawlish pointed to the workshop building. "You can rest there. I'll support you. Can you make it?" He took his elbow.

A headshake. "I've men, what's left of them." Speech was an effort. A gesture to a half-dozen troopers slumped in a coach's shadow. "They need water."

Dawlish released his arm and ran back to the water tower. While he refilled the buckets, he glanced back to see Nadaud, tottering, threading his way back to his men through the other wounded. Pails brimming now, water sloshing as he hurried, Dawlish caught him up.

He recognised three of the wounded dragoons. One was Sergeant Morvan. A torn tunic was draped around his shoulders and his entire torso was bound by dirty bandages through which fresh blood was seeping. His eyes were dull in his waxen face and didn't flicker when Dawlish spoke his name. His lips didn't accept the water lifted to them.

Nadaud drank only when the others had. Dawlish helped him sit down, back against a coach wheel, then sat with him.

"This won't kill me," Nadaud mumbled. "But Morvan's finished. Poor Bechard too, his wound's mortified. The rest will live."

"What happened?"

"A battle. A big one."

The story came out slowly, painfully, but Nadaud was intent in telling it.

Durand had evacuated Guzmán before the Juaristas arrived to launch a new assault. It was a masterpiece of its type, Nadaud slurred, meticulously planned, accomplished in silence in a single night, taking infantry, artillery and supplies down the reopened *Camino* towards the railhead. Partway along, near the post where Nadaud and Dawlish had parted company, half the retreating force had been placed in ambush, artillery well concealed, infantry positioned in hastily dug entrenchments on steep brush-clad slopes to either side. Nadaud's troop, and others like it, had scouted to the north, watching for a Juarista advance. They found it two days later, pushing south in force from now-occupied Guzmán, and rode back to inform Durand.

It had begun, as intended, as an ambush, but developed into a two-day battle. Repulsed in the first fury, the Juaristas attacked again and again, took heavy losses but gained ground. They'd held it overnight and brought up reserves and artillery for another assault next morning. No further progress, their forces repulsed on one flank and falling into panicked retreat and Durand launching a successful counterattack on the other. The Juaristas retreated with heavy losses.

"But we retreated too," Nadaud said. "Back under darkness to the railhead. No time to bury our dead, though we brought our wounded. Hundreds of them."

"And yourself? Your troop?"

"That was a day later. We met Juarista cavalry reconnoitring northeast of the railhead, two or three troops to our one. Bad, very bad. This is all that got away." A nod towards his wounded. "Morvan took a lance through his right lung. But we made it back to the railhead."

To which the Juaristas had not yet advanced and which Durand now held with a force that included his personal guards. Given Juarista losses, it was unlikely that an assault on it was imminent. The majority of Durand's depleted forces, and all but a fraction of his artillery, had fallen back to Colima. It was now a fortress, its earthworks strengthened by labour-conscription of its occupants. There were dozens of wounded there still and another trainload would be due in Manzanillo soon.

"What about the mine?" Dawlish asked. "Are the Belgians still there?"

Nadaud tried to shrug but the effort made him wince. "They are. Durand finds them useful for protecting his left flank. Not that they'll make much of a fight but if the Juaristas eliminate them, it'll buy time for him to retreat to Colima."

Sudden coughing. Morvan was convulsing, blood bursting from his mouth, body arching, then suddenly falling back, limp and still. No pulse. Dawlish helped Nadaud draw a blanket over his face.

That man saved my life. If nobody else remembers him, I will.

The mule-wagons that brought the first of the most badly wounded away were back to take yet more. It would be hours before Nadaud's pitiful remnant would have its turn. Dawlish wanted to remain longer, even though there was little he could do for them. But he had another duty.

Report to Weatherby.

*

270

Sprightly's gig was carrying Dawlish back to her when he saw two sailing craft at the bay mouth, ghosting shorewards on light airs. They seemed to be in company. Though difficult to judge head on, one seemed to be a large topsail-schooner and the other a brig. They were the first visitors to Manzanillo in weeks. He had no time to wonder about their identity, for the gig was drawing in to *Sprightly's* side.

Weatherby listened in silence and told Dawlish to return in an hour.

He went on deck, saw Lieutenant Ashton leaning on a rail, studying the new arrivals through a telescope. The schooner was already dropping anchor. Ashton called him over.

"Take a look, Dawlish." He handed him the glass. "Can you make out the ensigns?"

He focussed on the brig. The flag was hanging limp at the counter, green at the staff, white and red below. Mexican colours, claimed by President Juarez and Emperor Maximilian alike. Only when a weak breath flapped it did he glimpse for a moment the crown-topped crest at the centre.

"What do you think, Mr. Dawlish?"

"Imperial, sir."

"I think so too. And there can be damn few civilian traders flying it. I believe *Quetzal's* been busy. They're prizes."

Dawlish went to sponge-wash and change, eager to put behind him any trace of the foulness at the *Ferrocarril* sidings. When he presented himself again at Weatherby's quarters, he was subjected to further questioning.

And then his orders.

"Kindly have a message to sent to Colonel Macquart. That I'll visit him at six o'clock. You'll translate. And another to Mr. Turnbull. I'll see him afterward."

A tone of determination.

Weatherby had come to a decision.

Chapter 24

Macquart proved cooperative, perhaps because Weatherby wanted no decision from him other than agreement to provide places on a train to the railhead that was scheduled to leave the following morning. He understood there were to be discussions with Colonel Durand and didn't query their substance. Weatherby would be welcome to bring an escort of his own. It would indeed be a welcome supplement to the French guards travelling with the all-but-empty train. That was the pattern now – empty trains up the line, laden ones down. And Macquart had good news too. A train that arrived today had brought word from Durand that the remainder of the silver stored at the railhead would be carried down to Manzanillo in the next two days. It would be received and stored in the fort's magazine as the previous shipment had been.

"Damn good news, that," Weatherby said to Dawlish. "Tell him I'll witness the formal opening and counting when I get back – I'll talk Durand into agreeing to it. In the meantime, the boxes should be stored with the silver that arrived recently."

Once back in *Sprightly*, preparations had to be hurried. The escort would consist of Grove and a dozen marines. Rations and equipment were to be landed at first light and loaded on the train. Departure was scheduled for eight.

It was preferable to travel in the open wagons, or to join the French guards in the sandbagged railcars at front or rear, for the coaches still reeked of the wounded. Dawlish sensed a light mood among the marines, that this journey was a welcome change from the monotony of recent weeks at anchor. Weatherby too had an air of cheerful resolution about him. Only Dawlish felt uncomfortable. The prospect that he might encounter Clothilde again oppressed him.

The track was notably better guarded than before, the posts strengthened, new redoubts manned by French troops in platoon strength at the longer bridges. They probably had demolition charges beneath them already but the question was one that could not be asked.

They reached Ciudad de Armería before nightfall – the defences of the rail-halt and passing-point there had also been strengthened. To Weatherby's delight, a train had stopped there to pass the night. It looked as heavily protected by sandbagged railcars as that which had carried silver to Manzanillo previously.

"It might be the silver, Dawlish," Weatherby said. "Find the train commander. Tell him I want to see it. And also get us accommodation in some of those huts. Wretched places but better than sleeping in one of those foul coaches."

Dawlish found he'd once met the French captain in command during a convivial dinner at the railhead with Major Flandin. He was friendly and cooperative, was looking forward to the relaxation – he winked – that Manzanillo would offer. The train was transporting thirty-two boxes of silver he said, four ingots to each box, he'd been told, and Weatherby would be welcome to inspect them. And when shown the letter, signed by Macquart, that requested all possible assistance to be provided for Weatherby's party, the captain didn't bother to read it. He was happy to assign four adobe huts and regretted he could offer nothing better.

The boxes were stacked in two open wagons, out of sight behind the high sides. Rope handles, PMC stencilled in black, padlocks closed. Weatherby counted them, Dawlish checked also. The lead PMC seals were intact. Two men on guard at all times.

Plutus Mining would still have to reach a settlement with the Imperial Government – if it still existed – about the level of the royalty but that was minor by comparison with the fact that the silver itself was no longer at risk of seizure by the Juaristas.

One British Interest out of danger. But one more remained.

El Glorioso itself.

*

They reached Colima without incident next evening. It was indeed a fortress now, its earthworks extended, cannon withdrawn from Guzmán grinning from their embrasures. More guns and limbers stood in rows along the sidings' tracks, ordered piles of stores nearby. All troops to be seen were able-bodied – the last useless mouths from Guzmán and the casualties of the recent battle had been evacuated by now.

Major Flandin was now in command here.

"Colonel Durand insisted on holding the railhead himself with a small force," he told Weatherby and Dawlish. "As long has he can. A matter of honour. He'll be the last to leave."

Like Marshal Ney, the last man to step back across the Russian frontier during the Retreat from Moscow, plucking glory from the catastrophe of defeat. The sort of calculated gesture that makes a man a national hero.

"You'd better stay here tonight," Flandin said. "I'll lend you horses to get to the railhead tomorrow. We've ripped up sections of rail. Trains can't reach it anymore. But your marines will have to march. I suggest they make the best of the morning coolness and leave at dawn."

"What's happening at the mine?" Dawlish asked.

Flandin shrugged. "I don't think much. I've heard most of the workers have gone back to their villages. They know it's a matter of time before the Juaristas arrive, or worse still, *El Serpiente*, and they don't want to be at the mine when they do."

"The Belgians are still there?"

"They are, poor devils."

"No orders to bring them back here? Or to evacuate?"

Flandin shook his head.

"Maybe they'll never leave it," he said. "They're nobody's children."

They dined with him afterwards and the mood was sombre. The battle losses had been heavy and men disliked being ordered to fight in a cause already lost.

"The defences here look bloody impressive," Weatherby said to Dawlish afterwards. "But it's a rearguard post nonetheless and they hope there'll be no need to defend it. You saw those rows of cannon by the tracks? They're not positioned here, they're for sending down to Manzanillo. And they'll defend the town and port there only long enough for ships to evacuate them."

"Perhaps that's why *Quetzal's* taking prizes, sir?"

"Maybe damn good business for *Jennie Dixon* too," Weatherby said.

And he laughed.

*

A cavalry patrol was carrying despatches to the railhead and Weatherby and Dawlish could join it. The marines would follow a small mule-drawn wagon column, well protected by infantry, that was setting out at sunrise.

For part of the way, Dawlish rode alongside the dragoon lieutenant commanding the patrol. There had been no sighting of the enemy, he said, neither Juarista nor bandits, south of the railhead. Reconnaissance had however identified large Juarista forces to the north, and more troops were joining them by the day. They were biding their time, the lieutenant thought, perhaps hoping the French might withdraw without a battle. It had been a long war, all sides were sick of it, and the Juaristas wouldn't fight unless they had to. He wanted nothing more himself than to be home in France.

When they arrived at the railhead, now lacking rail connection, it was hard to judge numbers but it looked to be defended with a fraction of the troops seen there previously. Allowing for men who were resting after night duty, there could be scarcely more than a hundred. Half were wearing the blue tunics and red breeches of the smart cavalry which Dawlish had seen escorting Durand. The remainder were infantry and gunners. There were horses and mules in the pens. All but two of the twelve-pounders there previously had been removed and their embrasures filled with earth. The sight confirmed the suspicion that Durand was here for show only, ready for a fast retreat after a token defence.

275

They found him in the office previously occupied by Flandin. It seemed a great come-down compared with what he had occupied in Guzmán. He didn't rise when they entered and was as little welcoming now as he'd been before. He seemed like a man abstracted, his mind on more than the concerns of intrusive British officers.

Weatherby thanked him for the release of the silver and Dawlish translated. Durand shrugged. It was better for it to be stored at Manzanillo until agreement was reached on the royalty and permission given for export.

A difficult half-hour followed.

Weatherby asked what was happening at the *Glorioso*.

Durand was evasive. He had no immediate plans to withdraw the Belgian troops from there but doing so could not be ruled out. Military priorities would decide if, and when, it was appropriate. He clearly recognised Dawlish but he made no reference either to his appropriation of silver from the mine or to Clothilde's rescue. He must know about both. Dawlish wondered if he was so aggrieved by her desertion that he was virtually abandoning the mine, and all there, to punish her.

Weatherby emphasised the *Glorioso* was a British business undertaking. The investment had been great and was now at risk. He wanted to see the situation at the mine for himself. Only then could he recommend whether or not to close down operations and withdraw British staff.

Sarcasm dripped from Durand's voice. It was indeed a concern of British business interests, so perhaps Britain would prefer to defend it? Maybe with the dozen men Weatherby had brought with him? He was welcome to go there if he wanted, as long as he would not expect accommodation here at the railhead or the loan of horses or mules. Weatherby hadn't been invited and Durand would accept no responsibility for him or his people.

And Weatherby ignored the dismissive, insulting tone. It struck Dawlish he seemed even pleased.

He thanked Durand and looked forward to many years of friendship and cooperation between France and Britain. With that, the interview was ended.

Now to get to the mine.

On foot.

*

Weatherby and Dawlish sat until noon on a bench in the shadow of a thatched awning at the horse and mule pens, their baggage at their feet, studiously ignored by members of the garrison. There was at least water available from a hand-pump that fed the animals' drinking troughs. They were both in working uniform but, sweating as he was, Weatherby did not open a top button, nor did he remove his hat.

"We're Queen's officers, damn it," he said. "That blackguard's trying to humiliate us. He won't have the satisfaction."

Dawlish, broiling, could not but follow his example.

And yet for all the discomfort, and the prospect ahead of a brutal march to the mine once Grove and the marines arrived, Weatherby was buoyant. He said nothing about his intentions but conversed pleasantly about past experiences, Dawlish's as well as his own. And he made no secret of his contempt for Durand.

"I'll be surprised if his whole garrison isn't out of here in a week. He'll have no compunction about abandoning the Belgians. I take all that nonsense about him making a heroic stand here with a pinch of salt. He'll be gone long before the Juaristas arrive."

But all the time, the image of Clothilde was haunting Dawlish. She wasn't at the railhead — he was sure of that, for the accommodation was too Spartan. Did Durand care about her desertion? Had she already broken with him before she'd left Guzmán, or he with her? It was easy to imagine her as yet another in a long line of women he'd used and cast aside. She must still be with Damseaux at the mine. With the poor devils there, nobody's children . . .

He'd never mentioned to Weatherby that, as a boy, he'd known Clothilde, had been so close, had pledged his honour to his dying uncle

— a dying naval officer at that — to protect her always. And even at this moment he shrank from doing so, for all that he knew Weatherby would most probably offer understanding and advice. But he was ashamed, and afraid, and despised himself for being both.

Weatherby looked at his watch and snapped it shut. "It can't be long before Grove gets here. We'll meet him outside."

The sentries made no attempt to question or detain them. They walked south along the track of sleepers, now stripped of rails, for half a mile, then waited in a tree's shade. Soon after they saw the red coats approaching at a slow but steady plod. Footsore, weary and thirsty, they'd done well, twelve miles against the slope as the day's heat had grown. They'd imagined the railhead to be a goal, a place to rest before moving to the mine on the morrow.

Now Weatherby must tell them that they were just halfway. Their rest could be no longer than thirty minutes, then onwards to the mine. Grove would accept it without demur and, though the men might complain among themselves, they'd do it anyway.

The honour of their corps demanded nothing less.

*

It was hard on Grover and the marines but they had trained relentlessly ashore while *Sprightly* had lain moored at Manzanillo. It was hard for Dawlish too, but worst of all for Weatherby, who was twenty years older than any of them. He maintained the albeit slow, and slowing, pace mile after mile, insisting on carrying part of his baggage himself. He drank from his canteen only as much as Grove allowed his men at each halt of five minutes in the hour, and tottered when he arose again but somehow stumbled back into a painful trudge. Dawlish stayed close, ready to catch him if he fell, admiring him more at each step.

They didn't reach the mine that night but the first of the Belgian posts, which looked out across the *Glorioso's* valley, afforded shelter as the sun set. It had been strengthened further since Dawlish last seen it, the little loopholed adobe shack surrounded now by a low wall of sandbags and cactus. Lights were twinkling down in the valley but there was no pounding of the ore crusher. Work at the mine had ended a week before, the corporal at the post said. He looked relieved to be reinforced, if only for a single night, and did his best to provide food and scanty comfort. Like his men, like most of the Belgians whom Dawlish had met, he looked beaten and dispirited.

It was downhill towards the mine next morning but still a miserable plod on blistered feet and tired legs. No smoke drifted from the chimneys above the workshops and only a few figures were moving between the other buildings. But somebody had spotted the marines' red tunics on the track above, for a horseman came cantering up the track to meet them. He reined in. Dawlish saw it was Captain van Maarkedal. As always, he gave the impression of a man thriving on adversity, still full of energy.

Salutes, welcome, and surprise. And not the time for lengthy explanations. van Maarkedal looked shocked at Weatherby's exhaustion, still obvious after a night's sleep. He slipped off his horse and handed the reins to Dawlish.

"I'll wait here with these men. Ride down and find Atkinson. Tell him to send a horse for your captain. Mules for the rest."

Dawlish, aching, pulled himself up into the saddle.

"What about Colonel Damseaux?" he asked.

"Recovering slowly. But unable to command." No hint of regret.

Dawlish cantered down the track. He would seek Atkinson at his office first, hoping he was there and not at his house. Yet even so, his gaze drifted to that white wooden building. There were people on the verandah and, as he came closer, saw a figure lying on a couch. A woman in a blue dress and snowy-white apron was sitting on an upright chair beside him, seemingly reading-aloud from a book, a table with a vase of flowers on the opposite side. It hurt as much to see Clothilde with Damseaux as when he'd seen her with Durand. He looked away, fearful that Clothilde might lower her book and recognise him. It was likely unavoidable that he'd meet her soon but hoped it would not be now.

He rode past the Belgian troops' adobe barracks and on to Atkinson's office. He tethered his horse outside but his heart fell when he found nobody within. Going up to the house would be a last resort, he decided. On foot, he checked by the idle crusher and found nobody there either – in its silence it looked like a forlorn metallic Ozymandias. Only in a workshop did he at last find Atkinson speaking with the Welsh foreman and watching two mechanics repairing a lathe.

"What are you doing here?" Atkinson looked alarmed.

"It's not just me, sir. It's Commander Weatherby as well. With marines too. Come to support you."

"How?"

"Commander Weatherby will tell you, sir."

I've no inkling of what he intends.

Told that van Maarkedal was with Weatherby, and of his request for a horse and mules, Atkinson sent the foreman away to see to it.

"It's better you join me in my office, Mr. Dawlish. We can talk better there. I expected nothing like this and I must know what's going on."

And even if he'd known, Dawlish could not have told him. Weatherby would reveal his plan in his own good time. But he did draw from Atkinson as much as he could about what had been happening at the mine. Or not happening.

"We couldn't keep the workers after the bandit attack," Atkinson said. "Everything had to stop, the mining, the crushing, the recovery. Colonel Durand sent a troop to escort the last silver we had here. He said it would be sent to Manzanillo with the rest of the ingots at the railhead. Since then, we've had no word from him."

"The first load arrived safely, sir, and we met the second as we were coming up. But how's the situation here? Any sign of the bandits, or Juaristas?"

"Nothing of either, though van Maarkedal thinks they may have us under observation. But no move as yet. And we've heard nothing from the French either."

"And Baron Damseaux, sir?" It was hard to ask.

"The poor fellow damn nearly died. If you hadn't brought that lady here, Mr. Dawlish, he wouldn't have survived. She never left his side, still hasn't." Atkinson paused. "It's a delicate matter, Mr. Dawlish.

Who is she exactly? My wife's heard scandalous talk that she was Colonel Durand's . . . friend, a very close friend indeed."

Impossible to tell the truth.

Dawlish shook his head. "I understand she's the widow of a young officer killed earlier this year up beyond Guadalajara. The colonel took pity and was helping her get back to France. She was on her way when the column she was with was attacked."

"She seems wealthy."

"Well connected. From an aristocratic family, I believe."

"A tragic story." Atkinson sounded like he believed it. "I'll tell my wife not to press her about it. Madame Sapin has trouble enough already."

And I'm lying for her now, as I would lie about her to my uncle, were he still alive. It would have broken his heart to know the truth.

Time to meet the line of men, horses and mules straggling down the hill.

To what purpose?

Only Weatherby knew.

Chapter 25

Dawlish rode up the ridge north of the mine just after sunrise. It was two days since Weatherby revealed his plan and put it into action with Atkinson's assent. The morning inspection of the observation posts was now routine.

He reached the crest, turned towards the post a half-mile to the west, conscious his profile was silhouetted against the skyline. It was better to be seen, Weatherby had said. Some Juarista officer might scrutinise the strange uniform through his field-glasses and wonder about the British union-flag now flying above the post.

A marine shouted a challenge as he approached, demanding he remain fifty yards distant until Lieutenant Grove agreed to him coming forward.

"Any movement?" Dawlish asked Grove when he did.

"Nothing. I don't think they're out there at all."

It was the post at which Dawlish arrived after the retreat from *El Camino* with Sergeant Morvan and the other French.

With Clothilde.

Grove had two marines with him. No Belgians. There was a similar post a half mile distant to the west, manned by a corporal and two men. A mile to the east was the post on the track that led from the railhead. There too the Belgians had been withdrawn and a marine sergeant occupied it with two men. Union flags, carried in knapsacks from Manzanillo, were now stirring on poles above all posts. If nothing changed, Dawlish would be relieving Grove in two days' time, bringing fresh marines with him from those held in reserve at the mine. He didn't relish the prospect. The Belgians manning the redoubts would have some hope of survival should there be an attack. The observation posts had almost none. A Juarista commander might recognise the significance of a British flag. *El Serpiente* and his savages wouldn't, nor care if they did.

He took Grove's glasses. *El Volcán* was directly to the north, smoking as ever. No threat from there. Its bare slopes extended far to the west – little chance of approach from that direction either. But he scanned the scrub-clad lower slopes to the north-east intently. On the retreat, he had come through there himself with little enough difficulty and *El Camino Real* lay close, but out of sight, beyond. He saw nothing but pointed that way.

"They're out there, Grove," he said. "They're watching us and wondering about our flag. Some young Juarista officer doesn't know what to do and he's probably reported back and waiting for a reply. Maybe his senior's uncertain too and has referred it up the line also. But sooner or later they'll come. Depend upon it."

"And if it isn't the Juaristas? *El Serpiente*? What then?"

"Run like the devil to Number 6 redoubt. You probably won't make it, so say your prayers on the way."

Half joking, whole in earnest.

He remounted, rode to the two other observation posts. Nothing to report at either. Then back down to the mine.

Weatherby's logic had aligned with Atkinson's. It was not unlike the proposal he had intended to present to the Juaristas at Guadalajara weeks ago, before Durand turned him back. The mine was a British interest. Its operation would be profitable not just to the shareholders of the Plutus Mining Company but, through royalties, to the Mexican government – whatever that government might be. Plutus had a licence from the Imperial Government. Should another government replace it, honouring that licence would reflect well internationally on the reputation of the new government. Investors wouldn't hesitate to make further commitments. Plutus would be in the forefront of doing so and ready to agree to reasonable modifications to the licence as regards royalties and other matters.

It would all depend on the existing investment being left undamaged during current hostilities, in which Britain was unreservedly neutral.

But there was one objection, a strong and reasonable one.

"Durand will have us butchered if we retreat without orders," van Maarkedal had said. "And if we surrender to the Juaristas they'll slaughter us without hesitation." He paused. "They've a lot to hold against us from further north. Reprisals, shootings, villages burned. They won't have forgotten."

"You'll have the protection of the British flag," Weatherby said. "That or our lives. If they want to slaughter you, they'll have to kill me and my people first. When Juarez is president again, I doubt he'll relish explaining that to Her Majesty's ambassador."

He hadn't raised his voice, had looked van Maarkedal straight in the eye. He meant every word – Dawlish knew him well enough for that by now. Weatherby might be gambling again but was prepared to pay the price of losing.

van Maarkedal was impassive as Dawlish translated. He waited a full minute before replying.

"How can you guarantee it?"

"I can't," Weatherby said. "You'll have to take my word for it. The word of an officer. And if you don't, you know the options. I'd recommend neither."

"Damseaux must approve it. His signature on a paper, not mine. I don't want to face a firing squad in Belgium either."

"Write your paper," Weatherby said.

Dawlish translated van Maarkedal's draft into English. Weatherby made a few modifications, than had it translated back into French.

"Satisfied, Captain van Maarkedal?"

"As long as Damseaux signs it."

Obtaining a meeting with him proved difficult. It would have to be in Atkinson's house and sensible that he himself should arrange it. He looked amused when he came back to Weatherby.

"That damn woman," he said, "she told me in Spanish it wasn't convenient today. The baron needs rest and can't see more than one person at a time besides herself. Not for longer than five minutes. And if he gets agitated, she'll insist on everybody leaving. She couldn't guarantee he'd be up to it tomorrow either."

"Did you leave it like that?"

Atkinson laughed. "I retreated and mentioned it to my wife. She went to see her. I could hear loud voices but didn't investigate. When Josefina returned, she told me Madame Sapin had agreed we could see him on the verandah at three o'clock."

Dawlish had no option but to attend as translator.

They found Damseaux on his couch, supported by cushions, still pale but not feverish or in noticeable discomfort. Clothilde was standing by him, hair immaculately coiffured, pearl-grey cotton dress protected by a white apron. She looked demure and vulnerable.

"The gentlemen are here, André." Her whisper was loud enough for all to hear. She squeezed his hand. "Don't fret. I'll be close." She looked towards the visitors. "Five minutes, gentlemen, no longer."

When she stepped back a pace, she laid her hand on Damseaux's shoulder. She had seen Dawlish but looked past him as if he were a stranger. He was grateful for that.

It took less than five minutes. Weatherby explained, Dawlish translated, Damseaux listened, van Maarkedal had his say. Clothilde leaned forward and pressed Damseaux's shoulder and his hand rose to touch hers.

His voice was tired when he spoke. It was all regrettable, very regrettable, but he could see no other option in the circumstances. Empress Carlota's Legion had done all it could and more. There was no dishonour in this step. Clothilde was nodding. She leaned over and whispered in his ear, just loud enough for Dawlish to hear.

"It's for the best, André. Set your mind at rest."

He turned to her and asked for a pen. She returned with a writing slope, laid it with exaggerated gentleness, on his lap after asking if he could bear the weight.

Damseaux signed. Authorisation of van Maarkedal to surrender, should the situation become hopeless, so avoiding needless loss of life and property.

There was a paragraph beneath and Weatherby signed it both as captain of HMS *Sprightly* and as Her Majesty's Consul at Manzanillo. That Britain, as a neutral party, would exert its best efforts to ensure strict observance of the rules of war as they affected surrender.

Atkinson witnessed both signatures. Weatherby produced a second copy, for his own retention, and he and Damseaux signed again.

"You must leave now, gentlemen," Clothilde said. "The baron is fatigued."

Within the hour three Union flags had been raised above the advance observation posts.

And the waiting began.

*

Three uneventful but anxious days passed. Dawlish had replaced Grove at the post up on the ridge. It was mid-morning now, the heat growing, difficult not to drift into a torpor.

"Beggin' your pardon, sir." A marine private was pointing north-eastwards. "Something's down there."

Dawlish swung his glasses over, sharpened focus on the thinning brush some four-hundred yards distant. He caught brief glimpses of uniforms – faded blue, some with crossbelts, similar to those of Juarista troops he'd seen at Zihuantanejo – moving from cover to cover. And then nothing, no further advance.

He had wondered if he should hope for, or dread, this moment. Now he knew. His heart was pounding, hand trembling.

"Get the white flag," he said.

It was made from a bedsheet donated by Atkinson and nailed to a long pole.

"Leave your rifle and follow me," he said to the marine.

They clambered over the wall.

"Start waving. Slowly."

Dawlish led the marine thirty yards to the right. It was important to stand outlined against the sky, Weatherby had stressed, essential to convey a message of willingness to parley.

Three minutes passed. No movement in the scrub but twice a flash of sunlight on what might be a lens. Chilling awareness that, even at this range, a skilled rifleman could score a hit.

"Stop waving," Dawlish said. "Drop the flag and stand still."

He raised his left arm, pointed back at the Union flag above the post and held the stance.

More sun flashes, now from the edge of the scrub. He was being studied. There would be a discussion in progress there, argument and counterargument about how to respond.

"Sweep the white flag again," he said to the marine. "Ten times, very slowly. Keep it low. Then stay where you are."

With luck, this might be interpreted as willingness to negotiate. He walked back to the post, pointing to the Union flag all the way. It was drooping and he would have wished for an Atlantic gale. He climbed up the wall, reached out, caught a corner of the flag and drew it out as far as he could. They must see it now. There could be no doubt what it was.

His gaze was locked on the scrub-edge. Two figures emerged. They were looking up through field-glasses, sun flashing on their lenses. He fancied one wore an officer's uniform but the second was clad in black.

And then, at last, response, a man was called out from the scrub behind them, carrying a white flag over his shoulder. This could not be the prelude to assault.

"Wave again!" Dawlish shouted to the marine with the flag. "Ten times."

The Juarista flag-bearer halted ahead of the two men already in the open. He was looking back, awaiting orders. When he got them, he also swept his flag ten times. Dawlish called for another ten as answer.

An eternity passed before three horses were led out from cover. The man with the flag mounted, the two others also. Dawlish called for his glasses.

Gold braid and epaulettes identified the officer as a colonel at the least, perhaps even a rank more senior. But the man by him was a civilian, clad in black but for the white of his shirt above his waistcoat and an elegant straw hat, its broad brim turned down at the edges. Civilian or not, he was riding with the same assurance as the officer beside him.

They were picking their way up the slope now and Dawlish went out to meet them. A wave from the officer instructed the rider with the flag to pull aside. He came on with the civilian.

The two horsemen drew rein just before him. The officer returned Dawlish's salute.

"*Teniente Nicholas Dawlish del barco de Su Majestad Británica, Sprightly.*"

"*General de brigade Diego Ortiz.*" Perhaps fifty, with the look of a seasoned campaigner, a Mexican counterpart to Durand.

The civilian was younger, darkly bearded, and spoke in English. "Of the ship that raided Zihuantanejo?" From his accent, he might have been American. He didn't introduce himself.

Stand your ground.

Dawlish answered in English. "From the ship which helped repossess a British merchant vessel unjustly seized."

The civilian pointed up to the Union flag. "So, in reprisal, Britain's claiming part of Mexico?"

"No, señor. Just waiting to discuss common interests." He paused. "I haven't had the honour of knowing your name, señor."

The civilian held out his hand.

"Rafael Jiménez. Onetime consul-general of Mexico in New Orleans, now a personal representative of President Benito Juarez."

"My captain will be glad to see you," Dawlish said. "I'll send one of my men to alert him."

"If we've come this far, we can afford to wait a little longer," Jiménez said. He swung down from his saddle. So too did Ortiz.

Jiménez reached inside his coat and produced cigars.

"These might pass the time," he said. "And maybe something stronger too."

He reached out a silver pocket flask.

"French cognac, lieutenant. We captured a lot of it in Guzmán."

*

Weatherby came riding up, leading another horse for Dawlish.

288

Salutes and introductions, a compliment on Jiménez's English, hope of mutually agreeable resolution of difficulties.

"This is a damn poor place to discuss matters, gentlemen," Weatherby said. "I suggest we meet in more comfortable surroundings down there." He might have been inviting a brother captain to visit his ship. He glanced down at Ortiz's buttoned holster and said to Dawlish, "Tell the general he's welcome to wear his sidearm and sword. And no need for blindfolds either."

They rode down the steep and narrow pathway leading to the mine, Dawlish at the rear. Past the white house – no Damseaux or Clothilde on the verandah – and headed towards Atkinson's office. The general was riding next to Weatherby but Jiménez dropped back to ride alongside Dawlish.

"Where are the Belgians?" he asked.

The question was reasonable. There was an absolute silence, a deadness, about what had been a busy industrial site. Nobody to be seen in the open, not at the doors of the workshops, nor in the laneways between the adobe barrack huts.

"They're manning the defences." Dawlish pointed to one of the redoubts on the ridge to the south. "Anybody resting is confined to their quarters."

Jiménez was looking around, obviously impressed.

"Where's the actual mine?" he said.

Dawlish pointed to the drift, and the rail track also that carried loaded cars from its mouth.

"And what's that?"

"It's the machine that crushes the ore. And there, in those sheds, it's treated with mercury to extract the silver."

Jiménez, nodding, seemed fascinated. He pointed to the workshop sheds. "And there?"

"Where they repair the machinery if it's damaged."

"And all this is unharmed? No explosive charges in place?"

"That's correct, señor. I understand everything was functioning normally until it was attacked by *El Serpiente*. No damage was done to it then. I happened to be here on my captain's business."

"Aaah," Jiménez said. "*El Serpiente*, Javier Belarra. Well named. Useful to us for some time but an embarrassment now victory's imminent. We've dispensed with his services and he's taken himself off. We'll deal with him after our government's installed again in Mexico City. It won't be long."

Dawlish knew he was being pumped for information but had told nothing Jiménez wouldn't be hearing shortly. Besides, he wanted to do some pumping of his own. Information, however trivial, could be of value.

"You speak like an American, señor," he said. "How long were you in New Orleans?"

"Thirty-seven years, three of them as consul. I was born there. My father had a business. A good one."

"But you came back?"

"As soon as Juarez was ousted. Some things are worth more than profits. And Juarez found me useful."

They had arrived. Atkinson was standing outside his office to meet them.

*

van Maarkedal wasn't present, just the two Mexicans, Atkinson as manager of a British company, Weatherby as both consul and naval officer, here to assure the security of British investments. In courtesy, the meeting was conducted in Spanish – Atkinson was fluent and Dawlish sat by Weatherby to translate.

Weatherby left no doubt as to the reason for the meeting – agreement on measures to protect the investment of Globus Mining Limited. It would perhaps be better if Señor Atkinson was to explain the nature of the mine. Ortiz waited to assent until Jiménez agreed.

Atkinson was well prepared, account ledgers lying open on the table, details of allocations of investment, a large-scale map of the facilities, weekly records of production. And an open pan heaped with ground ore beside a single silver ingot.

General Ortiz listened in bewilderment. Jiménez had taken up the ingot, was weighing it in his hands, as he listened, interjecting searching questions at intervals and jotting in a notebook.

Atkinson kept the best until last. He unrolled another map, indicated locations for further drifts, opportunities for doubling production in two years, doubling it again two years later. It would of course be dependent on the willingness of whatever government might be in power to reissue, in its name, the licence granted by the Imperial Government. But what mattered for now was that the existing facilities remain undamaged. Any destruction would deter future foreign investors.

"How long before you can extract silver again?" Jiménez asked.

"Within a fortnight if we can get our labour back." Atkinson said. "They fled to their villages out of fear. Once security's guaranteed they'll flock back."

"General Ortiz can do that," Jiménez said, without consulting him.

Ortiz nodded assent anyway.

Now, as arranged, Weatherby had his say.

"There's one slight complication, gentlemen. The Belgian troops already here. They've been abandoned by the French. If they're attacked, they'll fight because they'll have nothing to lose. But everything here could be wrecked before you finish them." He waited, let the words sink in. "However, they might be willing to surrender. Under acceptable terms."

"What terms?" Jiménez said.

"Guarantee of their lives. Disarming but for officers' sidearms. Freedom to depart with myself as British representative to oversee their transfer to Manzanillo and ensure observance of the terms."

"You think the French will accept that? Their Colonel Durand?"

"He will because France can't afford to offend Great Britain. It's had a bloody nose here and there's trouble brewing in Europe. It doesn't need more enemies than it has already. So France will accept it. And leave Durand to me."

"These Belgians are hated here," Jiménez said. "They've charges to answer, atrocities, villages burned. Are they to walk free?"

"Just as you'll let the French walk free. They're even now falling back on Manzanillo and for one reason only. This war's damn nearly over. Your country's suffered enough. Just let the Belgians go. I'll see they'll be shipped out. You have my word."

Dawlish translated.

Long silence before Jiménez looked towards Ortiz.

And Ortiz nodded.

"We want to talk to the Belgian commander," Jiménez said.

Weatherby sent Dawlish to bring van Maarkedal.

Another step forward.

But still a long way to go.

Chapter 26

It was easy for van Maarkedal to confirm his willingness to surrender in Atkinson's office. But the Mexicans demanded a more formal ceremony which was impossible to arrange before the Belgian troops were reassured capitulation would not mean massacre. The danger was of despairing and futile mutiny by frightened men. It was agreed the ceremony should be delayed until the morrow. Weatherby and Dawlish escorted Ortiz and Jiménez back to the ridgetop post, shook hands, and watched them ride down to their own force. By the time they would return next morning, with a single company of infantry and a troop of cavalry, the Belgians should be ready to disarm themselves and be prepared for departure.

When Weatherby and Dawlish returned, van Maarkedal had paraded those of his men not on duty in the redoubts. He told them of his decision to surrender and asked Weatherby to confirm they'd be evacuated, unarmed, under the protection of the British flag. Shuffling and sidelong glances in the ranks, low muttering, shock and fear on the faces of men who'd dreamed of deliverance for months but now confronted by the risks it demanded.

"We're not sheep to be slaughtered!" an unseen voice shouted from somewhere at the rear.

A sergeant called for silence but others were joining in, refusing to give up their arms, that all was a plot to abandon them, that they were betrayed, would never see Belgium again.

And yet the ranks held. van Maarkedal waited for the noise to lessen and spoke again. They'd known him as a hard but just commander, he reminded them. One who'd shared their dangers, hunger and fatigue.

"Private van Temse! Where are you?" he shouted.

An arm raised.

"You were wounded at Amacueca. The Juaristas would have had you if I hadn't carried you on my back under fire! And Corporal

Renkin! You hear me? I went back and held off five of 'em 'til help came when you went down at Barranca San Lorenzo."

"You did, sir! God bless you!"

"And Private Theunis, you salopard! The baron would have had you shot when you violated that child at Estipac, had I not spoken for you!"

Shouts of derision for Theunis, a few weak cheers for van Maarkedal.

"So you know me!" he shouted. "Do you think I'd agree to anything but the best bargain I could get for you? A bargain that means I'll run the same risks as you. I hate this place as much as you do. I too want to be gone. But there's no other way than to trust this British officer and the protection his flag can give. It's that or stay and fight without hope here. And each of us keep the last bullet for ourselves."

Now wavering. Doubt or confusion on faces, cohesion loosening in the ranks that still somehow held, men arguing, calls for silence from junior officers and sergeants ignored, heads nodding or shaking. Then quietening at last, the starkness and logic of surrender accepted.

van Maarkedal spoke again, more-matter of fact now, then walked along the ranks, briefly listening to some man's concerns, moving on, pausing when he recognised a soldier to tell him he was glad to have him alongside – they'd already come through a lot together.

It took an hour or more but in the end the majority seemed to accept. Now they were to be sent to relieve the men manning the redoubts so they too could hear van Maarkedal.

And all of them would stand under arms for one last night.

*

Now the long night for Belgian officers copying out paroles on scraps of paper, the first short paragraph on each in Spanish, the second in French. Undertakings that the bearer would refrain, upon pain of death, from bearing arms again on Mexican soil. Space below for a name and signature – or an 'X', as many of the Belgians were illiterate.

Then the parade at dawn, each man with his unloaded rifle and ammunition on the ground before him, his pack, filled canteen and rolled blanket ready for the march. A table with pens and inks and boxes containing the parole slips, three chairs behind it. One waiting for a Mexican officer, one for van Maarkedal, the third for Weatherby, to sign as witnesses.

The other preparations.

Ten Globus-owned mules to carry two-days' rations as far as the railhead and return afterwards to the mine. Atkinson's two-wheeled trap to carry Damseaux and Clothilde. Two mule-drawn wagons for Belgian sick and horses for Weatherby, Dawlish and van Maarkedal

Then the arrival of the Juaristas just after sunrise.

Ortiz and Jiménez riding down the ridge ahead of their escorting troop of lancers. The infantry company appearing directly after – it must have spent the night in cover just below the crest. They came without haste, alert but expecting neither trap nor resistance, confident they would face not just a beaten enemy, but one willing to admit it.

The slow humiliation of the ceremony.

Formal salutes on arrival. The Juarista lancers drawn up on either side of the Belgians, their infantry in front and behind. van Maarkedal reading out the surrender document's terms to his troops, then signing. Ortiz and Jiménez following and Weatherby last. Handshakes. Shouted Belgian commands. Rank by rank, each man to take up his rifle and ammunition, come forward in single file, throw down both on growing piles overseen by Juaristas. Then another pile, bayonets pulled from scabbards and cast on it. To the table then, one by one, writing their names and ranks on a parole slip if they were able, having it written for them by a Belgian sergeant if they were not. Then the signatures and 'X's and final release to join the column waiting to depart. The half-dozen remaining ex-Confederate guards signed last, bitter they must discard their weapons brought from Texas.

And all the while, the merciless sun beat down.

This is defeat incarnate. Not just capitulation but degradation, the surrender of pride, the recognition that all endeavour, all sacrifices, had been futile. Dear God, may I or my country never experience this!

The moment was over. It could never be forgotten.

*

It all took so long that the march began just after midday, the worst time for it. There would be no option now but to bivouac halfway to the railhead, for most of the dispirited Belgians were poorly shod. Weatherby and van Maarkedal rode at the column's head, two marines on foot behind them, taking it in turn to hold aloft a Union flag. Damseaux and Clothilde followed in the trap. It was loaded with her baggage and she insisted on driving herself while he sat crouched and all but comatose, grimacing each time the vehicle lurched over a rut. Juarista lancers rode along each side of the straggling line and Grove and his marines brought up the rear, also flying a Union flag.

Dawlish, determined not to have contact with Clothilde, ranged back and forth along the line on horseback. He wondered how Durand would receive her. Would he resent her desertion of him in favour of Damseaux or welcome the relief from a burden he had tired of? He had certainly not come for her, or even sent a message offering help, since she'd reached the mine. If so, Atkinson would have known.

And Atkinson had not left the mine, nor had any of his British staff. He was glad to accept its guarding by Juarista forces and slowly accommodating himself to the reality of their inevitable rule. In strict letter of law, royalties on the silver in storage at Manzanillo were due to the Imperial government. Even before the ingots could reach Europe however, the title to those royalties might have passed to a new, internationally recognised, Juarista government of Mexico. Lawyers might squabble, but there would be no Imperial government to accept payment.

At the second halt – five minutes in the hour – Weatherby summoned Dawlish to join him. He found his captain writing in pencil in a notebook, a wagon's dropped tailboard acting as desk.

"It's for that blackguard Durand," Weatherby said. "To warn him of what's happened and ensure we're not attacked on sight when we get to the railhead, flags or no flags. I wouldn't put it past the scoundrel ordering it after the Mexican lancers will have us two miles from there."

Dawlish was nodding, not doubting who'd have to carry it and translate it.

"And you've seen how so slowly this column's moving, Dawlish. These poor Belgian wretches have hardly a pair of decent boots between them and most are lame already. So I'm appealing to Durand, one officer, one gentleman to another, to send out mules from the railhead to meet us in the morning."

"Am I to carry it, sir?"

"You're a resourceful young chap, Dawlish. You'll be there long before sunset. I want you to translate this note and argue with Durand for the mules. Don't hesitate to refer to the value of warm Anglo-French relations, that sort of thing."

"Very well, sir. I'll leave immediately."

An ambitious young officer should relish such a task.

But his mouth was dry and his heart pounded nonetheless.

It was only eight miles or so, he told himself.

And he had his revolver.

Always a last resort.

*

He rode most of the way at a fast trot, slowing to a walk on glimpsing the outpost a half-mile outside the railhead fortification. French and Imperial flags drooped on poles above it. He drew closer. Lone horsemen must be an unusual sight and would draw attention. He expected to see a head raised above a parapet to study him but saw none. That made him fearful some rifleman there was perhaps drawing a bead on him through a loophole, but he could only press on.

It was a small sandbag-walled redoubt with an adobe shack within to accommodate the four or five men normally manning it. He'd passed through here before. There had always been a challenge when still forty yards distant, even when with a French dragoon escort. But this time, no challenge, and its lack chilled him. He came closer. Still no sign of life. Past it now. He dismounted on the far side - the entrance was there – and he threw his reins over a hitching rail. It was better to enter to explain himself, he thought. The idea of a shot in his back as he rode onward to the railhead frightened him.

The gap in the sandbagged wall was open, the *cheval-de-frise* that closed it from within pulled back to one side. At its far end a body lay sprawled, flies buzzing over it, a French infantryman, his head split and almost black with drying blood. It looked as if he had been struck down in the act of drawing the barrier aside.

Sickened, terrified, Dawlish fought back the urge to flee. He drew his pistol and cocked it, could see no other body in the open. He moved around the back of the hut but froze when he heard a whirr of wings. He edged to the corner and looked with one eye around it. Alarmed by his approach, however silent he had tried to be, several raven-sized birds were flying skywards. Now around the corner. There was another body, this one on its back, black sockets where the eyes had been pecked away, mouth locked open in a final scream of agony. One hand pressed against the stomach – flies swarming there – and the other thrown out to one side, a great gash across the palm. He'd been killed by bayonet, his last despairing action being to grasp the blade plunging into him. Just beyond, faint tendrils of smoke still drifted from the remnants of cooking fire. A cast iron pot lay on its side there, a stew of beans and meat spilled from it, and nearby an overturned coffee pot. Whatever happened here must have been on the previous day, for the body was already bloating and the ashes, when Dawlish held his hand over them,-had only a vestige of warmth.

He steeled himself to enter the hut. The buzzing was even louder there, the smell of corruption already strong. Three more bodies. One crumpled on its knees, face against the ground, back of the tunic soaked black with congealed blood. The two others lay on cots as if surprised in sleep. No gunshot wounds, death in all cases inflicted by bayonet or sabre, no sign of resistance, nor any rifles to be found. He choked back vomit, retreated from the hut. There had been no storming of this post. Whoever entered had been admitted without suspicion and the killings unexpected.

298

Hesitation, a strong urge to race back to reach Weatherby before darkness. But he could see the railhead ramparts, with flags hanging limp on poles above them. Was it possible the garrison there knew nothing of this silent slaughter? He would approach and, if anything there threatened as he neared, wheel his mount around and urge it into a gallop. It was foolhardy, he knew, but curiosity was stronger than fear. He untethered his animal, mounted and rode forward again at a slow walk.

And, as when he'd approached the post, he could see no movement, not on the ramparts, not through the embrasure from which one of the remaining twelve-pounders gaped. Large birds circling overhead, unmistakable as zopilotes. Closer, and still no challenge.

He was under the ramparts now. All seemed as quiet and lifeless as the small post had been. Dread was strong within him now, less fear for his own safety than revulsion at what he now knew he would find.

The entrance on the southern face, through which the demolished rail track once entered, was open and unguarded. Outside, over to the right, he saw marks of horse and mule hooves, droppings too. They disappeared into the scrub to the east. No traces of wagon wheels.

And silence. He rode inside, saw bodies in the open but did not approach them. Large black zopilotes flapped away as he passed but returned immediately to their feasts. He tethered his mount to the fence of the large pen that had previously contained dozens of animals. But none now. He climbed over the top rail, examined horse and mule droppings. Some not wholly dry. All this must have happened during the day or night before.

He walked towards Durand's office, saw more dead, paused three times to turn bodies over with his foot. Uniforms identified two as infantry, the other an artilleryman. Only one had died of gunshot, but the others hacked down by sabre chops, telltale hoofmarks circling around them. He moved on, found others, the impression also of them having died while fleeing. He saw only one rifle, half-hidden by the corpse sprawled over it. Whoever did this had taken away every weapon they could find.

Fear was mixed with horror now, all the more terrible for the silence, the desolation. The door of the long adobe building housing Durand's office was open. In one corner of the outer room, two bodies lay behind a table thrown on its side as improvised defence. One more in a corridor beyond, ledgers on the floor by his side, another clasped in his arms, as if he'd been surprised from behind in the execution of some mundane clerkly task.

The door to Durand's office was closed. Dawlish, cocked pistol in hand, kicked it open and darted to one side. No sound within but that of buzzing flies. He waited before entering, decided there was no danger, then stumbled across a body just inside. It lay on its front, head towards the doorway. A sheaf of papers half visible beneath, soaked by the blood pooled and dried around it. Braid on the shoulders told this had been an officer. Durand's desk beyond, a few papers on it, his chair empty.

Dawlish forced himself to ignore his revulsion and bend over the corpse, grasp its tunic and roll it on its back. In that moment the body was an 'it' no longer – he recognised him. A young infantry lieutenant once seen when dining with Major Flandin, though he'd never spoken to him. He remembered he limped badly from a recent wound, that he'd likely been assigned temporary administrative duties. He had been busy with just such tasks when he died, head dragged back and his throat gashed open, dead in seconds as his lifeblood fountained from him. He must have been walking towards the door, unsuspecting, then grabbed from behind and killed with a single slice.

Only one man could have had the trust and the opportunity to have done this.

Dawlish left the charnel house, gulped lungfuls of hot dry dusty air that gave no protection from the sense of evil now palpable about him. He hungered to go but knew he could not.

And it got worse.

In the adobe barracks he found half-dressed men, who must have been sleeping, bayoneted on their cots, others who had awakened and struggled to their feet to be cut down in futile resistance. Outside the building where the officers had messed – where he'd dined himself several times – he saw bloodstains on the sand, but no bodies, heel marks indicating they had been dragged away. The windows were barricaded but the splintered door hung open. Furniture piled in a makeshift barricade, blood but no bodies on the floor before it, and a gap torn in the middle. The eight men beyond – five officers, a corporal and two privates, both mess servants – had died hard, three by gunshot, the remainder by bayonet or sabre. In addition to other wounds which would not have killed outright, two had slashed throats. All but one of the officers – an artillery lieutenant – wore infantry uniforms. There was surprise here too, and desperate resistance, but the bodies of the attackers they had killed had been dragged away.

Numbed, Dawlish went from one building to another, found more bodies – he began counting now – in other barracks, in the railway sheds, in store rooms. Everywhere the impression of unexpected attack – of trust betrayed – and, only in a few places, of futile resistance. The magazine was locked, so too the bomb-proof shelters by the gun embrasures. Almost no food stocks remained.

Shadows were lengthening and sunset was a half-hour away. Unpalatable as the idea was, it would be safer to spend the night here than ride back in darkness to report to Weatherby. He'd make good use of the light remaining, exploring the fortification's entire interior, noting how many dead had been infantrymen – forty-one – and how many artillerymen – seventeen. And not a single cavalryman, whether officer or trooper, none clad in the blue tunics and red breeches of Durand's loyal troop he had seen here last. He went outside the redoubt again to look closely at the hoof tracks leading eastwards into the scrub. He dared not follow them more than two hundred yards and was about to turn back when noticed five low mounds just off the track.

Each six-foot by three.

Hoof-prints showed animals had been led back and forth across to make them blend into the surroundings. Even had he a spade, Dawlish wouldn't have needed to dig, for he knew what would be found.

Scarlet-topped kepis, blue tunics, red breeches.

He went back to Durand's office, in a hope he realised must be futile, to find some explanation. He stepped carefully around the body

301

there and opened the door behind the desk and found himself in Durand's accommodation – a bed, a closet and a wash stand. No personal items remained, no clothing, no shaving tackle. He returned to the office and riffled through the papers on the desk. All concerned routine matters. Nothing significant in the drawers either until he pulled out the last and heard a faint rattle. He reached to the very back and, behind papers, found something like a metallic bar some four inches long and three-quarters in diameter.

And it explained everything.

The sun was down, the pink glow in the west rapidly fading. Shocked by what he'd found, Dawlish went outside, led his horse into the corral and found adequate fodder for it in a manger.

Then to spend the night in a tool shed at the railway sidings.

He'd found no bodies there.

Chapter 27

Dawlish started back to meet the column at first light. He rode hard, arriving as it was readying to lurch into movement. He dismounted, sought out Weatherby, saluted.

"If I may, sir, I suggest we stand apart while I report what I've seen." He dropped his voice. "It's serious, sir. Very serious."

Weatherby nodded and they walked twenty yards off the track, eyed from a distance by two Mexican lancers.

"What's this about, Mr. Dawlish? Durand being uncooperative?"

"Worse than that, sir. He's gone."

"Gone?"

"I'd better tell it from the beginning, sir."

Weatherby heard him out, growing shock on his face, and kept his questions to the end.

"Could it have been *El Serpiente's* people?"

"No, sir. There would have been stronger resistance. They'd have left dead cavalry too, not just infantry and gunners."

"You're convinced Durand's responsible?"

"Almost certainly, sir. And not just because the hoof tracks are headed east rather than Colima." Dawlish fished in his pocket, pulled out the metal bar. "I found this in his desk."

Weatherby took it, turned it over in his hand, focussed on one end and recognised instantly the significance Dawlish too had seen.

Three letters, PMC, in cursive script, enclosed within an octagon.

"I understood only Atkinson held a seal," Weatherby's voice was quiet, that of a man dreading to accept the implications. "That there was one only. He showed it to me, said that he alone could mark each seal before a box of ingots left the mine."

"It wouldn't be that difficult to copy if somebody had access to it even for a minute, maybe less. Somebody who could press it against an inkpad and then on a piece of paper."

"Who?"

"Somebody Atkinson trusted. Maybe even one of Captain Clayton's people. Perhaps they're with us now. We'll never know."

303

Weatherby was scrutinising it. "But somebody must have been able to make this damn thing."

Dawlish had been turning that question over in his mind through an almost sleepless night.

"Any of the mechanics at the *Ferrocarril* workshops could have done it," he said. "It would have taken hours, dozens of 'em, filing and scraping and polishing to get the letters this sharp but they have the necessary tools there. And see here, sir," he ran his finger around the octagonal frame outside the letters. It's brass wire, brazed on, then filed almost flat. That was something, at least, to speed up the job."

Weatherby looked ashen. "Those boxes of ingots we saw on the *Ferrocarril* when we were coming up . . ." His voice trailed off.

A long minute passed – his brain must be racing, churning explanations, admitting the unthinkable might indeed be possible. Then he said, "Fetch Grove and van Maarkedal, Mr. Dawlish. Not a word of this to either."

Both men had been ready for departure, were surprised at being summoned.

"Mr. Dawlish has brought bad news," Weatherby told them. "Colonel Durand hasn't enough animals available to send us. He's evacuating the railhead, retreating to Colima."

Dawlish translated for van Maarkedal, who listened in silent but obvious anger.

"I'm riding to see Durand with Mr. Dawlish to get what I can from him," Weatherby said. "I'll do my best but don't offer much hope. As for the column, it's better to branch off before the railhead and meet the *Ferrocarril* trace south of there – that'll cut off a few miles – then south to Colima. If Durand does release a few animals, I'll bring them to meet you along the trace."

When translated, van Maarkedal reacted badly. "It'll kill some of my people if we don't get mules and I want –"

Weatherby cut him off. He might not understand French but recognised protest. "Tell him he's no choice," he said to Dawlish. "He's put himself under my protection and will damned well do what I direct. And you might remind him that Lieutenant Gove's marines are

304

escorting him. They're armed and none of his troops are. Grove has my full confidence – you hear that, Grove? You'll take no nonsense from this Belgian."

Grudging acceptance from van Maarkedal, then the last details fixed. The column to turn south-east a mile short of the first observation post on this side of the railhead. The Juarista lancer escort would, as per agreement, have left them by then.

Five minutes later, the column was getting under way.

And Weatherby and Dawlish were already out of sight ahead.

Cantering towards a truth no others must yet suspect.

*

Weatherby didn't dismount inside the railhead fortification. Dawlish guided him around. No need to say anything. There were even more birds now, the corpses more desecrated, the stench stronger, rats sighted at barracks doors and scurrying back inside as the horses approached. In the now-baking sun, in the dreadful silence, the overall impression was of the aftermath of a hell unleashed, now spent but for a lingering but invisible miasma of evil. This hadn't been war. It was something far worse.

"I've seen enough," Weatherby said. "Show me how they left."

They followed the track that led off through the scrub. There had been none there before and nothing now but a pathway newly beaten by countless hooves, winding between the patches of brush, skirting rock outcrops, here wide enough for several animals to plod on abreast, in others so narrow only a single horse or mule might pass through. And no matter how convoluted the twists, the overall axis of advance was eastwards. There were hills in the distance, and probably valleys beyond, but without a map it was impossible to guess where the advance was headed.

They rode on further than Dawlish had done the previous day, almost two miles, before Weatherby called a halt. They could learn nothing more here. It was time to go back and follow the *Ferrocarril* trace to Colima. By all indications, Major Flandin knew nothing yet of any of this.

If he had, he'd have given the bodies decent burial.

*

An earthen track, used during construction, ran alongside what had so recently been the railway. There was no sign of Grove and the Belgians having reached it yet. Their progress would be too slow for that and they'd most likely have to bivouac another night, maybe two. Dawlish wondered how Clothilde would cope. Probably well, he decided, determined and demanding, resourceful in ensuring every comfort for Damseaux, binding him ever closer to her.

The sun had passed its zenith but the heat still intense. The horses were tiring. Weatherby and Dawlish walked them at first, then dismounted and led them, resting briefly in whatever shade they could find, alert for signs of water, finding nothing but a few stagnant pools between rocks in dried-up streams.

An air of depression was hanging over them both, awareness that something wholly unpredictable, vast in its implications, had happened. Weatherby was withdrawn, brooding, and said nothing. It must be worst for him, Dawlish thought. Until now, he'd played an impossible hand well, taken risks that had paid off, made an imaginative and daring interpretation of his vague orders to protect British interests. Unspoken between them was fear of what might be found in the boxes awaiting opening in the Manzanillo magazine, fear this mission would end as cruel farce and Weatherby's career with it. Men like the Plutus directors in London, men with influence enough to have a Royal Navy vessel sent to protect their interests, would not forgive.

They covered the last two miles to Colima in darkness, were challenged by the sentries, not allowed in until permission had been sent for and granted by Major Flandin.

It was a long night – Dawlish was fighting off sleep as he translated for Weatherby – and Flandin found it hard to believe the story at first. Two wagons with food supplies, and escorted by a dragoon troop, had reached the railhead three days earlier and returned with a message from Durand. That everything was quiet north of the railhead and he was expecting no immediate Juarista assault. And now, as Flandin listened in shock to Dawlish's account, backed by Weatherby's, he shook his head as if denying it as an impossibility.

"It must have been *El Serpiente*," he said several times, each with less conviction. "You're sure there were no dead cavalry? None of Durand's own bodyguard? And Durand can't be dead – he'd have gone down fighting like a lion! If he's captured, may *Le Bon Dieu* spare him from those monsters' cruelty!"

But each protest, each objection, collapsed in the face of details. That there was no evidence of attack from without, only unsuspecting men slaughtered during their exercise of mundane duties. That the butchery was also entirely by bayonet or sabre. That the action must have been initiated at several points simultaneously so resistance, what there was of it, was fragmented. That the young lieutenant in Durand's office had been attacked from behind with papers still in his hand.

And that particular killing hurt Flandin most of all. "*Hélas!*" he said, shaking his head, "Poor Gauthier. Poor, brave Gauthier. He'd been wounded, needed time to recover, so was my administrative aide when I had command there. He was ..." He fell silent.

"He's not convinced Durand's behind it," Weatherby said to Dawlish, "Show him this." He handed him the counterfeit seal. "Ask him if he'd ever seen it. He'd used the same desk when he was in command."

Flandin showed no sign of recognition, or of dissimulation when he examined it. "What is it?" he asked.

Dawlish explained. No, Flandin had never seen it, neither had he ever closely inspected the actual lead seals on the ingot boxes when they'd arrived from the mine for storage. He'd only checked they were unbroken. And the two thick-walled adobe huts in which the boxes were stacked had been guarded night and day with the utmost rigour.

"He'd swear to that on his honour on an officer, would he?" Weatherby demanded.

The question was insulting and Dawlish hesitated before asking.

But Flandin was too shaken to take offence. He'd swear not just on his own honour but his father's and that of his grandfather, who'd died at Austerlitz. But he still didn't want to admit Durand was responsible. He wanted to bring the session to an end, needed to prepare to send a force to the railhead to investigate further, bury the bodies and recover the cannon there.

"Tell him there's more," Weatherby said. "Tell him the Belgians have surrendered the mine, that they're coming here under parole, that they have a British escort and British protection, and I want to get them to Manzanillo."

Flandin fought to control his temper. The surrender was infamous, he said, a cowardly breach of trust and honour, a betrayal, treasonous. But he'd never thought much of the Carlota Legion anyway, they'd been a liability from the start, not real soldiers. He was damned if he'd let them enter Colima, much less help them on their way. If they wanted to get to Manzanillo, they could march. There was no train here anyway.

Weatherby heard him out, didn't interrupt. Then, in a calm voice, he said, "I understand you need to take measures to send troops to the railhead. That's more urgent than the matter of the Belgians – they won't be here for another two days. Mr Dawlish and I will be happy to wait until it's convenient for you to talk to us. And in the meantime, we'd welcome a room where we can rest. Food too. We'll be available whenever you can see us."

Flandin called in an aide and ordered him to summon three officers he named.

And see to accommodation for his two British guests.

*

They didn't get underway until ten o'clock next morning. Flandin had been calm when he sent for them soon after dawn – they'd had six hours' necessary sleep. He'd sent a dragoon troop to the railhead at sunrise, with orders to follow the track beaten eastwards by so many hooves. For one day only, then bivouac and return the next, no matter

308

what they'd found, or hadn't found. He was now the most senior French officer north of Manzanillo but looked worried since Weatherby had confided his suspicions of Durand and their implications. There could be few ways of addressing them, perhaps none at all. He seemed anxious, though didn't admit it, to push the responsibility for further decisions up to the next level of command. And that was Colonel Macquart in Manzanillo. If there was to be a bearer of bad news, Flandin must have decided it would better be Weatherby initially.

The problem of the Belgians seemed trivial by comparison, especially when Weatherby stressed the value placed in London – and most surely, he imagined, Paris too – on warm Anglo-French relations. The Belgians were already disarmed, he said, and posed no threat. And he needed his marines back in HMS *Sprightly* urgently, so was trusting to Flandin's honour as an officer to respect the Belgian paroles, even in the absence of further British presence.

And, in the end, Flandin agreed to admit them at Colima, though he could provide no more than half-rations for longer than a week. In that time Weatherby would arrange rail transport to bring them back to Manzanillo and agree coverage of their costs with Colonel Macquart. The silver Dawlish had brought by railcar, and which Weatherby had turned into his own currency, would be enough for that. As he had said before, the lawyers, British and French and Belgian, Imperial too, if that still meant anything by then, could thrash out what was due to whom later.

The meaning of 'appropriate measures' stretched to the limit, an entire career staked on redemption of what we both now fear. Could I ever dare to be such a man? Would I ever want to?

And the answer always the same.

Yes.

There was no locomotive at Colima, none expected for days. But Weatherby accepted Dawlish's suggestion they use a railcar as he had done before. Two similar cars would be made available to Grove when he arrived and he'd follow with his marines to Manzanillo immediately.

Flandin, eager to have Weatherby on his way, offered three French privates to join them to guard and pump. Dawlish glanced back as the privates pushed the car into motion, then hopped aboard. He saw *El Volcán's* cone on the northern skyline, smoke wisping from it and hoped he would never see it again. Then the familiar descent down the inclines towards Ciudad de Armería, he the only veteran of such travel, manning the brake, judging which tightening turns would need it, calling for pumping on the level sections. When he'd come this way with the ex-Confederates, he hadn't hesitated to take his own turns on the handle – he felt a fellowship with them – but doing so in the presence of Frenchmen was unthinkable. He was a British officer, Weatherby would have reminded him. The French were here to pump, and pump they would, when needed. The day was hot but the breeze generated by the vehicle's forward motion made it bearable. Weatherby said little, seemed sunk in contemplation. The French privates, elated to be heading to Manzanillo, were no doubt hoping to find some way of not returning to Colima, and pumped gladly on the flat sections.

They reached Armería long before sundown and Dawlish, still craving sleep, hoped they'd spend the night there, as on the way up. But no, Weatherby said. There were two more hours of daylight and they must press ahead. It was too dangerous, the French sergeant commanding the post advised. There had been no bandit activity in the area recently, but that was no guarantee. Weatherby brushed the objection aside. They'd go on.

It earned them another twelve miles, mostly pumped, and they pulled into a passing place as darkness fell. They ate their rations cold and the three privates, along with Dawlish himself, acted as sentries in turn.

And sleep, even when fully clothed and booted, wrapped in a single blanket on hard ground, was welcome.

*

They started again at first light and passed the French posts outside Manzanillo in early afternoon. The harbour came into sight – *Sprightly*, spruce as ever, *Jenny Dixon* fully masted again and returned to her old self, the two prizes *Quetzal* captured, anchored close inshore. The ironclad herself was absent.

Dawlish expected Weatherby would go directly to *Sprightly* – both were sweat-soaked and dishevelled, their uniforms crumpled and dusty – to wash and change before calling on Colonel Macquart. Instead, they went directly to the French headquarters.

Though surprised to see them, Macquart's welcome was courteous. He paled however on hearing what happened at the railhead, and was as incredulous at first as Flandin had been, even when the counterfeit seal was put in his hand. He queried the evidence and implications point after point, as if delaying the acceptance he must increasingly know to be inevitable. It must be agony, Dawlish thought, humiliation for this decent man to hear evidence from two Englishman about the dishonour and treason of a senior French officer.

Even at the end, Macquart found himself unable to accept it, though his demeanour indicated he already had.

"There must be some mistake." He was comforting himself rather than trying to convince them. "A bandit attack perhaps, and the brave Durand in pursuit as they made off. Flandin's sent a patrol to investigate, you said. They'll confirm it. And Durand's not the man to give up. He'll track the brigands down and destroy them. Yes, that's it."

Weatherby was impatient now.

"We're wasting time, Dawlish. Tell him as politely as you can I want to see the boxes of ingots stored here. And I want him present when they're opened. No argument."

Macquart could not refuse. He called for an aide to join him as witness and then they walked, all four together, up to the fort. French troops at the entrance, two more on guard outside the magazine where the boxes were stored, two *Sprightly* bluejackets sharing the duty with them and springing to attention at the sight of Weatherby.

Then a delay. Macquart's aide had not brought the right keys – none for the magazine were held at the fort – and he had to go back for them. Long, uncomfortable minutes passed in a silence heavy with foreboding.

At last, keys grating in the three separate locks, down the steps into the deep arch-roofed chamber. The lanterns raised by Dawlish and the French aide cast pools of light on the stacks of boxes. To the left those of the first consignment to arrive, that which Weatherby and Dawlish had witnessed being lodged here unopened. To the right, the second, which they'd seen on the train halted at Ciudad de Armería, en route to Manzanillo, when they were going up to Colima.

At Armería, the lead seals had been intact. They looked as untouched now as they were then and the braided wire binding the boxes just as taut.

"Go up, Mr. Dawlish, fetch a bayonet from one of the bluejackets," Weatherby said.

Dawlish returned with it.

"Now ask Colonel Macquart to select a box at random."

He did, from the first consignment. Dawlish and the French aide dragged it into the passageway between the stacks, then stood illuminating it with their lanterns.

The familiar black-stencilled PMC on the rough wood. Then holding the lights closer, all eyes focussed on the seal. Weatherby held the end of the counterfeit bar against it. It fitted snugly, into the cursive letters, into the hexagonal frame.

"Open it, Mr. Dawlish," Weatherby said.

"The lock keys are aboard *Sprightly*, sir." Those Atkinson had entrusted to him when he'd brought the first boxes by railcar.

"Just open the damn thing, Dawlish! Any way you can! Hurry!"

He slipped the bayonet tip between wire and wood, ran the blade's blunt side to the edge and began to twist. The wire parted with a snap. Next he thrust the bayonet beneath the lid and ran it in as far as he could before jerking it up. At the fifth effort, the hasp tore free. He threw the lid back.

A layer of straw within. He began to tear it away. A glimpse of rust. He dug further, felt a curved metal surface, ripped out more straw, exposed what lay beneath.

"Roundshot, by God!" Weatherby said.

Six pieces, nestling close together.

Dawlish hooked his fingers around one – some five inches in diameter – and saw that there was another layer beneath. Twelve in total then.

Weatherby took it from him, weighed it in his hand, then handed it to an aghast Macquart.

"Ask him if he knows what it is, Dawlish," Weatherby said.

It was hardly necessary.

The railhead fortification had once bristled with twelve pounders. There were two there still.

Twelve roundshots per box, almost identical in weight to four silver ingots.

Another five boxes chosen at random and broken open. The findings identical.

And then French troops and the two British bluejackets set to smashing open the remainder.

Only roundshot, not a single silver ingot.

This was the explanation for Durand's delays over royalty rates. For the detention of the silver at the railhead, for the efficient massacre there of any but his personal guards. For the disappearance of every beast of burden from the pens. For that track heading towards the distant mountains in the east.

And for Durand's dismissal of Clothilde from Guzmán. She would have been an encumbrance for what he planned.

To escape with enough silver to bankrupt the Plutus Mining Company.

A British interest.

Chapter 28

It might just be a coincidence but . . .

Jesse Rogers, captain of *Quetzal* since the affair at Zihuantanejo, had travelled weeks earlier to Guzmán to meet Durand and receive confirmation of his command.

Durand was heading eastwards with a silver-laden mule train.

And *Quetzal* was at sea, her location unknown.

There would be a rendezvous, a high probability of it, Weatherby and Macquart agreed.

A soldier and his renegade supporters who'd forsaken their own country, were marching to meet a warship manned by mercenaries and commanded by men who had already lost theirs. Men, who felt no allegiance to any flag, were in possession of an ironclad – the most powerful warship in the Pacific – and one which would find a ready buyer in any country along the Central and South American Pacific coast. When outright war did not exist between them, civil conflict seemed always to fill the gap.

Or Durand might be yet more ambitious.

With his faithful Praetorian Guard, with silver to buy more recruits, *Quetzal* as his one-ship navy, and Rogers and Welborne his admirals, he might make himself master of some small republic. It could be Guatemala, El Salvador, Nicaragua or Costa Rica. The idea was not impossible. An American filibuster, William Walker, had briefly gained control of Nicaragua in the late '50s and made himself president with nothing like the resources Durand could now control.

Unless . . .

The maps available in the French headquarters were mostly of Spanish-colonial origin, a half-century old or more. They were of small scale, showed little more than roads linking large towns and it was likely those other than *El Camino Real* were little better than tracks. Hilly and mountain terrain, valleys and rivers – which might or might not be dry in season – were indicated, but not in any detail. To supplement these maps, Weatherby sent Dawlish to *Sprightly* to collect charts of the coast. Lieutenant Ashton was to accompany him back.

And now the maps and charts were spread out on a large table in Macquart's office. He and three of his senior officers – shocked as badly as he had been when they learned what happened – were poring over them with Weatherby, Ashton and Dawlish. Discussion was slowed by the need for translation.

It was obvious Durand must reach the sea as far as possible to the east of Colima lest forces from there should attempt to intercept him. It would mean traversing an area on the map that was all but blank except that it was mountainous and a single river, the Coahuayana, ran a sinuous course through it, north to south, reaching the coast some forty-five miles east of Manzanillo. Five miles further to the east, the chart showed a coastal village called San Juan de Alima. It was most likely a tiny fishing community, for no track was shown leading inland from it, nor westwards towards Ciudad de Armería. There was no harbour there, not even of an inlet on a great bare arc of beach down to which the mountains dropped. It seemed the closest point on the coast to which Durand could head.

"How long would he take to get there?" Weatherby asked.

"We know his track was eastward," A French major was leaning over a map. "He'd be wise to keep going that way, across the mountains towards the valley of the Coahuayana."

"And follow it down to the sea?"

"No." Colonel Macquart intervened, was shaking his head. "Durand's too old a fox for that. He could move down it faster but knows we could land troops at the river mouth and send them up to meet him. He'll continue further east through the mountains before turning for the coast."

Dawlish translated.

While he listened, Weatherby's gaze was fixed on the chart rather than on the map. His finger traced the shoreline to the east of the Coahuayana's mouth. It stopped some twenty miles further on, where the coast angled sharply north-eastwards. And there, at the point of turning, another village, identified as Bucerias. It might be linked by a track along the shoreline to San Juan de Alima, though the map showed none. It did however indicate the place was likely to be closed off from the hinterland by mountainous terrain.

"What do you think, Mr. Ashton?" Weatherby asked.

They bent close over it and Dawlish craned to see what had drawn their scrutiny.

A crescent bay a half-mile wide, the village at its centre, bounded to the west by a headland, off which two islands lay in line, the first a quarter mile seawards and the second as much again. Ragged edged, neither could be much longer than a hundred yards. They looked like mere rocky outcrops, tips of a mostly submerged extension of the peninsula.

"I'd expect a degree of shelter," Ashton said. "Some obscuring of the view from seawards too."

"A possibility," Weatherby said, and to Dawlish, "Ask our friends how long it would take Durand to get there."

Dawlish explained and pointed to the spot. Macquart directed a French officer to draw a straight line on the map, directly eastwards from the railhead to well beyond the Rio Coahuayana, then another to Bucerias. He measured it and checked the scale.

"About a hundred and thirty kilometres."

"In straight lines," Macquart said. "Half as much again, perhaps more, because the country's mountainous and Durand will have to find a way through. Assume two hundred kilometres."

Dawlish did a quick mental calculation. "About a hundred and thirty miles," he said to Weatherby.

"How fast could he move?"

Macquart shrugged. "In that sort of terrain, with so many animals? Maybe ten kilometres on a good day, less if the going is really difficult. Even then, Durand might make eight. He'll be driving hard."

Twenty days at the least. And five already since leaving the railhead.

"So we've fifteen days," Weatherby said. "But let's assume less in case Durand's lucky. It could be twelve. We can be there with *Sprightly* in a day."

"Waiting for *Quetzal* to arrive, if she's not lying there already?" Ashton said. There was the slightest hint of alarm in his voice.

Dawlish understood why.

Sprightly was unarmoured, wooden, had no weapon capable of making even a shallow indent on *Quetzal's* thick iron flanks. And one shell from any of her three large guns could blow the fragile gunvessel apart. A confrontation would be over in minutes and with only one likely outcome.

"Wait for her? Weatherby said. "We'll discuss that later, Mr. Ashton." And then to Dawlish, "Suggest to Colonel Macquart that we meet at nine tomorrow. Tell him I've no doubt there are aspects he might want to discuss with his people before then. And if he dissents, tell I'm leaving anyway and taking you with me. We're both bloody tired and deserve a wash, clean clothing and a bite to eat. And there is some work to do before we meet these fellows again."

Macquart protested but Weatherby was standing already.

No further argument.

*

A cloud of black dust drifted from *Sprightly* as the crew coaled – the most loathed of all duties – from a lighter moored alongside with anthracite purchased, without discount, from *Ferrocarril* stocks. Elsewhere in the vessel, under Ashton's direction, other preparations were underway, for departure, for combat. Weatherby had issued the orders when he arrived on board. But he said nothing of his plans, if indeed he'd yet decided any. He was seated now, with Dawlish, in the sternsheets of his gig on his way to the morning's meeting with Macquart.

But not directly.

The gig had circled the topsail-schooner taken as a prize by *Quetzal* three times already, was doing so again, even more slowly. Weatherby studied her in silence. Several curious heads leaned over her top rail and two bored-looking French sentries watched the gig from her stern. There must be thousands like her on every ocean of the world, workhorses of trade between lesser ports and capable of long-haul voyaging with small crews. The name above the hawsepipes was *Esmeralda* but that told nothing. Dozens of vessels between here and Cape Horn must bear the same name.

"Talk to that fellow, Mr. Dawlish." Weatherby pointed to a man now standing on the bulwark, steadying himself against the foremast shrouds. He looked weather-beaten, middle-aged and was wearing a nautical cap. "Find out where this vessel's from. Why *Quetzal* took her. On what grounds."

The gig approached, backed-water, held stationary.

Dawlish hailed in Spanish, exchanged brief courtesies. And, even before questioning, the man's indignant words were flooding from him. He and his crew were being held wrongfully, had been about their lawful occasions, had been taken by a pirate. He was Vincente Cordero, captain and half-owner, he would be beggared, he and his entire family. There was no consul of his country here to get him justice and he hadn't seen a single French officer and –

"*Dónde está registrada su nave?*" Dawlish broke in on him. Where was this ship registered?

"*Guayaquil!*"

Ecuador then. No party to this war in Mexico.

Dawlish continued the questioning.

What had she been carrying?

General cargo. From San Pedro in California to Ecuador.

Arms?

No arms! But that was the accusation when the great iron war-steamer ran us down and detained us. That we were carrying arms for Mexican rebels.

Were you searched? Were any found?

Certain items that must have been loaded in error. He knew nothing of them. There had been no markings on the crates and –

Dawlish ignored him. He gave Weatherby the gist.

"I'll wager he's guilty as sin, Dawlish. That craft's ideal for running into small ports. *Quetzal* may have had justifiable reasons for detaining her. She's probably a lawful prize."

The French sentries had approached Cordero and were shouting for him to come down.

"Ask if his crew's still on board, Dawlish."

A short answer before the sentries dragged the man away.

Yes! All eight!

"We need to hasten now," Weatherby said. "I don't want to keep Colonel Macquart waiting."

And he was smiling.

*

The *Esmeralda* had indeed been carrying general cargo, but along with five crates of new Springfield rifles, Macquart confirmed. Too few to represent a serious shipment, but always easy to trade either in Mexico or anywhere to the south. Cordero had persisted in swearing that he knew nothing of them. That didn't matter. *Quetzal,* while flying the Imperial ensign, had detained the schooner off the Mexican coast and Macquart accepted she was a legitimate prize. And what of the cargo, Weatherby asked. Macquart smiled and said it had been taken ashore and was being attended to.

"He won't go home poor to Paris," Weatherby told Dawlish and he'd laughed.

And Weatherby had what he wanted.

Macquart had agreed almost too eagerly, as if glad some action was being taken for which the main responsibility would not lie with him. He hadn't sufficient troops available, not here in Manzanillo or up at Colima, to detach any to find or intercept Durand.

Not when he knows the Juaristas are capable of one last irresistible push. He'll pull the last French forces back from Colima soon, will use them to man the defences here, hold Manzanillo until ships appear to evacuate them. The Juaristas may not even storm it, may just wait. That's all Macquart cares about, not a tuppenny damn about the silver's loss. If it's lost for good, he can argue with reason that the blame was Durand's alone. And if Weatherby recovers it, he'll have done enough to share the glory.

For Weatherby had the *Esmeralda* now, lent under a signed agreement with Macquart, on behalf of the Imperial Mexican government, that she might be used in recovery of the silver.

And now *Esmeralda,* with her captain and crew still aboard, was being towed across the bay by *Sprightly's* cutter to moor close to *Jenny Dixon.* Workers from the nearby yard, and her own carpenter and crew, had done *Jenny* proud and she was all but ready for sea. Now they would be diverted to another task.

One to be worked on night and day and completed within the next thirty-six hours.

Weatherby had sent Dawlish on another errand.

"Go over to the *Ferrocarril* workshops," he said. "Find out if there's blasting powder and slow fuse there – there must be some left over from railbed construction."

"Should I see Mr. Turnbull about it?"

"No. He'll probably refuse. Talk to one of your mechanic friends there, they'll know. Come back and tell me. I'll deal with Turnbull myself."

And Dawlish recognised Weatherby was gambling again.

*

Grove and his marines arrived late that evening. They'd left Colima before dawn on two railcars, had pumped the last, level, stages along the coast in darkness and narrowly avoided shooting by nervous French sentries when they reached Manzanillo's outer redoubts. All were exhausted and sweat-soaked but elated that they'd managed so quickly. Weatherby summoned his other officers to hear Grove's report. He'd reached Colima with the Belgians at noon the previous day.

"They weren't welcome," he said. "Major Flandin made that clear. There isn't much accommodation for them – most will have to bivouac until they can be brought here. And Flandin demanded that in the meantime they'd need to labour on the earthworks he's strengthening."

"What about Major Damseaux?" Weatherby said. "And that woman with him?"

"Flandin allocated them a little adobe hut. The lady made a scene. She demanded he let them have his own quarters. Damseaux was a baron, she said, he deserved nothing less. And he, poor fellow, hardly noticed. The journey had half-killed him. But it got her nowhere." He paused. "Major Flandin seemed to know her of old and enjoyed it."

It was from Flandin that Grove heard of what had happened at the railhead. The cavalry patrol sent to investigate had followed Durand's track eastwards for twenty miles before turning back. All they found was a mule with a broken leg and a bullet hole between its eyes.

"I'll let Mr. Dawlish tell you about the silver," Weatherby said as he dismissed them.

Exhausted as he was, Grove seemed eager to hear. He grew more sombre when he learned about the *Quetzal*.

"You mean Weatherby's going after her, Dawlish?"

"He's not giving up."

"It's madness. Even if she's found, we won't last five minutes."

Dawlish felt the same and guessed Ashton did also, though he'd never say it. Neither would he himself, though he had felt an increasing sense of dread all day.

"You'd better keep that sort of talk to yourself, Grove. Weatherby's got some idea in mind – that's why we're modifying that schooner *Quetzal* took as a prize. He'll share his plans in good time."

He spoke with a conviction he did not feel. The likelihood of death or maiming was as great now as at any time since he'd come to Mexico. And something else was troubling him.

Welborne and Vázquez were in *Quetzal*.

He'd served with both, risked life and limb together, and counted them as friends.

But if it came to it, he'd kill them or they'd kill him.

That was the way of it.

I'm a commissioned officer and Weatherby's my captain. That's all I must remember.

But that did not diminish the dread.

*

The work on the schooner took a day longer than Weatherby demanded, but was finished at last and she was ready for sea.

She was *Esmeralda* of Guayaquil no longer but the *Luisa-Maria* of Callao, Peru. She was a topsail schooner no longer either, the yards on the foremast gone and the mast itself shortened. The mainmast was shorter too, and the main gaff had been lowered. *Sprightly's* sailmaker had laboured a full day and night to modify the sails to fit. The jib boom had been cut back also – no possibility of carrying a flying jib now. She would sail more slowly and less handily than in her previous configuration and, with luck, might look like a different vessel from a distance.

There were other changes too. The nameboards above the hawsepipes bore the new name in white letters, darkened by thinned black paint wiped across them. The word 'Callao' appeared under the name at the stern. Axes had chipped the hull in a few places, not enough to damage but show brighter streaks of bare wood beneath the black paint. The small deckhouse was now ochre-coloured, using paint carried by *Sprightly* for her funnel. The sailmaker's assistant had fashioned a convincing Chilean ensign.

And she was underway now, ghosting out of a calm and moonlight Manzanillo Bay on the midnight's offshore breeze and heading south-east only when five miles from the shore.

Dawlish sensed Sanderson, *Sprightly's* second lieutenant, had accepted command of *Luisa-Maria* only because Weatherby him no option. He had protested that he could not communicate with her captain and half-owner, Vincente Cordero, and his crew, now manning her on the promise of the return of their ship when this affair was settled. Sanderson couldn't speak Spanish and without it he was unable to trust them.

That was easily remedied, Weatherby had said. Dawlish would accompany him as translator and second officer.

But Sanderson was pleased the schooner was carrying Grove and six of his marines. He spoke to him and Dawlish just before departure.

"That Cordero blackguard and his people won't hesitate to cut our throats at the first opportunity. Watch them closely. At the first sign of unrest, I'll want Cordero shot. That'll keep the rest in line."

Neither he, nor Dawlish, nor Grove nor the marines were wearing uniform. They were clad in poor second-hand clothing bought at a market-stall in the town and looked little different to the schooner's own crew.

The land was off the port beam now, the mountains a black irregular silhouette against the starry sky. Luisa-Maria was making barely five knots. Cordero at the helm, Dawlish and Sanderson flanking him. Grove, as ordered, was standing three paces behind, his revolver in its holster although its butt was exposed.

Cordero glanced back, then said to Dawlish, "*Su jefe cree que estoy loco? Tenemos familias a las que regresar. Haremos lo que nos digan.*"

That he thought Sanderson was crazy not to understand he and his crew had families to return to. They'd do what was ordered. He didn't raise his voice but there was anger as well as dignity in it.

"*Somos hombres, no perros a los que hay que disparar sin piedad. Díselo a su jefe.*"

Tell Sanderson they were men, not dogs to be shot without mercy.

"What's he saying, Dawlish?" Sanderson said.

"That it's a beautiful night, sir, and he's pleased to help us."

"Good. Better for him he keeps thinking that."

"*El jefe dice que no se preocupe,*" Dawlish lied to Cordero. "*Esta solomente una formalidad. Todos queremos llegar sanos y salvos a casa.*"

That Sanderson said not to worry. That the guard was just a formality. Everybody wanted to return home safely.

Some fifty miles to Bucerias. They'd sail past in the bright light of noon.

Hoping to be seen as a humble trader making slow progress in neutral waters.

Chapter 29

Dawlish was high on *Luisa-Maria's* foremast with a telescope, scanning the coast, some four miles distant. He'd been there for three hours already, baked and thirsty in the noonday sun. The schooner was crawling in the lightest of airs and two hours had passed since sighting what must be the village of San Juan de Alima. Had any vessel larger than a fishing boat been there, he would have spotted it. Now, close off the port bow, he could see the two islands that identified the headland shielding Bucerias. If estimates of Durand's rate of progress were correct, it was days still before he'd reach it. But that didn't mean that *Quetzal* wasn't waiting there already. The thought was daunting. He half-hoped, wholly feared, she might lie beyond those islands.

The schooner was holding a steady, undeviating, course and the islands drew close with agonising slowness. Other than at narrow inlets on the northern sides, patches of light surf broke along the islands' steep, rocky, shores. Low humps, neither island could be higher than twenty or thirty feet but both were topped with thick green vegetation.

Further out, streaks of white foam identified what must be a reef close to the surface. He called a warning down – Cordero was still at the helm and he acknowledged. A marine stood close behind him. Sanderson was on the forecastle, his telescope also focussed on the islands.

At last, the anti-climax, passing the reef with a mile to spare and seeing the small crescent beach beyond. A few fishing craft, little larger than canoes, were drawn up before a string of huts.

And no *Quetzal*.

The schooner held course for another two hours, could spot no thread of smoke ahead or out towards any point on the ocean's horizon. If the ironclad was anywhere off this coast, she was staying far offshore, possibly under sail to conserve precious coal.

Sanderson called Dawlish down and ordered a sixteen-point reversal of course. *Luisa-Maria* crept back towards San Juan de Alima even more slowly than she'd come, Grove now replacing Dawlish on the foremast. He saw nothing either.

By sunset, San Juan lay five miles off the starboard quarter and *Luisa-Maria* was turning again. She'd slip past Bucerias in the darkness, loiter beyond, and come again just after dawn to take more observations, then continue back to Manzanillo.

Where Weatherby was waiting with impatience.

*

The night passed quietly and Sanderson seemed easier in his mind. Dawlish suspected he'd be happy to continue this patrol for weeks, provided nothing was encountered. But he had established a watch-keeping routine and there was time for sleep.

Luisa-Maria ran on towards Bucerias. No sight of *Quetzal* on the horizon, none either of smoke. What had been a faint onshore breeze earlier had strengthened enough to raise low waves, some breaking into whitecaps.

Sanderson called for Dawlish, pointed to the south-west. A streak of grey cloud was growing over the horizon.

"I don't like it, Mr. Dawlish, and I like a lee shore even less," he said. "Have Cordero take us out for more sea room. Six or seven miles."

"And then, sir?"

"On to Manzanillo."

The schooner came about sluggishly. Cordero snarled to Dawlish that she was maimed, his beautiful vessel crippled forever. She'd turned like a dancer before, and was now a crippled hag.

"What's he saying, Dawlish?" Sanderson said.

"That you've made a wise decision, sir."

"It didn't sound like that to me."

"It's just that he's angry about the weather, sir. He'd been hoping for a calm passage."

Noon passed. Bucerias lay off the starboard beam. *Luisa-Maria* was now so far offshore that it was hard to distinguish the two islands from the shore behind them. Heavier surf was breaking there than before. Dawlish went aloft to observe, saw no *Quetzal* as they passed the small crescent bay.

Course maintained for a half-hour before the first squall struck, lashing the schooner with heavy rain. It lasted some five minutes and, when it passed, others were visible to the south-west and south. The wind continued to gain strength, stripping white foam from the crests. *Luisa-Maria* was handling poorly, and Cordero swore again that she was ruined forever.

Driving rain now, yet higher wind, no longer a squall but the promise of a minor storm that might persist for hours. No sense of threat or danger – every man on board had experienced far worse and, even in her present mutilated state, the schooner was well capable of enduring. Sanderson ordered she stand yet further out to sea, but resume her course to Manzanillo thereafter. The shore showed only intermittently through the grey curtain but, by now, Bucerias must be somewhere off the starboard quarter.

The schooner ploughed on – Dawlish was impressed by the efficiency of Cordero and his crew in adjusting sails and rigging. The rain was warm when it fell, beating through soaked clothing like tiny hammers, but quickly chilled flesh under the wind's blast.

And then a call from a seaman at the bow. Something sighted ahead. And no, not a ship, smaller, far smaller. Sanderson sent Dawlish forward. The man had only a glimpse, hadn't seen it again, and it might have been nothing, for it was hard to be sure in these conditions.

Minutes passed. The bows were rising high on a wave crest, were about to fall and then, down in the trough beyond, they spotted a boat to port. Not a simple fishing craft, but well fashioned, larger than a whaler and smaller than a cutter, flat-transomed, most probably a ship's boat. It was wallowing, almost swamped, no sign of oars, and the shreds of a sail were flapping from its remaining mast. A half-dozen men were cowering in it with two more bent over the gunwale, trying, but failing, to drag another aboard. It lay a half-cable off the port beam after the schooner topped the crest and dropped into the trough beyond. Some aboard had seen *Luisa-Maria* and were waving.

It was now that Dawlish's view of Sanderson changed.

"We're going to save them." He seemed a different man, voice strong, determined. "Stand by me to translate."

With Cordero at the helm, he suggested rather than ordered, accepted the other man's familiarity with his own vessel, left the detailed direction of the crew to him, but left no doubt salvation of those wretches in the boat was paramount. Cordero responded and, hardly noticing that their words were transmitting through Dawlish, they worked together as if they had done so for years, united by the urge to save fellow seamen.

Immediate rescue was impossible – the chance of the boat, upwind, smashing into the schooner's hull was too great, both men agreed. The solution was to drive far ahead, come about sixteen points to port in a wide arc, claw ahead with the wreck off to port, before coming about again to port, dropping the gaffs to kill forward speed and drifting down on the wreck.

Time meant nothing. The stricken craft was frequently lost to sight for minutes at a time. One of Cordero's crew was high on the foremast shrouds, shouting down sightings, most of his words lost in the wind.

And it succeeded, though the lookout called that the man in the water had disappeared. The boat heaved and ground against the schooner's hull and three of the men aboard caught the ropes with bowlines at their ends that were dropped to them. Others were too weak to assist themselves and seamen lowered to recover them. The last man was slumped in the sternsheets, water around his knees resisting all efforts to assist until the others were onboard. When hauled to his feet, his legs buckled beneath him as the line was passed under his armpits. He collapsed on reaching the deck. He sat there, crumpled, eyes glazed and uncomprehending until he was carried to the small accommodation.

And Dawlish recognised him.

Ignacio Vázquez, with whom he'd shared so much at Zihuantanejo.

The empty boat was drifting away, a thing of beauty in its time, hull now battered, a golden stripe running just below the gunwales. And one word on the transom.

Quetzal.

*

Sanderson ordered Dawlish to elicit whatever information he could from Vázquez. He was still dazed, aware of nothing except he had survived. Stripped, like the other survivors, he was muffled in a blanket. He didn't look up nor recognise Dawlish when he came to sit with him. Dawlish didn't enlighten him.

"You're safe now," he asked in Spanish. "What's your name?"

"Vázquez. Ignacio Vázquez." Answered as a young child might, without thought.

"What was your ship? Has it been wrecked? Are there other boats?"

"*Quetzal.*" And nothing for another minute as Vázquez drifted back towards awareness. "Where am I? What ship is this?"

"*Luisa-Maria.* Of Callao."

Vázquez must have been present when, as *Esmeralda* of Guayaquil, she'd been taken prize. He hadn't recognised her in the new configuration. It was best to play on that.

"What is – what did you call it? – *Quetzal.*"

"An ironclad. A Mexican ironclad." Said with a hint of pride.

He's coming to himself.

"Did she sink? In this storm perhaps? Or maybe earlier?"

Vázquez shook his head. "She's far out at sea."

"Why were you in that boat?"

"I'd been sent ashore on business." A pause. "The Emperor's business." And again, something of pride.

"Emperor Maximillian?"

"His Majesty." Even in that weak voice, a tone of reverence.

Is it possible he's a dupe, that he suspects nothing of Rogers' intetions?

"Where did you go ashore?" Dawlish said.

328

"A village called Bucerias. We were returning to the ironclad when the wind began to rise and –" He had turned to Dawlish and suddenly recognition – warm, joyous recognition – dawned. "Nicolás! My friend! You saved us. Thank God, Nicolás, thank God you came!"

"Why were you sent to Bucerias, Ignacio?"

Vázquez stiffened. "It's not a British affair, Nicolás, not like Zihuantanejo. It's a Mexican matter, Mexican and French. I can't talk to you about it."

Time to lie.

"But we British are involved, Ignacio." Dawlish's mind was racing to fabricate some explanation. He lied, despised himself as he did. "The Juaristas have Manzanillo under siege."

"You mean the French have retreated?"

"All the way from Guzmán and Colima."

Vázquez groaned.

"It's a debacle," Dawlish said. "And *El Ferrocarril's* workshop is under fire. That's a British interest. But *Sprightly* has engine problems and can't do much to assist. We've appealed to the French and they're at their limits. Colonel Macquart, their commander, wants *Quetzal* back in Manzanillo for support. He asked us carry a message to bring her back. Only this schooner was available."

It was a wild cock and bull story, but Vázquez, in his debilitated state, accepted it.

Because he trusts my word, would never suspect me of lying.

"We need to find *Quetzal* quickly," Dawlish said. "Her guns can change everything at Manzanillo. Where is she?"

"South-west, over the horizon. Cruising north to south and back each day. Captain Rogers doesn't want to come inshore yet."

"Yet? So why did he send you to Bucerias, Ignacio?"

"To assess water depth, to know how close to the beach he could bring *Quetzal*. I took soundings with a lead."

"Did he tell you why he'd want to?"

"He would be meeting a French column that had marched from Colima, hunting bandits. They were to reach the coast here any time soon. *Quetzal* would take them off the beach and return them to Manzanillo."

"They'll be welcome there," Dawlish said. "With the Juaristas pressing so hard there, every man is needed." He paused, then said as if mystified, "Why doesn't Rogers bring *Quetzal* in to Bucerias to be present when this French column arrives?"

"He's concerned about being caught on a lee shore if the weather deteriorates. This storm proved him correct."

"And how's he to know when the column has arrived?"

"Each night, a boat – mine or *Quetzal's* other – is to stand inshore, looking for a light signal from the column. We'd carry the news back to her." Then, as if realising the full implications of his boat's loss, Vázquez said, "Can you bring me to *Quetzal* as quickly as possible? Captain Rogers needs to know what's happened."

So does Weatherby.

"I'll see to that," Dawlish said. "Just rest for now. You need to sleep."

And he went on deck to speak to Sanderson.

＊

Luisa-Maria slipped into Manzanillo seven hours later, urged by a wind that weakened in late afternoon. She anchored and *Sprightly's* gig came to bring Sanderson and Dawlish for immediate reporting to Weatherby. They'd kept Vázquez below while underway. Now, when brought on deck, he was stunned to see where he was.

"Where's *Quetzal?*" he said.

"We couldn't find her," Dawlish said.

"This is Manzanillo. I don't hear gunfire here."

"Maybe the Juaristas have been repulsed. That's good news, isn't it, Ignacio?"

Vázquez didn't look convinced, and sat hunched in sullen silence as they were pulled across.

Weatherby received them in his quarters, was surprised to see Vázquez but didn't query his presence. He listened to Sanderson's report first – Bucerias, its bay and its two islands, and then the storm and rescue of the crew of *Quetzal's* boat.

"Damn well done," he said, when Sanderson finished. He gestured towards Vázquez. "What did you learn from this fellow?" he said to Dawlish.

"Do you believe him?" he said when he'd heard him out.

"Every word," Dawlish said. "We trusted each other for our lives at Zihuantanejo. He wouldn't lie to me."

Though I did to him.

"Ask him if he's still loyal to Emperor Maximillian, Dawlish. There's a bible here. Ask if he'll swear on it."

And Vázquez was loyal, he wouldn't betray the Imperial cause, could not forget his uncle and cousins murdered by the Juaristas. Yes, he'd swear, but not on a Protestant bible. If a Catholic one was brought from a church in town, he'd swear on that.

"He's been a bloody gullible young fool," Weatherby said. "Tell him he's lucky he was rescued. Otherwise, he'd be facing a firing squad when we've dealt with *Quetzal*. And tell him too about Durand and the silver, the French troops he massacred, and Rogers' complicity."

The story of the betrayal left Vázquez white-faced, shaking with anger.

It was good he did.

Vengeful men are always useful.

*

The French were also intent on vengeance. What had happened at the railhead was now common knowledge, both at Colima, which was still being held, and in Manzanillo. Infantry once stationed at the railhead defences, and artillerymen who'd manned the guns there, realised they too would have been victims had Durand unleashed his massacre

331

earlier. There was the shame of it also, a senior officer's treachery that outraged and dishonoured the entire French officer corps, the betrayal of enlisted men who'd served some four years under him in Mexico. Some of them had been with him in Algeria, the Crimea or Italy also and revered him as a leader. Delegations of officers, sergeants and corporals, and even private soldiers had come to Colonel Marquard, volunteering for any opportunity to bring him to justice.

It had been easy to identify the most experienced and most bitter. Easy too to form them in a single company, equip them with two light six-pounders, assign a battle-hardened Major Rouvier to command it. Easy too, in theory, to land them from the sea at Bucerias to await Durand's arrival.

Easy if *Quetzal* were not a concern. From the bay her guns could shred the village and surroundings.

Success demanded her elimination.

At the last conference before the joint Weatherby-Macquart plan was set in motion, only Weatherby seemed confident he'd accomplish that.

But probably he wasn't, Dawlish thought.

A seasoned gambler always willingly accepted the chance of failure.

*

Late the following morning, *Lusia-Maria* left Manzanillo, the timing calculated to arrive off Bucerias in the first hours of darkness. Sanderson was in command again, with Cordero acting as first officer. The rescue had fostered mutual respect and they were communicating in broken English and Spanish sufficient for what must follow. Dawlish was also on board, but he had other responsibilities now.

The schooner was crowded and it was good the airs were light, for crew could only move about the deck with difficulty. Grove and his dozen marines shared space with five of *Sprightly's* seamen and as many hardened French, commanded by a major named Rouvier. *Sprightly's* whaler, heavily loaded, was following under tow in the schooner's wake. The sun beat down and many slept, glad to escape the sense of foreboding that hung over them. Most had seen *Quetzal* previously and knew the brutal power of her artillery, the massive iron on her flanks. As they knew of *Sprightly* with her punier armament and eggshell hull.

Try as he might, Dawlish could not escape his own gloom. He'd risked his life before and knew the worst moments were waiting for action to begin. His mind drifted back to the letter he'd posted before leaving Britain to join the Pacific Station. It was addressed jointly to his father, his brother and his sister with the instruction on the envelope, *'To be opened only in the event of my death.'* He'd tried to say in it all he felt – love and gratitude, no regret for his choice of profession, pride in what he had given it, his desire that his loss be not excessively mourned. He included a separate note for his old nurse, Mrs. Gore, who was now the family's housekeeper. The words had been inadequate, he knew, but if he were to write it again now he could do no better. Death in itself did not frighten him – though not excessively devout, he trusted in a merciful God – but the prospect of serious wounding or maiming did. If that came, he prayed he would endure it with dignity.

But one concern occupied him above all, as it had for weeks.

Clothilde.

His sister, his so treasured and self-dishonoured sister, for whom he'd pledged to his beloved uncle to care. He'd seen what she'd become, feared worse in her future and was powerless to intervene.

The sun was dropping in the west. Soon a sickle moon would rise to give light enough to identify the two islands off Bucerias.

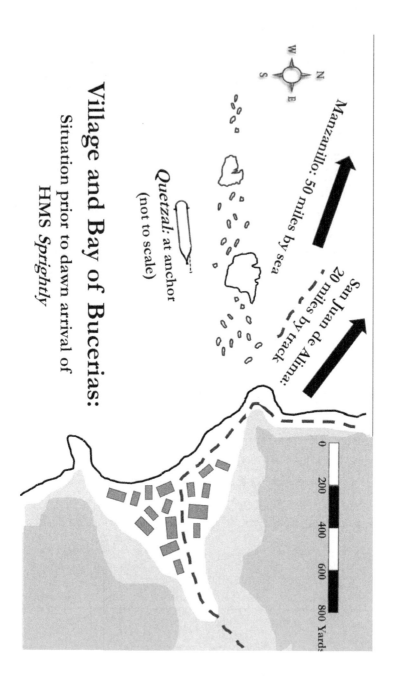

Village and Bay of Bucerias:

Situation prior to dawn arrival of
HMS *Sprightly*

Quetzal: at anchor
(not to scale)

Manzanillo: 50 miles by sea

San Juan de Alima: 20 miles by track

0 200 400 600 800 Yards

N
W · E
S

Chapter 30

The islands lay some four miles ahead when *Luisa-Maria*, hove-to, as close inshore as Sanderson risked bringing her. It was two hours after sunset, giving eight of darkness for the night's work ahead. The whaler was drawn up alongside and five *Sprightly* seamen dropped into her first, raised both masts and readied the oars. Grove and his marines followed, squeezing themselves between the thwarts and loaded cargo. Dawlish boarded last, after a few words with Sanderson, and took the tiller. The schooner would loiter here unlit and, with luck, he might return within three hours. The French troops lined her bulwarks to watch as the whaler pulled away sufficiently to raise sail, catch the light land breeze and steer towards the islands.

The sea was calm, its surface broken by only the slightest ripples. No pinpricks of light, no sign of human habitation, on the dark mass of land to port. The headland now being neared, and the islands at its tip, shielded the approach from any villagers of Bucerias who might be awake. But it was not them that Dawlish feared, it was that *Quetzal* might already be anchored inside the bay. He steered the whaler towards the outer of the two islands and, when three cables off, ordered the gaffs dropped, the jib taken in, and oars out.

Closer. The moonlight was strong enough to show no sign of foam at the base of the rocky shore ahead. Now the most nerve-racking part of the approach, Dawlish's eyes straining to identify the narrow inlet spotted previously. Only when directly outside did he find it, a deep-shadowed gash leading to a tiny beach. The whaler entered, stroked forward with caution and the bows grounded. Marines dropped into knee-high water to pull the craft higher.

Dawlish and Grove jumped ashore. Before them lay a steep slope, edged at the top with scrub some twenty feet above. They scrambled up, found patches of brush ahead and crept forward, hugging the shadows. forty yards brought them to the island's southern side, where the land fell away in a cliff. Beyond lay the tranquil bay.

No *Quetzal*. No lights in the village.

The hard labour began, seamen and marines manhandling the frame of *Sprightly's* six-pounder ashore, its wheels and barrel next. And then boxes of shells and charges, two signalling lanterns, kegs of fresh water and rations to last a week. It would be hard-lying among the scrub, no shelter but a blanket from sun or rain, no cooking fires, hardtack biscuit and canned meat only, water measured in mouthfuls, absolute silence. Dawlish did not wait to see the gun or supplies brought up. He shook hands with Grove, wished him luck and headed back to *Luisa-Maria*, reaching her just before midnight.

Transfer of the French troops, supplies and six-pounder to the whaler took almost an hour. Under command of Major Rouvier they too boarded. Under sail again, Dawlish headed back towards the islands. He looked astern – *Luisa-Maria* was already pulling away and should be back in Manzanillo by midday. On reaching the inner island he found, without difficulty, the short west-coast inlet that led to a landing point. There too, access to the island's upper level was possible, though backbreaking if all was to be offloaded, dragged up and hidden before daybreak. He climbed to the top with Rouvier. This island was slightly larger than the other and the scrub was thicker. It too provided a fine view of the bay. Even from there, there was no indication of any human presence on the outer island. Grove must have his six-pounder assembled and positioned by now, his men and stores under cover. One glance at the seasoned Major Rouvier was reassurance that he'd exert discipline as iron as Grove's in the coming days.

An hour later, with still an hour of darkness in hand, the whaler was heading seawards under sail to commence her own lonely vigil. It would be an uncomfortable home for Dawlish and his five seamen for uncountable days ahead. Holding station just over the horizon, masts lowered to reduce her profile, moving inshore again in the darkness for sight of a winked signal from Grove that *Quetzal* had, or had not arrived, and then to relay it to *Sprightly* further out, for she'd be on station shortly.

If *Quetzal* didn't find her first. And butcher her.

*

Sun was the greatest torment, blistering exposed skin, dazzling aching eyes by its reflection on calm water, making lookout duty an endless battle against drowsiness. Dawlish instituted a two-hour watch system, allowing three seamen at any time to find uncomfortable rest between the thwarts. He rationed himself to less, constantly scanning the horizon for sight of a sail – *Quetzal's* remaining boat perhaps, running in to Bucerias or, worse, the ironclad herself. The danger of sun-flash had precluded bringing a telescope and the nightglass carried would be reserved for use in darkness. His only aid to station-keeping was a compass, that and the profile of distant mountains on the land horizon.

Nothing sighted during the first long, endless, day. Only the occasional half-hour of pulling to maintain position, and the issue of cold food and tepid water, broke the monotony. But the fear Dawlish had felt was gone now, lost in concentration on the challenge of the moment and admiring the stolid resilience of his crew. Back in Manzanillo, *Sprightly* would now be readying to depart under sail alone to reach her station during darkness. And tonight, *Luisa-Maria* would be landing French troops five miles north-west of Bucerias, the first of two nightly trips that would bring a full company ashore with a six-pounder to drive on the village when the situation warranted.

The sun fell. In the last light, the masts were stepped, sails set, and the whaler headed shorewards. It had spent the day some eight or ten miles north-west of Bucerias and steered towards it now. No lights visible yet on the dark mass of land. An hour passed before a lookout announced he could spot a faint cluster of pinpricks. His eyes must have been sharper than Dawlish's, for it took him two minutes with the nightglass to identify what must be Bucerias village. Closer in, and the headland and islands could be identified against the moonlight's silver on the water. Grove must be searching seawards now, hoping for Dawlish's signal.

The dark-lantern was fired already. Dawlish took it himself, aimed towards the outer island and raised and lowered the shutter three times across the red glass.

No response.

Five minutes later, another attempt and with no better result.

A small voice within him whispered the worst might have already happened, that Durand might already have arrived. That the French and the marines on the islands had been detected, that they been massacred, that …

Stop!

Imagination could be a curse. Better to wait another five minutes and try again. Then twice more.

At last, the reply, three green flashes only, enough to confirm nothing had reached Bucerias, neither by sea nor land. A single red flash confirmed reception. Then seawards again. The land breeze was persistent, enough to riffle the smooth water and break the moon's reflection. By midnight, now cruising slow racetracks some five miles off the coast, close enough that the islands were just discernible, Dawlish lay down in the sternsheets to snatch an hour of cramped and uncomfortable rest.

It seemed only minutes before he felt a hand on his shoulder and heard a whisper.

"Mr. Dawlish, sir! There's something you should see."

He was instantly awake, recognised Rawlins, one of the lookouts.

"*Sprightly*," he said. "Have you seen her?"

Rawlins shook his head. "No, sir. But maybe a small boat."

Dawlish took the nightglass from him, followed his pointing finger, took almost a minute to identify the dim grey shape. He looked landwards for bearings, then back. South-westwards, the glass's inverted image resolved itself into what must be a sail. It looked to be moving away.

It could only be *Quetzal's* boat, the twin of Vázquez 's wrecked craft, watching also for a signal from Bucerias. It was better it be left to alert the ironclad when Durand arrived. Weatherby's plan demanded *Quetzal* be allowed to anchor within Bucerias Bay, that she be approached in the first light of day when the night's dying land breeze would have weathercocked her bows towards the shore. The massive three-hundred pounder jutting above her ram would be unable to bear on any approach from seawards. That was *Sprightly's* only hope for survival.

But this boat of *Quetzal's* was a danger. Should it detect the whaler now – and there was no indication yet that it had – it might alert Rogers in *Quetzal* that action was in the offing.

An immediate decision needed. Take in sail and lower masts, drift without oars, the crew crouching below gunwales in the hope that, if spotted, the whaler might be dismissed as driftwood. And if not, and the boat should come to investigate, there were still rifles and cutlasses.

. .

It was accomplished quickly and in silence. Only Dawlish's head was above the gunwale, nightglass focussed on the other craft. And yes, it was still drawing away and heading-south westwards.

Quetzal must be loitering below the horizon there.

Valuable information – *Sprightly* would have to remain well to the north.

Dawlish watched the tiny patch of grey sail until it was just a dot, then headed north-westwards under oars.

At last, two hours later, with only the tips of the mountains visible over the horizon, Rawlins was first to spot another sail – no, not just a sail, a vessel – to the west.

Sprightly had arrived to start her vigil.

Time to signal her – three agreed red flashes, repeated at five-minute intervals – that *Quetzal* was not yet at Bucerias. Three attempts before a green light winked from *Sprightly*.

Dawlish slipped the red glass from the lantern, slid a green one in its place. Another pre-arranged signal. Two green flashes.

Indication that *Quetzal* was to the south.

Should *Sprightly* have to run, she'd have a head start that might just save her.

*

A day passed, no more eventful than the first and Dawlish caught as much sleep as he could during it. He was resolved to remain on watch throughout the hours of darkness. Night came on and he brought the whaler close inshore again, north of west from the islands so his answering flashes would be shielded from direct view from Bucerias village. He signalled and Grove replied. *Quetzal* had not slipped in during daylight. Further signalling at midnight indicated no change. And all the while he was watching for presence of *Quetzal's* boat on her own observation mission.

Two hours before dawn, his patience was rewarded with a series of red flashes in the darkness to the south-east. It could only be *Quetzal's* boat. Heart thumping, he waited until confident it was on its way back to her, before daring to signal a query to Grove. The reply was instant.

Five green flashes. The pre-agreed signal.

Durand, or perhaps his advance party, had arrived.

The whaler had been under oars all night. Now, masts stepped and sail raised, it headed north-westwards, hoping to get a signal to *Sprightly* before sunrise. The faintest ribbon of brightness lined the eastern horizon when the gunvessel responded to the fifth signalling attempt.

And the reply was, as expected. Six flashes, predetermined.

Join Grove and observe.

Though weakening, the land breeze was an impediment that necessitated a long series of tacks to allow an approach to the island from the north-west. It was daylight now, impossible to disguise the whaler's sails, but they were essential for speed. Dawlish was watching with trepidation for sight of *Quetzal* to the south-west. It was almost ten o'clock, and the outer island still two miles distant, when Rawlins called that he had spotted masts and topsails just above the horizon. Dawlish strained his eyes – there was no doubt of it.

Immediate lowering of the whaler's masts now, oars out, stroking powerfully, fear that an observer on *Quetzal's* foretop might have detected it. The ironclad was still hull-down when the whaler slipped into the island's lee. Shielded, it crept along the rocky shore towards the narrow inlet leading to the beach.

Grove was standing there. Dawlish jumped from the bows as the whaler grounded.

"You've spotted her, Grove?"

"Under full sail. She'll be here within the hour."

"And Durand?"

"A few men arrived last night. We saw them signalling seawards. Another lot this morning and there're still more on the way. Have a look yourself."

Leaving the seamen to drag the whaler up the beach, and remain in strict silence, Dawlish followed Grove up to the scrub above. They passed through the thickest part, then crawled the last ten yards to look out on the bay beyond.

It was still empty but there were men in uniforms – French uniforms, blue tunics, red breeches – in the village and horses tethered where there was shade. But others too – peasant clothing, bandoliers, high boots, great circular sombreros and rifles. They were supervising what must be villagers to unload boxes from a half-dozen mules, then sending them staggering to the beach to pile them there.

"Look up there," Grove whispered and pointed.

The track through the narrow valley extending inland from the village was part-obscured by scrub but, in the gaps, more laden mules, led men with large-sombreros, were plodding down it. There were horsemen too, some uniformed in blue and red, but others cross-bandoliered Mexicans. Even at a distance there was an impression of exhaustion. This was the longed-for end of a brutal journey.

A memory flashed in Dawlish's brain. He was galloping down a track and, in its centre, fifty yards ahead, a sombreroed man was dropping to one knee, raising a rifle, holding him in his sights. No option but to urge the horse onward, hoping only the man's nerve would fail.

It could only have been Javier Belarra, he realised.

El Serpiente.

Whose murderous band had served Durand before changing allegiance to the Juaristas. The two men, treacherous and callous alike, must have maintained secret contact . . .

It all seemed so obvious now.

It was *El Serpiente* who guided Durand's column through rough, unmapped, country between the railhead and here in return for a share of the silver.

Dawlish tore his gaze away and looked seawards. *Quetzal* was hull-up, coming on with all sail before what was now a weak but steady sea breeze. Closer, and he saw the muzzle of the massive three-hundred pounder jutting through a port below the bowsprit. Towards her stern, the port seventy-pounder was also run out. Its twin on the opposite probably also ready for action.

"Have you seen anything of our French friends over there?" Dawlish nodded toward the inner island.

"Nothing," Grove said. "Not a glimpse and quiet as mice. It must be eating their hearts to see those blackguards in the village."

"They'll have their turn soon enough." Dawlish returned to studying *Quetzal*.

The long ram, the mighty guns, the rust-streaked armoured flanks and the knowledge that her high bulwarks hid citadels with iron walls some five inches thick were terror to behold. Dawlish felt fear creeping back, not just for himself but for the flimsy *Sprightly* and every man aboard. When Weatherby shared his plan, it had seemed beyond recklessness. Now it verged on the insane. And yet it would go ahead, driven by the will of one man, and he a gambler.

Like Hawke at Quiberon Bay and Nelson at the Nile, a small voice reminded Dawlish.

It should have comforted him but didn't. Others, no less daring, had been lost in the oblivion of failure. But it made no difference anyway. He had a part to play, and play it he would.

Quetzal was heaving-to outside the bay, taking in sail and dropping her single remaining boat. It took her in tow – slowly, infinitely slowly, even though her oars were double-manned. There were figures on the bridge – one, by the helmsman, was most certainly Rogers – and Welborne was unmistakable on the forecastle, commanding the anchoring party.

There were marksmen among the marines and *Quetzal* was crawling into their killing range. With Rogers and Welborne down . . .

Dawlish felt gratitude that Weatherby's orders for strict adherence to his plan precluded it. It was one thing to kill a man – and, if it must be, a friend – in impersonal battle but something shameful about cold-blooded assassination.

The ironclad was well inside the bay now and an anchor splashing down. Dawlish fancied he recognised a shouted command as Welborne's. Recollection came unbidden – so strong he could almost choke on acrid gunsmoke and feel his eyes sting, as it billowed inside *Odin's* turret. Two years before, brothers in arms, they'd directed her guns to tear bloody lanes through ranks of Prussian troops storming Danish defences. And now this . . .

The anchor held, its cable had run out and was secure. *Quetzal* weathercocked slowly under the sea-breeze to lie with her ram pointing directly out to sea. She'd rotate as much again during the first hours of darkness when the land breeze gathered strength. Smoke was beginning to drift from her spindly funnel – Rogers must intend departure under steam from Mexican waters. Her boat was now stroking towards the beach and that was surely Rogers in the sternsheets. Directed by French troops, villagers were wading out to draw its bows up on the beach. And, waiting there, in red-topped kepi, blue tunic and red breeches, stood Durand. Rogers jumped from the bows and they advanced to meet each other, shook hands, then turned to disappear into the largest house in the village.

Rendezvous successful.

*

Both Dawlish and the whaler's crew had snatched several hours of sleep during the afternoon. They pushed off from the island's tiny beach after sunset, stroking north-westward for an hour before raising sail. They encountered *Sprightly* two hours later, loitering under partial sail. Her engine was not powered but thin smoke confirmed her boiler had been fired and cautiously building pressure.

Dawlish came aboard and the whaler was recovered. Weatherby interrogated him in detail, asked him to sketch the bay, the islands and *Quetzal's* position on the back of an old chart. Ashton and Sanderson were present also. So too was Ignacio Vázquez, still smarting over Roger's betrayal of the Imperial cause. He had prepared a rough drawing of *Quetzal's* interior, and the hatches and accesses to it. Dawlish had already tried to memorise every detail – his life might depend on it. The mood was sombre, but determined, with each invited to comment as the previously agreed plan was tested against the new reality.

Only a few modifications needed.

The crew had been rested through the day, the engine checked, small arms issued, the guns loaded, the bulwarks that hid the 110-pounder dropped – the weapon itself was trained to fire on the port beam. The twin 32-pounders' ports were open, the whaler suspended outboard, ready for dropping. Each man knew his role – and probably feared it, for they all had seen *Quetzal's* might before.

Nothing to do now but wait.

Chapter 31

Hidden from the bay and village by the islands and with the dawn only a faint pink glow above the distant mountaintops, *Sprightly* was crawling north-easterly towards Bucerias, under steam alone. Other than the engine-room crew, and two seamen with rifles in the fore and maintops, all were on deck. Weatherby was alone on the bridge, calling down to Ashton at the secondary steering position below it, where the bulwarks provided some protection. Sanderson was with the 110-pounder crew and gunner's mates were commanding the 32s aft. A four-man crew at the forecastle, and counterparts at the stern, would be vital for initial success. The remainder, some three dozen men, were gathered with Dawlish and Vázquez behind the port bulwark amidships, eyeing the coils of grapnel-tipped rope on which so much would depend.

Dawlish could sense their fear, knew it to be no different from his own, the thumping heart, the dry mouth, the hollow stomach and private terror of losing bowel-control. As if for reassurance, they were fingering their weapons – cutlasses for the most part, but two had only heavy canvas bags hung about their necks, each with a rifle-armed seaman as partner. Dawlish found himself repeatedly tugging the lanyard linking him to his revolver and his hand occasionally drifting towards his cutlass-hilt. He noticed Vázquez's lips were moving in almost silent prayer.

The sky had lightened. He moved towards the gap in the bulwarks and looked landward. *Sprightly* was a mile off the coast, the islands half that distant. Somewhere along the mainland's shoreline, still hidden by brush, the French company landed by *Luisa-Maria* would be moving towards the village, was perhaps already in place. Their compatriots, commanded by Major Rouvier on the inner island, like Grove's on the outer, would have *Quetzal's* deck in their rifles' sights now, their pea-shooter six-pounders ready to be run forward. *Sprightly* slowed and dropped the whaler with a coxswain and five oarsmen. It headed for the outer island's inlet.

Now *Sprightly* was heeling over as Weatherby ordered her into a four-point turn to starboard, straightening then, speed building, so the light surf on the reef off the outer island lay off her port bow.

And still undetected . . .

Maybe, just maybe, this will bring resolution, an end, good or bad, to this Mexican nightmare of cruelty, greed and betrayal . . .

The sun was up now and *Sprightly* must be making her maximum eleven knots. It was minutes only before the reef was two cables off the beam and Weatherby, statue-calm on the bridge, called for the last turn to bring the gunvessel racing in a wide curve to port into the anchorage.

Rifle-fire crashed from Grove's island and a moment later it blazed from the French-held island also.

Now Dawlish saw the bay and all in it, frozen for an instant, as if caught in the lens of a camera.

Quetzal, still weathercocked by the weakening land breeze, her unseen ram and main armament pointing harmlessly towards the beach her transom seawards.

Dark smoke drifting from her funnel as if readying for departure and figures on deck and forecastle scuttling for cover.

Several boats, her own and fishing craft, clustered along *Quetzal's* port flank. Men in uniforms – French uniforms – climbing from them to board and a boom attached to the foremast still swinging a load across to lower it on deck.

The lash of rifle-fire had already triggered panic at the boats – men still scrambling up to the sanctuary of the deck, dragging others aside and flinging them into the water or jumping themselves. One crowded fishing craft had already broken from the cluster and was heading beachward.

And then the first six-pounder bark, a flame lancing from the outer island, seeking but not finding *Quetzal*, elevation too high. A moment later the similar French weapon, incapable of doing more than knock paint-flakes off her armour, struck her flank. But that didn't matter. What did was the panic it fed and which grew as *Sprightly* drove onwards.

For she was well within the bay's mouth now. Dawlish could see only *Quetzal's* transom, that and the barrel of the seventy-pounder protruding from the starboard port of her citadel aft. In two minutes, *Sprightly* must shave past its muzzle, close enough to let it rip along her bulwarks.

If it's not already manned, or if it can't yet be manned in time . . .

Quetzal was a cable ahead, sharp off *Sprightly's* port bow. Weatherby, his hand gripping the handle of the bridge's telegraph, was shouting down to the helmsman for her to nudge in further, then straighten to lay her hull-to-hull alongside the ironclad. The gunvessel lurched over, steadied, and Weatherby ground back the handle, shrilling a message in the engine room for full revolutions astern.

"Ready, lads. Ready with the grapnels." Dawlish forced calm into his voice. "Nobody else move 'til you get my word."

He glanced towards the forecastle – four men crouched there with hawsers, one end already bent around a mooring bitt – and aft, at the counter, a similar party.

Both the British and French six-pounders had established their rhythms, hurling shells at forty-second intervals – three hits on the hull, one bursting against *Quetzal's* foremast stays, another striking the foremast but inflicting no obvious damage. Both light guns must fall silent soon as Sprightly, slowing now as her reversed screw churned foam beneath her counter, drew closer to the ironclad. Then Grove's weapon scored the most significant hit, its shell striking halfway up Quetzal's funnel, tearing a hole through which black coalsmoke began to jet. The rifles were still rattling from both islands, no longer volleys but separate aimed shots. Anybody caught on the ironclad's deck must be sheltering behind the port bulwark.

Quetzal was almost dead ahead, as if *Sprightly's* bowsprit would crash against her stern. The gunvessel now at no more than a walking pace and still slowing. Weatherby was ringing the telegraph again to stop the engine, then calling down for the slightest nudge to starboard to avoid collision against the ironclad's stern.

Dawlish had lost all sense of time – the last two gliding minutes might have been an aeon. He didn't notice the islands' rifle-fire die, nor their six-pounders fall silent, though was aware of the fire now crackling down from *Sprightly's* fore and main tops onto the ironclad's open deck. His eyes were locked now on that seventy-pounder barrel jutting from *Quetzal's* flank. A single shot from it could cripple the gunvessel and end the action. His only fear now was that his nerve might fail, that seamen might die because of him.

"Any moment now, lads! Grapnels ready!" he called.

He glanced forward. The 110-pounder trained directly to port, its crew at their stations. Sanderson leaning out at the deck-edge to look ahead, gaze fixed on the protruding barrel, judging its hight above *Sprightly's* deck, calling orders to the gun crew to raise elevation two degrees.

Dawlish nodded to Rawlins, one of the two seamen with bags. "Have one ready. Throw only on my word! After that, two more. Then follow me!"

Rawlins reached in for a cylindrical meat-can with four inches of slow fuse trailing from it. It was filled with blasting powder and pebbles. The length of fuse was critical, the result of endless timing experiments with samples of the roll obtained from the *Ferrocarril* workshop. Too long and those targeted might have time to hurl it back, too short and it would blow up before throwing. And despite all the time-testing, trials of actual bombs at Manzanillo had shown variations, anything from four to seven seconds before detonation. Rawlins' rifle-armed companion produced a box of lucifers. His hand was shaking.

Sprightly shuddered as her bow struck *Quetzal's* starboard flank, was driving forward, fragments of the shattered bowsprit thrown aside, sundered cordage whipping. The gunvessel's wooden flank was grinding against the ironclad's and still slowing. The foremast drew level with the muzzle of the seventy-pounder gaping from *Quetzal's* starboard port, with Sanderson's 110-pounder just abaft it and –

Flame blasted up from it, the only chance there was to inflict damage, for it could do none against the ironclad's armoured hull. But now Sanderson's explosive shell was hurtling up into the open gunport. It must have shaved past the barrel, for a split-second passed before it burst within. Smoke billowed from the port. The gun was not dismounted but its crew – if it had indeed been manned – could not have survived.

The ripping of wood on iron killed *Sprightly*'s last momentum, laying her length to length alongside *Quetzal*. Weatherby was roaring his command to board. The riflemen in the tops were cutting down any opposition to the cutlass-armed mooring crews fore and aft, who were leaping across to lock the two vessels together with hawsers. Once lashed side-to-side, *Quetzal*'s monstrous 300-pounder could not be brought to bear.

Dawlish glanced up – the ironclad's bulwark looked like a high and unscalable cliff. The funnel rose beyond it, smoke jetting from the rent torn in its side.

"Now, Rawlins!"

The seaman struck a lucifer and thrust it against the fuse. He blew on the tiny glow, saw it sputter, then stood back and hurled the can. It crossed the gunwale above, fell out of sight and, even before it detonated, Rawlins had the next in the air. Then the crash, and another. Somebody, unseen, was screaming and the third can was already in flight.

"Grapnels!" Dawlish shouted.

The seamen equipped with grapnels had been swinging them in circles at the end of their lines to build momentum. At Dawlish's command all five soared aloft. Three held.

"Go!"

Dawlish caught the nearest line and began to haul himself upwards, boots seeking purchase on the hull-plate rivets. A seaman was ahead of him to his right, and another yet higher on his left. The two grapnels that had missed first time were recovered and sent flying up once more. They held..

One seaman reached the bulwark-top and had thrown a leg across before a rifle-shot caught him full in the chest and hurled him back and down.

Now Dawlish's arm was hooked over the bulwark. He raised himself, saw bodies on the deck before him – one was crawling – and figures in blue and red scuttling for cover behind the box-like casing at the base of the funnel. He swung his leg over, rolled across the top and landed on his hands and knees. Others to left and right were over the bulwark. Surprise and shock were with the attackers, but the advantage could not last long.

He dragged his pistol from its holster, struggled to his feet and raced towards the funnel casing – six feet tall and some twelve long. He gained its cover as rifle-fire, a ragged volley, crashed from around the corner at its far side. He glanced back, saw Vázquez close behind. Two seamen who'd been following were down, but the others, Rawlins among them, had all but reached him.

"Two more bombs!" He pointed around the casing edge. "Into the scuppers."

Another lucifer, another glowing tip, then Rawlins flinging the can low across the deck to roll into the port-side scuppers and sending the second to follow before shrinking back into the group that had joined Dawlish.

A cry from the other side of the casing told that someone there had seen the cans, that a brave man was perhaps dashing towards them to throw them overboard.

Two explosions, almost simultaneous, a hail of pebbles blasting past the forward side of the casing, cries of agony beyond.

"Follow me!"

Dawlish dashed around the casing, saw two Frenchmen bleeding on the deck, another reeling, then collapsing, and others falling back towards the stern, only one dropping cooly to one knee to fire back. The seamen had reached the slowest already, were hacking with cutlasses. A seaman carrying a rifle with fixed bayonet charged at the kneeling Frenchman but was too late to stop him dropping another seaman heading towards him. An instant later he rammed his spike into the Frenchman's throat.

Distinguishable by their clothing, some of *Quetzal's* seamen-were scattered among the retreating French. But for a few throwing themselves on their knees with hands raised, all were heading towards the citadel at the stern or disappearing down a companionway.

Sprightly's men were crowding behind them, chopping, thrusting, shooting and stabbing as they advanced between the dead and wounded.

Dawlish shouted for Rawlins to join him at the head of the companionway. Shots were crashing up from below to deter following.

"Two more cans down there," he said. "Two more again if anybody attempts to break out."

They exploded almost simultaneously. No more shots.

The after citadel's blank bulkhead extended bulwark to bulwark. There was no entry from the deck, Vázquez said, only from below. Lined along it, confronted by the attackers' fury, aware there was no escape, the enemy were throwing down weapons and raising hands in surrender.

"You, you, you and you!" Dawlish shouted to four seamen. "Cover them and shoot the first who makes a move." He turned. "The rest of you, follow me for'ard." Then, to the second man with cans in his bag, "Stay close to me."

The deck ahead was clear – the remaining defenders must have retreated below through the companionway abaft the foremast and had perhaps gained the shelter of the forward citadel. Two cans were hurled down that companionway also, men stationed by it to block any attempt to charge up.

Silence on *Quetzal* now, but not yet victory. The French below, or in the two citadels, were showing no willingness to surrender. But there was other rifle-fire now, more distant, that could only mean the French company landed by *Luisa-Maria* to the west of Bucerias was now driving forward to capture it. There were six-pounders in action too, perhaps the French piece on the inner island supporting its sister with the advancing troops ashore.

Dawlish climbed to *Quetzal's* bridge to call across to Weatherby.

"The deck's secure, sir! We've about a dozen prisoners and the rest are trapped below, some probably in the citadels also."

"You've got Durand? Rogers?"

"Neither, sir!"

Nor Travis Welborne either. My friend.

351

"We'll have to clear 'em out, Dawlish! Those blackguards won't hesitate to blow the magazines!"

Tempting for men whose lives were already forfeit.

"Ashton, Sanderson and the gun crews are coming across," Weatherby called. "And Grove's on his way!" He turned, pointed astern. The whaler was approaching with the marines. "Just keep the scoundrels below until they arrive."

Seamen surrounded both companionways, ready to kill anybody attempting to emerge. There was an open hatch further ahead, close to the rear wall of the forward citadel. Dawlish glanced down, saw ladder rungs set into the shaft's side, and nobody at its base.

"Leading into the citadel?" he asked Vázquez.

"Yes, but not directly. There's a passage leading forward that steps up into it."

The urge to drop a bomb down the shaft was strong. But no – better to wait. He called two seamen to guard it.

"Take me to the roof vents, Ignacio!"

When he'd toured *Quetzal* with Welborne he hadn't mounted to the forecastle or quarterdeck, both atop the citadels. But Vázquez had told that there was no roofing armour, only iron-supported wooden decks with vents to clear the inevitable gunsmoke when the guns recoiled.

They climbed up to the forecastle. The mooring crew there had done well– *Sprightly* secured by hawser and two bodies sprawled on the deck. They were directly above the forward citadel now and Dawlish had no eyes for anything but the hinged five-foot-square hatch cover that closed the vent. Dogs along its edges locked it down. He put his ear to it, fancied he heard sounds below.

"Do you want it open, sir?" a seaman said.

"No. Only the dogs. Don't hinge it back 'til you're ordered."

He hurried aft. The prisoners there were on their knees now, faces touching the wall of the after citadel, hands clasped behind their necks. He selected one, a grey-haired French trooper, and rammed his pistol's muzzle below his right ear.

"Is Durand on board?" he asked in French.

No answer.

"I'm counting to three. One . . .." He was unsure if he'd have the nerve to squeeze the trigger. "Two …"

"He's here," the trooper said.

"Where?"

"I don't know. He came last night. I haven't seen him since."

Dawlish left him, was greeted on the quarterdeck by the mooring party. A *Quetzal* crewman's body lay in pooling blood close to the bitt to which they'd secured *Sprightly's* hawser. And there too was a dog-locked hatch. He ordered it to be readied like its counterpart forward, then returned to the main deck.

Sanderson and Grove – faces black with gunsmoke – had arrived with their men. Ashton boarded and took command. Dawlish summarised the situation.

Ashton heard him out, asked a few questions, then allocated duties. Sanderson and half the *Sprightly* seamen now on board would descend through the sternward companionway and, guided by Vázquez, gain entrance to the after citadel. Grove, with his marines and most of the remaining seamen, would go down through the forward companionway and the access shaft to reach the citadel at the bows. Each group included a man with bombs.

But first, to offer a chance to surrender, an opportunity to avert the nightmare battle that would rage in *Quetzal's* passageways and closed compartments.

Dawlish took two bombs and a handful of lucifers from a bag-carrying seaman. Ashton joined him and they climbed to the forecastle.

The seamen there were standing by the unhinged end of the vent's hatch, the dogs open.

"Lift it!" Ashton said. "Throw it back!"

It rotated, crashed on the deck. No voices from below, only sounds of movement.

Ashton dropped to one knee, leaned as close to the void as he dared.

"Is Rogers down there?" he shouted.

A pause, then, "Who are you?" Accent unmistakable as Rogers'.

353

"Ashton. Her Majesty's Ship *Sprightly*!"

"You're offering terms?" Rogers called.

"Is Durand with you?"

"He's here. What are your terms?"

"Is the silver on board?"

"Most of it. We can make a deal, can't we, an' –"

Rogers' words were cut off amid a sound of scuffling. Then an incoherent cry, silenced just as quickly.

Now another voice., no less unmistakable.

"C'est Durand! Voulez-vous une réponse? Ça y est!"

Three pistol-shots as answer, one round ricocheting off the vent edge. Ashton started back. He nodded to Dawlish.

"Drop them!"

Crouching, Dawlish struck a lucifer on the vent's metal hatch, applied it to the bomb's slow match. He waited for the spluttering sparks, then dropped the deadly package inside. Shouting below – those who realised what it was must be hurling themselves behind any cover.

Then it blew. Even as smoke rolled from the vent, somebody was howling in pain. Dawlish dropped in the second can.

Both detonations had been signals to launch the attacks further aft. Other bombs were dropping, down the access shaft abaft the forecastle, down both companionways, down the vent above the after citadel.

Now the assault.

Grove's and Sanderson's groups rushing down the companionways as the smoke was still clearing, driving forward and aft through the passages towards the citadels. Little shooting, dazed survivors stumbling ahead of the attackers, some chopped down in the act of surrender, a few making brief ineffectual stands. On the forecastle and at the stern, marines were shooting down through vents, their ricocheting bullets as deadly within the iron walls as direct hits. In three minutes all was silent but for the moaning of the wounded.

Dawlish went below through the access shaft forward, stepped across a body at its base. Choking smoke was thick in the passage but through it he could see dim light ahead. There were other bodies, one at least still moving. Once he slipped and almost fell on what must be blood underfoot. He groped his way to the steps and found himself in the twilight of the forward citadel, illuminated faintly through the murk by the vent above and the port of the massive ten-inch ship-killer above the ram.

Grove met him, gesturing around. No need for words. It was a slaughterhouse. Marines and seaman were turning bodies over, propping the still-living against any vertical surface. Several prisoners were hemmed in against the rear bulkhead hands raised.

"Any sight of Welborne?" Dawlish didn't know what he would feel if he'd been found, either alive or dead.

My friend.

Gove shook his head. "He must be somewhere aft."

"And Rogers?"

"Over there."

He was lying on his back, blood pooled on the deck around his head and throat slashed from side to side to forestall any attempt at surrender, probably silenced by Durand even before the first bomb dropped.

It was Durand whom Dawlish now sought. He went from dead to living to dead again, dragging aside bodies sometimes heaped one on another, turning others over.

He found him at last, slumped on his knees below the huge barrel, hands locked on the bottom edge of its port as if in an attempt to crawl out through it. Durand was still alive – just. He turned his head as Dawlish bent over him, pistol in hand. Blood was bubbling from his mouth and there was no recognition in the dimming eyes.

Memories of a sister and brother playing together in Pau, she laughing as she corrected his French, an innocent and beautiful girl whom a dying man had loved as his own daughter, a promise – unfulfillable – to a beloved uncle.

And afterwards . . .

What she now is.

At this moment of witnessing nearing death, Dawlish realised he felt no pity, only loathing and hatred, bitter and corrosive of his own soul. And yet he embraced it.

He leaned forward, put his lips close to Durand's ear.

"Clothilde." He whispered. "Remember her. Remember Clothilde Sapin of Pau."

A flicker of recognition in Durand's eyes, of surprise at the mention of the name. His gaze fixed on the revolver in Dawlish's hand. Then a gurgling sound, an attempt to speak, words choked off by more blood but understandable at last.

Une balle. Pour l'amour de Dieu, une balle.

A bullet. For God's sake, a bullet.

Dawlish shook his head. He crouched there to watch him die. It took a minute, seemed centuries.

I've killed him just as if I'd put a round through his head.

He didn't know what he felt.

But it wasn't satisfaction.

*

The French force that attacked from the west had taken Bucerias village easily, though it found only a few renegade countrymen there. *El Serpiente's* force had left the previous day, taking its share of the silver with it, and already melted into the wild country inland. There were insufficient French troops to follow.

But the French had other work to occupy them – shooting all of Durand's men they could find, including those who'd surrendered in *Quetzal* and been shipped ashore in fishing craft. Weatherby had refused use of *Sprightly's* boats for the purpose. There was no court-martial, no distinguishing between injured and able, save the wounded were spared digging trenches for graves and despatched with a shot to the head rather than standing before firing squads. The French dead on the ironclad were flung into the sea but the survivors of *Quetzal's* crew were spared.

Dawlish had gone through the ironclad, searching for Travis Welborne. He found him in a cabin where he'd barricaded himself, but the door had been smashed down and a bomb thrown inside. Welborne must have died instantly, for his revolver, with only two rounds remaining, was still grasped in his hand.

He would have been proud to die that way. Undefeated.

It must have been his own cabin, for a tattered Confederate ensign that was fallen from a drawer in the already looted closet. It might have been had one Dawlish had seen streamed above *Odin* when she reverted to the name *Galveston* and followed the Danish battle line to with the Austrian squadron off Heligoland two years before. He laid it over Welborne, recited in his mind what he could remember of the burial service. It hurt him that the body – and it was that now, a thing, something that had so little of the man he'd known - would soon be cast overboard without further ceremony. Hands shaking, he removed the ensign, folded it and took it with him back to *Sprightly*.

She had lost six dead – they'd be buried with full ceremony at sea – and eight wounded, one badly enough to lose an arm as soon as a French surgeon could be reached at Manzanillo. Weatherby had taken possession of the silver and the boxes – forty-two of them, all containing ingots – were lugged across to *Sprightly*. *El Serpiente* must have taken the remainder for his services.

Weatherby handed *Quezal* over, nominally to Vázquez as an Imperial officer, but effectively to the French. She was still seaworthy, still Imperial property, still valuable. The boiler and engine rooms were intact and their crews had survived. Vázquez could at least get her to Manzanillo.

Three hours after she had entered the bay, *Sprightly* steamed from it, at maximum revolutions for the sake of the seaman needing amputation. Other than the shattered bowsprit and long scourings along her port flank, she was undamaged. Repairs at Manzanillo would take days only.

But there was no joy of victory.

Least of all in Dawlish.

Chapter 32

Sprightly's repairs were almost complete and she was due to leave for Esquimalt in three days. Witnessed by Weatherby and Colonel Macquart, the recovered ingots had been counted and weighed.

Since Plutus was a British company, Weatherby in his role as consul, suggested *Sprightly* take them all with her. Plutus could make its own arrangements for collection and for settlement of royalties thereafter. Macquart accepted without argument – he had more urgent concerns now. Two civilian passenger-vessels, chartered at Panama by the French government, now lay in Manzanillo harbour and more were expected. The first stage of evacuation was underway. Colima had been denuded of defenders – two trains were already scheduled to bring more to Manzanillo in the coming days. The Juaristas had made no move, were biding their time to let the French leave without further battle. The Mexican Imperia troops, soon to be abandoned, still had theirs to fight and the prospects weren't good.

*

"I don't think much of the fellow, nor that woman of his either," Weatherby said, "but it would be churlish to refuse." He'd had Dawlish summoned to his quarters to translate a letter.

In two days' time Baron André Théodoric Honoré Damseaux de Vérac would marry Madame Clothilde Marguerite Joséphine Sapin at a private nuptial mass in the church of San Pedro de Arbués, Manzanillo.

Damseaux's hand-written invitation was addressed to Weatherby but included Dawlish also. It asked that he'd act as a witness.

"I don't want to be there, sir," he said.

"Damn it all, Dawlish, the man's being polite. You saved that woman's life, didn't you? She probably requested it – a better gesture of thanks than I'd have expected from her."

"I've personal reasons, sir." Words hard to say.

Weatherby smiled like an indulgent father. "You're a sly one, Dawlish. Smitten, were you?" He laid his hand on his shoulder. "It

359

happens to us all in youth but we see the folly of it later. You're too young for this sort of thing. You'll find some decent English girl in years to come who'll be worth ten of her." He winked. "Just make sure she has no brothers, her father's well-heeled and his estate isn't entailed."

"It's not that, sir. It's something –" He couldn't bring himself to say more.

The squalor and calculation of her bargain. Worse than with Durand.

"Forget about it, Dawlish, and grit your teeth. You'll have to handle worse in your time. I'm attending and I'll need you there to translate."

"Is that an order, sir?"

"Yes, Dawlish. It's an order."

*

Across the harbour, *Jenny Dixon* was also readying to sail, in her case to Panama. She'd be carrying paying passengers. Dawlish went to La Galina that night to bid farewell to some of them.

He found Sorderer, Clayton and Tom Bryce at their usual table. They welcomed him without warmth.

"You've heard what happened to Rogers and Welborne?" he said.

They had. *Quetzal* was anchored in the harbour, mute witness to their fates. In Manzanillo's cantinas, *Sprightly's* crew and Major Rouvier's men had been voluble in their cups.

Then uncomfortable silence.

Dawlish broke it. "I've heard you're going to Panama. Are you planning to stay there?" He guessed they wouldn't, that there'd be nothing there for them.

"Going further south, maybe," Sorderer said. "God knows where. We'll find something. It'll be hardest on Pettigrew. He tried his darndest here."

Dawlish had never met the man but remembered the name and the fields mottled with stunted maize that Bryce had identified from the train during the first journey inland.

"Is anybody going back north?" Dawlish regretted the question even as it passed his lips.

"Not a single one of us." Sorderer spoke with the vehemence of a man trying to convince himself. "We're damned if we'll swear the Yankees' loyalty oath."

And yet it was easy to imagine them drifting back in the months and years ahead, shamefacedly, one by one, swallowing pride, accommodating to the reality of defeat, accepting it as endurable if not palatable. But this was neither the time nor place to suggest it.

Time to go.

Dawlish had brought a paper-wrapped package. That he placed on the table?

"Open it when I'm gone," he said. "It was Travis Welborne's. I spread it over him when I found him. And then I thought he'd have preferred you to have it."

They shook hands in silence and he left.

*

Behind the recently constructed defensive earthworks, Manzanillo was a place of desperate people waiting for evacuation. Even the hapless Belgian Legion had been brought back from Colima, condemned to live in shelters constructed by themselves from anything they could find. Only Damseaux and Clothilde had found comfortable accommodation in what was previously the residence of the deputy alcalde. They too would be leaving aboard *Jenny Dixon*, Dawlish heard from a French officer. At Panama, the Baron and his new Baronne would cross the isthmus by rail and travel on to Switzerland to convalesce there. The other Belgians were the French's lowest priority for evacuation.

When Dawlish accompanied Weatherby to settle payments for anthracite with Turnbull at the *Ferrocarril* yard, they found him perhaps the only man in Manzanillo who was unconcerned by the Juaristas' likely soon arrival.

"I told you, when you first came, they'll need us," he said after he'd offered cigars. "The French will destroy a few bridges when the last train leaves Colima, but the line has no long spans, so we'll have 'em repaired in a matter of months. We'll have to grease a few Juarista palms but we're greasing French and Imperial ones already, so it'll make no difference. And with luck we might have the line extended to Guadalajara in three years."

A British interest that had never needed protection in the first place.

*

Clothilde, demurely dressed, played her role to perfection at the wedding. Damseaux still seemed frail and looked at her with adoring eyes when she entered on Colonel Macquart's arm. Dawlish noticed that neither van Maarkedal nor any other Belgian was present. He had never attended a Catholic service before, but it seemed to be hurried. If so, the priest might have good reason – he too might be contemplating flight. The Juaristas were known to be merciless in their treatment of clergy who'd forged close links with the Imperials and French.

And at last the vows, Damseaux's words low and heartfelt, Clothilde's, sweet and grateful, hardly audible to any but him. She choked back a sob of joy as he slipped the ring on her finger.

Dawlish watched without emotion, as little as he saw in Clothilde's eyes when, after he'd signed the register, she thanked him with such apparent sweetness and grace that even Marquart and Weatherby seemed impressed. He hadn't just saved her life, she said, without him she would never have found her dear André. Her hand moved to touch Damseaux's and he took it and held it to her lips, tears glistening in his eyes. He mumbled his thanks to Dawlish. They sounded sincere.

Then it was over. Urgent matters aboard *Sprightly* prevented tarrying, Weatherby said.

And Dawlish felt neither anger nor contempt now. Clothilde, Baronne Damseaux de Vérac, was not just dead to him. It was as if he'd never known her.

But he wondered if he would ever trust another woman.

Sprightly departed a day after *Jenny Dixon* sailed and she'd carried with her not only an incongruous mix of passengers but a tangle of legal documentation likely to make lawyer's fortunes even if nobody else benefitted.

The passage to Esquimalt would most probably be uneventful, Dawlish expected, the greater part under sail, for the bunkers were almost empty. He wondered how appropriate Weatherby's measures to protect British interests would be judged. The *Glorioso* mine had been spared destruction and Atkinson must be forging cooperative relations with the Juaristas, now so close to victory. Turnbull of El *Ferrocarril del Pacífico* had never asked for support and was looking forward, after some initial inconvenience, to profitable business in a restored republic. And *Jenny Dixon* had not just been recovered, but restored.

The price had been high, not just in lives but in assumption of powers for which Weatherby probably had no right under British Law or Admiralty regulations. Depending on how his actions were judged as a success or a failure, he might be hailed as a new Thomas Cochrane or derided as a reckless fool meriting dismissal if not prosecution. The Pacific Station Commander would probably not commit himself either way and merely forward Weatherby's report to the Admiralty without comment. Dawlish knew he must be mentioned it in himself, and his spiriting away of silver in the railcar might boost, or prejudice forever, his own prospects for advancement.

Better not dwell on it.

At the worst, he told himself, he could make a career as a translator.

It was a meagre comfort.

The End

A message from Antoine Vanner & Historical Note

If you've enjoyed this book, I'd be most grateful if you were to submit a brief review to Amazon.com, to Amazon.co.uk or to Amazon.com.au. If you're reading on Kindle you'll be asked to rate the book by clicking on up to five stars. Such feedback is of incalculable importance to authors and will encourage me to keep chronicling the lives of Nicholas and Florence Dawlish.

If you'd like to leave a review, whether reading in paperback or in Kindle, then please go to the *"Britannia's Interests"* page on Amazon. Scroll down from the top and under the heading of "Customer Reviews" you'll see a big button that says "Write a customer review" – click that and you're ready to go into action. A sentence or two is enough, essentially what you'd tell a friend or family member about the book, but you may of course want to write more (and I'd be happy if you did since readers' feedback is of immense value to me!).

You can learn more about Nicholas Dawlish and his world on my website www.dawlishchronicles.com. You can read about his life, and how the individual books relate to events and actions during it, via www.dawlishchronicles.com/dawlish/

 You may like to follow my weekly (sometimes twice-weekly) blog on www.dawlishchronicles.com/dawlish-blog in which articles appear that are based on my researches, but not used directly in my books. They range through the 1700 to 1930 period.

By subscribing to my mailing list, you will receive updates on my continuing writing as well as occasional free short-stories about the life of Nicholas Dawlish. Click on: www.bit.ly/2iaLzL7

Historical Note

The last French forces left Mexico in March 1867, having fallen back on the port of Vera Cruz in the previous months. Emperor Maximillian refused to abdicate and opted to remain in Mexico to fight the now victorious Juaristas with the Mexican Imperial units that remained loyal to him. He was captured in May 1867. He might have been allowed to return to Europe had it not been for his approval of the "Black Decree". Court-martialled, he was sentenced to death. Despite clemency appeals from European royalty, and even liberal heroes such as Giuseppe Garabaldi and Victor Hugo, the sentence was upheld by President Benito Juarez. He was shot with two of his generals in June 1867. The execution was later the subject of a painting by the Impressionist Edouard Manet (who had not been an eyewitness). His body was subsequently returned to Austria and placed in the Imperial Hapsburg crypt in Vienna. Empress Carlota had returned to Europe in 1866 to appeal to both the French Government and the Pope for continuing support. Her attempts failed and severe mental illness followed. She never fully recovered. A tragic and disturbed figure, she lived on in various Belgian palaces until 1927, dying at the age of eighty-six.

The Mexican venture had been expensive for France in terms of wealth, lives and prestige. In retrospect it seems like a prologue for the even greater humiliation and defeat she would suffer during war with Prussia in 1870. Preoccupation with its own civil war from 1861- 65, had prevented the American government enforcing its Monroe Doctrine. This dated from 1823 and warned European nations that the United States would not tolerate further colonization or puppet monarchs in the western hemisphere. Following Union victory however, substantial material support was provided to the Juarista forces, and the threat of possible United States intervention against France reinforced diplomatic pressure for evacuation of Mexico.

Benito Juarez continued as president of Mexico until his death in 1872. Unrest and political infighting continued during this time, though Juarez's wisdom and prestige were calming factors. One of the Juarista generals, Porfirio Diaz, a hero of the war against the French, emerged as a new strongman and ruled as virtual dictator for the next three and a half decades. Under his rule a significant degree of modernisation was achieved and foreign investment welcomed for mining, railroads and some industrial development. Education was expanded, reformed and secularised. Many prospered in these years but not rural communities which, to a great extent, were left behind, with living conditions little different to those a century earlier. Unrest was common and often repressed with violence. Revolution erupted in 1910, bringing with it ten years of civil war between shifting alliances. As many as a million people may have died in this period. The country was devasted and recovered only slowly. The delayed postscript to the revolution was the savage Cristero War of 1926-28, triggered by Catholic opposition to implementation of secularist and anticlerical laws regarding education and worship. The government response was pitiless. The human cost of this war has been estimated at some 250,000 dead, with a similar number fleeing to the United States.

British investment in Latin America rose through the 19th Century and constituted what was virtually an unofficial empire. Activities included railways, mining, cattle-raising, meatpacking, street-car systems, utilities and a multiplicity of other ventures, often demanding engineering solutions on an epic scale. (Such investment is a driving theme the *Dawlish Chronicles* novel *Britannia's Reach*).

The ironclad *Quetzal* in this book is portrayed as a sister of the CSS *Stonewall*, ordered by the Southern Confederacy in 1863, one of a pair of armoured rams intended for service against the Union Navy. The key figure in arranging construction at the Arman Frères shipyard at Bordeaux, France, was James Dunwoody Bulloch (who plays an important role in the *Dawlish Chronicles* novel *Britannia's Innocent*). When *Stonewall* was nearing completion, the French government caved-in to United States pressure and arranged for the vessel to be purchased by Denmark, which promptly sold her on to the Confederacy. Now commissioned as a Confederate Navy vessel, she was hunted by the Union Navy and had reached Havana, Cuba, when the American Civil War ended. Here, *Stonewall* was seized by the US Navy and taken to the Washington Naval Yard and laid up.

Seen as surplus to requirements in a time when the US Navy was being reduced for peace-time service, *Stonewall* was sold on to Japan's Tokugawa shogunate in 1867 for $400,000, a vast sum at the time. Renamed *Kōtetsu*, she would see action in the Boshin War (1868 to

1869) between forces of the ruling Tokugawa shogunate and a coalition seeking to seize political power in the name of the Imperial Court. *Kōtetsu* participated in the naval battle of Hakodate in 1869. The war ended with the defeat of the Shogunate and the consolidation of the emperor's power in what became known as the Meiji Restoration. Subsequently renamed *Asama*, and reduced to secondary statues, the ex-*Stonewall*, ex-*Kōtetsu* participated in Japan's occupation of Taiwan in 1874. She was scrapped in 1889.

Stonewall had one real-life sister, also ordered by the Southern Confederacy but not delivered. She was purchased from Arman Frères by Prussia in 1865. She was found to be poorly constructed (a surprise, since the *Stonewall/Kōtetsu* seems to have been structurally sound) and leaked badly. She played no role of value in the Franco Prussian War and was scrapped in 1878.

Our Authors

Rick Spilman is the founder and manager of Old Salt Press, an independent publishing company that provides the umbrella for a number of authors who write nautical fiction. As well as keeping up a hugely popular blog, "Old Salt Blog", Rick has published three very successful nautical books — *Hell Around the Horn*, *The Shantyman*, and *Evening Gray, Morning Red*, plus a novella, *Bloody Rain*. *The Shantyman* won a Kirkus Reviews Indie Book of the Year award, and deservedly so. All four are absolutely first-class reading.

Alaric Bond, an English Old Salt Press author, is the producer of the hugely popular "Fighting Sail" series, set in the Napoleonic Era, the latest of which is *Seeds of War*. At time of writing, he is working on the fifteenth book in the series. He has also produced two stand-alone books, *The Guinea Boat, Turn a Blind Eye*. He has recently begun a series set in WW2, concentrating on the role of Royal Navy coastal forces. The first two books are *Hellfire Corner* and *Glory Boys*.

Joan Druett became a maritime historian by accident. While exploring the tropical island of Rarotonga in the South Pacific, she slipped into the hole left by the roots of a large uprooted tree, and at the bottom discovered the centuries-old grave of a whaling wife. Because of this, Joan became a noted expert in the history of women at sea, leading to ten novels and 17 works of nonfiction, including the bestselling *Island of the Lost*.

Linda Collison is American and has written the Patricia Macpherson nautical adventures series, the first being *Barbados Bound*, the next two books being *Surgeon's Mate* and *Rhode Island Rendezvous*. Linda has also published other works independently, including biting satires under the 'Knife and Gun Club' banner, and *Redfeather*, which was a finalist in Foreword's Book of the Year Award. A fourth book published with Old Salt Press is *Water Ghosts*, a haunting tale that was a number one Amazon bestseller in the Young Adult category.

Seymour Hamilton is Canadian and the author of *The Astreya Trilogy*. His work, though maritime, is very reminiscent of Tolkien's carefully wrought fantasy worlds. He also set *Angel's Share*, which was beautifully illustrated by Shirley MacKenzie, in the *Astreya* world.

The list also features V. E. Ulett, the nom-de-plume of a very successful Californian writer who normally specializes in steampunk adventures. Her three maritime novels, are published under the Old Salt Press colophon: *Captain Blackwell's Prize,* *Blackwell's Paradise,* and *Blackwell's Homecoming*.

And there is also Antoine Vanner – author of the *Dawlish Chronicles* series of historical naval adventures set in the late 19th Century. Twelve books in the series so far, and still counting!

Visit: oldsaltpress.com/about-old-salt-press

Printed in Great Britain
by Amazon

44147631R00205